HAWK

The River Bend Series

TJ MAKKAI

For information contact:

info@makkaibooks.com
makkaibooks.com

Editing: Starr Waddell with Quiethouse Editing
Cover: Jason Van Winkle
Formatting: Bad Doggie Designs
Website: Scott Oine with LittleBox Social

ISBN: 978-1-7354-778-7-9

BOOKS BY TJ MAKKAI

River Bend Series

Crow September 2020

Hawk October 2021

Pigeon Coming Soon

I dedicate this book to the best club ever.

WWRDT
"I was asked about a book club . . .
and this is what I got."
—Mary Seward.

Eva Sippel
Debbie Reiner
Molly Stretten
Krista Ghaman
Mary Seward
Alexis Cole
Tracy Johnson

CHAPTER ONE

CLAUDIA - RIVER BEND, WISCONSIN

It wasn't the most uncomfortable moment of my life, but it was not the most pleasant. It reminded me of seven years ago when I was in my public speaking class during my sophomore year in high school. One of the speeches I'd had to give had been well prepared, but I had been wearing pants that were too tight and barely long enough to touch the top of my shoes. One sock had lost the elastic binding, causing it to slouch at my ankle. I looked fine to others, but underneath, I was a mess. I was grateful to hide behind the podium and knew it was my words that counted.

The eyes of my classmates saw one thing, but I felt another. Like now, the hawk in the tree behind me could spy on its prey, but it did not know which one was the weakest inside and which one would put up a fight.

Sitting on a park bench on the Mississippi River bank, I was waiting for my boyfriend, Aaron, to show up so I could break up with him. I needed to control my life and make decisions based on moving forward and not taking what was just in front of me at the time.

The mosquitos relentlessly pecked at me, and the heavy humidity caused a black blood paste to form on my arm when I managed to smack one down. The only exit plan I had was my breakup speech, and words don't do much to mosquitos.

Looking back, I would never have guessed that, in a week, I would give anything to be back at this moment. It was the last snapshot in time before people thought of me as a victim and a killer.

Despite Aaron being a good guy and handsome—really handsome—I needed to make things happen for me. I felt like I was standing knee-deep in mud and not able to move. Even if I fell into the mud, it would have been a new direction. Something like going down a rabbit hole would give me the force I needed to get moving in life.

I'd never pictured myself stalling at the age of twenty-two. I had graduated from college ninety-six days ago and was freeloading at my aunt's house. My job—not career—but job was 50 percent court-ordered community service hours and 50 percent an hourly wage. The small income kept me fed and able to drink in a small town.

At that moment, I was sad but also irritated. I had lived in the Midwest all my life, and I would not—could not and refused to—get used to mosquitos.

Growing up in St. Paul, Minnesota, attending college near Milwaukee, and now, sitting on the Wisconsin side of the Mississippi River, I knew my only hope of reprieve would be wind sweeping the minuscule missiles off into the sunset or for Aaron to show up so we could leave the waterfront.

My hair was matted down and hidden by a baseball hat because my arm was still in a sling from being involved in a hit-and-run accident seven weeks earlier. The humidity dropped, but the long summer heat lingered. My summer dress clung to my body and might as well have been tattooed on me. I had a rotation of three—actually five dresses, if you counted the two my roommate, Sherrie, had donated to me—which had become my summer uniform. It wasn't easy to use the bathroom if I had to button or zip anything because my primary arm was in a cast.

Only two fishermen remained along the shore, and I watched them spray themselves down with bug repellent. As I watched them, I couldn't help feel again that someone was watching me. I felt like a circus clown without the circus. I had to use my hat as a battering ram against the mosquitos, but it was a losing battle. I wished I could have left, but I was waiting for Aaron. My phone had died, so I couldn't call and meet him elsewhere.

We had started dating back in June, just a day after I'd broken up with my boyfriend, Jackson. I knew it was tacky because the timing was a bit fast. I had barely let out a breath before I tumbled into a new relationship. One step forward was all I needed to keep going.

I would miss having him in my life, but he would still be around a lot. River Bend was a small town. Plus, my parents and his Aunt Jan were going into business together—opening up a commercial kitchen to mass-produce Jan's famous pies and bread. Aaron had been instrumental in scouting locations and designing the kitchen. On top of that, my roommate, Sherrie, worked for him at his bar. I had to move forward, and I would have to learn to balance the loss with gaining something for myself.

I had been with Jackson for over a year and a half. Overall, Jackson was a decent guy, but he was stuck in the now. Forward-thinking was not his strongest asset. Especially if it involved someone else, he could plan things for the day, maybe two days from the present or next weekend, but would never commit fully to something over a week out. Sometimes, that was fine, but you had to be looking forward when you were nearing college graduation. And, if you had been dating someone for over a year, they should be part of the planning process. There was thinking for yourself and thinking by yourself.

My first few weeks in town had been chaotic, and Aaron had been a great friend and someone I could really talk through things with. He was a good listener and a great sounding board. He would wait for me to speak, ask questions and challenge me to think logically and then with my heart. He was only five years older but seemed to be from another decade and had a multitude of life experiences to draw from.

He was also handsome. Not just cute but handsome. Blue eyes to melt your heart, brown hair you'd want to run your fingers through, a chest like a wrestler, and legs of a runner.

After high school in River Bend, Aaron had enlisted in the army, and after his service, he'd come back to River Bend. He and his brother, Chuck, opened their own bar, named BAR (stemming from Aaron's full name Bart Aaron Rhoimly), while taking classes at Jameson College. While he had been fighting terrorists in the Middle

East and setting up a career and finishing college, I finished high school and graduated college and was currently struggling with what to do with my life.

BAR had reopened last month after two months of renovations and just in time for the Jameson College students to return to River Bend for the start of the fall semester. Chuck was a silent partner and was currently a contract employee with a private firm with military security contracts. He was gone on assignment but expected to return shortly.

I'd learned not to ask too many questions about Chuck because Aaron's answers, most days, were very dismissive. His usual replies included I don't know, don't care, or can't answer, yet I felt they had a strong bond. They talked once or twice a week, and that was with Chuck being in the Middle East. I knew a couple of brothers that lived two miles apart but only spoke at family gatherings.

The problem between Aaron and me was that he had never stopped trying to mentor me. I valued the friendship but sensed the balance of our relationship was off. I wanted a partner, not a life coach. The sex was great once we figured out how to maneuver around my broken arm. Our schedules became more jagged when he started working more nights. Our dating life was filled with text conversations and meals between our work schedules. I thought I might have been invested in the relationship for convenience.

Aaron had said he would meet me after the second bartender showed up for the night. I hoped the bartender was on time because if I had to choose between being the person who waits and gets eaten alive by mosquitos and the person who saves themselves, it would be an easy decision for me. My legs bounced up and down, and I couldn't decide if it was from nervousness, trying to contain my sadness, or defense against mosquitos.

River Bend was a typical small town that seemed not to offer much upfront until you had gotten to know it. The population hovered under twenty thousand, and the jewel of the town was either the town square or the Mississippi River's beautiful shoreline. The heart of downtown centered around Town Square Park, which had a children's play area and a butterfly garden. It also hosted a monthly artist bazaar and farmers market. Summer concerts and one too many weddings were held in the white gazebo at the center of the park.

Just when visitors thought the town had nothing more to offer, a few blocks off the square were a few bars that catered to Jameson College students. Main Street, aptly named, guided visitors from the highway, past gas stations, one old motel and two nice hotels, one too many fast-food joints, and a beautiful park. The street continued past the town square to the sprawling Jameson College campus, only a mile from downtown.

Each fall, 8,500 students returned to school, adding another dimension to the town. Several dorms and the administration building held some of the best views of the town and the river.

Between the centuries-old brick buildings on campus, the town square, holiday parades, homes with white picket fences, and the annual Christmas tree lighting and caroling jamboree, even Norman Rockwell might have found this too inspirational. But despite the postcard images, every town had a dark side, and this town's shadow hovered out there, or at least, something was hovering.

CHAPTER TWO

Aaron approached just in time, carrying two paper coffee cups. I was dying out there, and he had stopped for coffee! I crossed the parking lot and met him at the walking path.

"Do you mind if we walk and talk? It might help if we walk away from the swarming air force of mosquitos. What did you bring us?" I eyeballed the cups.

He extended a cup to me. "Sorry, I'm late. Jo-Lee was late for her shift. I tried calling you, but you didn't answer."

Raising my phone, I showed him the black screen. "I forgot to charge it."

He looked at me pointedly. "You should keep it charged in case of emergencies."

I shrugged in response.

"Anyway, I only asked her yesterday when I realized I'd screwed up the schedule. She said she had a conflict but would make it work. It is slow, but I didn't want to leave Pete by himself." He handed me the paper cup, shrugging, and walked away from the river.

"Wait, let's go this way, and we can still see the sun setting."

"If we go this direction, we're closer to EG's house. I figure when you break up with me in five minutes, we won't have that awkward, silent walk back." He turned and started walking again.

I didn't move. "How did you know?" I asked but was not surprised when he'd said it. I took a sip and coughed out some of the cocktail. "What is this?"

"It's a rum and Coke. I figured something was up this past week, and I pieced it together. I hoped we could toast to a good summer and an easy breakup." He stopped walking and stood there with a smug look on his face, clearly proud of his reveal.

My leg bouncing had changed to my stomach flopping, but I had to maintain my composure. "Seriously? You are making this too easy. What's your endgame? Are you going to pretend to put on a nice face, but really, you will spend years pining for me and then we end up in a shoot-out twenty years from now? Are you sticking with the no-drama breakup? The no-one-more-chances speech? Sherrie will appreciate having to cook for only her and me now. Although, I still hope to get some of your homemade pies."

"Claudia, we will always have your sense of humor and Sherrie. Sometimes, I felt like it was the three of us dating."

"Well, with her living at EG's house with me and working for you, I guess she was always around. Maybe you should bring her a rum and Coke when she gets back in town tomorrow." I shrugged. "I appreciate how easy this is. I will miss you."

"Just because we're not dating doesn't mean we can't still—"

"I am not a friend-with-benefits kind of girl."

"That wasn't what I was going to say. If you're staying in town, it would be in our best interests to be on friendly terms." Aaron extended an undeserved olive branch.

"Are you sure you're not the girl in this relationship? Friends? Hang out together? Should we sync our periods?" I was nervous about confrontation, and here he was being the bigger person. My knee-jerk response was probably a subconscious effort to shoot down the goodwill he had put forward.

"With talk like that, you are making this

breakup a lot easier for me." He grinned, and then his face changed. He looked away. "Maybe it's my ego. I say we're friends, and I don't have to show my broken side."

"Oh." That was a hit to my gut, but I deserved it. "I will stop with the jokes. I would like to be friends, but I may flinch once or twice the first time I see you with some new coed." I held up my cup to his, and we toasted. "To the end."

"To the end," Aaron echoed.

"Do you have to go back to the bar?"

"I got Pete bartending, and Jo-Lee is there now. They will close and lock up tonight."

We walked silently for several blocks through town to EG's house, which was a beautiful white two story. The only person we passed was a teenager walking a dog, his head in his phone and no acknowledgment of my wave or that we were even on the same street as him.

We walked up to the house, and I suddenly stopped.

Aaron stopped too. "What's wrong? Second thoughts?"

"I didn't have any lights on when I left the house, and now the light is on upstairs."

"Which one do you think it is?" he asked. "The town's ghostly Gray Lady from the hill or the relatively new Spirited River-Bone Man?"

I took a step back. "Watch what you say. The

Spirited River-Bone Man is my grandfather!"

CHAPTER THREE

"Claudia, don't get snide with me. You're the one who came up with that name last month. This is just about halfway between the river and the hill; maybe the two spirits of River Bend are having a little rendezvous in the attic. Plus, from what I have been told, he was an ass." Aaron clearly noticed I didn't move or say anything. "Hey, I'm just joking. Is EG here, or is Sherrie back yet?"

"I spoke to EG earlier. She just got to Saint Paul and will be gone for a few days. Sherrie's not supposed to be here until tomorrow. Their cars aren't here. And just because I named George the Spirited River-Bone Man does not mean you get to be flip about it."

Lowering the cup from his mouth, he wiped away the rum and Coke off his top lip. "That is exactly what it means. You give a bag of bones—actually—you giving your dead grandfather a name fit for an alternative rock band or a nineties slasher film antihero means I do get to be flip."

My mind flashed back a month when a local fisherman discovered a bag of bones in the river, and it was revealed that my aunt, EG, was really my birth mother and that bag of bones found in the river by a fisherman was my paternal grandfather. I hadn't known him or that he even existed, much less that he had been missing for twenty-plus years. I had no emotional attachment to the man. Right or wrong, I named him the Spirited River-Bone Man. As far as the ghostly Gray Lady on the hill is concerned, didn't every town from the 1700s have a legendary ghost that claimed a spot for themselves?

Aaron's arm on my shoulder brought me back to the present. "Are you sure you didn't leave a light on?"

"Positive. It was light out when I left, and the porch light's burned out. I didn't want to be late, so I left the house dark."

"Do you want me to call the police?"

"Do you mind if we just wait a minute?"

Calmly, Aaron started towards the neighbor's house. "I'll see if Jorge is home, and the two of us will check it out."

EG's neighbor, Jorge, was a world-class

mechanic, expert wood craftsman, and overall decent guy. I'd met him three years ago at one of EG's famous book club meetings.

EG was only forty-three and had lived alone before Sherrie and I moved there. I didn't care how old or young a person was; I worried when they lived alone. I would never have admitted it to EG, but I'd had Jorge check in on her sometimes when she hadn't answered my texts. I hoped they would get together; however, she wouldn't date men more than ten years younger than her. She wouldn't budge despite Jorge being just eleven years younger. It probably really had to do with the fact that she was five inches taller than him.

We walked towards Jorge's house when the music of nineties pop group Spice Girls came blasting out of EG's house.

I stopped, dropped my shoulders, then sighed and sat down on the grass, sprawling out like a snow angel, surrendering between the two houses. "It's Sherrie. She must have come back early," I said flatly. "The fact that she scared me will only add to her joy of moving here."

Looking down at me, Aaron asked, "Are you sure? I don't see her car."

"She knows EG is gone for the weekend, so maybe she commandeered a spot in the garage for a few days. At least, I hope she's in there because I don't know if I can handle a ghost with a taste for retro music." I sat up and crisscrossed my legs.

"What's up? Are you ok?" Aaron asked. "You look a little pale. Maybe you should slow down with the cocktail."

"Actually, to be honest, I'm not settled. There is some strange stuff going on. I didn't want to say anything because I didn't want to sound . . ." I didn't know how to finish the sentence.

Understanding I was not getting up anytime soon, Aaron joined me on the grass. "After breaking your arm in a hit-and-run accident and learning your real family history, you get to be spooked."

"The funny thing is that doesn't bother me. The hit-and-run was solved. The lady who was the cause of all the commotion is locked up." I did not have time to finish explaining that the family stuff didn't have me rattled because, apparently, Aaron had more stuff to say.

"Come on now. You have to be unsettled. I understand you would be spooked by things." I started to wave him off, but he shut me down. "Hold on. I'm not finished. In the past six weeks, you also found out that your aunt is actually your birth mom, the guy you knew as Pastor Theo is actually your birth father, Teddy, and the bag of bones that was discovered in the Mississippi River was your grandfather. I don't care how great of a life you had and that your parents—who, by the way, I think are great—gave you an idyllic life, but all that new information is not something to gloss over."

Those words did not faze me. Twilight was settling in and the sparse wind had brought some small relief, but something was sucking the breath out of me, strange feelings and odd things that had been going on.

"I am actually content with that—well, mostly. I can reconcile all that. I am blessed with great parents, and EG has been amazing. After learning the story of EG becoming pregnant with me wildly unexpectedly and my mom and dad offering to raise me, I feel more love than anything for my family. Teddy being my birth father is a bit odd. You know we got together for coffee, and we are doing lunch tomorrow. I am still leveling that out. I see him as a person in my life, maybe like a distant uncle, but no more than that. The hit-and-run was solved, and I am about to be out of this arm cast. I just have this feeling that someone has been watching me. I swear, a few days ago, I came home, and the outside kitchen doormat had been moved."

I held up my hand to stop him from interrupting and, more importantly, from judging. "I know noticing a doormat being moved is odd and it maybe could have been an animal or my shoe snagging it, but it was like someone was looking for a key. Please don't roll your eyes at me. How can I detect a doormat shifting a couple of inches means someone is looking for a key? I can't rationalize it. I can't explain the vibe that hit me when I saw the mat. I also think someone was following me last week after I had coffee with Teddy. When I left the coffee shop, someone came out of the shop next door and was just walking at my pace, and it all felt so strange. I quickly got in the car and drove away. Today at the river, I looked behind me several times, and it seemed as if someone was in the woods. I don't know how all that adds up to something or for that to make sense. I just know that I feel a shadow on me."

"I'm sorry I didn't pick up on this sooner. So much for being a good boyfriend. I never saw you freaked out. I wish you would have said something sooner."

"It's probably no big deal. I want it to be no big deal, but yet I can't—"

"You don't need to justify anything. As long as you're safe."

I nodded and sat there for another minute, and then I picked up the cup and tried to take a large sip of the cocktail. My power move of taking a swift, deep drink was like watching an old helium balloon mercilessly and slowly wander to the ground as it lost its stability. I never imagined how difficult it was to swig a cocktail with ice from the small opening of a coffee cup lid. I understood why

Aaron kept wiping his upper lip when he drank.

"Help me up. Let's go turn on better music before Sherrie claims the right to be DJ for the night," I said.

We walked to the highlight of the house, a screened-in porch that wrapped almost all the way around the front. I looked behind me as I had been doing these last few weeks. I didn't see anything unusual, but I didn't feel anything comforting either.

CHAPTER FOUR

A few months ago, I'd planned to come to River Bend after my college graduation to take care of EG for the summer as she underwent chemo treatments before I moved to Chicago for a job in September. But things had snowballed, and I'd decided to stay in River Bend while I figured out what I really wanted to do in life—all in the same week I'd found out my Aunt EG was my birth mother.

EG had made a great career for herself as a writer. For most everyone in the community, EG was the apple of their eye. She wrote one series of books that were set in the town of River Bend, which brought fame to the small town. I thought some women were intimidated by her independence and success. She had a loft in

Chicago and spent a good deal of time there if she was not teaching at the college or traveling the world.

Teddy—or as I knew him, Pastor Theo—was my birth father. He'd had no idea that EG was pregnant before he disappeared from his life and returned a few years later as a pastor.

My parents, Katie Lyn and Matthew, raised me and my brother, Connor, in St. Paul, MN. They had always been rock-solid and had given me everything I wanted while growing up—not in the materialistic way of buying me a thousand toys, but in the form of love, guidance, and support but not smothering. They were my biggest cheerleaders for whatever I chose to do.

Maybe that was my attraction to Aaron. He was a younger version of my father. That was also probably why I had broken up with him.

Perhaps that was what had drawn Sherrie and me together as instant friends. She was the polar opposite. She instantly cheered my decisions if she agreed; otherwise, I'd have to listen—and really listen—to why she believed my judgment might be flawed, and then she supported whatever I chose to do. To be fair, she was loving and loyal.

Her chaos amazed me. She'd come up to visit in the beginning of the summer at EG's request, figuring I'd want a friend around when EG gave me our family history.

Soon after I had decided to stay in River Bend, Sherrie quit her job and moved there to start a graduate degree program at Jameson College. Before she had even been accepted at the college, EG had extended her home to Sherrie. Before one box was officially moved in, she had a job at Aaron's bar. Within a day, she found someone to sublet her old apartment, packed up everything she owned and could fit in her VW Bug, and made the move. Chaotic but decisive.

Two girls. Same house. Two different directions. I was sputtering around in life, figuring out what I should be doing, and she was doing. I was watching her and taking notes, hoping to learn something.

Aaron and I walked in the front door and stepped into the living room. I went to charge my phone, and then I belted out, "Yo, Sherrie. Turn down the nineties and come join us for cocktails."

The music was softened slightly, and then, with hair flopping and bare feet pounding down the stairs, Sherrie blew into the living room. "Hey, I thought you guys just left."

"What makes you say that?" I took the couch while Aaron went to the fridge and grabbed Sherrie a beer.

She took the tall wingback chair, pushed back the recliner, and greedily accepted the beer. Aaron sat on the love seat.

"I heard the back screen door shut just as I entered the front door. I figured you were in the basement and didn't hear me yell hello or just went out the back, hoping not to help me unpack."

"Where is your car?" Aaron asked.

"When I pulled up, I parked out front and Jorge was outside. He came over and opened my door and told me I had one minute to pull out anything I wanted from my car for the next twenty-four hours. I asked him what was going on, and he said I better start grabbing stuff because I only had forty-five seconds left. I ran around back, grabbed my stereo, two crates of albums, and my overnight bag. I barely shut the back door when he left me standing on the curb. I carried a load in, heard the back door, went upstairs, turned on the music, and made two more trips in the house with my stuff."

Aaron looked at me, and I just gave him the I-told-you-so look, which he did not seem to acknowledge before he asked Sherrie, "How many albums do you have? Are you still collecting or just holding on to what you have so far?"

"If I find a group I like and come across the vinyl, I will definitely add it to the collection. Most of my new music, I download, but I am always on the lookout for different stuff. So did you guys make a coffee run at this hour?" Her head toggled like she was at a tennis match, flipping back and forth between us.

"No, we are toasting with a cocktail. We can't exactly walk around with beer cans in our hands in this town—or actually most towns," I said with half a smile. "It was Aaron's idea."

"Don't tell me you are celebrating some sappy two-month anniversary."

I said nothing and let Aaron flatly comment, "We are celebrating our breakup."

Sherrie's head toggling back and forth from Aaron to me and back was now nonstop. Waiting for one of us to break the silence, she sprung the chair back forward. "You are kidding?"

"We just broke up a few minutes ago. We are trying the friends thing," I added, and my stomach flopped again.

After a long slow gulp of beer, the only thing that came out of her mouth was "Interesting."

"That's it?" I asked. "You have nothing else to say? You have to be thinking something."

"I am always thinking something. If you are asking, I am saying interesting. Before you ask for more, I will tell you. You are both good people. As a couple, you were ok people. Too much of the same thing in one couple."

Aaron stared at her blankly and shrugged when he looked at me.

I concluded the conversation with "I guess drama-free breakups do exist." I raised my cup, and the other two raised theirs. "To a drama-free fall, Sherrie and I living together once again, the two of you working together—"

"Ahem . . . excuse me?" Aaron pulled back his raised arm. "Sherrie's working for me, not . . ."

My hand still raised, I continued. "Yes, Sherrie working for you, boss man, me being a regular at the bar with special friend pricing and—"

"For the love of god, can we just toast!" Sherrie said. "Yes, drama-free blah, blah, blah. Cheers."

If I had to guess, Sherrie had spoken for her and Aaron with that declaration. We stood up and tapped our beverages and drank.

"Sherrie, can you go put on better music?" Aaron asked.

Without hesitation, she finished the beer, handed him the empty bottle, and bounded up the stairs.

He looked to the now-empty stairwell and turned to me. "I don't know about drama-free."

CHAPTER FIVE

"What do you mean? Not drama-free? Sherrie is not always drama . . . sorry, I can't finish that sentence with a straight face. She is full of fun but not always take-the-stage drama." I giggled.

Aaron was not smiling or moving. "You do not lie or exaggerate. What about her hearing the back door open and close when we weren't here? Maybe you're right and somebody is watching you or, worse, was inside the house?"

He watched me slowly step back. I was determined to stay standing and hold my footing despite my knees shaking a bit. "Now, you are freaking me out. It is one thing to have these secret thoughts, but to hear them echoed back is a little unnerving."

Neither one of us said anything, and the

music of Elvis Presley started playing.

Sherrie returned, watching us from the bottom of the stairs. "Strange vibe going on here. Don't tell me you're back together? Thank god I didn't give my real opinion about the breakup."

Aaron seemed to wait for me to explain what we just hit upon, but all I could think to say was "This is better music?"

"Yes," Aaron and Sherrie answered in unison.

He broke some of our tension when he turned and tapped her on the shoulder. "Tag, you're it."

Sherrie looked at me, and I shrugged my shoulders. I was as confused as she was.

"Claudia gets her cast off in a few days, and since I am no longer on boyfriend duty, you are now on nurse and housekeeping duty since EG is gone," he said.

My jawed dropped, and my heart was pounding. "I don't know if I should be flattered or pissed. Take care of me? What am I, five years old? Am I your property?"

"Ease up there, civilian. Stand down." Aaron was direct, but his voice was even. "Every time EG leaves town, she hands me a list of things to keep an eye on. She said she was living with the one-armed bandit, so she made sure things were easy for you. I had to make sure the lids on jars were loose, all chip bags and cracker boxes were preopened and sealed with just a clip for easy use, and my personal favorite, any bread I brought to the house had to be presliced."

Now my jaw was on the floor, and before I could say anything, Sherrie laid it out. "Oh, mmmmmyyyy god. You are the same person. You and EG. EG and you. Add to that, your mom. You, your mom, and EG. Last year at college, if Mia, Sami, or I had broken an arm or leg, I can't imagine what you would have had concocted for apartment protocol! Remember the flu outbreak last fall? You went full-on nuts on everyone." She looked at Aaron. "She packed up Mia, Sami, and herself with three days' worth of clothes, their laptops and books while they were in class, and found couches to crash on within the hour of me coming into the apartment with a fever and throwing up. She systematically checked on me two times a day dressed in a homemade hazmat suit. I thought you were going to switch your major to be premed or pre–Nurse Ratched. So don't get all huffy. This is what you, your mother, and EG do—nurse, dote, and nurture all with love." She turned on her heels to face Aaron, raised her arm in a salute formation. "By the command of EG, I accept all orders and will perform these duties, sir."

She walked between Aaron and me to the front door to let Jorge in. We just stood there soaking in all things Sherrie.

I leaned in and whispered, "Drama-free?"

Aaron raised one eyebrow and shrugged. We returned to our seats on opposing sofas.

We heard Sherrie squawk, "You want to tell me what is going on with my car?"

Jorge entered the house and shook hands with Aaron and gave me a smile. He turned to Sherrie and said, "I am fixing the muffler on that thing. Your father called earlier today and asked me to fix it for you immediately. You'll have it back tomorrow. I'm hoping you didn't have plans this evening that involved your car."

"It's great it is being fixed, but I don't have the money. Wait, my dad called? How does he know you?"

"Last week, when he delivered some of your boxes, EG brought him over and introduced us. She wanted me to show him the renovations I've done to the first floor of my house. We talked again a couple of days ago about something I installed in the kitchen. Today, he called and gave me his credit card number and asked that I fix the muffler as soon as you got back."

"That is sweet of him, but did you have to do it before I unpacked?"

"How long has he been asking you to get it fixed?"

Sherrie put her head down like a toddler in

trouble.

"Plus, I've been listening to that thing these past three weeks. I was either going to fix it or steal it and sink it in the river. Just be happy it is getting done and say thank you."

She looked up, smiled, and threw her arms around his neck. "Thank you, thank you, thank you." After the hug, she slugged his arm. "Next time, you could tell a girl what was happening." She bounced back to her chair.

"No way and risk you darting off because you have just one more thing you have to do. I promised your father I would take care of it immediately. As I said, you will have it tomorrow." He turned to look at us and took a step to the door. "Good to see all of you."

"Wait, before you go. Can we talk to you about something?" Aaron said to Jorge, then nodded towards me.

I wasn't sure I wanted to include more people in my theory about being watched, but since I couldn't think of something else to say, I might as well come out with the truth. The three of them were now back in their same seats in the living room, but this time, Sherrie sat on the edge of the chair with her head toggling between all of us, clearly unaware of where Aaron was going with the conversation. He stayed silent and let me begin.

"Jorge, have you noticed any unusual

activity around the house? Have you seen anything or anyone around here?"

"Has something been going on?" Jorge asked me and looked at Aaron and Sherrie. He was standing near the door but stepped forward with no intention of leaving. He went to the dining table and pulled a chair out and sat in it backwards, then motioned for me to continue.

Sherrie moved to speak first, her voice teetering between nerves and rousing excitement. Like the upward climb on a rollercoaster—you don't know if you want to get to the top, but know you don't want to turn back. "Did I miss something? I have been gone for two days. Don't tell me more soap opera stuff is going on? Didn't I just say there's a strange vibe in the house?"

"Easy there. Sherrie, sit back and pull your fingernails out of the cushion of the chair. Jorge, can Aaron grab you a beer?"

Jorge nodded, and Aaron was out of the chair before I finished asking the question. He returned from the kitchen a minute later with drinks for Jorge and Sherrie, then resumed his position on the love seat.

"It's no big deal, really. I have this feeling somebody has been watching me for the past few weeks."

Sherrie responded first. "Is it just a reflex from the hit-and-run?"

"I don't think so. None of that spooks me." I began grinding the last of the ice from the cocktail.

Aaron circled the conversation back to the present. "She thinks someone was looking for a key because the back doormat was moved and that someone was watching her at the river today and a few other times."

"What has EG said or seen?" Jorge asked.

"I haven't said anything. Even though she got a good prognosis after her chemo treatments, it's still a big ordeal, and she also had a lot happen earlier this summer. And now she is traveling again and doing a lot of writing. I didn't want to interrupt her positive rhythm she has going. She has barely been around these last three weeks, and I didn't want her to slow down because of some weird feelings. Why spook her when I am not even sure what this all means."

Everyone was waiting for me to continue, but I had a question for Aaron. "What I don't understand is why you decided to hold court here with everyone. I thought you would politely downplay my theory that someone is following me, but instead, you're being rational about it."

Waiting for him to crack a joke and call this all nonsense, I realized he was taking his time to answer, and the hair on my neck tingled.

I almost felt like stopping him from answering, but he said, "I didn't think anything of it at the time, but last week Jo-Lee said some guy had been asking about you. You came in when Sherrie's shift was ending. That night you guys were going to see a movie, and I met up with you here afterward, remember? You sat at the bar and had a beer."

Sherrie spoke up. "I remember that because it was strangely busy for a summer Sunday because the Brewers played the Twins. Jo-Lee had caught on quick to everything the week before, but she kept screwing up the lunch special. I had to spend some time straightening out her tickets before I could leave. Aaron's right; you were sitting at the bar waiting for me. He was bartending, and you were talking to Bobby and Nick."

"I chatted with them for a bit, but they were mostly watching the game and talking about the fall hunting season with the two older guys on the other side. What exactly did Jo-Lee say?"

"It was a couple of hours later when we were closing up. She said someone had been asking about you. Like if you were a student at Jameson or a townie. It was mostly all regulars because the students aren't back yet. Most people know who you are. It struck me as odd."

"You have cameras all over that place. Did you look at the surveillance from that afternoon?"

"I didn't look because I didn't think much of it at the time. Some of the stuff Jo-Lee asked threw me off a bit as well, but then I think she was just trying to make conversation with her new boss by showing interest in you," Aaron said.

"I'm sure she was just trying to make conversation with you." I tried to sound convincing.

Sherrie added, "She is an odd one. Don't get me wrong, she is a hard worker, but there is something off about her. She can ask a thousand questions, and she pretends to relate to you, but if I ask her a personal question, it's like I slapped her."

"What do you mean? Her father, Victor, is a long-haul truck driver on the weekends. He does part-time welding work during the week, her mom is not around, and she has no brothers or sisters. She split from her boyfriend, Adam. She's easy to talk to, and she has been going through some serious shit. You're right; she is a hard worker. You did her reference check, and I told you how to ask the right questions when you called," Aaron reminded Sherrie.

"Can we stop the staff meeting and get back to Claudia?" Jorge asked.

"I don't know if this is something or not, but someone was checking out your car a few days ago," Sherrie said.

"That car?" Jorge and Aaron said together.

"Don't make fun of Debby!" I had named my car Debby after the '70s one-hit wonder Debby

Boone. "I plan to let her go at the end of summer, but be kind. She has been with me on some epic adventures."

I could have sworn Jorge rolled his eyes when he turned to Aaron.

Jorge continued. "I guess I get your attachment to the car. Our point was, why would someone check out your car? It is not a classic or antique or anything despite your peculiar affection for it."

Sherrie added, "I saw the person staring into your car. I said something like, 'That car is not going anywhere for a while.' The person just made a comment about checking the meter. That struck me as odd because other spots were open. I just thought the person was checking for valuables and got nervous when I caught them."

"What did the person look like?" I asked. I looked down and saw I had moved past fraying the edges of the paper cup and had begun shredding it, the remnants falling on my lap and the couch cushion.

"I have no idea. They had a hat on and a windbreaker and baggy sweats. Couldn't see a face. I remember thinking the person was way overdressed. Rain was expected but not until much later that evening, but I thought if they were casing cars, they would not want to be recognized. Honestly, I don't know about age or if it was a guy or girl. My height, I guess."

The message tone on my phone beeped, and I read, I am sorry I can't make lunch tomorrow. My brother and his kids are in the hospital. It was from Teddy.

CHAPTER SIX

I relayed Teddy's information to the group after a few more message exchanges. Two days before, Teddy's brother, Christian, and his son had been in a car accident. They were fortunate to have made it out alive, because a driver in another car was killed. Christian had some fractured ribs, a broken leg, and both he and his son had some deep cuts and bruises. Full recovery was expected, but the next few months would be difficult for them.

"So much for things that spook me. I guess they have it much worse than anything than what might be following me."

"I can't imagine what it's like for Christian's wife or Teddy to get that news," Jorge said.

"You almost lost relatives before you even met them," Sherrie said.

"This is sad and horrible, but I really don't think about them as family or even Teddy's kids as half-siblings. I would like to meet them one day because they are important to Teddy. To be really honest, I see Teddy as someone in my life but not necessarily as family. Maybe that will change over time. EG made peace with leaving Teddy out of the picture all these years, and my mother and father are more than anyone could ask for, so I don't know about expanding that side of the family tree."

Aaron's phone beeped this time with an incoming message. Pete, from the bar, sent a message that the south side of the town square had lost power, and the power at the bar had flickered but seemed to be operating fine. Business was picking up more than expected because some of the other bars had to close. After a brief phone conversation, Aaron apologized for having to leave before we'd settled things.

"Let me go, and you can stay here. I need the money," Sherrie said.

"Thanks, but you have been drinking, so that is an easy no thank-you."

"You have been drinking as well."

"Yes, one drink, but I own the place. There is a difference. Pete and Jo-Lee can handle the crowd. I just want to make sure the register is still online and the backup generators are set to go for the coolers if power loss hits our side of the street.

Plus, if you stop drinking before the hangover phase, you can ease into your work as EG's temporary deputy in charge since I am off boyfriend duty."

Hearing Aaron repeat that, I have to say, stung a little. I know the breakup was my doing, but with him being so cool about it, this final decree hit me like a cold bucket of water.

I stood but felt strange just standing there. "We could walk with you to see if we can find out more about the power outage," I blurted out.

Sherrie did not protest or contribute a snarky comment about me insisting we all go for a walk. "I'll turn off the music and be back down in a minute," she mumbled.

Everyone was standing now, and Jorge thankfully brought the conversation back around to all things that spooked me. "We never came up with anything conclusive tonight. I know you need to go, Aaron, so I will keep this short. I'll keep an eye out for anything funny. Claudia, ask EG about installing one of those doorbell cameras. I know you have my number, but make sure Sherrie has it as well."

"Will do. I'll check the back door and the windows on the lower level." I went through the kitchen to the back door and locked it.

The guys were talking in a low voice, and Sherrie was traipsing down the stairs.

We all walked out together, and Jorge said, "I'm going to walk around the house before going back home. I'll be in and out of the garage and in the kitchen if you need anything tonight."

CHAPTER SEVEN

The three of us said goodbye to Jorge and started down the sidewalk. My eyes floated between the teens on their bikes racing down the street and Sherrie and Aaron walking ahead of me. The empty space beside me was loud. This was the first time in two years I did not have a boyfriend.

I would see Aaron again—probably a lot since Sherrie was working for him, and oddly enough, my parents were going into business with him—but I felt the loss of his attention on me. The breakup was the right thing to do, but it left me with another gap in my life plan that I was working on. More gaps for me to watch out for. I hoped I wouldn't fall into the gaps.

Aaron led at a brisk pace. Business was business. He spent the few minutes texting and calling the other bars in town to get a handle on what was going on.

After a few blocks, we turned on Main Street. North towards campus, lights were on, and south towards the town square, power was sporadic. We walked a couple more blocks towards BAR, and a few bar patrons strolled down the street and a few sat on park benches. Some carried bottles of beer or plastic cups. Apparently, when the bars had lost power, everyone just left and those with cocktails exchanged their glasses for plastic cups, and nobody seemed concerned about walking around with alcohol.

We were about to enter BAR when Aaron gave us an update. "A transformer blew from near the construction site behind the hardware store, causing the outage. Power should be restored in a few hours. I am going to stay and make sure the beer coolers are good."

"Are you sure you don't need me to help?" Sherrie asked.

"Positive. From what I can see inside, three of us can handle it. If it slows down and Jo-Lee or Pete want an early night, I will relieve them or just crash upstairs for the night and monitor the power situation."

"Gotcha, boss. Let's head back to the square. I saw Kay and Jenna walking around with cups."

"I'm not sure if I'm in the mood to party in

the square," I said.

"Come on, let's say hi, and then we'll head back together."

I hadn't thought about what I was going to do these next few days. If I hadn't been working or driving EG to chemo, I'd been with Aaron or waiting for him to finish at the bar. I was determined not to get spooked out by everything we had been discussing, but that didn't mean I needed to go back to an empty house. "Ok, I'm with you, girl."

"Well, that's it then." Aaron pulled the door open. "I will see you . . ." He looked at Sherrie and finished with "At your next shift and . . ." He looked at me and just concluded with "Later." He turned and walked in.

Ouch. Self-inflected wounds might hurt the most.

I was slightly irritated he was handling this so well. If he'd been being a dick about the breakup, I could have at least been mad at him.

CHAPTER EIGHT

Sherrie locked her arm around mine and trotted us off to the square, waving like a five-year-old trying to stop an ice cream truck. Kay and Jenna motioned for us to join them. Kay reached below the bench they were sitting on and pulled out a bucket of beer and offered us each one. It seemed to be acceptable now to openly drink tonight in the park because of the blackout.

I'd met Kay at Chambray Senior Living Center, where we worked. I had initially gone there to complete an absurd amount of community service hours after my former boyfriend—well, former former boyfriend—got a ludicrous number of parking violations in my car, and I had no idea it was happening. The judge reduced the amount that had to be paid but replaced it with community service hours for me.

I met Kay on my first day there. She had a striking look with her purple-and-red-streaked hair, nose ring, heavy eyeliner, and pale complexion with beautiful skin. If someone was to judge her by appearance, they would not place her at a facility for seniors but probably behind the bar of some dive joint that doesn't open until ten p.m. She loved working there, and all the residents adored her.

Her roommate, Jenna, was attending college part-time to become a paralegal and was working part-time for a judge in town.

My community service hours eventually turned into a paying job. The work was dull, but with one good arm, I was limited to what I could do. I was fortunate enough that they found different jobs for me.

Usually, once a week, I went for drinks with Kay, Jenna, and Sherrie. The three of them were generally scoping out the bar scene, looking for boyfriends. All three had high hopes for when the postgrads returned in the fall.

"After we finish these beers, we're heading over to Peach's Café. On Fridays, they have acoustic music and food specials. I promised Vivian—you know the nice lady in the condo with the bright-yellow car and the little runt of a dog—that I would listen to her grandson Jacob play and report back to her. Want to join us?" Kay asked.

"That's cool," Sherrie said.

"Not really. I am only doing this because I really like Vivian. Since she fell last week, she is not so mobile. She's so funny. She insisted I take twenty dollars from her to buy a drink for me and whoever I could get to come with me and then put five dollars in the tip jar next to the piano. She doesn't think he is very good, and is scared many people will leave once he starts playing," Kay said.

"She is so sweet. I have seen him around, visiting her. I have no idea about talent, but he is pretty cute," I said.

Leaning back on the bench with her leg crossed over the other and bouncing up and down, Jenna said, "Oh la la. Look at you having eyes for another man. What would your boyfriend say?"

"We . . ." My stomach flopped. "We are no longer together."

"Really?" Jenna said.

They looked at Sherrie for confirmation, and she nodded.

"Yes, it's all good. Happy with my decision." I needed to explain it had been me doing the breaking up. I couldn't help but wonder if that was my ego or me needing to reassure myself.

"Well then, let's use that to our advantage and head over to the café. Maybe this Jacob music guy has some cute friends that came to hear him play. A group of four girls looks like a girls' night out as opposed to three girls out picking up dudes," Jenna said.

My phone beeped, and I rolled my eyes.

Sherrie knew what it was. "The douche is late. He must be sitting home thinking about his favorite defendant. Do you think he is enjoying a nice Chianti or sipping some jug wine from his mother's pantry while he texts you at this hour?"

"Let it go. Hopefully, this will be the last of it. I just have to figure out how to send him on his way."

"Don't tell me you already have a man lined up to date you. Please share," Kay said with a wink and a smirk.

"Not this creep. You do not want him. It's the judge who assigned my community service. Once or twice a week, he asks for an update of my community hours and then tries to make it personal. I have tried polite, I have tried rude, I have tried ignoring, I have tried official. Remember, Jenna, when I called to confirm my hours were recorded? I have tried, I have sooo tried. He says he is just following up on his court cases."

"I have never heard of a judge maintaining contact with someone they had in their courtroom, especially without a lawyer," Jenna said. "I have only been with Judge Konrad a few years, but I think that is strange. Creep-ola."

"My hours wrap up soon. Hopefully, he just fades away. I am just gonna ignore him. I'm not going to play his games. This can't be right."

"Let me know if you want me to talk to Judge Konrad. I could get you some time with her."

I just nodded and pushed him out of my mind.

She understood and decided it was time to keep the evening going. "If we are done with creepy dude, let's head over to Peaches."

"I told Jim we would return the bucket to the bar. It's only a block away from the café. We can finish these beers on the way," Kay said.

Both girls uncrossed their legs at the same time, stood up, and Kay grabbed the bucket and led us away from the square.

We were walking in the opposite direction of Aaron's bar, and I couldn't help but turn and look.

Because I slowed down for a second, Sherrie turned and waited. She spoke to the other two up front, "Hold up, ladies. You guys go ahead and return the bucket. We may meet you at Peaches. I want to check in if Aaron needs help. Who knows what's going to happen with the power on that block."

"You want to come with us?" Kay asked me.

Before I could formulate an answer, Sherrie latched onto my arm with a death grip and said, "She will go with me tonight wherever I go even if it is back to Aaron's. Hopefully, we'll see you later."

Kay and Jenna accepted that and kept going. Sherrie took three steps in the opposite direction, throwing her beer bottle in a garbage can. She stepped into the doorway of the closed tailor shop and started texting.

"What's going on? Aaron made it clear he didn't want 'drinking Sherrie' working tonight."

"You didn't see what I saw, did you?"

CHAPTER NINE

"See? What did you see? What are you talking about? Oh, shit, did you see someone watching me? Us?" My hand shook while still trying to hold the beer bottle, which suddenly needed to be drained. I closed my eyes and gulped it down, trying to let the beer calm me, but apparently, the situation was not all about me.

Sherrie still had her head in her phone. "What are you talking about?" She looked up at me. My face must have been pale. "Sorry, no. I didn't mean to panic you. I just saw Jo-Lee running from the alley behind the bar. She still had her apron on and looked scared. I just texted Aaron to see if he needs help. Should we go see?"

"We?"

"Yes, we. You are not going anywhere by

yourself."

"Thanks for thinking of me, but I don't need a babysitter. Let's not blow everything out of proportion."

Thirty seconds earlier, I was ready to pee in my pants, and now, I was declaring my independence. Sherrie was my great equalizer—my partner on the seesaw of life.

"Maybe she has a date with her boyfriend, Adam."

"I don't know. Maybe late for a date. She looked frightened."

Her phone beeped, and she read the message. "No help needed. Seriously don't come to the bar. Stay off the square tonight."

She looked at me and added, "That is to the point and weirdly directive. What do you think it means?"

"I think it means we should just go home and call it a night. I am not in the mood for music at the café."

"You don't think it is code for"—Sherrie inhaled deeply and spoke in a throaty voice imitating Aaron—"help, we're being robbed, come save us."

"That would be cool, but the dude is ex-military and doesn't need two girls rescuing him. Let's get out of here. He suggested we leave the square, and when has he been wrong?"

"Only about you." Sherrie laughed.

"Hardy har har," I said.

We stepped out of the doorway together and headed back to EG's.

"You know, since we are living together again, you will have to work on your sense of humor," I said.

It was getting close to eleven o'clock, and we got back to EG's fairly fast. Approaching the house, we had to pass Jorge's. The faint sound of an electric grinder of some sort came from his garage. The garage light was on, and the door open.

For the past seven months, he had been remodeling his house, each room and every detail. We stopped in the driveway, and he looked up and gave us a nod like a father checking on his daughters. He was less than ten years older than us, but he seemed a lifetime ahead of us. We said goodnight and kept going.

We walked onto the screened-in porch, and Sherrie fumbled through her pockets for the key. We didn't always lock the door if we were going out for the evening. EG was fairly loose on security. Hook the screen door shut and lock the back door when the last person went to bed were the general rules. Tonight was different.

"How do you feel about everything earlier? Did I sound like a lunatic?" I asked.

"The breakup? I think that was for the best."

"That's not what I mean."

"I know. I was trying to lighten the mood. You feel what you feel. I wouldn't freak out if I were you. Let's use common sense, and we'll figure it out."

"Keep a level head. Got it."

She pushed open the front door, and we stepped into the living room. "How about we crash in our own rooms tonight and no one takes the porch couch?" Sherrie said, locking the door.

My eyes were drawn to the big window that looked into the porch then out to the street. I glanced at Sherrie and then back to the couch on the porch that suddenly didn't look so comforting. "Good idea. I'm just going to check the back door and kitchen windows."

Everything was still locked. I walked back from the kitchen and looked through the side window just in time to see Jorge's large door close and him going inside for the night. If I had to guess, he had waited for Sherrie and me to return. You don't find many good guys around like that these days.

And I told myself the car that had just driven past really slowly was only a cautious driver and not someone watching the house.

CHAPTER TEN

Saturday morning, we both slept in. I woke up with the sun in my eyes and felt refreshed. It had taken some time to find that deep sleep. I'd kept my window open for some air since we didn't have air-conditioning in the house.

I had lain in bed and stared at the rotating ceiling fan, thinking about each strange interaction I'd had and what Aaron and Sherrie had witnessed. Doormat, someone strangely walking behind me, watching from the woods, casing my car, asking about me, the car slowly driving past the house. With each whoosh of the rotating blades, I repeated mat, walking, watching, casing, asking, driving by. That eventually lulled me to sleep.

I sat up and did one of those satisfying morning stretches that powered through my whole body.

I looked down at my cast. Two more days and I am free.

I glanced at the closet, longing to wear any number of shorts piled up there. Hating cold feet, I grabbed a pair of socks and put them on. Then I used the lotion from the nightstand to begin my daily ritual of trying to get it on my arm underneath the cast. I was battling dry skin and losing the battle.

I was careful not to make any noise going down the stairs. The third and fourth steps on the way down made a creaking noise if they weren't traversed quite right, the wooden planks grinding against the wood trim and creating a high-pitched squeak that could wake up anyone.

I successfully made my way into the kitchen without stirring Sherrie and then realized the coffee was made and there were a bowl and spoon lying on a dish towel drying.

Sherrie had left a note that said, Bike. Damn thoughtful. She hadn't left a text message that could have woken me up.

I opened the refrigerator and touched all the jars—pickles, jelly, mayonnaise, and all the caps were on but loose. In the crisper was a bag of presliced apples. The English muffins had all been presliced. The toaster was on the counter instead of the top shelf of the pantry, and the panini press was sitting next to it. EG had thought of everything. She and my mother were two of the best women I know.

EG had offered to let me stay as long as I needed. Sherrie had come to visit, and within a few days, EG had offered her the third bedroom.

EG enlisted a few rules upon us. No rent was to be paid. We all had to buy our own food, but if we cooked, it was for whoever was home. Snacks were everyone's domain, but if a favorite goodie was to be saved just for yourself, you could put your name on it, but no more than two items at a time could be saved just for you. She said she wanted us to feel at home and that her stuff was our stuff but understood coveting a favorite comfort food or snack.

Sherrie's father, Robert, thought that was unfair and unbalanced. EG said she welcomed the company and was delighted to have young people in the house. Robert laughed and said Sherrie attending graduate school was helping guarantee she would not return to his house. He and his wife were delighted to be empty nesters. He insisted Sherrie at least be responsible for the grass cutting and snow shoveling.

When he was here last week, he'd had a new lawn mower delivered. He also met with Phil, the owner of the hardware store. Phil was to call him the day the snowblowers arrived for the season. EG didn't have the heart to tell Robert that the high school kid she paid to cut her grass would be out of a job. Instead, she told the kid to cut the elderly neighbor's yard and paid him under the condition he didn't tell the couple who was paying him.

Sherrie returned, and we decided to head to the farmer's market in La Crosse forty minutes away. Jorge had not returned with her car so I tossed her my keys, and she was happy to drive.

"When are you going to put Debby down to rest in peace?"

The odometer had stopped working several months ago. My parents had offered me the down payment on a new car as my college graduation gift. I had been saving money for an electric vehicle, something small and easy to park in Chicago, but ever since I had decided to stay in River Bend, I'd had my heart set on something else.

"As soon as my dad or Jorge come across my dream car at a reasonable price. It doesn't have to be new, but the right car and, more importantly, the right price. Do you know where you're going?"

Sherrie had just started driving, not knowing the best route but just moving forward. Driving and in life, she was always moving forward. God, I envied her.

We turned off 13th Ave. onto Main Street.

"Not really. I was just going to head to the freeway from Main."

"Let's take Highway 25 on the Minnesota side and then we can cross back over the river farther south. That way, we can stop in fifteen minutes at the gas station that has those amazing doughhhhnutttsss . . ."

Sherrie semi-slammed on the brakes and did a U-turn.

"What are you doing?" I screamed.

"I've heard about that gas station. Aaron and Jo-Lee were talking about it. Her dad, Victor, being a truck driver, always talks about places on his route. I didn't know it was so close."

"Easy with Debby. She is not much of a car, but she has to last me a little while longer. Do you know how to get to Highway 25?"

She did not immediately answer and then spoke slowly like she was focused on something outside of our conversation. "It's on the other side of the campus, but . . . Just do me a favor. Don't ask questions and don't freak out. Lower yourself in the seat." She had two hands on the wheel and was looking from me to the rearview mirror to the road in front of us. Soon, she was just looking ahead and in the mirror. Sherrie reached her arm out and pushed on my shoulder like she was trying to shove more sweaters into a suitcase.

"Oooh, ok." I slid down and waited.

The radio was not on. Not by choice. It stopped working last month. Sherrie was making a few turns that were not leading to Highway 25. She stopped where she had to, but I didn't know if I would have called them complete stops. She was not reckless but determined to keep going. I could see just enough to know we were headed out of town and into an area surrounded by farms. The only air-conditioning vents that worked in the car flowed up from the floor area. The cold air was blowing up my dress, goosebumps were on my legs, but my pits were dripping with nervous sweat. I tried getting back up, but each time her right arm held me in place.

"Why, what . . ."

Practically ignoring me, Sherrie pressed on. "Shh, quiet. Let me drive!"

We were passing cornfields on the right and a bean field on my left for several miles, but I had no other sense of direction now.

She suddenly turned left down a dirt road. Dust was flying on both sides of the car. She slowed down and did a careful U-turn, then put the car into park and lowered our windows. She waited a minute before softly saying, "You can get up now."

"Please explain! What was that all about?"

"Don't freak out." That was the second time she'd said that, but I started to get really worried. "I think—actually, I know—there was a car following us. I noticed it when we turned onto Main Street. I didn't think anything of it until I did the U-turn. It also turned around and followed us until I turned down this shit bucket of a dirt road. I guess all that crap you said last night is the real deal. It's not like I didn't believe you but to—"

"Don't worry. I know it sounded far-fetched. Did you get a good look at the person driving?"

"You won't believe me. This is all too late-night-cable-TV-bad-movie stuff. The person had on sunglasses, a baseball hat, and a hoodie."

I just looked at her, unconsciously scratching around my cast.

"Aren't you going to say something!" Sherrie said.

"This is where you or I usually make a bad and inappropriate joke, but I got nothing. You?"

She shrugged. I looked down and saw a collection of dead skin gathered on my lap. I opened the door, stood up, and wiped everything off. Sherrie got out, dabbing sweat off her forehead.

We sat on the hood of the car. The warm metal was like a comfy blanket. We looked at each other and started laughing. The sun was beating down on us, but a soft breeze made it comfortable.

"I guess it's cool neither one of us has a boyfriend. We have no phone signal out here, but we also have no one to call," Sherrie said.

I leaned over, curling my hand into a fist, and turned awkwardly to her, looking for a fist bump. "There it is—the inappropriate joke—it has been less than twenty-four hours, and the lack-of-boyfriend jokes have started."

She met my fist with hers, and we laughed.

"Let's start from the beginning. God, I sound like my mom, but anyway." In a high-pitched but loving voice, I said, " 'Girls, when there is a problem always start at the beginning.' " That was one of her many favorite quotes. "There was a car following us. Was it in front of EG's house?"

"I only noticed it when I was turning onto Main Street. I sat at the stop sign for longer than expected for a car to pass before pulling out for the left turn. I thought the car behind me would honk because I could have gone before the second car passed, but I didn't want to push Debby too hard."

"That lasted about four blocks, and then you made that gnarly U-turn on Main Street. My old gal Debby held on strong." We each gave a knock on the hood. "Do you know the make or model?"

"A reddish wagon or hatchback of some kind."

"Plate numbers?"

"No, I tried to look, but I was too busy making turns."

"The car kept going and did not turn around and drive back past this road. Well, at least not yet. So the car is headed to whatever direction that is." She raised her arm and pointed left.

"From what I can tell, that must be east. It is

almost eleven a.m., and the sun is bearing straight down on us. I think that road would eventually lead to Interstate 94 or at least to Marshall and then the interstate."

We didn't say anything for a while. A farmer's tractor was working the fields not too far from us.

I finally asked, "Why did you have me lower myself in the seat?"

"I figured the person is after you. They would eventually see me and drive on. It is not like we could be confused as the same person. I mean, my hair is so much prettier."

I held up my arm next to her dark-brown arm. "Maybe if I work on my summer tan and I had two working arms, I could have prettier hair."

"No matter how pretty your hair is, it will never be a match for my fine Black woman's hair."

We laughed, and I said, "You're right. No one could confuse us. Now what? We can't sit here all day. We have no phone signal. I'm sure we will have it in a couple of miles, but who are we going to call? My parents left on their anniversary cruise two days ago. I'm not bothering EG with this yet. This is her first fun weekend since chemo ended. We can tell her tomorrow when she returns. I don't think anyone from our gang will drive a hundred miles to assist us. Do we go to Aaron or Jorge? The police?"

"I say we talk to Aaron and Jorge again. Have you told anyone else about the strange stuff going on?"

"Like I said last night, I didn't think—or at least I was hoping—it was all my imagination that someone was watching me."

"No idea who or why?"

"None."

This time, Sherrie conjured up my mom's voice. "Girls, let's start at the beginning. Who has Claudia pissed off?"

Neither one of us had an answer.

We slid off the hood and got back in the car. Despite Debby taking a beating this morning, she purred right up. We turned the air off and put the windows down. We heard the farm tractor but not much else. She drove slowly down the dirt road but still managed to stir up a dirt cloud.

We changed our minds pretty fast and rolled up the windows so we could talk.

"I didn't think I was ever enough of a bitch to have enemies. I broke up with Jackson seven weeks ago. I only got two texts from him asking if I had some stuff of his, and he tried to visit. Insisting that I had some backpack of his. Like you said last night, he does not have the cojones to do anything this thought-out. He was sore about the breakup, but it's not like he is out there pining for me. He's moved on."

"What about Aaron? Did he have a jealous ex-girlfriend?"

I shook my head.

Sherrie started talking as if she was a game show contestant. "For five hundred dollars, I will take 'Who did Claudia piss off?' "

We got to the end of the dirt road, and Sherrie made the right-hand turn back to town. She eased Debby onto the road, and less than a quarter of a mile later, she said, "Oh shit."

And she never got to answer her question.

CHAPTER ELEVEN

Sherrie pushed the gas pedal to the floor and tried gunning it. I looked in the side mirror. A car was barreling down on us. Debby was no match for whatever was behind us. Sherrie's options were limited. It was a two-lane road and had farm fields on both sides. Sherrie started to veer right.

"No!" I screamed. "The ditch is too steep. We won't get out of it."

She crossed the lane, and the car followed, then bumped us. Her foot hammered the gas pedal harder, and Debby pushed a little faster. I imagined we were just inches ahead of the car behind us. We couldn't outrun the other car.

I saw our only hope. "Left!" I screamed.

She saw the dirt road and cut the steering wheel hard. Our bodies swung with the swaying of the car. The back left tire dipped into the ditch, but we motored onward. The car bounced, and we bounced harder. It turned out not to be a road but about a hundred-foot-long dirt path that led to some type of water basin and a sprinkler system.

Sherrie kept her hands on the wheel, but the turn was wide because she overcorrected when the tire dipped. She forced another turn to avoid the water system. We went off the dirt lane and careened into the cornfield. We were probably four or five rows in. The corn was as high as the windows.

We bounced, we swayed, we rocked, we jiggled, and we stopped moving probably twenty seconds after the car stopped.

Thanks to my father, I heard the words to the song "Rock and Roll All Nite" by KISS. He could always find lyrics from bands from the '70s or '80s for almost any situation, appropriate or not.

I pushed those lyrics out of my head and came back to the moment when my body stilled with the car. I released the hand clutching the dashboard, and my legs relaxed from the position of straight posts bracing myself from flying into the windshield only to start shaking slightly.

Sherrie finally turned the car off, and we undid our seat belts, opening our doors but remaining in the car.

We didn't know where the other car had

gone, but we were pretty confident it wasn't in the cornfield with us.

We looked at each other, holding our breath, and let it out. In unison, we said, "Hells bells."

We had said that since our third year of college. We fought over who'd had started it, but it became our slogan. After a minute, we stepped out, and Sherrie looked over the roof of the car towards me.

Putting her arm on the door and the other arm on the roof, she passionately implored, "Seriously, who did you piss off?"

I had nothing to say.

From somewhere in the cornfield, the farmer yelled, "Are you ok? Please be ok. It'll be ok. Hello? My wife has called the police."

"We're here, and we're fine," I yelled.

"Lordy, girls. Good to see you both standing." He came up from behind the car following the broken stalks that Debby had laid down as we'd skidded into the field. He stopped and rested his hands on his hips. His T-shirt was spotted with sweat, and the jeans looked like they had been on the farm for a decade. He was probably sixty years old and had a big old grin on his face. "Darn good to see you're ok. I wanna give you both a big hug but don't want you thinking I am one of those old creepy guys you hear about on TV."

"We're fine, sir," Sherrie said.

"Unbelievable. I spotted you girls when you made that crazy first turn. The dirt was flying! We've had a lot of drag racing down this road. Keeps gettin' worse. I got up in the tractor, hoping to see what cars were making trouble. I couldn't hear you leave because I got the Brewers game on inside the cab, but I saw the dirt come up again. At first, I thought it was a game—I saw the other car sitting around the bend and suddenly take off, but I knew something wasn't right. I radioed my wife, Carole, to call the police. We gotta use radios or talkies as some folks call them. Can't use those fancy phones out here." He seemed to realize he was rambling and shrugged. "Right, well then, I hope you're good folks. Carole always tells me to stay out of things, but you haven't shot me yet, so I'm thinking you two are good folks."

"Yes, sir. I'm Claudia, and this is my friend Sherrie." High-stepping over some of the crushed cornstalks, we made our way to the back of the car near the farmer. I raised my right arm showing the cast and extended the left hand for the awkward handshake I have become accustomed to these past few weeks.

He said, "I'm Marty." He pivoted to Sherrie. "Mighty fine driving. I wasn't sure this car of yours would make it."

We heard a car on the road, and Sherrie and I froze. The blur of a blue sedan passed. We let out our breath.

"Girls, it's ok. Carole and I have you. The police will be here shortly. That's probably them goin' up to the house to see my wife. Carole is always saying, 'Stay out of things,' but I am happy you're ok, and I can see for myself you look ok."

Two minutes later, dirt rose over the corn before we heard the car.

"Let's step out to the road. I didn't know where you were headed when I radioed Carole. She will be expecting me out on Milligans Road there so she can spot us. They got it listed as County Road 14 on the maps, but if you have been out here as long as I have, you know it as Milligans Road. If you don't feel comfortable, stay here, and I'll make sure it's just the police and not something crazy."

He lumbered through several rows of corn—stopping twice to check his crops. Sherrie and I followed, and when we got to the edge of the cornfield, we saw a four-wheeler and a squad car following it. We were amused to see sixtysomething-year-old Carole handle that machine like a cowboy riding a horse, who had been on the range for decades.

Before they came to a stop, Sherrie looked down at the ditch and said with serious confidence, "I could have made that cut in the ditch and switched back behind that car."

"I don't know what most of that means, and

sometimes, I don't know what to say to you. But as long as you think you're that good of a driver, please stay away from my Debby from now on."

Carole stepped off the four-wheeler like she had done it all her life. She wore a 4-H Club T-shirt and jeans. Her hair was hidden by a red bandana. Not one speck of makeup, but her skin was flawless. The tall rubber boots seemed to be too much since we haven't had rain for a week.

She caught me looking at the boots. "I've been in the chicken coop, cleaning it out and hopefully haven't dragged anything out with me."

No apologies for the appearance, just a straightforward explanation. I wished I were that confident.

"Hi, girls. I'm Carole. I have to admit I'm surprised to see two girls. Bad on my part, assuming it was going to be boys. We have had trouble with kids drag racing out here, so I put in a call to Holton." She waved to the officer still in the car. He put up his finger to signal he needed a minute. "I wasn't sure where you were exactly, so I had him come to the house. I didn't know what we would find coming out to the main road."

Marty said, "Some crazy stuff. These girls almost got run over. Mighty fine driving by this one."

Sherrie elbowed me and whispered, "Mighty fine driving."

"They were being run off the road by some crazy man."

The officer stepped out of the squad car, and I recognized him from my hit-and-run.

"Afternoon, Marty. Carole tells me you've had some trouble again out here."

"Thanks for coming. Oh, it's not the drag racing this time. These two nearly got ran off the road. Some car was waiting and went straight for them. If it wasn't for her good driving, I think they would be in the ditch."

Sherrie went to elbow me again. I stepped sideways to avoid another round of her self-promotion, but I stumbled and nearly ended up in the ditch. She grabbed my arm, keeping me upright. I couldn't turn and face her. She was enjoying this way too much.

"You again?" the officer said.

"Hello, Officer Holton," I said.

"It's actually Officer Patrick. Officer Holton Patrick. No one gets it right. My parents did me no favors selecting a last name as my first name. Then to match it with a surname name like Patrick. I have had more issues with official government documents than I care to remember or you care to hear about. Right now, with this rambling, I am beginning to sound like my Uncle Marty."

A belly laugh came from Marty, and he lightheartedly slapped Officer Patrick's back .

"Tell me what's going on here?" Officer Patrick said.

"I was on the tractor, and I saw the dirt wind up."

"Excuse me, Uncle Marty. Let me take the girls' statements, and then I will come to the house and get yours. If you want to get back on the tractor, I'll have Aunt Carole radio for you when I'm ready."

Marty smiled. "Always the polite one in the family, aren't you, Holton? Just tell the old man you need some privacy. I can take it. Come on, Carole, let these folks do their business."

"Sir," I said, "thank you for watching out for us. Sorry about the corn. I'm sure we owe you something."

"Don't worry about the corn, but I appreciate it. Are you ok getting the car out?"

Sherrie jumped in. "If I can get it in there, I can get it out of there."

"Darn right, miss. Well then, if you need anything, let us know." Marty turned towards his wife.

She said, "Girls, please be careful. Holton, when you are done here, come to the house and you can get your uncle's statement and some lunch. I have a roasted chicken that I think you'll enjoy. Girls, you are invited as well. Turn left on the gravel road, and you'll see the house on the left."

"Thank you for the offer, but I think we'll head back home once we're done here."

Marty followed Carole to the four-wheeler and held out his hand to help her step up. She certainly didn't need the help but clearly enjoyed having him at her side. He waited until she drove the quarter mile down the main road and turned off. When she wasn't visible any longer, he walked back into the field towards his tractor. I envied everything I had just witnessed. Still in love after all these years.

Sherrie called him back. "Marty, sir."

"Yes, what can I getcha?"

"The Brewers, you think they got a shot at the Series this year?" She knows how to talk to anyone.

He smiled like a little kid. "You betcha. They're gonna take it all the way to the Series this year." He lifted his hat towards us and then walked back to the tractor.

Officer Patrick turned the focus to me. "I recognize that cast. How is it healing?"

"Nicely. Almost out of it. What are the odds of me seeing you again so soon?" I held my hand over my eyes to shield them from the sun.

It was high in the sky, and the heat was radiating from the sun and hot pavement. The light breeze was not doing much to save us from the heat.

"Pretty good as there are not that many of us on the squad. I should be asking what are the odds of me seeing you so soon. Would you like to give me your statements?"

Sherrie and I recounted what happened separately. I hoped she would only begin with today's escapade and leave out my theory about being followed. Although if there were ever a time to tell someone, this would be it, but I didn't have anything concrete to put on record—well, until now.

Unfortunately, we didn't have much of a description of the car. We were hoping his uncle could help with that, but we were doubtful what kind of view he had from the tractor.

After Sherrie gave her statement, the two of them walked back towards me. The standard bounce in her step was not there, but she still had an easy stride. Her adrenaline was probably dropping from the chase, but her self-confidence would always be with her.

Officer Patrick said, "Unfortunately, we don't have any physical evidence, like tire marks or paint scratches. Hopefully, Uncle Marty will have a more detailed description of the car."

We again declined any medical attention, and he asked if we needed a tow truck.

"Absolutely not. It will start." I paused and considered my approach. "Holton, I don't know what the protocol is, but if I were to ask you to remove the car from the cornfield, are you able to help us? I feel if Sherrie or I tried, we would do more damage to your uncle's crops."

"Understood."

We walked with him between the rows of corn to the car.

"The keys are in it," Sherrie said.

I was so proud but not surprised when Debby started right up. We followed Debby as he backed the car out the same way we had come in. He got out and left the door open. Sherrie got in, and he closed the door for her.

Then he came to my side, opening and closing the door for me. "Girls, I am going to follow you back into town before I talk to Uncle Marty. I'm sure whoever was out here is long gone, but be careful, and should something like this happen again, call for help and don't engage with the other drivers."

"Thank you," we said.

He turned towards his car. "No problem."

"Wait!" I yelled. "What can we do for your uncle and aunt? They were so kind."

"They are not expecting anything. That's the type of folks they are. Someone needs help—they help. I will pass on your gratitude."

While we waited for Officer Patrick to return to his vehicle, Sherrie and I downed anything we could find to drink—our tepid coffee from this morning and two half bottles of warm water. On the ride back to EG's, we reviewed what we'd said in our statements. We had done nothing wrong, but when questioned by the police, one tended to be nervous.

We turned onto Main Street and waved goodbye to Officer Patrick.

"You never answered my question," Sherrie said.

"What question would that be?"

"Who did you piss off? Aaron's ex?"

"I am Aaron's ex."

"Yes, but most of this started before you were the current ex."

"I can't imagine Aaron dating someone whacky." Sherrie started to interrupt, but I held her off. "Easy, now. No comments about his choice of girlfriends."

"Anyone stalking EG. We are living in her house. I have only been there three or four weeks and only sporadically until now."

We turned off Main Street and onto 13th Ave. and were just a few blocks from the house. I thought about what Sherrie asked before I said anything. "I can't imagine EG having any enemies. I am clearly not her, and this is clearly not her car."

We were just about to the house, and Sherrie stopped short. I lurched forward. When I pulled myself upright again, she raised her arm and pointed.

"But that is clearly her house, and someone is on her porch. I just saw someone duck."

"Hells bells," we whispered together.

CHAPTER TWELVE

We sat there frozen until he stood up. Chuck crossed the porch and shifted a ladder we had not seen, then moved it. We sighed and looked at each other, forcing a laugh.

I couldn't imagine what he was doing there. He presented no threat, but I was unnerved by the thought of anyone being in the house. My hands were shaking a little. Sherrie didn't crack a joke, so I know this got to her too. It had only been twenty seconds since we'd discovered it was Chuck and her pulling into the driveway, but we didn't say a word.

When I tried to unbuckle my seat belt, my hand was sweating so much, it slipped. I broke a nail and scraped my knuckle on the center console, peeling off some skin. I swore, startling Sherrie.

She dropped the keys on the floor mat and reached for them, bumping her head. "Goddamn," she whispered.

We continued in the most ungraceful exit from a car ever by both of us—my skirt was caught in the door, and Sherrie hit her head on the low-hanging visor.

We walked around to the front of the house. Chuck was holding open the screen door for us.

"Hello, Ms. Claudia Middleton. Rough morning, ladies?"

We passed him, not saying a word. I collapsed onto the oversized chair. Sherrie tossed the key ring to Chuck and face-planted on the couch opposite.

Sherrie rolled over. "Yeah, and you didn't help. Get us something to drink."

"Of course." He turned to the front door, looking for the right key. "When you say drink, do you mean water or a drink?"

"Both," we said unnecessarily loudly.

He returned ninety seconds later with two glasses of ice water and two beers. We sat up, grabbed the beers, and drank quickly, ignoring the water. He set down the glasses and watched us.

Chuck and I had met a few times, and we sometimes laughed that we'd once had the best date ever. One night, I'd met Aaron at his loft above the bar for dinner. Aaron had just finished making a fantastic dinner when Chuck called from the Middle East. They talked for a minute, and Aaron got a text—there was a problem with the credit card machines at the bar. He told me to start eating and said he wouldn't be gone long. Somehow, I ended up with Aaron's phone, so Chuck and I talked for an hour until Aaron returned. I had a great meal, and we shared a great conversation. Chuck said he'd had a good time and hadn't even had to cook or pick up a restaurant check.

"What are you doing here?" Sherrie asked.

"What she means to say is nice to see you and thanks for the drinks. Chuck, you remember my roommate Sherrie." I inclined my head toward her. "Why do you always use my first and last name?"

"Nice to see you again. I always had a hard time remembering names, and someone once said if you repeat both first and last names when meeting someone, it will be easier to remember. I probably say it out loud unconsciously as my way of confirming I know the person's name."

"So long story short, it's just a weird habit?" Sherrie asked.

"Yes."

"Lawrence, Sherrie Lawrence," she said and went back to her beer.

"Now, what the hell are you doing here?" I yelled.

Sherrie was midsip and spat some out when she laughed.

Chuck stood there and looked down at me. I was holding my beer with my left hand and used my cast arm to push the hair out of my face with the finesse of a toddler who had been playing in the dirt. I would have bet I smelled as nice too.

"Just relax, Chuck. I'm sure Aaron told you some stuff." He didn't say anything, so I kept talking, "It's ok. If Aaron trusts you, it's ok."

Chuck seemed to be carefully evaluating his words. "Hi, Sherrie Lawrence. It's actually Charles Adam Rhoimly. Moving on from the introductions, I was at the loft this morning, and Aaron had this new doorbell camera system sitting on the table and I asked why he needed it for the loft. He said it was for EG. I owed her a favor and thought I'd get it taken care of for her because Aaron is busy with the bar and the new facility set up."

I got lost in my own thoughts for a minute. Damn. I broke up with Aaron last night, and he still goes out of his way this morning to buy the doorbell camera. He will always be one of the good guys. Mythical unicorns do exist.

Chuck was still talking. "I didn't realize I was going to set the two of you into a state of unrest." He remained standing and looked at both of us.

"That seems to check out. Come, sit with us.

Grab yourself a beer if you like."

He looked at his watch and stepped into the house.

He was tall, muscular, and built to play football. You could see the resemblance between the brothers—the facial features, dark hair, and blue eyes. Aaron was not as tall, and his legs were his strength.

"I guess he will join us." I tilted my head towards the house and shrugged. "Are you ok?" I asked Sherrie.

"I should be freaked but this is weirdly entertaining."

"Of course, you would think that."

Chuck returned but remained standing.

"Come and sit," I said.

He looked around the porch, finally stepping over the table between Sherrie and me, and took the second comfy chair. Sherrie stretched out on the couch with her feet near Chuck and her back propped up with pillows on the other end. I threw my legs on the coffee table and adjusted my dress as not to offend anyone.

Chuck sat back. "So, what's this soap opera I stepped into?"

I didn't say anything, so Sherrie offered up, "Just start with this shit. You know you will tell him everything, and as of thirty minutes ago, it is police business."

That got Chuck's attention, because his right eyebrow arched. He took a second swig of beer.

The next few minutes, we related everything, including the car chase. He didn't interrupt, just nodded. Sherrie ended her story with him ducking on the porch, but she was more like yelling at a cook who had given her the shits from serving bad meat.

He took a third drink of beer and set the empty bottle on the side table. "I wasn't ducking. I didn't even see you approaching. I was looking for the wiring, trying to install this thing, but the wiring is ancient. It has not been updated since the house was built. I'm surprised the lamps work and the ceiling fan hasn't caught the house on fire yet. I was tracing the wires across the baseboards. Nice stealthy approach, by the way."

"Hey, don't knock my driving. It's because of my driving we are alive today."

"Oh my god, stop with self-indulgent driving accolades." My stomach rumbled for the whole room to hear.

We ordered pizza and wings, and while we waited, Sherrie and I took turns freshening up. For me, that involved putting on a hat and using cold water to wipe down my face. I had learned quickly six weeks ago my limitations when getting ready.

"Just a few more days," I repeated to myself, or at least I thought it was to myself.

"What did you say?" Chuck asked as I walked into the kitchen.

"I didn't know I was talking out loud. I was saying just a few more days until this thing comes off."

"That's cool, but I was talking to Sherrie." He smiled and laughed.

Sherrie stood up from behind the island, holding paper plates. "I was saying I found the plates but no napkins, just paper towels."

"Oh. Good to know. Well then, now you know I get this off in a few days."

We sat around the island eating. I was devouring pizza and avoiding the wings. Chuck offered me some, but I said I couldn't and burped.

"Why, it's not ladylike? Pizza and burping are acceptable but not wings?"

I raised my cast. "Normally, I use both hands for wings. You know I am a lady and can't gnaw on wings like they're turkey legs at a Renaissance Fair. I was eating fried chicken once, and it slipped between my fingers and hot grease slid down into the cast. Ever since then, I have been a one-handed lady while eating." I put down my slice and, wiping my hand clean, took off the hat. I tried pushing my hair back before putting the hat back on.

Sherrie got up and washed her hands.

"Come to the sink," she said, motioning me over.

I did as I was told. She removed my hat and had me bend over the sink, and she lightly wet my hair, pulled it back, and then put the hat back on. "You white chicks and your hair, can't you figure it out yet."

A large truck beeped, as if it was backing up, and for a brief second, we stopped moving, then returned to our seats at the island.

"You two need to relax. If that noise freaks you out, you both are gonna lose it. Take control of the situation. Until you figure out what's happening, you need to control your environment."

Sherrie swiveled on the stool and stood back up, lowering her beer. She looked Chuck in the eye. "How?" Determined not to lose eye contact, she stayed still. "How? We just walked into this crap today."

"I understand that. In the military, we learn to know what we can control. Like here, EG's house—"

"Wait! I get it. I get it," Sherrie said excitedly as if she was on a Broadway stage. She recited, "When I don't have control of the ball, what do I do? I press to get it back. It's a way of defending. Pressing or taking the offense is taking control." She repeated the quote.

"When I don't have control of the ball, what

do I do? I press to get it back. It's a way of defending."

"Johan Cruyff." Chuck high-fived Sherrie. "What are you doing, quoting Cruyff?"

"I played soccer all through high school and two years of college. One of my favorite coaches was always tying inspirational quotes with that of real-life problems. I could probably quote Vince Lombardi's famous speech if you give me a minute. But back to Johan, take control."

She was so confident and proud of making the connection she eased back to her stool but didn't realize she had stepped forward, so when she went to sit, she missed the seat. She grabbed for the island, catching the pizza box instead. Chuck tried catching her and the pizza box but failed on both accounts. As she landed on her butt, the box hit her on the head before it fell on the floor. Chuck stood there, mouth agape, holding two slices of pizza. We laughed so hard, I had tears coming out of my eyes. Besides all the heaving from laughing, nobody could move. Until we heard a voice from behind me.

CHAPTER THIRTEEN

I screamed. Chuck threw the pizza slices up, pulled me down, and assumed a protective squatting stance between us and the interloper.

"Goddammit." Chuck fell with ease onto the floor once he saw it was Jorge.

The laughing continued for several minutes. Jorge watched us and eventually became bored. He rattled Sherrie's key ring. She popped up from the floor, and he tossed her the keys. She let out a yelp of excitement.

"We didn't hear you or the car," Sherrie said.

"That was obvious. It was also the point of fixing your muffler," Jorge said.

Chuck and I were now standing, picking up pieces of lunch off the floor. We were lucky the wings and sauces had not taken the fall with us.

"Are you sure I don't owe you anything?" she said.

"Your father took care of it. Call and thank him. I am just happy I don't have to listen to you coming and going. Chuck, if you're done with the ladder, I can take it back with me; otherwise, keep it as long as you need it. If I am not around, just leave it on the side of the garage."

"Will do. The wiring work is way above my pay grade. Maybe you can take a look at it."

"I can do some basic stuff. I can take a look at it, but if you think it's a bigger project, like a complete rewire of the porch and stuff, I will call my sister's husband. He's the electrical guy."

"Whoa ho, hey guys. I appreciate this and I'm sure EG would as well, but can we talk to her first? This is her house."

"Of course. Sorry, I assumed she knew," Chuck said.

"Let me know what I can do to help. I will be home or at the shop this weekend. The garage shop is not open again until Monday, but I'm backed up on repairs, so I'm headed back in a few hours."

We said goodbye and finished cleaning up.

Chuck said, "Back to where we were before Sherrie's one-woman act that took us all down. Control. You need control. Look at how calm you are once you called off Jorge and me off the doorbell project. You set the rules of this being EG's house. You didn't need to wire the house, but just giving direction to us gave you control."

I stood there in the kitchen, calm, with the overbearing heat beating through the windows, pizza still on the floor, needing to tell EG someone may or may not have been stalking me in her house. My greatest source of strength, my parents, were unreachable by phone for another seven days but I had a moment of tranquility. "I like control. I want more control. But what can I do?" I sat back down on the stool and looked at them.

Chuck leaned back against the sink and crossed his arms just like I had seen Aaron do multiple times. I closed my eyes for a second and refocused to see Chuck, not Aaron. My hand went to my cast, playing with the frayed edges. I looked at Sherrie, who had thrown herself on the counter next to Chuck.

"Don't look at me. This is not my plan. But I am hoping to get in on the action. Control!" She raised her arms in the air like a champion boxer.

Chuck pointed his finger at me. "Let's get rid of that now."

"What?"

"Your cast. You said you get it off Monday. Let's do it now. Take control. Do something for yourself."

I looked at Sherrie, who was suddenly

focused on her phone.

"What? How?" I was confused. I looked down and saw I had pulled more of the frayed edges, and again, dead skin was gathered on my skirt.

"Right now, let's go next door. Jorge has a dozen different saws. I'm sure one of them is not much different from what they use in the doctor's office. I've done this before. It's easy. Take control."

From Sherrie's phone whooped the deep boom of beating drums and a trumpet soaring, illuminating the kitchen—an anthem one might have heard before the start of a basketball game. It would have had the entire arena on their feet.

Boom boom roar boom boom soar.

Each beat of the drum echoed "Control" in my head, and the trumpet made me jump off the barstool. I bounced on the balls of my feet. "Yes! I'm in. Let's do it. This is me taking control."

"Really?" Sherrie hopped off the counter and was halfway out of the kitchen. "Let's go. This is going to be fun."

Jorge was still home, and he was more than happy to participate. In the garage, he had me sit on his workbench. He stacked two cinder blocks and set my arm on them. "Don't worry. I did this last year with my nephew."

The large garage door was open, flooding the area with sunlight. My legs were swinging nervously below the workbench.

"I want control. I want control," I repeated.

"I want control, I want the ball back, I press to get it back, I want to roar, I want control, I want the ball back, I press to get it back," Sherrie said.

We chanted while Jorge plugged in the cord and put on safety glasses.

I put on my sunglasses, and the purr of the blade made me jump. "Wait! I need a minute. I'm nervous. Just a minute."

Jorge turned it off. Chuck was standing close to me. I could smell the coconut shampoo when he bent down and pulled over a sawhorse for me to rest my feet on. Chuck was coconut, and Aaron was spring fresh. I don't know why I was comparing the two of them.

Sherrie was seated on a camping chair, chanting, "I want control, I want the ball back, I press to get it back." With this rhythmic tone, she had me repeat the new mantra.

"I want calm, I want control, I want me back, I press to get it back, I want calm, I want control, I want me back, I press to get it back."

"You don't have to do this. It has to be your decision," Jorge said.

I had a big smile on my face. "I want to do it. I just want a minute. Savor the moment of taking control."

"This is so exciting. I can't stop bouncing,"

Sherrie said. She played "I'm So Excited" by The Pointer Sisters on her phone. A pop hit from 1982 with an infectious chorus that upped the energy to the next level.

Without moving and with a deadpan voice, Chuck said, "Why don't you get up and do your dance? Work out that energy."

"I love to dance." She stood up and kicked the chair back. Back with the Broadway dramatics, she threw her arm out towards Chuck and said, "Dance with me."

With a more flat tone but a sinister smirk, he said, "No. No. Do *your* dance."

Sherrie, now frozen in place, and Jorge and I eagerly watched this exchange, waiting for the next move. She tilted her head. Barely moving her lips, she said, "What dance?"

A big grin on his face, like he was moving the winning chess piece, Chuck said, "Your dance. Like you dance before the bar opens, and you're there by yourself. Dancing from table to table as you clean."

Not moving anything but her legs, she lowered her arm slightly.

Chuck pressed on. "Come on, show them your dance. I know you know the cameras in the bar are always on. I've seen the dancing."

Can someone say checkmate?

"Oh my god. What did you see?" Sherrie's

hands were on her hips. Completely not embarrassed.

"We only saw two different routines. The first one is obviously your salute to the eighties movie Flashdance, but we have money riding on the second one. I can only pick up video and not audio."

"We?"

"Almost every day, I check the security system. I set it up when Aaron and I were putting the bar together. One day, I checked the video feed when I was in the Middle East a couple of weeks ago. I was sitting around with some other guys, and they wanted to know what I was laughing at. Don't give me that look. I was not spying like a peeping tom. I had a twenty second clip of you moving from the back hallway, down the length of the bar while you were doing some dance and talking to someone out of view of the camera. We were placing bets on your choice of music but couldn't figure it out. I put the video on a loop, and it broke up some of the monotony of our evenings there. Apparently, you have fun while opening the bar."

"I have fun every day." She flung her head to the side, flipping her hair. "I don't know this Flashdance movie you refer to, but I could have been dancing to Gene Kelly's 'Singin' in the Rain,' not to be confused with the other opening routine I have to 'Uptown Funk' by Bruno Mars. Come to the bar next week, and we can make a video together."

Chuck blushed. Sherrie had managed to flip the conversation on him and had held her ground.

She returned her focus to me. "Back to our victim, I mean patient, I mean master of control!"

Jorge turned on the saw, and I yelped. I couldn't believe I was doing this. Breaking doctor's orders but taking control.

My left hand was squeezing my knee. My eyes were closed. I was taking control, but I didn't need to watch the saw come close to my arm. I opened my eyes to find Sherrie looking over Jorge's shoulder and Chuck looking over mine. The cast released from my arm. Joy surged through me. I looked at Chuck, wrinkling my nose. "Couldn't you have stepped out of the garage?"

"What? That smell didn't come from me. I appreciate the thought that all bodily smells come from men, but that smell is all you and your arm."

I raised my arm and could only get it halfway to my nose before having to pull it back. It was horrible, and I shouldn't have been surprised.

"It will be sore for a few days. I would still go to the doctor and have it checked out," Jorge said. "If you guys don't need me anymore, I am going to head back to the shop. Thanks for letting me play doctor."

We said our goodbyes, and the three of us walked side by side by side back to EG's house.

Aaron pulled up in his truck, and Chuck stepped back three feet as if he had been caught in an intimate embrace with someone else's girlfriend. Aaron parked on the curb under an old oak tree and got out but remained by the door. Rita, his golden retriever, was ready to hop out of the rear seat, but Aaron told her to stay put. I spied the look he gave Chuck, and I waved at him. Sherrie tried waving him into our little group, but he stayed put.

"I can't stay. I was driving past and saw all of you out here. I need your help tonight at the bar."

"I can be there in an hour," Sherrie said.

"Sorry, I was talking to Chuck."

"Oh, I could use the shift, or is the power back out again?"

"It's nothing like that. I need other help." He looked directly at Chuck.

Chuck clearly understood something we could not. He walked up to Aaron, and they talked in nearly a whisper. Chuck had a defensive stance but relaxed after a minute.

The conversation broke up, and Chuck said, "I gotta go to the bar. Let me take the ladder back to Jorge's, and I'm out of here."

Aaron was halfway back in the car when he stood back up and yelled, "Hey."

"Yes," I answered quickly and walked towards the truck.

"Oh, ah, this time, I was talking to Sherrie,"

he said.

I turned pink, and we both turned uncomfortable.

Sherrie watched the exchange and removed herself, so she was not physically halfway between Aaron and me but more in the background. "Can I switch your eleven a.m. shift tomorrow to Monday night?" Aaron asked.

"Sure, whatever you need," Sherrie answered.

"Thanks. It will help me, and you can stay away from the square for another night."

"Coming from Peach's Café?" I asked.

He looked at his shirt and brushed off powdered sugar that wasn't there.

"I was at Phil's."

"I see the brownies sitting in your truck. I assumed they were from Peach's. But now that I look closely there, they are too ordinary-looking—like something I would bake."

"I doubt that. Molly, Phil's sister, was there and gave these to me," he said.

"Are you sharing?"

"These brownies are not for sharing." He must have seen my look of disappointment. "Maybe Jan has some at the café for you." He got in his truck and left.

Not sharing the damn brownies pissed me off. He had gone out of his way to buy me a doorbell camera this morning but held back on baked goods! He was concerned about safety but not sharing the brownies. He was starting to shut me out. I guessed I deserved that since I had broken up with him.

When the anger wore off, I felt empty. Maybe he was upset about the breakup. It wasn't right, but that made me feel better because it made me feel like I was worth losing as a girlfriend.

The porch door swung open and shut. Chuck came out, carrying the ladder. "You two in for the afternoon and night."

I wasn't sure if that was a question or suggestion.

"I haven't given it much thought. We never thought much past the farmers market we never got to."

"That was some ride you were on today. Between that and your arm—I mean, it not my place to say anything—but I would just take it easy." Chuck looked at both of us. "Stay off the square tonight. Your adrenaline will drop and you guys will crash, and you still have someone out there who was trying to run you down."

The sun was high in the sky, casting shadows everywhere, but everything he said came out with vivid clarity. Surprisingly, Sherrie was quiet. He had my attention. My left hand slowly caressed my newly freed right arm. The smell had not gone away and snapped me back from Chuck's admonition for a moment.

"Maybe we'll just grab some food and head back here," Sherrie said.

"It is none of my business, but I would recommend that you guys stay together and stay off the square."

He walked towards Jorge's garage. "Let me know if you need anything or if you hear from the police. I don't think they will have any information, but you never know what someone may have seen, especially if the car was stupid enough to speed through River Bend or back through Marshall. I should be at the bar most of the night."

We walked into the house and took spots in the living room, sitting as if we were stains on the furniture. We were comfortable and dug in. No one turned on the television.

"So, all that just happened," I said.

"Car chase, cornfield, talking to police, Chuck on the porch, Jorge in the kitchen, and your cast." Sherrie rattled things off like she was looking in the kitchen cabinets and gathering the ingredients I needed to put together a meal.

I raised my right arm and confirmed everything she said with an "Amen."

"That thing does smell," she said, then mumbled something I couldn't understand.

I was too dazed to ask her to repeat it.

We sat there for five or ten minutes, and neither one of us said anything. We may have taken control and had a good laugh, but we ignored the point that someone had come after me.

"I could stay here all night, but I need to shower. Do you want the remote?" I stood up and, without waiting for an answer, tossed it to her, but she let it slide to the floor.

"Do you know what's strange?" She paused, and I didn't know if it was for dramatic effect or if she was considering an answer to her own question. "Both Aaron and Chuck said the same thing."

"What do you mean?"

"Stay off the square. Aaron said that last night and today, and Chuck said it twice just now. Don't you think that's odd?"

"I haven't thought about it. They're brothers, so they are bound to talk in a familiar pattern."

"It's not that. It's a direct order. Not a suggestion."

I leaned against the bookcase. "What are you getting at?"

"Do you think they know something?"

"Like what? Who came after us?"

Looking for a clue in the words from the brothers, Sherrie kept softly repeating, "Stay off the square. Stay off the square. Stay off the square."

"Let me know if you come up with any answers," I said and headed to the shower.

Sometimes, it was really straightforward, and we should have just stayed off the square.

CHAPTER FOURTEEN

My arm was free. I was free and in control. I put shampoo in my hand and ran all my fingers, all ten fingers, through my hair. I repeated that with conditioner. I used soap on my arm, and I was careful not to overdo it. I even used the master bathroom off EG's bedroom to use her unique soaps. She had always brought back locally made soap when she traveled. I felt clean, really clean.

In my room, I put on shorts I hadn't worn in weeks. Shorts with a zipper and a button. I took a couple of ibuprofen to stay ahead of the pain game.

I was giddy with excitement and bounced down the stairs. I wanted to share my joy, so I picked up my phone to call Aaron, and I then realized I had no right to call him anymore. I got my arm back but still felt a part of me was missing.

Sherrie sat at the island, leaning back on the stool while mindlessly eating pistachios and gazing out the window.

I stayed silent, standing in the living room. I just realized that whoever was watching me was more or less watching Sherrie and EG as well. I was thankful that EG was gone for a few days.

Sherrie was with me and in my car. Whatever was going to happen to me was going to happen to her.

CHAPTER FIFTEEN

I joined her in the kitchen, just realizing it was close to dinnertime. We'd never made it to the farmers market and had only eaten half the pizza. I was not in the mood for floor pizza. I stared into an almost-empty refrigerator as we contemplated our options. That took some time despite our choices being limited.

This time, we heard the car pull into the driveway. We stayed still, suddenly aware of everything around us. The back door remained locked, but the front and porch doors were open.

The only movement was dust floating through the air in the light coming through the kitchen windows.

Sherrie slowly stood up and moved quietly towards me while facing the doorway. I closed the fridge door, listening to footsteps and the rapid opening of the screen door.

"Hellllloooo, girls." EG rounded the corner and floated into the kitchen, smiling before landing on a stool. "There you are. Are you all right? You look like you saw a ghost."

I nudged Sherrie back to the island and took a seat, relaxing but holding my guard. I casually tossed a kitchen towel over my arm, and Sherrie understood. We were under strict instructions from Mom, Dad, and just about everyone to make sure EG had an easy summer. It was an odd position to be in because it was usually her orchestrating orders for others.

"Just trying to figure out our dinner options and who would be pulling into the driveway. That's all. Everything ok? Why are you back from your weekend so early?"

"Couldn't be better. I got a call from my book agent. Earlier this year, I was invited to be a guest speaker and special panel guest for this forum. I turned it down because I didn't know where I would be with chemo. Long story short, another author dropped out at the last minute, and they asked if I would still be interested. I said yes. It's a five-day cruise set up through the alumni association as an academic extension course hosted by the university. A mix of sightseeing, mixed-art education, and socializing. Art being a broad term for everything ranging from writing courses, cooking classes, anthropology excursions, blah blah blah.

"Sometimes these things can be dreadful, but it's a free trip and a change of scenery. I have been here almost all summer, and I'm exhausted at everyone being so, so nice to me and trying to do things for me. I appreciate the kindness, but this is over-the-top Hallmark Channel cheesy good-heartedness, and it's too much for me. It always has been. Maybe that's why I write suspense thrillers and teen slasher books."

It was such a delight to see EG smiling and having something tangible to look forward to. She had gotten a lot of writing done this summer but hadn't left the house much. Chemo had been reasonably easy on her, but she'd had her tired days.

"When do you leave?" I asked.

"Tomorrow. That's why I'm here. I need to pack and then turn around and head back to the Minneapolis airport. I have an early flight, so I booked a room at an airport hotel and I can leave my car there." She picked up a paper plate and fanned herself.

"Is this cruise going anywhere fun? Are you crossing paths with Mom and Dad?" I asked.

"Not at all. They are still cruising through the Mediterranean. I board the ship in Fort

Lauderdale and stay in the Gulf region and move west towards Mexico before returning to Florida. I am going to pack and be out of here. Are you girls good? It has been a long time since I've had people living with me. Is there anything you need from me before I go?"

"No, we're fine. How soon are you leaving? Can I do a load of wash for you?"

"Don't be silly, but thanks for the offer. I should have enough to get me through the cruise; otherwise, I just may have to shop when we hit a port. What you could do is open the windows and get some fresh air. It is stifling in here." I started to get up, but she waved me off. "I was talking to Sherrie. I see what you did with your arm. How does it feel?"

Can't sneak anything past her. "I just did it."

"You?" EG joked.

"Not me. Jorge. Could you see me with a saw?"

"No, but I could see Sherrie with a saw." EG laughed.

"Absolutely! But Jorge wouldn't let me near it, so I just had to watch," Sherrie said.

"Why is everything locked up? You girls going somewhere?" EG asked.

I paused, and Sherrie busied herself with the window lock.

I finally said, "We were just tired of hearing

Jorge work in the garage. Normally, it's not so bad, but he was doing some cutting in the driveway, and the Connors next door had friends over that smoke. Between the noise and the smell, we thought it was better to be a little hot."

Sherrie understood our goal was not to let EG know that something was going on and happily played along. "When I was back home this week, my dad gave me one of those doorbell cameras. My mom had purchased it for my other place I had before deciding to come here. They offered it to you. I didn't want to install it without your permission. Well, let's be honest, I didn't want to ask someone to install it before talking to you. If I'm not allowed to handle a handsaw, I should not be allowed to mess with electrical wires."

"That is sweet of them. I thought about getting one of those. If you find someone to install it while I'm gone, let me know what I owe you. Next time you head home, can you make sure they get one of Jan's or Aaron's pies? With them only ninety minutes from here, I bet you could deliver it still warm."

Jan was Aaron's aunt and the owner of Peach's Café. People had been known to barter services for Jan's pies and bread. A pie could have gotten your driveway shoveled; two pies and some bread could have gotten someone to drive you ninety minutes to the Minneapolis airport.

Sherrie squealed with delight, but EG said, "Easy, kiddo. You do know that pie is for your father and mother and not you."

Sherrie put her head down and slumped her shoulders like a toddler who had been scolded. She walked over and gave EG a hug before she headed upstairs.

"What are your plans for the evening? Aaron at the bar?" EG asked.

I was not about to tell her about the breakup. I wasn't keeping everything from her, but I didn't want to sour her mood or answer any questions. "We are going to grab something to eat and then figure out our plans. I hope you don't mind I used your shower. I wanted to treat myself to some of your fun soaps."

"Of course not. But stay away from the round green bar. I keep meaning to throw it out. Green tea, cucumber, ginger, and amber with a salt scrub does not do anything good for my skin or smelling sensation."

"That is so funny you say that. My arm was smelling so badly that I wanted something natural and healing, so I thought your soaps would do the trick. It took me several attempts to realize it was the soap and not my arm that was smelling up the shower. The oval blue one is the best. Where did you get it? Thailand? Costa Rica?"

"That came all the way, a long journey,

crossed a river and back, traveled north on this trip." EG's voice rose like a football announcer doing the play-by-play about to tell you the team just scored, but then her voice faded back to: "And it was a forty-minute drive from the farmers market—"

I finished the sentence for her. "In La Crosse" I laughed and thought, Sometimes, what you need is right in front of you.

CHAPTER SIXTEEN

EG left forty minutes later, and once again, Sherrie and I dropped ourselves down on the porch sofa. We put up our feet on the coffee table and were relieved when EG's car left.

My stomach rumbled again as Sherrie mumbled, "Stay off the square, stay off the square . . ."

My phone beeped. It was Jackson asking again about his backpack. This time, he was asking if Sherrie had it.

"How many times do I have to tell this idiot I don't have it? It's not here."

"Teach him a lesson, take control. Tell him to listen to you. Better yet, give me your phone."

I tossed it to her. She typed, I said I don't have it—you don't agree, so if you are not here in seventy-two hours, I will toss it in the river.

She passed the phone back, and I read the text she'd sent.

"How is that taking control? I don't want to talk to him, much less see him. Why are you inviting him up here?"

"Control is action. Control is not just harsh words. You told him you didn't have it. Multiple times you have said it, and nothing has changed. He can either accept that you don't have it or contemplate that you might and that you'll get rid of it. You make him take action by accepting your words or forcing him to drive several hours to determine if you're telling the truth."

I should have been proud of this insightful information from her, but all I could do was roll my eyes and slink lower into the couch. We listened to the crickets and let the wind coming through the porch screen cool us off. My phone beeped again, breaking up the meditative lull we had fallen into.

Jackson replied, WTF?

Sherrie tried to grab my phone, but I held firm and said, "Control. I got this." And I typed, You read it right. Believe me that I don't have this backpack of yours, or I will take what I do not have and toss it into the river. No mind games. No more texting. The only thing I want from you is to know if you will be here in seventy-two hours to watch me throw nothing into the river. You text me anything else, and I will block you from my phone and all other forms of communication. Don't even give me a thumbs-up emoji to this text.

"Damn, girl. You got it! Control."

"Control, yes. But that message is sorta messed up. How am I throwing nothing into the river?"

"Control is action. Put up or shut up, and if Jackson is too dumb to figure it out, let him waste his time and gas money on stupidity."

A couple of kids rode their bikes down the street, shouting at each other. Then an old man went by, walking his poodle, looking around to see if anyone was watching when his dog took a crap in the yard across the street. We pushed the coffee table on the floorboards to make some noise, and with some reluctance and a showy effort, the man pulled out a plastic bag to clean up after the dog and then waddled off.

The sounds of crickets brought us back to a relaxed state before Sherrie pulled me out of it and sent us on a quest for control.

"Claud, I got the plan we need. Let's go."

CHAPTER SEVENTEEN

"I didn't know we needed a plan, but whatever. Does this plan involve 'control'?" God help me, I used air quotes on control. "Can this plan involve food?"

"Absolutely, food and control. Stay off the square, my ass. We are going to find out why Aaron and Chuck pushed us out of the bars tonight. While I get my shoes on, text Kay and Jenna and find out what's going on in town. Don't commit us to anything, but if anything's happening, they will know."

We met back in the living room three minutes later, after locking all the windows.

I had no news to report. Kay had left that morning to see friends in Rochester, and Jenna was with her sister.

I wanted to give Debby a rest for the night, so we hopped in Sherrie's VW Bug.

Earlier this summer, her car had rolled over to two hundred thousand miles, and it showed every mile on the inside and outside. The once-yellow color was speckled with rust, and dents decorated the bumpers and doors. The front seats had lost most of the cushioning, but Sherrie had gotten beaded seat covers at the flea market. The air-conditioning worked and so did the radio, which was a step better than my car. The windows did not always roll up, so it was a gamble when you opened the window. She once had gone a week with the passenger window down when the temperature never rose above twenty degrees.

We drove out to Towne's diner and ordered food to go. Sherrie insisted on getting extra drinks with high caffeine content to counterbalance our dinner of meatball sandwiches, onion rings, and cheese curds. She didn't want us falling asleep on our stakeout.

We ate the onion rings and cheese curds as we drove back to town and the square. I reached into the paper bag while holding a napkin in the other hand, enjoying the simple pleasures of using both hands to eat. The right arm was still sore and looked a little funny, but it was functioning nicely.

Sherrie side-eyed me. "Do you think you could not put your scaly arm into the food bag?"

I was slightly perturbed but understood. "Fine then."

I wasn't sure what we were looking for, but I was along for the ride literally and figuratively. The conversation drifted between all the clothes with zippers and buttons that I could wear now, the expectation that I would have a better hairdo, and how we would convince EG to put in air-conditioning before next summer.

We drove around the square, past the campus bars, and to the river.

A few boats lingering on the water before dusk settled in and cast their fishing lines. We watched in amusement as one lady tried to back a boat trailer down the ramp and her husband idled in the boat, readying to drive the boat onto the trailer. It was indeed a lesson in physics and patience. Watching the lady turn the vehicle one way and the trailer move in the other direction and nowhere close to her waiting husband was a spectacle. I gave him all the credit in the world for his patience.

It helped that no other boats tried to come off the water at the same time. The dock was four cars wide, and she needed every foot of space. We laughed when a young girl, not much past sixteen, jumped out of the truck and her father yelled, "Not bad for the first time. Maybe next time you can do it in under thirty minutes."

She did not hesitate to bounce it right back. "Give me a break! I have had my license for two weeks, and this was definitely not on the test. What are we going to have for dinner tonight, one of the three fish I caught, or are we just going to think about your fish that got away?"

We left them laughing and turned around in the parking area.

"What are we looking for?" I said.

"I wasn't sure what to look for, but it was odd Pete's car and Jacob's truck were parked near the bar. I thought Jo-Lee was supposed to work tonight. With Aaron, that makes four and maybe Chuck. That's five. It's Saturday night, but no one is on campus yet and I don't think there is a baseball tournament this weekend."

"Head towards the bar. I want to see who's parked behind the building. Don't go down the alley. Just slow down. We can see everything, and we won't be on the camera that sits above the back door."

"I thought you would think this stakeout was crazy. Welcome to the club."

Not much activity was happening around the square, and plenty of parking spaces were open. We turned off Main Street, slowing down, and spied down the alley. All we could see was Chuck's Jeep. I didn't know why the thought came to me, but I told Sherrie to turn around, back to

Main Street, and head towards the freeway but turn right before the library. She was giddy with excitement but seemed disappointed that we weren't headed onto the freeway.

I pulled out the sub sandwich and ate as I gave her directions.

"That smells delightful. Give me my sub," she said.

"No way. Two hands on the wheel. We're almost there. After the row of mailboxes, turn left."

We were traveling down a country road lined with old houses with large wraparound porches and enormous yards. Houses eventually gave way to woods on one side and a tall grassy marsh area on the other side.

"I will be done in a minute, and then I can drive when we turn around at our destination. Here's the turn. Go kinda slow."

Her left leg bounced with excitement. "What are we looking for?"

"Control." I laughed.

"Don't mock it. Either take control or be controlled, but don't mock it," Sherrie said.

"Whatever. Just trying to lighten the mood."

"Why? I'm having fun. I should become a private investigator."

"Slow down. Pull over here. I'm trying to figure out the back way in, but I have never seen the road from the other side. Actually, keep going.

I guess we will have to take this way in. He shares the main driveway with the Douglas Farm. His driveway splits off just beyond the big oak tree."

"Who is out here? Who is 'he' that you keep referring to?"

"This is Aaron's place."

"Why does he live in the boondocks? Is he hiding bodies in the basement?"

"Not that I know of. Remember, he splits his time between here and the loft above the bar. He bought it to fix up and flip. I don't know if he'll be able to sell it. There's a small lake back there, and he likes to fish. He only stays at the loft above the bar on nights he works late."

"Seriously, why are we here? Are we looking for dead bodies?" She seemed to want to laugh but also taken aback by my silence.

I didn't say anything. I rumbled in my head, Control, take control, control. Oh boy, help me. I am becoming Sherrie.

At least I wasn't thinking, *Press to get the ball back.*

Her hand snapped in front of my face.

I shook my head, gathered myself, and told her to go down the driveway but to veer left and then a quick right. "Aaron's driveway goes to the right, the old Douglas Farm is to the left, but that middle road will take us to the water. I'm assuming your car can handle the road."

"If there's a road, I can handle it. Just ask that farmer from this afternoon." Her overconfidence was nerve-wracking but inspiring.

I had half the sub sandwich left, and when she turned off the main road onto the shared gravel driveway, we hit two bumps and I squeezed out a meatball and it went rolling down my leg. I bent down and tried to catch it but missed. As I was bent forward, she hit another bump and my head hit the dashboard. I thought I had gotten control of my right arm but had lost control of the rest of my body. Sherrie laughed and kept going at a slower pace.

She veered left at the oak tree and quickly found the right-hand turn to the lake. The lake was probably a half mile or the equivalent of eighty oak and maple trees. Sherrie's VW had to travel at a low speed to make it down the dirt road. The trees created a canopy, and the road was always damp even in the hot summers. Too bad I had broken up with Aaron before autumn because the area must have been postcard perfect when the trees started turning.

The trees gave way to an open grassy area probably two hundred feet wide. The water was maybe fifty feet away. I told her to park anywhere. The lake was about eight to ten acres big. The shoreline around the lake varied from grass, marsh, and a gravel beach area. It was shared but the four surrounding properties. Each owner was responsible for maintaining the shoreline in whatever fashion they desired.

We got out of the car, and I picked up the lost meatball and threw it into the woods. Sherrie leaned against the hood of her car, eating her sandwich while I went to the water to wash the sauce off my hand and leg.

"What are we doing out here? What are you looking for? I love a good scavenger hunt, but give me some clues."

"I will once you're done eating. Hurry up before the mosquitos come out in full force."

She must have been as hungry as I was because she was done in about three minutes. I started up a path, and she walked quietly next to me. We passed a small boat shed that Aaron had built. It was barely large enough to hold a small rowboat and fishing gear.

It was about a quarter-mile walk through a wooded area to the edge of Aaron's yard. I stayed behind the tree line and remained frozen in place. She watched and waited for me to react. I had nothing to say. I just was taking in the scene. I could see Aaron's truck and Jo-Lee's blue hatchback. From the tree line, we watched Aaron come out of the house and grab an overnight bag from the back seat of Jo-Lee's car.

She must have been in the house with his

dog, Rita, because we only saw him. I didn't know how long they had been there. Had we just missed them when we turned down the gravel driveway? Had she been there all afternoon? Is that why Aaron had wanted Chuck's help at the bar tonight so he could be with Jo-Lee and why we are supposed to stay off the square tonight? Why had she left the bar yesterday during her shift? Had she gotten ready for a late-night date with Aaron? It hadn't even been twenty-four hours since we'd broken up. Everything except control was swirling in my head. Had he been dating both of us? Is that why he was so accepting of the breakup?

"Claudia, I am really sorry. This sucks." Sherrie's voice was a blend of pity and understanding. "Do you want—"

"Don't say take control. Screw control right now. I just want to get out of here." I didn't remember the walk back to the car. I barely remembered closing the door. I snapped back into the moment when Sherrie turned on her headlights as she turned onto the main road.

"Can I ask a question? If it's not the right time, you can tell me to back off," she said.

I shrugged my shoulders like I didn't care.

She asked, "How did you know? I mean, did you suspect something? You never told me why you broke up with Aaron."

"Something strange hit me when we were

coming back from Jorge's this afternoon. When Aaron pulled up, Chuck jumped back from me like we were caught doing something wrong when we were laughing and standing so close.

"Aaron and Chuck get along great, but the one bad thread between them was something about a girl. Aaron would never tell me the story, and I didn't pry. Instead of being angry at Chuck, he seemed to push him into helping at the bar tonight, and he wouldn't look at me. When you said it was all guys working tonight, I knew something was up. Aaron always likes to mix up the bar schedule with both guys and girls working. He had some strange theory about staffing. All guys make it appear to be a sports bar for guys; all girls working makes it a Hooters. He was always careful with the schedule, and for him to mix it up, something must be going on. I didn't imagine it would be this.

"Last night, maybe she wasn't running from something scary, but she was getting ready for a date. Maybe, that's what he was telling us. The whole 'Stay off the square' mandate was so I wouldn't run into them and make their date weird.

"As for why I broke us up . . . I guess I was looking for control before I knew I was looking for control. I felt as if I had stumbled into the relationship instead of choosing it."

"So? Who cares how you found the relationship? Do you like him? Are you guys good for each other?" she asked carefully.

"He is here, and I'm not sure where I want to be literally and figuratively. My career is not Chambray Senior Center."

"What did he say about that?" Sherrie asked.

I didn't answer, and she didn't press. Why hadn't I talked to him about it? Could I be uncertain about my future professionally but secure romantically? Could I merge these two worlds? Why did I have to start fresh with my career and my heart? I guessed not talking to him about it was going to be worse than losing him.

Right now, I was too mad about Jo-Lee spending the night to be sad.

CHAPTER EIGHTEEN

We left Aaron's property, and I told Sherrie to drive past the bar and head back to EG's. I was not in the mood for a stakeout or whatever she had in mind for the rest of the night.

She drove up slowly to the house, looking for any signs of someone hanging out. She pulled into the single-lane driveway and parked behind Debby. We got out, and I walked towards the porch, but she stood by the car.

"I feel like we should be doing something," Sherrie said.

The evening twilight had faded, and there was no moon to light the sky. The weight of the darkness pressed on my shoulders. I stood on the steps to the porch, the dim outside light casting shadows on my face. I knew she saw me roll my eyes.

"Don't give me that attitude. I mean, we should be doing some type of therapy or maybe a shot of something. We have to get you past this relationship. He has moved on and so should you," Sherrie said.

I opened the screen door and walked onto the porch, holding the door open for her.

While she fidgeted with the front door lock, she rambled on. "So what are the seven stages of grief? One is anger. I think you got that. Two is denial, and you are not yet there, but please don't start to justify what we just witnessed. The third stage is acceptance, which may be a bitch of a step to get through. But we will come up with something for that. There's depression and guilt and something about upward turn. I know I'm missing one."

"Would you just open the damn door? I think you're missing reconstruction or something like that," I said.

Sherrie finally jiggled the key into the door, and we stepped into a hot box, otherwise known as the living room.

"I can't stand this house being locked down. I'm opening the windows. Doors will remain locked. We need fresh air flowing in this place," I said.

I struggled with the first window because

my arm was still sore, so Sherrie helped and opened the other two windows in the living room, but we left the kitchen windows closed.

My arm's release from the cast seemed forever ago, and the chase into the cornfield felt like it had happened on a different day. This afternoon, when we'd left Jorge's garage, he had given me a squeeze ball and told me it would help my arm and hand recover. I lay on the couch and picked up the ball, absentmindedly tossing it from hand to hand.

The breeze picked up, and the humidity was rising. I was beginning to think rain would be in the forecast for tomorrow. Like the previous night, Sherrie took the recliner and threw it back, picking up the remote. She flipped channels and landed on an episode of Cops.

"No." That was all I needed to say.

She kept flipping until she landed on a movie we had seen a hundred times.

"You got really quiet," I said.

"I am trying to come up with something for you. I—"

"Thanks, I get it. Not everything needs in-the-moment action. Let this all sink in. By the way, you also had a hell of a day. You were part of the car chase and Chuck and Jorge startling us. Let's not forget your early morning bike ride that left you tired."

"Don't deflect. You had a shit day."

"Yes, but you were there. I realized earlier what happens to me is also happening to you."

She laughed, but I wasn't sure at what. She waited half a minute before saying, "I am with you to the end."

"Nice. I appreciate it, but don't get all Thelma and Louise on me. We are not driving off the cliff together."

"Not with me driving! We are making it across the damn canyon!" Sherrie said.

I was too tired to give her an amen. I continued shifting the ball back and forth and realized sometime later that Sherrie had fallen asleep. I was not settled, but at the same time, I was not having a pity party for myself. I had broken up with him; he could start seeing someone at any point. This was a bit fast, but something was not right. My mind floated back to Stay off the square.

CHAPTER NINETEEN

At some point, I also fell asleep. I didn't think Sherrie had made it past ten, and it was probably ten thirty for me. No wild night on the town for us. Sherrie must have woken up and wandered up to bed, because I found myself alone and awake at five in the morning. I'd slept on the longer side of six hours, but it felt more like a power nap. I was fully awake, but I had a feeling I would crash by early afternoon. I lay there wiggling my fingers and decided to make the most of the day.

I climbed the stairs, careful not to make noise on steps six and seven. Sherrie's door was closed, and I took that as a sign she was still sleeping and not out bike riding. I showered and found another pair of shorts to wear. Hopefully, they wouldn't turn into my pajamas as had happened last night.

I made breakfast of an English muffin with almond butter when the nagging sensation came back to me. I sat hunched over the island, letting the sun pour over my back. I cracked a window, and the fresh air blew in, stirring emotions again.

This morning's version was slightly different: the 'stay off the square' decree now had me picturing the square and Jo-Lee's overnight bag dropping into the center, wiping out everyone around it like a bomb going off.

I busied myself cleaning the kitchen. Sweeping, wiping down the baseboards, straightening out the Tupperware lids, and reorganizing the gadgets and utensils so I could find things—although EG might be lost in her own kitchen when she returned. I had moved on to clearing the toaster of its crumbs when Sherrie came into the kitchen.

"So much for taking control and being in charge. For a nonworking weekend, that has to be the lamest Saturday night I've had since seventh grade."

"We may not have been awake to watch Saturday Night Live, but we did precede it with a pretty outstanding day."

Sherrie poured herself some coffee and plopped down at the island, watching me futz with the toaster. I stopped cleaning the toaster and took the stool opposite her.

"Speak for yourself. Yesterday, I just went for a morning drive, helped a friend feel better about her arm, and then drove out to the country. It was not like your day—you almost got run over, was convinced to let a neighbor get close to you with an electric saw, and then got to experience seeing your very recent ex with a new girl," she said.

"So what you're saying is your days are fine, but we need to work on your nightlife."

Sherrie opted for skipping breakfast and asked if EG would mind if she painted her bedroom. I assured her EG wouldn't mind and would even encourage her to do so. I sent her downstairs to look for paint supplies before heading to the hardware store for paint.

"If you can't find what you need down there, take a look in the garage. The key to the garage's side door is on the hook by the back door, or otherwise, grab my car keys and use the garage door opener. I'm going for a walk."

"Is that a good idea?" Sherrie asked.

"What do you mean?"

"Being by yourself?"

"It still stings seeing Jo-Lee's car and her overnight bag, but I am a big girl."

"That's not what I mean. Remember the joyride into the cornfield? Somebody is watching you. Chasing you down. I did what you asked and didn't tell EG anything, but I am not going to let this go."

Hearing that made me feel like I had been punched in the gut. Reality had changed for me and others. We had made jokes about it yesterday, but today, I had to live it. "I get it and I understand what you're saying, but I can't hide," I barked.

"I never said you were a coward. So please don't raise your voice to me. I just don't think you need to wander around by yourself. I am not your babysitter or your mother, just someone with common sense."

I spoke louder. "I can't be attached to someone twenty-four hours a day. I can't ask you or anyone else to do that."

Sherrie had her hands balled up on top of the island and squared off her body, looking directly at me. She spoke louder. "You are not asking, but maybe I am offering."

I stood up and grabbed the edge of the island. My body was rigid with determination to make my point. "I can't drag you into this."

We were both getting louder.

Sherrie said, "You are not asking. I am offering! No, I insist on being there for you."

I raised my voice louder. "I don't know if you realize what that might mean for you. We almost got run off the road yesterday. I am not pulling you in. The last time you tried to help, the sheriff's wife shot you."

"I understand. If you say you got over your hit-and-run in June, why can't I get over my arm getting grazed by Pistol Packing Jean. So . . ."

There was a fine line between speaking loudly and yelling. We were crossing the line when I said, "Do you realize we are getting mad and loud while trying to play the game of who cares the most about the other person!"

Sherrie boomed and pounded her fists on the island. "Of course, you dweeb! I get it. That was my whole point." Now smiling, she relaxed and continued. "The point was to be smart. People care about you! Bad people and good people can watch you like a hawk."

I had the last shout. "Ok!" I exhaled finally, sat back down, and asked, "Now what? I still need to get out and do something productive."

"How about you help me tape up the walls so I can paint? When I get the paint, I'll drop you off at the high school and you can walk around the track. No one is stupid enough to approach you on school property with a church across the street on a Sunday. I know the track is not as Zen as walking by the river, but that path has too many secluded sections. Does that work?"

"That's not a bad plan. I guess if you're gonna get in a car chase because of me, the least I can do is help with taping and painting."

Sherrie got up to look for tape and paintbrushes. She was on the top step heading into the basement when I called her back.

"Sherrie?"

She stopped and turned her head, waiting for me to speak.

"Are we good? You and me?"

Without hesitating, she said, "Of course. That was my whole point." She took one step down and looked back again and asked, "Do you want to hug it out?"

"Nah, maybe later. You haven't showered, or maybe I don't care that much for you," I said.

Sherrie pivoted on the step, and with her back to me, she raised her arm, gave me the finger, and started down the stairs. Laughing, she said, "Right back at you."

CHAPTER TWENTY

Twenty minutes later, we were upstairs in Sherrie's bedroom, with the furniture and EG's boxes pushed away from the walls. The room was quite large since it was the size of two rooms. When EG originally bought the house twenty years ago, she'd knocked down the wall and was going to make this a large master bedroom.

During the process, she had gotten married and Duncan had moved in. They used my current smaller room as their bedroom, and the downstairs room as her office. Before the remodeling was done, Duncan had died in an automobile accident. It seemed that she could no longer picture herself sleeping alone in the master bedroom, so she converted it to her office and turned the room downstairs into the master suite.

A month ago, when EG had offered Sherrie the room, she had said most of the stuff in that room could be purged. It was mostly old notes, research for her books, and files she had accumulated over the years. She'd put a desk in her room downstairs and moved her laptop there. A dozen boxes of varying sizes remained for her to determine what should be kept or tossed. The room was plenty big enough for Sherrie's bed, a desk, and the boxes.

Sherrie had offered me the larger room, and I'd thought that was generous, but I had no need of a larger room. To make me feel at home here, EG and my parents had decorated my room with vintage rock band posters and things from my childhood bedroom in St. Paul.

In the basement, Sherrie had found paintbrushes, drop cloths, and painter's tape. I wasn't sure about the tape she'd found. It appeared to have more dust covering it than adhesive. As she was trying to tape around the windows, I went to the garage to get the tall ladder because the ceiling had a pitched roof.

Many things that day and during the week were to go wrong, very wrong, but me opting to get the ladder was probably the first mistake of the week I can recall, and it was only nine in the morning.

I picked up the ladder, and my right arm

twitched from its weight. I quickly gained control before it crashed into the doorframe or the siding but not before it crashed into the light fixture by the door. The glass orb and light bulb shattered above me. Sherrie heard the commotion from the open window ten feet above. She raced down to see me standing there with glass in my hair and around my feet.

She gave me and the former light one look before she said, "You should have given me a hug an hour ago; it would have helped your karma."

"I recall you giving me the finger, so let's talk about your karma," I said.

She spun on her heels and left me standing there. Granted, she returned a minute later with a broom, dustpan, and paper bag.

I was fortunate no glass had come down on my face. I shook out my hair the best I could and went to get the hairdryer. Plugging it in outside, I flipped my head over and carefully went through my hair, and I did not find any pieces.

When I examined the light fixture, it was worse than I had expected. The ladder had clipped the metal arm of the light sconce. On the ground I found two old screws that were stripped from the siding. The fixture was hanging by one wire and another wire was not attached to anything. I hoped to get it fixed before EG got back.

The back door led into a stunted hallway.

One step into the house, we were forced to either turn left and take one step into the kitchen or turn right and head down the stairs where Sherrie had given me the finger earlier. I held the door for her as she tried to maneuver the ladder past the screen door. She couldn't move into the kitchen because of the wood door, so she had to shuffle down a few steps and narrowly avoided the overhead interior light bulb. We got the ladder successfully in the house through the kitchen, around the dining table into the living room, and to the stairwell before we had our next incident.

I remembered I hadn't closed the garage door, and typically, it would be no big deal around here, but if we were locking doors and windows, I didn't want the garage door to remain an open invitation for anyone who might be lurking around.

Overconfidence caused Sherrie to try handling the stairwell by herself. The staircase had three steps up to a landing before she had to make a right turn up the narrow curving staircase. The house had been built in the thirties, and wide, open staircases hadn't been the norm back then.

She made the turn on the landing, but at the curve near the top, she wobbled. She stepped back down two steps and regained her balance, but the rear of the ladder bumped the canvas print hanging in the landing. The canvas was in a heavy metal frame, and it slipped off the nail, hitting the side wall and denting the floor. I narrowly avoided getting struck in the head by the swinging ladder. The frame had punctured the wall, but not too deep that we couldn't patch it.

After a few swears and a couple of quick prayers, Sherrie managed to get the ladder in her room without further incidents. Upon entering the room, I heard a few disgruntled comments coming from Sherrie. The tape she put around the windows had come down due to the humidity and age of the tape.

Sherrie had not chosen a paint color yet or even the tone she wanted. She dropped me off at the high school track to walk off some of my unsettled energy while she went to the hardware store. Quick and decisive with life direction was one thing, but choosing a paint color could take her some time.

She had been at the hardware store for forty-five minutes before she called and asked if I was done or if she should come back in an hour. I wanted to walk longer, but several kids from the track team had come out for practice.

I felt like a poser on the track with these kids. I was probably only four or five years older, but my lack of running made me feel out of place. I wished I could have joined the two old ladies who had skipped early morning church and were walking the track instead of the mall, but I would have felt like a bigger interloper with them. I decided to take my energy and put it into helping Sherrie paint.

We went to Peaches Café for lunch to fuel us up for the afternoon. I had the insight to grab us some sandwiches for dinner that night. We had failed to get to the farmers market and never thought about the grocery store.

On the ride home, Sherrie realized she forgot the spackle needed to repair the stairwell wall. She pulled in front of the store, and I hopped out and ran in.

I stood in the aisle, determining which spackle was the best, balancing on one leg while using the other foot to scratch my itchy ankle. I reached for a small tube of spackle and nearly lost my balance when some guy turned the corner too quickly and tried avoiding me but ended up grazing me instead.

"Excuse me. So sorry. I didn't see you," he said.

I caught my balance, recognizing the voice before he recognized me. The apology seemed sincere. He extended his hand, but I refused to take it.

A long pause, and finally, Aaron realized it was me. His tone changed. "Oh. Didn't expect to see you here."

"Apparently, you didn't expect to see

anyone here, the way you took the corner." I continued using my foot to scratch my ankle.

"I was thinking of calling or stopping over today. I, um, ah. I don't know the protocol, but I was alarmed when Chuck told me about the car chase."

I didn't want to engage him in a long conversation. I wasn't sure how long I had until I cracked, not sure if I would cry or say angry things. I kept it simple. "It was crazy there for a minute, but we're fine. No need to come over."

He seemed taken aback for a moment. Our relationship had ended two days ago, and today, I truly felt disconnected from him. If I hadn't seen Jo-Lee's overnight bag, would I have been throwing myself into his arms right now?

Aaron noticed my itch dance and looked at my leg. "Looks like you may have gotten yourself into some poison oak." His face changed from an insightful doctor with a diagnosis and a raised eyebrow to a look like he'd had a flashback. His cheeks turned red. I was sure it was the same memory that had me shaking where I stood.

The first time I had gone to his property, he'd shown me around the house, and we'd walked to the lake, laughing and talking. He suddenly grabbed my arm and pulled me close to him. I took that as a sign he wanted to kiss, so that's what we did.

We stood in the same spot as I had last night, making out. It was only after we stopped ten minutes later that he did a little laugh. I asked what was so funny. He shyly admitted that had not been a make-out move, but he'd seen me heading towards the poison oak and had wanted to protect me.

I was steady. I was calm. I knew things that he didn't know I had witnessed. I needed the upper hand. I was going to take control. "Ironic that you are the one to pinpoint the rash."

"How so?"

"It must have come from the lake—Kettle Lake."

"You were there? When . . ."

My heart was pounding, but I was steady. I was not going to crack. "Yesterday. In the evening, before dusk settled in."

"Yesterday? Oh, so you saw . . ." He maintained his stance. He did not slouch or shrink like a criminal who had been caught, but he certainly was not acting like he'd won the breakup either.

"I saw lots of things, including a pretty good sunset. Excuse me now. Sherrie is waiting for me." I walked past him, and it took everything in me not to turn around. I went to the register, paid, left, and never looked back.

CHAPTER TWENTY-ONE

Sherrie was proud of how I'd handled the situation. "Walk out like a lady. It leaves them stunned," she said.

On the way home she ran into the pharmacy to get me something for the poison oak.

Her bedroom had windows on three sides, creating a decent breeze. I set up fans to circulate the air and help the paint dry. I taped the window, closet, and doorframes while Sherrie taped off the ceiling. We had not spoken much since the hardware store.

I would have bet that she'd have thumping bass music playing, but she opted for meditative music. At first, the music of Enya reminded me of those sound machines from the Sharper Image stores in the '90s.

After listening for a bit, I was transported to a train in the Scottish countryside. I pictured myself looking out the windows to green hills, mist covering the windows, and rolling fog. The music lulled me forward. The destination was unknown, but the journey and the clatter of the train was calming. The music didn't lull me into place; it was like a current that kept me flowing towards wherever I was supposed to be.

We pushed the bed away from the wall. Sherrie painted, and I propped up all the pillows and leaned back, stretching out one leg and letting the poison oak leg dangle off the edge.

I looked out the window for some time and noticed a car driving slowly past the house. The first time, I thought it was no big deal because some kids or something could be in the road out of my sight line, and the driver wanted to avoid hitting them. The second time I saw the car, the hairs on my arms tingled and sweat covered the back of my neck. I stood slowly and moved to the side of the window.

I looked over to Sherrie, and she was watching me. She put down the paintbrush, stepped around the old boxes, and moved to the other side of the window.

She whispered, "What's going on?"

"I just saw the same car twice in the last ten minutes, slowly driving past the house."

"Is it the same car as yesterday?"

"I don't know. It could be," I said in a low voice.

"Did anyone get out?"

I shook my head.

"Why are we whispering?"

"I have no idea." I laughed.

We sat on the bed and looked out the window. I lay down and put my feet up on the windowsill. Sherrie watched for cars, and I rolled over, looking at the progress she'd made. She had chosen blue, a cross between robin's-egg blue and a sky blue for two walls and a grassy green for the other long wall. The colors were balanced and complemented each other.

"Are you going to keep going with the green for the front wall?"

"I might just do a fresh coat of white." She shrugged. "So are you going to tell me what you have been thinking for the last few hours? You sat on the bed and watched me paint. Are you mad, sad, lonely? This quiet thing is disturbing."

"Confused. I have to say, slightly confused. I keep rattling in my head what you started last night—stay off the square. What do you think it meant?"

"I have no idea. Do you really think he was trying to hide a new girlfriend?"

"I would like to think not. I don't want to

think I have that bad of taste in men."

We heard a car pull up and park in front of the house. I rolled onto my side to watch Sherrie's reaction as she looked out the window.

"Let's go downstairs. I'm assuming he's here for us," Sherrie said without alarm.

I pulled myself off the bed and looked out the window. A patrol car was parked under the oak tree. I beat Sherrie to the living room because she stopped in the upstairs bathroom and appeared to be fixing her hair.

I opened the screen door to the porch before he knocked and let him into the living room.

Sherrie came down the stairs looking delighted to have a guest. Officer Patrick said he stopped by to tell us there had been no other sightings of the car matching the description we had given. He initially assumed it had been someone looking to drag race, but following us from the town square didn't seem like the typical scenario. We told him about the car driving past the house several times. He said they would patrol our neighborhood as much as they could, but he couldn't do much about a slow-moving car. He said not to engage in any activity with the car.

I felt slightly foolish because we had no concrete evidence that someone was watching me—well, really, that someone was watching us. If it had not been for Officer Patrick's uncle giving his side of the story, would we have appeared to be drag racing and to have lost control?

Sherrie was all smiles and chatty, asking all sorts of procedural questions. She had far more questions than we had problems. Officer Patrick happily answered everything. He stood there in his full uniform, and I noticed sweat around his hairline. Sherrie must have as well, and she explained that we had been keeping the windows and doors locked when we weren't in the room, and offered him some lemonade. He seemed to blush at the lemonade offer, but that could have just been the stiflingly hot room. He declined, saying he had to go.

I thanked him for stopping in, and he turned to leave but asked, "What does EG say about all this?"

"She's out of town for the week and actually out of touch—on a five-day cruise."

"Keep everything locked up, and we'll be in the area."

"I'll walk you out," Sherrie said.

They exited the house and talked for a minute on the driveway. Despite the turmoil in my romantic life, I was happy for Sherrie and her potential date. The only time I had seen her this nonstop chatty was when she had a crush on a guy.

She usually got ahold of herself the third time she saw the guy, but it was fun to watch.

This should be interesting.

CHAPTER TWENTY-TWO

After Officer Patrick left, we went back upstairs and finished painting. I even picked up a small brush and did some of the edge work.

Sherrie weighed the pros and cons of dating a cop in a small town.

"Why don't you try for a date before you plan out the year?" I said.

"This is not so easy. I have a feeling if you're seen with a cop in this town, it is big news, so do I even want to pursue him?"

"You are assuming he wants to date you. You are assuming he lives here." I raised my hands and flexed two fingers. "You can't assume a 'relationship.' That's right, I used air quotes for your fictional relationship."

"I know all that. I was thinking out loud if it

was worth my time. He is so nice and good-looking."

We kept painting, focusing on getting the paint where it belonged and not on the ceiling.

"He is definitely cute, but is that him or the uniform? Remember that bartender you dated junior year? You thought he was soooo good-looking. And then you went out on a date and realized he was not so handsome without the nice mood lighting above the bar hiding the bags under his eyes that made him look like Mr. Potato Head. He always had the sexy, wary look of twenty people begging for his attention even when not working because he constantly used his sweaty palms to push his hair back, thinking it was cool. The fact that you didn't realize he was three inches shorter than you—not that height matters—but for weeks before you went out, all you talked about is how big—yes, physically big—you thought he was. That was because you put the bar and his bartending job in the power seat. You figuratively made him larger than life. Don't do that with the uniform."

"Let me dream. Let me date. Isn't that the purpose of dating?"

"That was my original point," I answered.

Sherrie put down her paint roller and looked around the room. "Maybe he has a friend for you." She looked proud like she had solved a puzzle, trying to get me to help her snag this guy.

The two lamps began to cast shadows as the sun lowered in the sky and went behind some clouds. I went downstairs and grabbed the to-go containers from Peach's Café. We sat on the floor in her room eating, taking bits of each other's pie. Cherry and apple pies, the two best pies.

"Claud, why are you looking so glum?" she asked.

I looked at the pie and thought about what she had said about dating a cop in a small town. I had dated Aaron for six weeks, and I would be intertwined with him for the foreseeable future.

My parents going into business with his aunt would continuously pull us into the same circle. He had been more involved than just scouting locations. Once, he'd even mentioned he was thinking of selling the bar and becoming operations manager for the facility.

Maybe Sherrie and I were both right, and considering the pros and cons of a relationship might be the equivalent of a first date.

I was sitting on a canvas drop cloth with my back against the bed and legs stretched forward.

Sherrie was next to me, and she stood up, all giddy. "I don't know the best part of painting. Is it putting on the first brush of paint and knowing you picked the right color, or is it now when you get to pull the tape off the walls and trim?" She did a little two-step dance. Just a short hop, with her hair bouncing, a big grin spreading across her face.

"This is like when you get a new phone, and you get to pull the clear plastic cover off and it's all shiny and new."

She stepped towards a window, reaching out ceremoniously for the blue tape. She paused for dramatic effect and looked at me. She must have seen the color drain from my face and my body go rigid. "What's wrong?"

"Shhh," I whispered. I got up, and with my sweaty hand, I pulled her to the back of the bedroom, wedging us between EG's old boxes and the back wall.

"What's going on?" she whispered.

"Someone's in the house." My heart was pounding. I was on my knees, peering over a stack of EG's research material. I wondered if maybe there was some insight into what we should have been doing. EG wrote mystery and teen slasher novels. There must have been something in those boxes. I pinned our hopes on outdated material from twenty years ago.

"What did you hear? Did you see something?" she whispered, grabbing her phone and pressing 9 and 1, then looking at me for an answer.

My head was tight. I could hear every sound—the crickets outside, a dog barking in the distance, and the trees shaking with the breeze. "The lights. The living room lights. I saw down the stairwell, the lights went on. Someone is downstairs."

This crap is getting real. I looked at my Sherrie. "Hells be—"

She didn't join me. She had been squatting and balancing on the balls of her feet. Getting ready to spring forward but suddenly rocked back, fell against the wall, and started shaking.

I didn't know what had happened. Was she having a seizure or freak-out? She was always a rock in stressful situations. Maybe she was reacting from Jean accidentally shooting her in June.

I listened for footsteps or for steps six and seven to sound the alarm that someone was climbing up to us. I reached for Sherrie's phone to call the police and maybe an ambulance for her. I was going to save us. It was going to be me to keep us out of the ditch this time. I was going . . .

CHAPTER TWENTY-THREE

When I reached down to her, I realized she was not having a seizure or paralyzed in fear, but she was laughing. That kind of belly laugh that could make someone laugh so hard they couldn't breathe or make noise. Tears streamed down her cheeks, and finally, I heard heaving noises that resembled laughter. It was that contagious laugh and I started chuckling. I forgot about the intruder for a second. Only a second.

My laughter stopped. I glanced between the bedroom door and Sherrie about a hundred times. She righted herself into a semi-standing, semi–bent over position. In between breaths, she managed to get out, "It's me." Belly heaving. "Lights." Pointing at herself and more belly heaving.

I stopped looking at the door. I was

standing, not moving. Even the itchy poison oak seemed to have suspended its fury on me for the moment.

"Lights. Me." The belly heaving became lighter. After what seemed a lifetime, she was able to speak. "This morning, I bought timers for the lights. I thought it would help with security. The lights turn on and off by themselves." She wiped away tears. "I thought I told you. You watched me plug it in."

"What do you mean? Watched you? When were you fiddling around with the plug? I just thought you were grabbing your phone charger. Jeeesussss . . ."

In relief, I sat down on a box covered with a drop cloth. Unfortunately, I'd picked a box that was only half-full. It collapsed under my weight. My butt went down, my thighs folded into my stomach, and my feet went up. Sherrie once again doubled over in heaving fits of laughter. I couldn't move. All I could do was join her. She pulled me out of the box, and we continued giggling.

We pulled the tape off the walls and admired her work. At one point, when she was not watching, I dipped my fingertips of my right hand into the blue paint and then the green paint and let it trickle down my still-scaly arm and chased her as an evil light witch, flicking paint at her. Surprisingly, she was not as cool about my horror movie scene as I thought she would be. That was until she picked up the roller brush she had been using and used it as a weapon. There was still a lot of paint left on the roller brush, so I concluded game over.

Sherrie went to the basement to clean the paintbrushes and put everything away. I was at the kitchen sink running the water gently over my arm.

I thought I heard knocking on the porch screen door. I didn't want to freak out this time.

I grabbed a dish towel and wiped my arm. I walked past the island and was approaching the dining table when the living room lights clicked off. I pulled my phone out of my pocket. The time read 9:30 p.m.

Who turns off the timer at nine thirty at night? We are not ninety years old. What was she thinking? I stepped forward just in time to see a silhouette leave the front step and walk towards the driveway on the north side of the house.

The kitchen was well-lit. Whoever walked past the windows would have a better vantage point to see me than I would have to see them. I stepped into a dark corner of the living room to text Sherrie. Up now No Joke Someone here. A second after I sent the text, I heard the ding coming from upstairs. She didn't have her phone with her. I heard knocking on the back door.

Sherrie came up the steps, shouting, "You

lock yourself out?"

She was swinging open the back door, then looked in my direction and saw me standing in the kitchen. I had been waving my arms, trying to stop her. She seemed to be trying to focus on the person on the other side of the screen door, but with the outside light not working because of the ladder incident, she needed an extra second to focus.

A man said, "EG, is that you?" He wore jeans, a T-shirt, and a baseball hat that made it harder to determine if he was friend or foe.

"EG?" he said again.

With her dark skin, big curly hair, and being twenty years younger, there was no way to confuse Sherrie with EG. The voice was slurred but recognizable this time. I took Sherrie's spot in the crowded doorway.

"Teddy," I said.

"Ohh, hi, Claudia. I wasss hoping to EG was here."

This was all very strange for me. This man was my birth father. I didn't think I would ever be able to give him a title like dad, father, or papa. We'd met twice since the initial meeting. Once for lunch and once for coffee. Actually, I had met him before but without knowing he was my birth father, only as Pastor Theo, when my parents had sometimes taken me to his church in St. Paul.

My mom had always said we visited there

because she didn't care for our senior pastor when it was his time to lead the service. I never did ask her if there was more to it after learning about my connection to him.

That association of Teddy—my birth father and the man with whom I had shared a meal—is different from the man who preached from a pulpit. It was like when I was in grade school and I saw my teacher in a restaurant with her husband and kids, and thought, Who is this lady, and who are those strange people with her? Why is Mrs. Nellis, my second grade teacher, wearing jeans with a tear in them? And is that a T-shirt from a rock concert?

"Teddy, hi. EG is gone. Do you want to come in?" I didn't know how to link this man to the moment. It was Sunday evening, and he seemed to be slightly drunk. I wasn't scared of him, but I was not able to connect either. I unhooked the screen door, allowing him to step into the small vestibule, backing into the kitchen, and he followed. Sherrie was there taking it all in.

"Hi, Pastor Theo. Remember me, I'm Sherrie."

They had met previously one crazy night in this very house. That was a story for another time, a really good story if you were to ask me.

"Of course. Pleassse call me Teddy. I don't think thisss town will ever be ready to call me

Passstor. I'm almosst done with it anyway."

"What do you mean?" I asked.

"I am taking that job. Teaching. I was done withhh the church ssssoon," Teddy said, swaying just a bit.

My face still felt flushed from all the laughing, and under the bright kitchen light, I felt magnified, like I was onstage in some weird play, hoping for an intermission.

"Come and have a seat. Can I get you something to drink?" I asked because I couldn't think of anything else to say.

I went to open the refrigerator. Sherrie leaned against the sink and watched with a smirk on her face.

I will have to remember to ask her what she was thinking.

With all the weird stuff that had happened the last two days, I was no longer surprised by someone showing up on a Sunday night.

Each time we had met previously, I hadn't been nervous. I was curious now and slightly bewildered.

"Actually, I don't have much to offer. We never made it to the store this weekend. Does water work?"

"Sure," he said and squinted in the bright lights of the kitchen.

"Why don't we move to the porch? It will be

cooler than the house," Sherrie said.

We grabbed our waters and moved past the dining table, into the living room, and to the front door. The outside light provided little light, but I didn't think that was why Teddy stumbled when trying to get to the couch.

Sherrie turned on one lamp in the living room. The two lights together gave the patio a soft glow, and we could easily see each other.

I definitely saw the look on Sherrie's face. Now I was nervous. She tilted her head towards the yard, but I couldn't see what she was trying to point out.

Teddy took a seat on the couch. I made my way towards the far chair, but Sherrie casually pulled my arm back and led me to the chair opposite him. She sat on the armrest next to me.

"Will EG be back ssssoon?" he asked.

Sherrie jumped in. "What have you been up to? How is your brother?"

"Oh, physically, he and my nephew will be fine. Mentally, he is shaken up. They were minutes away from home when the accccident happened. What did you say about EG?"

Sherrie answered again. "She will be awhile."

Teddy took a long drink of water, and she elbowed me in the side.

"But my friend will be here soon. Have you

been with your brother this weekend? Were you at church this morning?"

It took him a while to answer. I wasn't sure if he could remember both questions. His eyes were half-open, and he was slipping deeper into the couch.

"I have been with them since two days, no three days. Today is what—ah Sunday. I went there Wednesday. How many days is that? Four? I have been driving my mother back and forth."

"How long of a drive is that?" Sherrie asked.

"From here, about nnninettty minutes. Three hoursss from Sssaint Paul."

"Do you have any recent pictures of your nephew?" Sherrie asked.

"My son is a soccer player, but this fellooooow will be a baseball player. See, here they are together." He held up his phone.

She extended her arm like she was going to try to hold the phone, but it seemed like a heavy iron ball in his hand and he withdrew before she could take it. His movements were very slow.

"They are adorable," she said, but I didn't think she had seen the picture. She started talking again, this time in a softer voice, rambling on about the neighbor boy back home who loved soccer. She was telling some irrelevant story that seemed to be going nowhere.

"This must be exhausting for you being with

them and driving back to your family," she said.

"I-I-I am managing," Teddy said.

"I don't think you should drive. Is anyone expecting you? Are you driving back to Saint Paul tonight?"

"No, I was going to stay here."

"Here?" I croaked out.

"Spend some time with my mom and a friend," he answered, but I was not sure who he was talking to.

"You're staying with your mom?" I asked with relief that he did not mean here in this house.

"Claudia and I will get something for us to munch on. Why don't you relax here a minute? Maybe EG will be back soon."

He nodded, and that was his only body movement.

Sherrie and I went into the living room.

"What is all this?" I whisper-yelled.

"Holy shit!" Sherrie pointed outside. "That is the car! The car from yesterday!"

CHAPTER TWENTY-FOUR

"What are you talking about? You think Teddy tried to run us off the road?"

"Shhhh. Quiet. Let the man sleep. I'm sure he's a minute away from passing out. He is loaded. I can't believe he drove here," Sherrie said.

"I can't believe you think it was him. Are you sure it was the car? It's dark out. How clearly can you see it?"

Sherrie paced between the dining table and the island, not answering.

I continued. "What should we do?"

We heard a car start and then drive away. We froze for a split second before we ran to the porch door and saw a car going down the street without headlights on.

Together we whispered, "Hells bells."

A snort came from Teddy on the couch. He shifted and straightened up. We walked back onto the porch.

I said, "We heard a car. We thought you'd left."

"I musst have dozed off."

"How did you get here?" I asked.

"I walked. I was with a friend at the bar. I saw your boyfriend."

I rolled my eyes and was thankful he couldn't see my face clearly.

"I ssshould get going."

Sherrie and I looked at each other in a panic. He was in no condition to be driving. "If no one is expecting you, why don't you stay?"

"I must be going," he said but did not get up.

"How about you stay on that couch? We bring some of those cheese and crackers we talked about. In the morning, we can go for breakfast."

"That's not a bad plan. Maybe I will get to sssee EG."

I pushed Sherrie back into the living room, and we left Teddy on the couch. We stood between the dining table and the opening to the kitchen, shaking our heads in disbelief.

"What just happened? Was there a car out front watching us? Watching Teddy? Was it the same car from yesterday?" I was asking a lot of questions neither one of us had answers to.

We heard Teddy grunt again. We crept to the window facing the porch. His stomach rose and fell like that of someone sleeping soundly.

Sherrie paced around the living room.

I went to the kitchen to make sure all the doors and windows were locked. I turned off all the lights in the living room and kitchen. The only light was the exterior light above the screen door. Sherrie and I sat side by side on the stairwell landing, our legs hanging down the two steps. Sherrie leaned against the wall. I looked up the stairwell, hoping for the explanation to come rolling down the stairs. I shuffled my butt back and leaned against the wall, watching my feet hang over the landing. My mind was circling.

"What do we know?" I said.

"Teddy shows up. Drunk."

"Thankfully, he didn't drive."

She nodded in agreement. "Someone in a car may have been watching the house."

"That is a maybe. I was not focused on the car when I heard knocking on the porch door. I had just seen someone step off the porch steps. I wasn't looking for a car. We don't know when it got there."

"We do know it left without any headlights on," Sherrie pointed out. "And it may or may not have been the car chasing us from yesterday."

"Why were you rambling out there about some kid that lives near your parents?"

"I was trying to get him to pass out from boredom. Then I thought to ask about his brother to get a timeline of where he was yesterday."

I rolled my eyes. She was always playing detective. "Why would he want to run me over? Sorry, I mean, us. Why would he want to run us off the road?"

"Why does he want to see EG so badly on a Sunday night. How much do you have to be drinking to pass out at nine thirty on a Sunday?"

"What should we do now? Let him sleep it off?" I asked.

"I've got an idea."

"I am not calling the police so Officer Hottie can show up again."

"Oh, no. It's too soon for that. I need a few days before I bump into him."

"Really? You are staging your sequence of run-ins with him? Can we focus on right now? What is this idea?"

"Let's take his phone and see if we can figure out where he's been."

"Are you kidding me? You want to sneak onto the porch, take the phone from him while he's passed out, somehow log into his phone, and try to track his movements."

"We can use his fingerprint. You hold the phone, and I will press his finger on the button."

"You have to be kidding me!" I whispered

loudly.

"Why not? What do we have to lose? He came here. It's not like we went breaking into his house."

We were whispering, but each time our whispers were louder than the last. "You can't be serious?"

"What do you really know about him? I've got your mother's voice in my head again." Raising her pitch to match my mom's, Sherrie said, "Let's start at the beginning." She continued in her normal voice. "Think about what all we learned about him earlier this summer. He thought he accidentally killed his father and took off for several years. Yes, it's true, he didn't actually kill him, but he hid the body! He didn't tell his mother or brother that his father was dead—regardless of the fact that his dad was a shit of a man, his mother and brother deserved to know. He was too selfish to tell them their nightmare was over. Then, he suddenly reappears as an ordained minister?" Sherrie shook her head. "You met him in June and what, twice since then? What do you really know about him?"

I had crossed my legs and arms, and my muscles were tight. I was mad. I wasn't mad at Sherrie, but because everything she'd said was true. Why did he get the benefit of the doubt? Because we were blood? Because he was a pastor? Because I thought most people were good unless proven wrong. I had let this man into my life and now EG's house, but how far did I have to take it?

"You got a point there; I really don't know him. However, I do know if that car"—I gestured towards the driveway—"was indeed the car following us yesterday, it's most unlikely Teddy was driving it then since it just drove off without him."

"Good point."

"Why is he asking about seeing EG? She has not mentioned anything. I told her about each time we got together, but that was all she spoke of him. I don't think they communicated since we were all together in June."

"So you are not going to go through his phone?"

"No, I am not going to look at his phone! Should we let him sleep it off?"

"Do we have another choice at this point?"

CHAPTER TWENTY-FIVE

Sherrie and I sat on the landing for ten more minutes trying to figure out if we should call someone. My parents and EG were all on cruise ships and unreachable. Sherrie's father and mother would either call the National Guard or take the other approach and think she could handle anything that came her way. She was also hesitant to tell them of any strange things going on for fear of them trying to make her leave town.

I clearly was not going to call Aaron. The police were already patrolling. We debated calling the nonemergency number, but what would we say? "We know you are driving past the house, just letting you know someone is sleeping on the porch. Yes, we let him in . . . No, I really don't know too much about him. Shoot, don't shoot, it's up to you.

Don't worry; us girls are not crazy." We couldn't figure out what to say. The only other friends I'd made in town were Kay and Jenna. We thought calling them would just add fuel to the fire.

Our last choice was Jorge. Unfortunately, that would not be an option tonight. He had worked all day at the auto shop, and he went to his sister's on Sunday nights. If he was not home by now, that meant he had been drinking with his brother-in-law. We decided to leave him a text stating Teddy was sleeping on the porch couch. We did not want or need him going all Rambo on us if he saw something or someone suspicious camping out on the porch.

We didn't know if this was silly, smart, or ridiculous, but we decided I would sleep on the small couch in Sherrie's room. Strength in numbers. We pulled off the boxes and dirty clothes she had piled on top of it when we started painting. It was not a pull-out sofa, and it was relatively short in length. I couldn't fully stretch out my legs. I thought it would be fine since I usually sleep curled up.

Our biggest issue was whether to lock the door from the house to the porch. We decided to shut the door and not lock it. We closed the door to Sherri's room and put two heavy boxes in front of it.

My gut told me Teddy was harmless. If he

was going to attack us, he would have done it already, and a lock on the front door would not stop him. It might slow him down but not stop him. I kept thinking about the car driving away without him. I was building a relationship with him and did not want to embarrass him by locking him out of the house.

I lay on the rock-hard couch with my pillow that was more than a third wider than the sofa, staring up at the ceiling. My left arm was dangling down the side, my fingers gently dancing on the hardwood floor.

My phone was under my flaky right arm crossed over my chest. The pain was still receding. I was looking forward to seeing the doctor tomorrow and hearing that taking off the cast yesterday was a good thing to do. My mind went back to that light bulb moment when Chuck was talking about taking control.

Why was I struggling with how Teddy might feel if he woke up, needing to use a bathroom, but found the door locked? I should have felt comfortable protecting Sherrie and me. No excuses should be made for someone else when it came to my safety. It should have been ok to look out for myself first. Then I realized I was confusing fear with pity and my need to make everyone feel comfortable.

Why should I watch out for him? I should

watch out for myself.

I was still awake at midnight. We only kept one fan on because we wanted to hear any noises downstairs or outside. Sherrie pushed the twin bed into the corner so her phone cord could reach her pillow. We were both ready to call 9-1-1 should we hear anything strange. She fell asleep pretty quickly, and I was grateful she did not have to listen to me constantly shift all night on the couch. I couldn't even say I tossed and turned because there was not enough room to toss or turn. I could slightly shift from lying on my back flat with my knees bent or on tilt on my left side with my left leg bent and the right leg stretched over the armrest.

I thought I'd managed a few hours of sleep, and finally, after five in the morning, I peeled myself from the couch and quietly shifted the boxes in front of Sherrie's door, used the bathroom, and headed downstairs.

I'd slept in the clothes I had been wearing yesterday and felt no need to change them at this point. I avoided making any noise on steps six and seven, and in the living room, I looked through the window. Teddy was still sleeping on the couch. At some point, he had gone from sitting slouched over to fully covering the length of the oversized sofa.

I sniggered at the ordeal Sherrie and I had made of him showing up last night. He looked harmless, but on the other hand, what did I know about him? He was a pastor, husband, and father. Those things were titles—not the person. They gave me no depth to the man nor added any meaning to my life. Sherrie's friendship meant more to me than this man who had given me life. Actually, my mom and dad had given me a life; this man had just donated his sperm.

I went to the kitchen and made some coffee. I sat at the island with both hands around the warm mug. The sun slowly filled the kitchen with light. I cracked open a window, allowing fresh air to flow in.

I scrolled through the news on my phone, and twenty minutes later, Teddy got up from the porch couch. I went to the front door. He stood with his back to the house and rubbed his face. He hadn't shaved in a few days, but it was a look most men would like to be able to pull off. It was far from being called a beard and was more than a five o'clock shadow, but he did not look unkempt.

I pulled open the door and said, "Good morning."

He seemed to blush behind the mock beard. He gave me a grumbled "Morning."

I offered him EG's bathroom and returned to the kitchen and poured myself another cup of coffee. He joined me a couple of minutes later.

He approached the kitchen quietly like he was waiting for permission to enter. Besides offering him coffee and a stool at the island, I let him speak first.

"It has been many years since I have done that," Teddy said.

"Drink too much?"

"Unfortunately, not that. I do enjoy a beverage or beverages quite often these days. But I mean showing up somewhere after having too many. I'm sorry if I made you uncomfortable."

I shrugged, giving a voiceless response of whatever and let him continue.

"The last few weeks have been crazy with the church, job change, home, and now my brother's accident. Melanie, my wife, is having a hard time with all this. I have been pulled to the limits on sleep and apparently on common sense. I apologize for last night. I should not have come over like that. I just wanted—"

I finished the thought. Not out of kindness, but I didn't want a change of subject. "You just wanted to see EG."

"Yes." He looked at me over the top of the coffee mug as he took a sip.

"You could have called."

"Ah, a voice of reason." He laughed and continued. "A voice of someone sober. I actually don't have her number. Believe it or not, but me putting the connection of you living with EG and you being able to connect me with her was not something I could put together last night."

"I understand. We've all done things we normally wouldn't have done if we were sober. Nobody thinks rationally after a few drinks."

"I appreciate that, but that does not excuse me for showing up or, worse, not leaving. Again, I am sorry if I made you uncomfortable."

"It's ok." I meant that. He seemed sincere, and there had been no real threatening behavior. He had no idea of the things that had transpired before his arrival. I hoped I was not making excuses for him. I thought I just understood him.

"Can I buy you breakfast before you head to work?" he asked.

"Thanks for the offer, but I'm not going to work until this afternoon. I have a follow-up appointment with the doctor about my arm." I raised my right hand.

It must have occurred to him for the first time that morning that I did not have my cast on, nor did he remember that today was supposed to be the official day it came off.

"If you're sure then. I should be off. I need to see my mom before I head back."

I didn't know if I should offer him a ride. It felt slightly condescending, but then again, he was the fortysomething-year-old showing up drunk and passing out. "Can I offer you a ride?"

"My car is just up the road in the lot behind

the square. I appreciate the offer, but the walk will help wake me up."

We stood up and walked towards the front door. I kept the coffee mug in one hand and put the other hand on the handle of the open front door. We'd usually just said goodbye. This was not time to start hugging goodbye, so I made an effort to look like that would not change today.

We made small talk for another minute, and I casually mentioned EG would be gone for a few more days but did not offer her phone number.

He rubbed his eyes. "Something about coming back to this town makes me act like I did when I last lived here at twenty years old, but the ringing in my head reminds me I am well into my forties."

I gave him a pity laugh as much for him as for me. I was still a decent person. He walked down the sidewalk with his hands in his pockets, and I couldn't help wondering what he was thinking.

I texted Sherrie. All good all clear.

A minute later, my phone beeped. It was Jackson. Please don't delete or block my text. Do I need to be there in 72 hours exactly or before it expires?

Another text followed a second later. I NEED that backpack.

I didn't have the emotional capacity for this. I texted back, Understand I don't have it!!!

I went upstairs to shower and get ready for my appointment. I couldn't help thinking about what I'd gotten myself into, forcing Jackson into action by threatening to throw something I didn't have into the river. Who cared if he didn't believe me. He had been in this house twice and all for less than thirty-six hours. I had only lived here for less than two months. I knew what possessions I had come with.

He should have known I didn't bullshit with anyone. What did he think I was going to drop in the river? What had him so freaked out that he was willing to drive several hours for a shitty backpack? He couldn't have been doing this just to see me. He didn't put that much effort into someone.

It finally dawned on me. He seemed desperate. What could be so important to him? As fast as that thought came to me, I let it go. It was not my problem anymore.

The morning had started strange and continued to evolve into a weird day, with one strange event unfolding after another.

CHAPTER TWENTY-SIX

During a breakfast of cold cereal and extra coffee, Sherrie and I talked about how to handle that day and the week. I appreciated her concern, but I was not going to be bonded to fear. The house would remain locked while we were gone and while at home. Our phones would be charged at all times. I would stay in public places or at the house. I wouldn't go for walks by myself, and Sherrie had to agree not to say anything to Aaron at work that night.

The best part of the morning was sitting in the doctor's waiting room. I struck up a conversation with the hotel manager from one of the nice hotels in town. Short of offering me the job on the spot, she highly suggested I come in for an interview. There were several job openings.

My volunteer hours at Chambray had evolved to half-volunteer and half-paying. The pay was medium at best. The work had been a breeze but boring. I would be forever grateful they were allowing me to complete my required volunteer hours and kept finding work for me. There was not much of a career for me there. Plenty of work but short on anything satisfying.

I wanted something to challenge me and take me places. Literally, I wanted to go places, travel, and see things. Why not work for a company like a national hotel chain or an airline that can help facilitate that love of travel? I had a degree in business, and I could mold that into almost anything on a job application.

Am I falling into a hotel job as I have fallen into work at Chambray? I'd heard people talk about luck versus being ready to take advantage of an opportunity when it presents itself. Had I fallen into my life in River Bend?

I sat in the waiting room for fifteen minutes after Gloria, the hotel manager, was called into the inner office. I could no longer fiddle with the frayed edges of my cast, and I instinctively went back to spinning my ring.

My mom had given me the five-dollar ring several years ago. We had been on a road trip and stopped at a gas station. She went to pump gas, and I went to get us something to drink. The rings were near the cash register, along with some fancy lighters. It was silver and had tiny red stones embedded in it. I thought about buying one, but I then saw a silver one with green stones and bought it for my mom. She went into the store to get something salty to snack on and saw the ring with the red stones and bought it for me, not knowing how I had admired it and bought her the ring with the green stones. It was one of my favorite gifts I have ever received.

I had taken the ring off when I'd broken my arm because of the swelling in my hand, and I was happy to have it back on. A little piece of me had been missing without it.

I wanted to talk to my folks about making the career move, not so much for advice but to share my excitement that I was making decisions.

I had this all worked out in my head. I would work at the hotel for a year, gaining experience, and determine where I wanted to live and then transfer with this company.

When I realized my parents were still unreachable for five more days, my immediate thought was to call Aaron.

It stung me when I realized I wasn't going to call him. It had been weird when I'd broken up with Jackson—I'd never had a moment of backsliding, regretting the breakup, and never had any thoughts to reach out to him about anything.

Even now, with Jackson texting about coming up here, all I want to do is avoid him. Maybe me seeing Aaron with Jo-Lee was preventing me from backsliding.

I was so wrapped up in these thoughts I didn't hear my name. I was one of two patients in the waiting room, and they might have said my name several times before I acknowledged the nurse. The elderly lady waiting for her appointment gave me a look meant for toddlers who have an accident in their big-kid pants. I was too excited about the new prospect of a career to care.

At this point, I wasn't nervous about seeing the doctor. My new career choice was empowering a new type of control. He was not surprised to learn I had removed the cast. He said, with people my age, especially with guys, there is a pretty good chance of it coming off outside the doctor's office. I got a good report from him and headed home to complete the application online before going to Chambray for the afternoon.

Sherrie had been home all morning and had spent the morning finishing her room. Moving the furniture to the right places and hanging several pictures. I said I would go through EG's old research boxes this week and figure out what we should keep.

She was happy to report nothing strange

had happened while I was gone. I had watched for cars following me and had even gone a couple of miles out of the way. I deliberately drove past the police station, and it gave me a sliver of comfort knowing it was there.

CHAPTER TWENTY-SEVEN

Before I left for my shift at Chambray, Sherrie tried telling me I should go in lockdown mode while she was at work. I was beginning to feel stifled. She reminded me that last Friday, she thought she'd heard someone leave the house when she was bringing in her stuff.

She got funny when I suggested that maybe somebody was watching her and not me. When we were chased down, she had been in the car; she lived in this house that someone might have been in and had cars slowly driving past. Someone just may have been looking for a prime parking spot and not casing my car. Maybe Jo-Lee was just making conversation with her boss. She didn't like hearing that spin on things and told me not to deflect the danger away from me.

Twenty minutes later, I hit send on my laptop and submitted the hotel job application. I danced around the kitchen island, weaving myself in between the stools to the music of Justin Timberlake.

"Yo, keep your head in the game. You may have a job, but you definitely have a stalker," Sherrie barked from the living room.

"Buzzkill," I bellowed and danced my way to the back door.

"Don't be a fool!"

I wanted to give her the finger, but she was out of sight so I opted for yelling one more time, "Major Buzzkill."

After my half-day shift at Chambray, I went to talk to my boss, Mrs. Baron. I know I did not have the job at the hotel yet, but I could not stay at Chambray. I was not going to settle here. If I gave my notice, I would push harder to find something if the hotel job did not work out.

Mrs. Baron was a straightforward person, all work and little play. What she lacked in fun, she made up for in kindness and common sense. With saying all that, I was a bit surprised how curt she was with me.

Seeing Mrs. Baron, one risked losing twenty minutes of their day just getting past her assistant, Cheryl. She was so efficient at her job, she had too much time on her hands. She spent her free moments dragging people into her net to talk about anything that came across her mind.

Cheryl's desk sat off the main corridor in the Administration and Activities building. Thus, Mrs. Baron's door was eight feet behind her, so it was challenging to see Mrs. Baron without seeing Cheryl. I didn't have an appointment to keep the outer office visit short, so I hoped for the best.

I walked down the hall and noticed two other staffers walking past Cheryl's desk with their heads down, either engaged in paperwork or their phones. I was curious if they were reading anything interesting or doing their best to avoid eye contact with Cheryl.

"Good afternoon, Cheryl. I was hoping to see Mrs. Baron if she is available."

"Hellllooo, Claudia. I have not seen you in a while. I see your cast is off your arm. You must be so happy."

I just nodded and pointed towards Mrs. Baron's door.

Cheryl continued. "When my nephew got the cast off his leg, he was so excited he started dancing around, tripped, and nearly broke his other leg."

I gave a little laugh. I needed to see Mrs. Baron, and Cheryl was my entry ticket. "That's a funny story."

From the office, Mrs. Baron said, "Is that

you, Claudia? Come on in."

Cheryl gave me an apologetic smile as if she was sorry she couldn't save me from seeing Mrs. Baron.

"I hope I'm not disturbing you," I said as I entered her office.

She motioned for me to sit. "I was expecting to see you sooner."

"Yes, my community service hours will be completed this week. I appreciate the opportunity to mix my work schedule with both paid and community service hours."

"And let me guess. You will not be continuing your employment with us. I have to say I am slightly disappointed."

I was sitting upright and stiff, spinning my ring. Mrs. Baron's desk was absent of clutter. In front of her was my paperwork for the court. She looked up before signing her name and continued. "I hope you will at least give us until the end of the week. I have signed off on your hours for tomorrow and that concludes all the court work. It would leave us in a bind if you leave before Friday, and two weeks is the standard time frame when giving official notice. I spoke highly of your performance here. Please let me know your final day as I am doing the schedule for next week."

"Of course."

I was stunned. Mrs. Baron is efficient, but

how did she know I was coming to give my notice? Had the hotel called to confirm my employment history before the interview? It had only been seven hours since I completed the online application.

My need to please people left me sputtering. "Of course, I will work this week and next week. Anything you need. I appreciate everything you did for me. Spoke highly of my performance?"

She slid the court form across the desk. "You will get your final paycheck on the standard payday. Please stop into Human Resources on your last day for any final paperwork. This completes our business for today. Just one piece of advice: I know you're young and new to the job market, but it is customary to tell someone you are using them as a reference so they're not caught off guard. I was happy to help you though." She stood up and grabbed her blazer off the back of her chair and put it on.

"Yes, of course. Thank you again. I will be here this week and next week."

"Three weeks. That's wonderful." She pointed to the paperwork and did me another favor by saying, "That is the only copy. You may take it to court sometime after tomorrow or have Cheryl scan and send it to the court. It's your option."

She was out the door before I could respond, but what would I have said—"Thanks for me not having to come back and talk to your assistant"?

I sat for a minute alone in her office. Three weeks. She'd said three weeks' notice. I had barely given her two weeks' notice. I couldn't sit there all day. I would just have to dash past Cheryl if I wanted to get home and have dinner before the sun went down, and I almost made it. She was on the phone and hung up just as I passed her desk.

"We're sorry to see you go. I knew you wouldn't stick around long."

I kept my head straight and continued walking. "I'll see you before I'm done next week."

"I knew when that lady called last week; it was only a matter of time before you gave your notice."

"Have a good night," I said, rounding the corner. I was one step away from avoiding any lengthy conversation when I stopped dead in my tracks and turned back to Cheryl.

She grinned, having tossed out the bait. I'd sucked it right up.

"Last week?" I stood there with one foot in the hallway and one foot on the carpet in the reception area. The air-conditioning blowing through the vent above me dropped the temperature about fifteen degrees. The hair on my arm stood up, but sweat poured down my back.

"Yes, when that lady called for a reference, I knew it was just a matter of time before you would be gone. I know it's none of my business, but I don't know about working for someone like that. She was asking all sorts of questions that aren't supposed to be asked." She leaned forward, looking around for a few seconds to make sure no one was around to hear her, and lowered her voice. "Mrs. Baron actually scolded me for saying so much. I just thought that I would do you a favor and talk you up. Honey, you can do anything you want. You are off to bigger things than this place. I don't know why Mrs. Baron was so mad."

My body was frozen in the same spot, but my voice trembled. "What day did she call? What was her name?"

"Now let me think. Last Tuesday or Wednesday? No, it was definitely Tuesday because Kara from the dining room brought me some cherry cobbler."

I didn't know how she'd made the connection between Tuesday and cobbler. I couldn't afford the headache of that answer, so I moved on. "Forget the day. What was her name? What did she ask?"

Cheryl leaned back, seemingly not liking my tone. "Don't worry. I talked you up. I let her know all that you do around here." She leaned in towards me again and whispered, "I didn't mention the community service hours. Are you ok? You look a little funny."

I couldn't move my body. Stuart Nicholas,

the director of Chambray Senior Center, walked in. Cheryl moved her focus to him. I knew I wasn't getting any more out of her today. She was done with her shift in ten minutes. I mumbled hello to Stuart and escaped down the hallway, not seeing anything that I passed. All the sounds faded as I recalled what Mrs. Baron and Cheryl had said.

Some lady called and asked questions about me last week. It could not have been the hotel job I applied for today, and from what Cheryl said, she asked all sorts of questions.

I pressed on the metal bar on the back door that opened to the courtyard. I stepped out and leaned against the wall. Bending over, I put my hands on my knees, crumpling the court papers in my hand. I heaved, but nothing came out of my empty stomach. Someone had been asking about me. Someone had tried to drive me off the road. Someone had driven past the house and might have been in the house. Someone just became one real person.

CHAPTER TWENTY-EIGHT

I walked to my car in a daze and got mad at myself for my stupidity. I didn't have my purse or keys. I was in such a state I wasn't thinking clearly, which would get me into trouble. I ran back around to the employee area and grabbed my stuff from the locker. On the way to Debby, I was hyperaware of every sound and shadow.

I pressed the car and house keys between my fingers and made a fist. I was ready if someone was going to jump me. My hand was getting stronger each day, but it had only been out of the cast two days. I wouldn't be able to deliver a brutal punch to the nose or face , but perhaps the person would be weirded out by my scaling zombie-like arm.

I realized I must have been ok at least mentally because I began laughing at myself. Of all the places I have been lately, was someone really going to jump out from behind a car at five thirty on a sunny Monday evening at a senior center? Then the smile faded from my face when my thoughts went back to a true crime podcast I had been listening to. The two ladies hosting the show had discussed murderers and psychopaths that hide in plain sight.

I looked around and thought about the obvious. Who could it be?

I got into my car. Do I need to start from the beginning or jump to the question of who did I piss off?

I wanted to talk to someone. Currently, my options were very limited. I was sad that I couldn't speak to Aaron. He'd made a big deal about remaining friends, and I had hoped we could, but now, I wasn't just sad about the man I thought I'd known, but also the man I realized I'd never really known.

I hoped Sherrie wasn't busy at work and I could talk it out with her. Instead of driving straight to the bar, I drove around, watching for anyone following me. Even with all the stuff going on, I felt rather foolish. Concerned but foolish.

CHAPTER TWENTY-NINE

I was lucky and found parking in front of the bar. I waited a minute before I got out, preparing myself in case I saw Aaron or Jo-Lee. I had no idea who was working tonight with Sherrie. I wanted to appear as if nothing was bothering me. The last thing I needed was for Aaron to think I was freaked out and for him to start helping or, worse, me wanting him to help.

I stood in front of the bar and looked through the window, trying to see if it was busy and who I would have to talk to if Sherrie was busy. It looked like I was in the clear. Pete and Sherrie were bartending, and it was not busy.

I turned around when I heard Kay and Jenna calling my name. They seemed to be ready for happy hour. Kay was wearing the same black shirt and black jeans she'd been wearing several hours ago at work. Jenna must have come from the judge's office. She was in pinstripe navy slacks and a blouse with a high collar. Very conservative and very unlike her rock concert T-shirt and cutoff jeans look she had been wearing every time I had seen her socially.

"Happy hour works better if you actually go in the bar," Kay said.

I had been practicing what I would say to Aaron or Jo-Lee, but I'd had no thoughts about talking to anyone else. I started to stutter out an answer but just stopped.

Jenna looked at me, concerned. "Are you ok?"

"Of course, you just caught me off guard."

I looked back in the window. Aaron was walking towards the bar from the back room.

Damn, I can't go in there now. Not with Kay and Jenna. They will want to talk to Aaron and see how uncomfortable I am. I can't be mad because I probably would have done that several years ago to any number of friends of mine.

"I was thinking of visiting Sherrie, but I think I'm hungry for a burger. Why don't we go up the block to Bumbles for food and beer?"

"Are you sure it's not just to avoid Aaron?" Kay asked.

We were walking side by side, and I went

ahead half a step, so when I spoke to them, I could look at them while looking behind me to see if anyone was following me. "I was about to walk in there but decided a burger with you was a better option."

Bumbles Bar and Restaurant is a plain wood-panel bar with neon beer signs on every wall, a decades-old jukebox and furniture that has been there since the seventies. What kept everyone coming back was the prices barely changing with each new decade, and the food was fantastic. The three of us walked in, and Kay went to a table next to the only people in the place, who were not sitting at the bar—of course, it was two guys. They appeared to be mid to late twenties, both with military-style buzz cuts and fit, drinking beer, and had no women with them. All the things my friends were looking for.

There had been nothing heartwarming about the place until I'd met the proprietors Denny and Rose. Denny ran the kitchen. Rose worked the bar and kept the customers happy. Today, like all the other days, she walked over to take our order. I had never seen her write down one item, and I had never seen her get an order wrong.

"Hi, ladies, what's going on today? Jenna, that business suit makes you look smashing. Kay, you can put about a dollar's worth of quarters in the jukebox before we switch over to the baseball game. Here you go." She reached into her apron and pulled out some quarters. As she bent over to slide them to Kay, she tilted her head towards the two guys and whispered, "They are handsome, but they are not for you ladies." She stood straight and continued. "Claudia, your arm looks great. Are you feeling ok? You look a little pale."

I guessed I was not hiding my earlier freak-out very well. I had been fiddling with my ring, and now fresh perspiration poured over the old sweat I had earned while running to my car as I'd fled work.

I had taken the chair so I could watch who came in. I glanced at the door before I answered. "All good. Just hungry." I had learned when one lies, they should keep it simple. The more someone forced a long answer, there was more for people to have to believe.

She left our table, and Chuck came in. He paused at our table to say hello. He pulled the headphones off his head.

"What were you listening to?" I asked.

"Cheap Trick's 'I Want You to Want Me.' " Chuck didn't sit and almost seemed uncomfortable as he shifted at the table.

Kay said, "That's Claudia's jam. Classic rock from the seventies and eighties."

Chuck was more rigid now and seemed relieved when the two guys waved him over. Some guys were intimidated to talk to Kay, but I'd never thought a woman could rattle Chuck.

Seeing the wave was all Kay needed. Ignoring the warning from Rose, Kay took the opportunity to engage with the two guys. Before our drinks had been delivered, Jenna, Kay, and the newly introduced Ryan and Brady had joined our two tables together.

Turned out, they had served in the army with Chuck. Brady had talked Ryan into coming to River Bend for a few days of fishing and maybe some golf before Ryan headed to an oil rig job off the Louisiana coast.

Chuck and I sat next to each other and watched the four of them chat each other up. We made small talk between us. It was like watching a doubles tennis game. Each team was flirting and watching who best returned it. I felt like an outsider and was pretty sure Chuck did too.

But we were both ok with that. Chuck was responding to emails while we talked, and apologized several times, explaining that he had a military contract coming up that involved another six months at an undisclosed location.

I was ok being lost in my own thoughts among a crowd. I felt safe in numbers.

I temporarily let my mind wander back to Cheryl's desk. Somebody had called and asked about me.

Who did I piss off?

The noise of the other customers talking created a buzzing white noise that wrapped me in a safe bubble.

My phone beeped, jarring me from my comfort zone. Judge Lobal was following up with concern since I hadn't returned his text on Friday. I decided no lying here. I was not going to waste my energy on him. Just continue to ignore and tomorrow, I would go to Jenna at the courthouse and have her process my final paperwork.

Kay never got the chance to play music. Rose remained behind the bar when two college kids came in and started waiting tables. The place was filling up fast.

The server delivered our checks with the food, and by that time, it appeared Kay was interested in Ryan. I thought it was mutual. Brady focused on Jenna, but it didn't appear she was into him. She sat back and looked at the television as a diversion rather than looking at either one of the guys.

I was lost in thought again as my conversation partner dealt with more emails.

I broke out of my own thoughts when I bit my thumb. I was eating a French fry so slowly and absentmindedly I didn't realize I had run out of fry and had bitten myself.

Jenna pulled me into the foursome.

"Claudia, how is that burger? You barely touched it."

I looked down and realized I'd only had two bites and had hardly touched my beer. I was not surprised. I had only came here to avoid seeing Aaron and his new girlfriend before I was ready.

"It's good, but I lost my appetite. Maybe I'm getting sick. More than one person told me I don't look so great today."

Chuck looked up and joined the group again but didn't say anything.

"You look good," Brady said.

He seemed to be reworking his game plan for tonight in case Jenna didn't respond to his advances.

"Thanks." That was all I could answer.

Brady continued. "Eat up. You'll need your energy if we're going to keep this night going."

"I don't think I'm in it for the long haul tonight. You guys have fun." I went from freaked out to lost in space to just fake smiling my way out of this group.

Chuck seemed to sense something was not right but didn't want to call me out in front of everyone. "How are things at home? Any crazy road trips for you and Sherrie lately?"

I completely understood what Chuck was asking. "No, we stayed in town for our load of crazy stuff, but all is good." That was my indicator for yeah, more weird shit, but I think I have it under control.

Ryan now entered the conversation. He seemed to know if he wanted to keep up his chances with Kay, he needed to have Brady occupied. "Come on. Things are good at home. Let's take our group to BAR. I want to see this place I have heard about—"

Before Brady finished speaking, Chuck said, "We can do that another time. Maybe on your next visit. Aaron is busy. Maybe if it stays slow at BAR, he'll join us at Draw Tavern. They have a good setup for watching the game. We can watch it there."

"It's got to be better than this place. I don't know if you can call that thing behind the bar here a TV. My laptop has a larger screen," Brady said.

"Let's pay up, and we can get there before the other game starts," Chuck said.

"You guys go ahead. I'm going to bow out and head home," I said.

Kay perked up. "Come on. We haven't been out together for a while. You bailed on us Friday. Wait a minute—are you going back to see Aaron?"

"No, I am not going to see him." I reached for my purse, giddy about using one hand to hold my wallet and the other, now-useful hand to unzip it.

Chuck stood and seemed to be rushing the

process of moving us out. "How about the four of you go on to Draw Bar, and I'll walk Claudia to her car?"

"Thanks, but I can manage. I'm parked right in front of BAR, and I want to see Sherrie."

He was too much of a professional to show his poker face. He didn't shrink in defeat, but he twitched.

I didn't know why until Brady spoke. "Wait a minute. Sherrie? Dancing Sherrie from the bar's security cameras? I want to meet her. We gotta go to BAR! We will walk you."

"How about another night," Chuck said. It was not a question.

Brady challenged him. "Come on, Chuck. We're not here for more than two days. You have been a downer since we got here. Let's go have fun."

Kay sat back. I thought she was calculating how this would affect her odds of getting together with Ryan. I didn't think she had to worry about what bar they went to, and she seemed fine with them only being here a few days. Jenna said nothing but grabbed the cash Kay and I had put with the check and walked to the bar to pay.

"Let's not disturb her while she's working. Draw Bar will have both games on, and the beer is just as good there." Chuck sat back down, bringing his voice to a casual tone. "I am at BAR almost every night. I'm back in town, so give me a break and let's go somewhere else."

I didn't understand that because I rarely saw him there. He was a silent partner in the business, which I took to mean absent from sight.

Ryan definitely seemed to be up for keeping the good times rolling and must have figured it would be best to side with Chuck. "Let's go with the original plan. The four of us." He looked around for confirmation from Kay, Jenna, and Brady. "We go to Draw, and Chuck will join us after he walks Claudia back. Claudia will convince Sherrie to join us when her shift is over." He smiled, obviously pretty happy with his plan.

I appreciated him maintaining a neutral zone in this standoff. "Ryan, I think that's a great plan. I'm not sure Sherrie will be able to meet you tonight, but she'll try if she knows she has fans to meet. I'm not sure anyone can cover for her at work, but I'll put in a good word for you guys."

I looked at Chuck for confirmation, and he nodded as his phone beeped again.

Brady gestured to Chuck's phone. "What's going on there? Lost in too much work? I have not gotten anything from them since returning. You have another assignment so soon?"

"I was supposed to go in two months, but they want to move it up a month with several weeks of training in Texas. It looks like I head out in ten days. I thought you were out of the security business. On our last assignment, you kept talking about finishing some family business—maybe our bosses heard you and counted you out for future missions."

"You're right. I have business with the family, but I will need other work."

Not completely ignoring the subtle request for a job reference but deflecting nicely, Chuck said, "Work is work. Let's go have a few drinks."

The guys threw cash on the table, and we stood to leave. Brady was the last in the group behind me as we walked away from the table. I glanced back as he threw five more dollars on the pile. I pretended I hadn't noticed what he was doing, but if I'd had to guess, one of the guys had shorted the gratuity, and I knew it wouldn't be Chuck.

He walked past and whispered, "He means well, but the idiot can't do math."

I laughed. Maybe Brady wasn't so bad after all.

CHAPTER THIRTY

Chuck held the door for everyone as we walked out. Kay and Jenna asked again if I would join them, but I declined. Chuck said he would meet up with them shortly but had to take care of some stuff. We waved goodbye, and they wandered down the block before turning the corner.

"You don't have to walk me back. It's only two streets," I said, suddenly nervous I would spill everything to him.

He would help without hesitation, but something was stopping me. Maybe it was my relationship with Aaron. We were no longer together, but sharing this chilling incident was almost too intimate to share with Chuck before I talked to Aaron about it. I couldn't put Chuck first. I would not get between these two brothers. I had no romantic feelings for Chuck, but I couldn't confide in him.

"I need to see Aaron. Tell me what you were saying back in there. Something else happen?"

"Not really. It's all good." We were stopped at the crosswalk, waiting for a car to turn. I changed the subject fast. "You see my arm." I raised it, and we stepped into the street. "I got a clean bill of health from the doctor."

"You don't hide your secrets so well."

"What do you mean?" I said, playing dumb when there was no other choice.

"You don't like my army mates do you?" he asked. "You can't walk any faster to get away, and I know you're not rushing to see my brother and you will see Sherrie at home." He put his hand on the small of my back to guide me away from spilled food on the sidewalk. His hand seemed to linger, and I again smelled his coconut shampoo.

"Nice detective work, but you're wrong. I don't think much of them." I shook my head. "That came out wrong. I just met them, and I don't know them well enough to judge them. Maybe I am a fast walker, and I do want to see Sherrie before I head home."

We thankfully arrived at BAR. Chuck held open the door for me. Sherrie was behind the bar, and Pete was cleaning off some dirty tables. The place was steady but not incredibly busy.

It usually picked up later since it was not a dinner destination. The menu was limited to pizza made in a small pizza oven and other hot items like tacos, sloppy joes, and pork sliders. There was no cook on duty—just ready-made food for the bartenders to serve efficiently. There was, of course, pie. I couldn't understate the goodness of the pies.

Music was playing, but I absolutely heard Sherrie shout from behind the bar. "Yo, look who's here."

My face grew hot as heads turned, but Chuck was not fazed. He scanned the room, and Pete pointed to the back room. I guessed there was an understanding that he was looking for Aaron.

"Are you going to be ok?" he asked.

"Yes, of course," I said.

He left me at the door, and I walked to the bar, taking the corner stool.

This was one of my favorite bars. On the walls hung old sporting equipment mingled with vintage beer signs. I leaned against my favorite wall. Above me, an American flag, probably ten-by-twelve feet, made from old baseballs and bats. The ceiling was lined with hockey sticks and skis.

No one ever smoked in there, and Aaron was a fanatic about cleaning. The place never smelled like bleach, but it was always obviously clean. His other trick to make it feel like a comfortable family room was to make a pizza just for the aroma. He'd give out a few free slices, and before you know it, half the place ordered pizza.

I had a good view from my spot and watched Sherrie clean some glasses. I could see the front door, the restrooms, Aaron's closet of an office, and the rear entrance.

Sherrie walked over and put a pint of beer down in front of me. She could fit in anywhere. I had always called this place a flannel-wearing man's cabin. She had taken that to heart and convinced Aaron to have uniforms. She found flannel button-down shirts that had been rejected from the buyer because they were the wrong color. They were priced low to get rid of them. The retailer was so delighted to have a buyer for the shirts, they sent triple the amount ordered.

The colors were definitely off. The deep-red and navy turned out to be deep-pink, aqua, and gray, but the colors blended nicely. It turned out they had not only been rejected for the color but because of faulty construction. Buttons were missing or would fall off after wearing just once, the plaid rarely lined up when the shirts were buttoned, and the fabric easily frayed. Aaron hadn't been mad about the money spent. He'd actually thought it was funny that Sherrie hadn't seen it coming because of what they'd paid for the shirts. True to form, Sherrie made the best of it and got the staff to wear them.

Today, she had on jeans, a tank top, and the flannel shirt with the sleeves cut off and a knot tied at the waist.

She had gone back to cleaning on the other side of the bar. "I'm assuming more shit happened."

I nodded. "How'd you guess?"

"It would take some serious crap for you to come in here and possibly run into Aaron. And you look like—"

"Crap. I know. I have been told. I was going to come in here earlier but saw him and froze for a moment. Then Kay and Jenna came along, and we went to Bumbles and ran into Chuck and friends. By the way, your fan club is here."

"What do you mean?" Sherrie looked around the bar.

"Dancing Sherrie. Remember when Chuck said they watched you dance around when the place was closed. The two guys wanted to come here and meet you, but Chuck sent them to Draw."

"He didn't recommend they stay off the square tonight," Sherrie said with a little laugh.

"He was preoccupied with work."

"So are they cute?"

"Not bad. Kay was playing for one, and Jenna didn't seem interested in the other. Rose from Bumbles did not appear to be a fan of them. But trust me, they want to meet you."

"Of course they do," she said nonchalantly. She filled some drinks and returned. "So what happened that has you coming in here?"

I looked around, but no one cared about what we were talking about. Still, I couldn't help but whisper. "Somebody called Chambray last week and asked questions about me."

"That's not normal."

"I know!" I finally picked up the beer and downed a large amount, burping it up before I even put the glass down.

"Easy there, sister. Let's figure this out. Just sit here while I take care of them."

A couple had come in and sat at one of the tables near the end of the bar. I watched Sherrie and drank my beer on a somewhat empty stomach.

"What did the person say?" Sherrie asked.

"I'm not sure, but Chambray took it as if it was for a job reference. I was leaving my boss's office and couldn't figure out why she was perturbed with me. Then Cheryl, her assistant, mentioned the call. The director came into the office, and she got tight-lipped so I don't know much."

"Let's review. We have someone possibly following you around town and may have entered the house, a car chase, driving past the house—maybe—and now calling and getting . . . getting what? Background information?"

"I don't know. Maybe my schedule."

"Would someone give that information out?"

"Probably not." My stomach growled.

"Good god, I heard that. Didn't you eat at Bumbles?"

"I ordered but really didn't have an appetite. What do you guys have today?"

"The usual pizza and chili. Chili in August is weird, but not my choice. Want some?"

"I guess, give me a cup. I gotta have something."

Sherrie strolled down to the small kitchen and came back a minute later with the chili. The pizza oven dinged, and she served the couple and came back. "Do we have enough to go to the police?"

"Not really. What are they going to do? Your cop buddy already said they would patrol our neighborhood, but I think that was friendly flirting and not so much police work." My leg bounced up and down.

The chili tasted good. Hot but good. I finished the beer, and both my legs started to bounce. I couldn't hold it any longer. I had to go to the bathroom. I had to walk past the office to get to the bathroom. I could do it. Just keep walking and maybe glance in and give a casual hey. The office barely held a desk, much less two guys, with one guy being Chuck's size, making it tight, so I knew the door would be open.

Sherrie read my mind. "Would you just go to the bathroom? Woman up! No conversation will be expected. I will have some pie for you when you return."

"No pie, please. I can barely afford this dinner—two dinners out in one night. I technically don't have the hotel job yet." I turned on the stool and hopped off. "Wish me luck."

"Just go to the damn bathroom, and I'll walk you to your car when you're done."

"I don't need a walk to Debby. Just be ready to interfere with some work-related stuff if you see an uncomfortable situation ahead."

I made my way to the bathroom and risked a glance into the office. The brothers had their back to me and were concentrating on some papers. I reminded myself not to get comfortable on the return. I exited the bathroom and cruised past the office, crowning myself champion for not only coming into his bar but also avoiding him in his bar. I went back to my barstool and put out money again for a second meal. At least I ate this time.

Sherrie and I reviewed our plan for the evening. She confirmed she and Pete would be closing the bar together and would text me when she was leaving regardless of the time, and I would text her when I was home.

Leaving the bar, I no longer felt like a champion but rather empty. Was I really beginning to miss Aaron? Does it matter that he had moved on? I didn't know why I'd thought I had to move forward without him. Isn't that what couples do, work to move forward in their relationship, careers, and life? Wasn't that one of the reasons I had broken up with Jackson—because he couldn't think like a couple? Here I had done the same thing, except this time Aaron was a good guy that I still liked.

CHAPTER THIRTY-ONE

I was glad to see Jorge was home. He was not working in the garage for a change. It was a comfort to know he was there inside his house. I wasn't sure what he could do if someone snuck into EG's house, but it was nice to know he was close. The house was still stifling hot because we had everything locked. We would not be able to keep this up once EG came back. She would quickly figure out something was not right. I was going to have to tell her sooner rather than later.

I changed into comfy shorts, a T-shirt, sports bra, and socks. I don't know if it was the beer or fear, but I was fueled up and not freaked out anymore.

I spent the evening cleaning the house, dusting, cleaning the hardwood floors, the two bathrooms, and even wiping down the stairs. I had turned my energy into something productive.

The television was playing softly in the background. I had all the windows closed except the living room window in the front of the house. A light breeze blew through, and I hoped for rain, which would bring a change of scenery.

With each swipe of the rag, I went through my memory bank.

Who could want something from me?

I would move three books, wipe the shelf, and check another person off my list. Pick a picture frame, wipe it down, and move on to the next person. I wiped down the window frame and checked off the next person. I went through my life—hometown, high school, college, all my jobs, and living here.

I was down to the last step on the stairwell. It was a good thing because I ran out of people in my life to examine. I couldn't come up with a person or find the trigger point of what I'd done to cause someone to come after me. I'd had a good life and a great time at college but nothing too erratic that would make me someone's target.

I kneeled on the stair landing, the same spot Sherrie and I had sat on last night while trying to figure out what to do with Teddy.

I had run out of people and steam. It had been a long twenty-four hours. I rolled myself onto my butt and pushed myself into the corner. I let my right leg hang down the two steps into the living room, and my left leg was stretched out, resting on the stairs headed up.

I studied each step going up, looking for a clue. The top of the staircase curved to the right, and I couldn't see the last step. Although I walked up these stairs every day, they now looked like a StairMaster without an off button. Each step I took was getting me no closer to finding an answer.

I didn't know how I did it, but I fell asleep sitting up on the landing, for several hours. My phone beeping woke me up. It was Sherrie telling me she was on her way home. The top of my shorts were damp because of the wet rags I had been using to clean the stairs had fallen out of my hands. My neck and butt were sore from sitting on the wood landing.

Sherrie was home in five minutes, and I managed to brush my teeth, pee, put lotion on my scaly arm, change into a dry pair of shorts, and fall asleep before Sherrie was done climbing the stairs.

I slept hard. No dreams. No stirring. I woke up with the sunlight hitting my face and drool on my cheek. Another morning without my cast.

It was six a.m., but I felt like I'd slept twelve hours. I showered, dressed, and was having coffee by six thirty, looking forward to the day. I felt like I could take on anything that came my way, but I wasn't ready for what was about to happen that week.

CHAPTER THIRTY-TWO

Tuesday, I had a five-hour shift in the morning. By two p.m., I would be done with all my community service hours. I had three more paying shifts this week and would take my paperwork to the courthouse this afternoon. Cheryl would send it over as well, but I wanted to make sure I was all done and got to say a final goodbye to Judge Lobal and all his creepy texting.

I would also have time to stop at the clinic before it closed and complete the drug test. I emailed Gloria, the hotel manager, giving her my availability for the next few days to set up a formal interview.

I didn't know what I would do about the hours I was scheduled to work next week. I didn't want to burn any bridges and leave Chambray in a bind, but I didn't want to be somewhere that was familiar to someone stalking me.

Security cameras were prevalent but weren't monitored. I didn't want to bring harm to anyone at Chambray. On the other hand, I felt safer where I was known to the residents, and I knew my way around.

I decided I would find Cheryl and get more info about who had called and what they'd asked. I was delighted to hear that Mrs. Baron had gone to a conference for the day. That would provide me one less major obstacle to avoid. I spent my day working with Chef David cleaning the storage area and mentally reviewing my tactics for getting the information from her. While she was overly chatty, I didn't want to come across as using her. I was so engrossed in reviewing my approach with Cheryl, I didn't realize I had mopped the entire room three times until Chef said something to me.

I figured I'd keep it simple and approach it as if I was there to say thank you for all the help she had given me these last few months. I am not sure what she had done for me besides providing coffee—actually very good coffee—but I had to stay friends with her. I might need Mrs. Baron's reference in the future, and Cheryl was her gatekeeper. At the last minute, I asked Chef David if I could take two scones. I figured coming with sweets would seem celebratory and not at all gossipy.

That plan evaporated quickly. My luck ran out with Mrs. Baron being gone for the day because Cheryl was training a new woman named Denise, who would fill in for her while she was out after knee surgery. This would not be the opportunity I had hoped for. I left the scones and wished them well.

My luck kept bouncing back and forth. After driving around town for an extra ten minutes to make sure no one was following me, I got to the courthouse. This town was not very big, and if I kept driving extra miles each time I had to drive two miles, someone would report me.

I texted Jenna from the car, and she said she was only there in the morning. She went on to say all my paperwork has been processed and sent back to Judge Lobal's office. There was no need for me to worry anymore. She did extend the offer again for me to talk to Judge Konrad about creepy Sir Creep Judge Lobal—her nickname, not mine, but I didn't disagree, or she would do it on my behalf. I declined the offer for now.

I sat in the courthouse parking lot, thinking, Could this all be Judge Lobal? Was he stalking me? He was a former college classmate of EG's, and she'd found him to be kind of peculiar when they were in school twenty years ago. I could have maybe understood him calling Chambray to check on my hours, but there was no way for him to be chasing me in his car. I will put him in the unlikely-but-not-forgotten-about category.

While I was at the clinic waiting to do the drug test, I confirmed my interview tomorrow at three p.m. This would not give me time to talk to Cheryl after my shift. I was going to have to catch her on my break or skip lunch.

It was 4:30, and the bar had been open for ninety minutes. I imagined it wouldn't be too busy and I would be able to talk to Sherrie. I hoped I could avoid Aaron and planned to be aloof as if everything was fine with us and me. With my luck bouncing up and down, I hoped my acting talent would kick in when I saw him.

I was driving to the bar and realized I needed to eat, but I couldn't afford another meal out. I stopped at the grocery store and picked things for the week, realizing I needed a drink to help me calm down.

While I was in the store, I got so paranoid when a lady looked at everything I put in my cart. She was wearing a baseball hat pulled down so low it was hard to see her eyes behind her glasses. I guess she was between thirty and fifty years old and looked like she could be anyone's mother in this town. I could have easily passed by without even knowing she was there except for the fact she seemed to have propelled herself to me. I really didn't need someone judging my shopping choices when I've got someone stalking me. Just let me have my rocky road ice cream and strawberry Popsicles.

I was getting ready to unleash on her when she finally spoke to me in such a sweet voice. "Sorry for staring, but I am just trying to figure out what to make for dinner. I am in such a rut, and my husband gives me no hints as to what I should cook. I'm just looking for inspiration."

"Go to the meat department. At the end of the cold cases near the produce, they usually have meal kits with everything you need. If nothing else, it might give you ideas."

"What a sweet idea. Have a good day."

"You look familiar. Have we met?" I asked.

"It's a small town. Everyone looks familiar," she said and walked out of the aisle.

It was strange—I didn't see her again while I rattled back and forth across the store because I kept forgetting things.

The rain finally started, but it was a light mist and the sun was gone. I parked next to the house instead of the garage forty feet away because I intended to go out again. I felt safer being able to see the car while I was going in and out of the house, unloading groceries.

I opened all the windows in the kitchen and living room and let the breeze flow through the house. The rain air made the place feel fresher than all the cleaning yesterday.

I had a salad and a glass of orange juice at the head of the dining table instead of my usual spot at the kitchen island. I put my feet up on a chair and tried to enjoy my meal. The weather dropped to a comfortable eighty degrees, but I wasn't enjoying the solitude. I turned on the television but couldn't find something to keep my interest and decided this silence was refreshing.

My mind circled back to this afternoon. I hadn't gotten to talk to Cheryl. My paperwork was complete; hopefully, no more creepy Judge Lobal; interview set for tomorrow; Aaron; a weird lady at the grocery store; and Aaron again. I was beginning to realize I missed him and us.

Why had I broken up with him? Because I had fallen into the relationship the day after I'd broken up with Jackson—guilt? It was too easy. Just because I'd stalled my life professionally, did that mean I had to change my personal relationships? I had given up that poorly paying temporary job in Chicago and was rethinking my last four years at college and my degree.

Can't I figure out my career and still have a boyfriend? Do I need to start fresh on everything at the same time? Why do I think I have to have a grand gesture in all aspects of my life to be more forward in this post-college life? Why are these same thoughts circling in my head?

The ice clinking in my glass made me smile. Aaron always drank his orange juice with ice. I'd put ice in my glass without thinking about it. I watched the ring of water grow on the table. Before I got up, grabbed a kitchen towel, and clean up, I thought, It doesn't matter how I feel about Aaron; he has moved on.

My phone beeped with two messages.

Jackson's message read, please don't delete. My car died. Give me more time. Please.

Whatever. I have no emotion left for him, I thought.

The second message was more intriguing. Sherrie said, Come to the bar for me. I beg.

The more-pleasing second message was easy to agree to. I quickly washed my dishes and went upstairs and changed out of my work clothes and put on a bohemian-style blouse, pairing it with light-blue shorts and sandals but changed my mind.

I had spent most of the summer being cold because of the air-conditioning at work and because I didn't want to put a sweater on over my cast. The bar would probably still have the air-conditioning on, and I was determined to be comfortable. I had no one to impress. I tossed on a T-shirt and a lightweight zippered hoodie, socks, and tennis shoes. I giggled with joy again at zipping up the shorts and hoodie. My arm was looking better, and I hoped to have it back to normal by the end of the week.

I hung my other capri pants and a green polo shirt on the closet door for work tomorrow. I also grabbed a blouse for my interview.

The drum music Sherrie had played Saturday afternoon, which helped empower me to take control, reverberated in my head. The beats lured me forward. Making stuff happen felt good. Just picking out clothes to keep me warm tonight and look professional tomorrow wasn't the pinnacle of having my shit together, but little steps each day.

I was about to leave through the porch entrance when reality hit me again. Normally, I would have walked to the bar even with the light rain. Now, I turned around to shut and lock all the windows and hopped in Debby for the four-block drive.

I scored a good parking spot again. I was across the street but directly in front of BAR. I waited for a few minutes and watched four cars drive past. Someone walked out of the insurance agent's office and locked the door, and a lady went into the salon.

I readied myself for whatever was to happen. Sherrie would not have called me into the lion's den.

The bar had a nice vibe when I walked in. The seats at the bar were full and about a third of the tables. Sherrie spotted me when I walked in and turned to Pete behind the bar, saying she needed five minutes. He gave her a nod of approval, and she whisked me around, grabbing my arm, and trotted me outside.

"What is that all about?" I asked.

"I just need to ask you a few questions." She kept her arm linked with mine and steered us into the doorway of the insurance agency I just had seen being locked up for the evening. She was smiling. "What did you think of Chuck's friends?"

"Not a whole lot. Nice, I guess. Ryan and Kay hit it off, and Brady was still a free agent when I left them. You got a thing for him?"

"I don't know. He is kinda cute. They've been in there for about thirty minutes, and we've been chatting."

"I don't think they're sticking around long. Ryan has some job in Louisiana, and I don't know what Brady does. Only here to fish and drink, I think."

"Fine by me," she said with a smile. Today, she was wearing the flannel shirt without sleeves, buttoned up, and tucked into shorts. She looked sporty and eyed her reflection in the windows, fluffing her hair. "Do you want to hear something weird?"

"Always."

"A new schedule for the week was posted. Jo-Lee wasn't on it. Before we opened, Aaron was there and told me and Pete that she's off the schedule, and if anybody asks, she was never here."

"Bizarre. Maybe she's back with her beau? What's his name? Adam? Serves Aaron right."

"Doubt it. Aaron said something about her leaving home because of something bad. He left after he spoke with us and said he would be back later this evening if one of us wanted to cut out early."

We walked back towards BAR. "Anything new with you? Did you talk to Cheryl?"

"I couldn't. I'll try again tomorrow." I shrugged. "My interview is tomorrow. I want to make a decent impression, so I'm not going to be here all night playing wingman."

"I get it. Just keep them entertained a bit. I got more shifts this week to cover Jo-Lee's sudden absence so I could skip out early. Pete owes me one. There is one thing I can't figure out. Maybe you can . . ."

I didn't hear her finish the sentence because I stepped back for a second thinking I saw Teddy walk into Draw Tavern down the block.

We went back inside BAR. The afternoon sun cascaded through the big front windows over the booths on either side of the door, highlighting the baseball bat flag and reflecting a colorful light off the skis on the ceiling. Pete must have had control of the music because Sherrie would never have selected anything from the country catalog that had come out in the last ten years.

I quickly switched gears when I saw Brady, Ryan, and Kay sitting at one of the tall tables near the bar. Kay gave me a wave. I went over to join them. They each had a beer in front of them, and two pizza pans with a few pieces left were scattered on the table.

Sherrie brought me a beer and quickly got back to work. She was swinging from cleaning, taking orders, and occasionally popping over to our table. She sat down for a minute, leaned over, and whispered, "Well?"

"Go for it," I said.

The other three at the table were engaged in a battle to name the best horror movie of the last decade. That gave us a moment to ourselves.

"Not that. What was I saying before?"

Before I could figure out what she was asking, Brady interrupted. "Which one is scarier?"

Sherrie stood up, wrinkled her nose at me before I could answer. "You have two different questions going on. Horror versus scary. You can have a psychological thriller without blood and gore and be scared shitless. You can also have a pure blood–and-guts slasher movie and be scared or find it comically implausible. Two different categories, gentlemen and lady."

This kept the conversation going for another ten minutes. Twice, Sherrie walked behind the guys and wrinkled her nose.

After the movie conversation faded away, I learned Ryan and Brady had been fishing all day with Chuck on the Mississippi River. Chuck had left them a couple of hours ago to take care of some business.

Kay had dressed in a black pleated miniskirt and a KISS concert T-shirt with black Converse tennis shoes. She totally made that outfit look cool. On me, it would look like some weird Halloween costume. When she leaned back, her navel piercing and a daisy tattoo above her right hip were visible.

She'd met up with Brady and Ryan about twenty minutes before I'd gotten there. I hadn't been able to connect with her at work today because she'd been conducting some type of class with the senior ladies. I could only guess things had worked out for her and Ryan last night. He had his arm on the back of her chair, and she put her hand on his knee. I wondered if they were a one-hit wonder and this would end when Ryan left town.

Jenna was nowhere to be found, and Brady kept flirting with Sherrie, so apparently, Brady and Jenna had not connected as Kay and Ryan had.

I finally realized what Sherrie had been

hinting at. There was a smell coming from the table, and I was beginning to think it was Brady.

The bar had little activity now, and Sherrie sat down with us but was still on duty. My phone was on the table and buzzed. I rolled my eyes when I saw it was from Jackson.

The message read, I had to tell them.

I had no idea what he was talking about and assumed he'd sent it to the wrong person. I finally decided to block his calls and texts before I got anything else from him.

"Who was that?" Sherrie asked.

I rolled my eyes. "Jackson. I blocked him."

"About time. Do you want to place a bet on whether he's stupid enough to drive here for a silly backpack?"

"I don't even care enough to do that," I said.

"What are you ladies discussing? You're over there being all secretive and stuff. Don't you want to share with the rest of the class?" Brady said, smiling.

Waving off the question, I said, "Just stupid stuff from a foolish person."

I was curious how I had moved on so fast from one relationship but not the other. When I'd broken up with Jackson, it had been an easy transition. I'd started dating Aaron the next day, but I had never looked back. I hadn't gotten sentimental for even a second when I heard music on the radio he'd introduced me to.

I never even wondered if he was still planning on going to Chicago for the fall as we had planned. Before I had sorted out my feelings for Aaron, I had seen Jackson for who he was and his true character. I knew he was not someone I wanted to be with. I didn't know if I had ever loved him, but I'd had feelings for him. I had been able to completely distance myself from him emotionally.

Is it that Aaron's a good guy and checks all the boxes of someone I want on my dating profile? Is it because it's hard to lose a good person in my life, or do I really have feelings for him? Do the feelings mean I want him back? I shook my head. I have got to stop this. As Grandma used to say, "Shit or get off the pot."

Sherrie nudged my arm when my phone beeped again. This time, it was Teddy asking to go to breakfast tomorrow. I didn't know why I was hesitant, but regardless, I agreed to meet him at Peach's Café at seven.

Sometimes not every opportunity should be taken.

CHAPTER THIRTY-THREE

Chuck and two other guys walked in. I had hoped I could make an early exit if the group got larger. Sherrie clearly didn't need my assistance with Brady, and Kay could handle herself with any group of guys. Three steps into the place, however, the two guys took seats at the booth on the right-hand side of the door. Sherrie left to take their orders, and Chuck pulled up a seat.

A day on the river had added fresh color to his already tan face and body. He appeared to be clean and fresh, while Brady and Ryan looked like they'd had a hard day's work.

While Sherrie took drinks to the new customers and put in a pizza for them, Pete brought Chuck a pint of beer.

"What is this?" Chuck asked.

"It's the new seasonal beer your brother and Sherrie think will be a hit," Pete said.

"It tastes like shit," Chuck said after he finished a third of it in one gulp.

"Exactly. Now tell your brother. I won't be able to sell that."

"Come on. It's not bad. I like it," Sherrie said.

"Keep the pumpkin in the pies and out of my beer. Tell me you will keep it out of our inventory, and I will let Sherrie be the one to leave early tonight," Pete said.

"I'm a silent partner. You will have to take it up with Aaron."

"Where is he? He never showed up on the river," Ryan said.

"Beats me. I figured he was here. How long did you stay fishing?" Chuck said.

"Couple of hours after you left, and then we came here."

"Oh my god, is that what smells?" I said.

Sherrie laughed, and Ryan and Brady looked at each other. Brady lifted his arm and smelled, and Ryan just shook his head and chuckled. Kay didn't seem to notice or wasn't bothered by the smell of sweat and fish guts.

"Probably," Brady confessed. "We were hot and wanted a beer, so we stopped here before returning to Clint's place."

"Who is Clint?" Sherrie asked.

Ryan answered. "Our former lieutenant. He lives over in Shallow Village. Why don't we take this group over to that place you were telling us about with the patio seating?"

"I have to end the evening for me now. It turns out I'm leaving this weekend, and I have a few things to wrap up before I go. I'll catch you guys for breakfast," Chuck said.

"I gotta work, but maybe I will catch up with you if you guys are still out when I'm done," Sherrie said sweetly but not committing fully. She returned to the pizza oven behind the bar and served the two guys.

I said, "Sounds like you guys have it figured out. I'm going to skip tonight's pub crawl. I gotta look good for tomorrow. When do you guys head out?"

Probably five seconds passed before Ryan answered, but the pause was loud. "It's supposed to be tomorrow, but we might push it out another day."

Kay picked up her beer and smiled. Brady's eyes followed Sherrie, and he waited for her to return to the group before he spoke.

"I want to explore the area. Ryan might fish again, and I might find a bike shop for a rental and cruise the bike trails that I heard are good in the area."

I didn't know if he was waiting for Sherrie

to offer herself as a tour guide or feared losing another prospect of hooking up with a girl as he had already lost Jenna, but Brady pushed harder for me to join them. Did he think if I was with them, it would be more likely for Sherrie to meet up with us?

"Join us for one until Sherrie gets done. I don't want to third wheel with these two here."

"How about you guys go shower, and then you can all meet up later," I said.

"I'm not sure how long I'll be, but text me when you guys are on the patio," Sherrie said.

"Let's just say an hour," Brady pressed. "This place is slow. I'm sure Pete can handle it."

"I don't know when Aaron will be back. We always have two of us here. We never leave one person working. Don't worry; I'll join you when I can. Plus, you guys need plenty of time for that shower."

Sherrie had her winning agreement. Kay, Ryan, and Brady departed through the front door. I watched them organizing the evening for a minute. It ended with Kay and Ryan walking off in one direction and Brady not looking too happy to go the other way. I had a feeling Kay and Ryan might not be seen again tonight. Chuck said goodbye and went to talk to Pete at the bar.

"What's your plan for the night? Are you going home to binge something on TV?" Sherrie asked me.

"I need to stop at the drugstore for some stuff, and then I was going to do some research about the hotel and the job."

"Hot time on the town for you. Have fun and don't get run over," Sherrie said.

"Amen."

A couple of women sat at the bar, and Sherrie went to serve them. I stepped out of the bar, watching my car for a minute before I got in it. The trip to the drugstore was uneventful and even relaxing. I spent fifteen minutes just browsing the cosmetic aisle, looking at everything for another ten minutes, picking out birthday cards I needed for the next three months. If I had remembered stamps at the checkout, I would have been on fire.

I got a text from Sherrie asking if I was still out and would I mind coming back to the bar. I was not in the mood for more drinks, but with everything I'd put on her these last few days, I couldn't say no.

My old parking spot was available, as were most of the other spots. The light rain kept most people away. Again, I waited in the car an extra minute and made sure no one was following me.

The bar was fairly empty. The guys who had walked in simultaneously with Chuck were still in the booth, and three new guys, who were about retirement age, were at the bar. The only woman besides Sherrie in the place was with someone who probably was her boyfriend. They were lost in their own world in the last booth at the far end.

Pete was behind the bar and clearly still in charge of the music because Luke Combs filled the air.

Pete was a grad student finishing his master's degree and had worked for Aaron since the bar had opened. He was a nice guy and cute, but always seemed preoccupied. He could mix and mingle with guys at the bar but was quiet with women unless they engaged with him first.

My favorite was watching him and Sherrie work together. They were like an old married couple that bickered but were better when together. He wore the pink-and-aqua-plaid shirt every day to work but had made himself a name tag with Sherrie's name. He also took a black Sharpie marker and wrote BAR in large letters on the back of each of his shirts. I didn't understand the humor, but he found it funny.

He gave me a wave. "Sherries in the beer cooler. She'll be out in a minute. Beer?"

"I'll just have some water." I took my seat back at the end of the bar where I'd been last night.

Sherrie came out and plopped herself on the barstool next to me.

"It's dead in here," I said.

"I'm not surprised. It'll all change in a few

days when the students are back. Thanks for coming. Until four minutes ago, I was the only chick in here, and those two guys at the front are weirding me out. They had a pizza, no booze, and have been nursing soda for over an hour. Pete has been in the beer cooler adjusting the keg tap lines, and the khaki-wearing, soda-drinking dudes keep scanning the room like they're waiting for the right moment to hold up the place. I could use someone friendly sitting here until my night starts. I promise if I see Aaron come in the back door, I'll let you fly out before he makes it past his office."

We chatted another five minutes before we heard some bad belly-yelling karaoke coming from outside the bar, and it was getting louder. We turned in our seats, and in walked Brady and someone I assumed was Clint.

Brady clearly had kept drinking, and he was inspired to sweep Sherrie off her feet. The men came in, belting out the lyrics to "Oh Sherrie" from the eighties rocker Steve Perry, former member of the group Journey. Brady scanned the nearly empty bar and finally focused on Sherrie and tried sliding in on his knees to where she sat but shorted it by eight feet.

Sherrie was rarely embarrassed and enjoyed this moment. I would have been mortified at the attention and would have found it a turnoff. He beamed with pride. He would probably remember the grand entrance, forget the off-key and wrong words and the lack of a large audience.

"Come with us," Brady said, winded, not getting up yet.

Clint took a seat at one of the tall tables.

"I appreciate the gesture, but I can't," Sherrie said.

"The place is dead. He can handle it." He made his declaration still on his knees.

Sherrie walked over and grabbed his arm, helping him up. He tried pulling her closer, but she casually stepped back. I wasn't sure how she was playing this. I knew she found the entrance adorable, but she took her work seriously. She did not do subtle well and was being direct.

"Listen to me. I am not leaving until Aaron shows up. Why don't you and . . . I am assuming you are Clint."

The thirtysomething-year-old, baseball-hat-and-tank-top-wearing dude nodded.

"Go on, and I will meet you later."

"Come on. I gave you a song. I want a dance." His hair was still damp from the shower, and the clean clothes and fresh smile added to Brady's charm. "I was in the Middle East, watching you hop around this place. I want a live version. Please."

He had the attention of all seven guests in the bar. For a second, I thought she would go for it.

"Listen to me. I'm working. Go have fun, and we can see each other later."

"Don't be a downer. This place is dead. Liven it up."

"Let me work. Go have fun," Sherrie said. She stood there, hands on hips, initially enjoying the debate. She rarely backed down from any challenge and enjoyed being courted by guys, but this pivoted quickly away from fun to Brady not understanding or willing to accept Sherrie's answer.

"Work? Not much work being done here. Actually, can we have some beer and you join us here."

"I am not going to sit. I am not going to screw up at work. I can chat while I work, but I'm not letting anything interfere with my job. Let me get some cleaning done, and if Aaron shows up, I will be ready to go."

"Can't you get someone to clean?"

"Yes, me. I have to do the cleaning. Go find Ryan and Kay."

"I think we lost them for the night. Ryan left with Kay and didn't come back to Clint's with me."

Sherrie sat at the tall round table and looked at them both. "I hear you. Now hear me. Let me work. No more drinks for you here. Let me get my stuff done. Go get a table on the patio." She squared her shoulders, steeling herself for a direct conversation.

Clint was obviously enjoying the back and forth. He had his arms crossed against his chest, slouching back. I had not moved from my barstool behind Sherrie. Except for the two guys in the booth, all the other guests had turned their attention away.

Brady casually hunched over, his arms folded on the table, and smiled like he was playing a game of chess. Unfortunately, he was unwilling to understand his opponent.

Sherrie maintained a steady approach with a slight smile. "You have already seen me dance, and I have heard you sing. Let's get you guys going." She did the power play move and tapped him on the arm.

Brady was not going to back down. "How about I go get some help? You need someone to clean. I will get someone."

She didn't move. "I don't know what to say to that, but this is over. Let me work."

"Let me take care of you. You said you have to do some cleaning. I will get someone to clean for me."

Sherrie pulled her arms off the table and sat upright. "I don't need someone to take care of me."

Brady didn't move. He didn't realize after the first or second time Sherrie had said to leave it had stopped being a game. "Come on. Lighten up.

Let me get someone. I saw the day-laborer guys standing in the parking lot of the lumberyard on the way into town. Maybe somebody is still there."

"What?" Sherrie said.

"You know, those guys. Begging for a job. They will do anything. My old man back home hired a couple of them to cut and clear some trees. The work was decent, but you had to stay on them. Make sure the work got done. Pete can watch them."

"What?" Sherrie said again. "Watch them?"

"Yeah, you know what I mean? They are here, taking our space, and their kids are going to our schools. At least they could do is work a bit. I mean, they do have to eat. Can't have them stealing."

My heart was pounding, and I wanted to stand next to Sherrie. Not because she needed it, but because I was her friend. I dared not to move, and let her finish this.

Her voice was steady and calm, but her attitude shifted. "Stealing?"

"They stole their way into the country. Can't make it too comfortable for them to want to stay, but they gotta eat. The trick is finding the hard workers. It's a sea of people waiting to be taken care of in my country. Pay per job so they are motivated to get it done fast and then maybe throw in a few extra bucks at the end if they are decent. Gotta keep them motivated."

"Motivated?" Sherrie's voice was slightly louder but still steady.

Clint stopped smiling. He was one of the two people at the table that recognized the tension building. "Hey, buddy. Let's listen to Sherrie and head out. She can handle it here."

"Thanks," she said.

"Come on. It will be twenty minutes, and I'll get someone here, and we could party all night long. Who knows when Aaron will get here. Give me the truck keys." Brady turned to Clint, but he didn't move so Brady turned his attention back to Sherrie. "Let me help you. What do you need? A clean-the-restrooms lady, those are harder to find in the labor lots, but I'll find someone for you or a clean-the-kitchen-take-out-the-trash kind of guy."

"Why do you think they're here?" Sherrie challenged.

"What do you mean?" Brady asked.

"Why do you think most of the immigrants are here?"

"We're the best. They know once they're here, they don't have to do much," Brady said.

"Except maybe find work for food?" Sherrie said.

"Yeah, you know. Have a kid here, and they're set."

Sherrie stood and pushed her chair back.

Clint even stood up, but Brady remained where he was, leaning on the table.

Her hands gripped the table, and her voice was steady. "You piece of shit. Get out of here and don't return."

"What are you talking about? Sit down," Brady said.

Not loud, not condescending but straight on point, Sherrie said, "You racist ass! Leave now."

"Easy. How can I be racist when I am into you?" He smiled and made to touch her hand.

Sherrie wrenched her hands away.

"Get out." She boomed this time, standing solid as a rock.

I was sweating enough for both of us.

"Come on! I voted for—"

"I don't care who you voted for." She took a deep breath and remained still. "Please leave."

"You can't throw me out. Chuck's got my back. Once in a unit, always in a unit. Even if he is not here, this place is half his."

"If she won't throw you out, I will" came from a voice behind me—Pete, behind the bar, just on the other side of where I was.

Sherrie did not turn around but held up her hand, signaling to Pete she had this.

"I applaud your service. I appreciate every minute you spent defending this country. You showed bravery and made sacrifices. Your family made sacrifices. You have done honorable things for this country, but that does not mean you are a man of honor. You live in a country worth defending. You have the opportunity to do something for this country. I owe you a thanks, and I will help make sure all service members receive benefits, insurance, and gratitude for their service. What you failed to see is what you were defending. These housekeeping gals and kitchen dudes you refer to . . ."

She stopped for a moment. Not for effect but to keep herself even. "You know why a lot of immigrants come here illegally and submit to ignorant pieces of crap like you?" She paused for a moment and glared at him. "Because it is still better than where they were living. They don't have the option to sign up for the military. Most of the time, there is little to no education for most kids over the fifth grade. The kids have the option to work in the drug fields for the cartels like most of their parents or join a gang for survival. Every day their kids are home alive is a win, and if the family is fed, it is a double win. A win but not a guarantee. Standing there in the lots begging for work is the best chance of survival most of them have. You had the option to serve. Those kids and parents don't have that option. They don't have a government to support or a government that supports them. They know what they are getting here—possible separation from each other, little to no chance of legal work, and it is still better than their other options. Here they have hope.

"One day, we will have a better system for all immigrants. Illegal crossing sucks for everyone, but nobody needs your condescending attitude. You got to fight for your country. They have to fight for their lives. You get a gun, and you think you have honor and superiority. What you don't know is what you were defending. Freedom, prosperity, education, and hope.

"Get out!" She was as solid as a wrecking ball and hadn't moved a muscle.

Brady did not move.

Clint tapped his shoulder and said, "Let's go."

"No." Brady crossed his arms.

I was so focused on Sherrie and Brady I didn't see Khaki Number One approach the table until he was closer to Brady than his own shadow. I gasped when I looked down.

Brady shook his head. "No."

Clint made eye contact with Khaki Number Two, who was still sitting in the booth and seemed to understand the situation. He looked at Khaki Number One and nodded.

Together, they picked Brady up by the arms, pulled him off the stool, and walked him backwards out of the bar.

Sherrie turned to me and dropped her shoulders. No expression was on her face but an obvious release of tension. One guy at the bar shook his head, but the other two old guys at the bar applauded, as did the couple in the back booth, who had stood up to watch.

The woman yelled, "I'll have what she's having."

I was sure one of the most-quoted movie lines of all time was lost on the guys, but it put a smile on Sherrie's face and that was all I cared about. I hugged her, and we sat down. Even Pete reached out and put his hand on her shoulder. She gave him a smile but turned quickly to watch the door. I had not seen Khaki Number Two leave, but he had disappeared.

The guys at the bar turned their attention back to the television, and the couple sat back down.

The front door opened. Sherrie and I froze as Clint walked back in. He took two steps in and looked at Sherrie. "I want to apologize—"

"Don't apologize for someone else," Sherrie bounced back to him.

Clint stood there with his baseball hat in his hands, in tank top, shorts, and flip-flops, looking like someone about to order a beer and wings, deciding if this was the place to do it. He stepped forward. In a soft but not condescending voice, he said, "I just want to make sure you're good."

"All good here. Just keep him out of here while he's in town."

Clint nodded and headed towards the door.

Sherrie called out, "Clint."

He turned and waited.

"Thanks for coming back," Sherrie said.

He nodded and left.

"I wonder what the khaki brothers are doing with Brady right now," I said.

"He'll be fine. All they're going to do is make sure he doesn't return," Pete said.

We swung around on the barstool to face Pete.

"I don't know about that. I think maybe we should call the police. Brady is a dirtbag, but Khaki Number One had a gun. I saw it strapped to his ankle."

"That's why nothing bad is going to happen. They both were carrying, and that is why they weren't drinking. They were probably off duty."

"They're cops?" Sherrie asked.

"Doubtful they're cops, or at least not anyone from around here. Detectives or DEA, but without Jameson having started classes, I don't think there's much for a drug cop to worry about. Probably just driving through town. They probably shouldn't have been in here or at least left the ankle holsters in the car, but since they weren't drinking,

I left them alone."

"You could have told me," Sherrie said.

"Why? Would it have made a difference? Would you have hit on one of them?" Pete said.

"No. But they were weirding me out by not ordering drinks in a bar and just sitting there. I made Claudia come back here."

"Jesus, woman. Relax. That is why there are always at least two of us here."

"Sometimes it makes a difference if there is another woman here," Sherrie said.

Pete's face got a little red, and his tone changed. "Can't understand that, but I was here." He walked backward and poured two draft beers for the guys at the bar, then cleaned the table where the khaki dudes had been sitting.

I leaned in close to Sherrie. "I don't think you owe him an apology for wanting me here, but I think you stepped on his manhood a bit, so careful how you play it."

"At least I'm leveling up on my share of the crazy tonight," Sherrie said with a small smile.

"You're getting close, but I'm still winning the game. Any idea when Aaron will be back?"

"Nope. It could be an hour or three. He never really said where he was going."

"Do you mean where they are going?" I said.

CHAPTER THIRTY-FOUR

What remained of the night was thankfully peaceful. I left a few minutes later after I knew Sherrie was calm. I was careful driving back and did what had become my usual—driving mindlessly around for an extra mile or two to make sure no one followed. When I pulled up to the house, it looked mockingly at me.

All the windows were closed despite the first decent temperature in weeks. The rain had stopped, but the clouds hid the stars and moonlight.

The living room lights were on because of the timers Sherrie had purchased. Just knowing a plastic device was turning on lamps, everything seemed artificial to me.

Was EG's house my home? I always said

house not home—let's go back to the house. She'd always made me feel welcome and permitted me to do whatever I wanted, but I lived in her home, not even paying rent. Rent would have given me some pseudo piece of responsibility or paying my own way, but I greedily accepted freeloading.

I pulled into the driveway but got a little unhinged when I noticed the backyard was completely pitch-black. I remembered us knocking out the light above the door and realized it was also a motion sensor light for the yard.

I was getting into my own head and didn't have the courage to pull into the garage and get into the house without giving myself the creeps. I wasn't sure if I should laugh or cry.

I backed up, leaving just enough space for Sherrie to park behind me on the driveway, and went in through the porch door. I turned on the kitchen light before running upstairs. I didn't know when Sherrie would be home, and I wanted a light to remain on in the kitchen because of the timers in the living room.

I grabbed a book and plopped on my bed with music from my phone playing. I wanted a diversion. I was close to falling asleep, still holding the book, when Sherrie texted that she was walking out of the bar. I reminded her to have one of the guys walk her to the car. She was home a few minutes later, and we were secure in the house.

I tossed and turned all night with maybe two hours of solid sleep but enough to get up and shower at six thirty. I was not prepared for the rest of the day.

CHAPTER THIRTY-FIVE

I got to Peach's at seven as Teddy was arriving, and he held the door open for me. It had definitely been him going into the bar yesterday. He had on clean clothes, but I could smell the remnants of last night on his breath and through his pores.

We walked to the counter, and I ordered coffee and an egg sandwich. The redheaded cashier asked Teddy if he wanted the usual. He nodded and paid for both of us.

"I hope that doesn't include any pastries," I said.

A burst of gentle laughter came from Teddy. He understood the implications of ordering anything sweet. Some days, even the English muffins and bagels were not safe from a dousing of powdered sugar.

Jan, the owner and Aaron's aunt, wanted a signature statement and opted to put powdered sugar on all plates. It was best to look into the kitchen before ordering. Some employees took Jan's direction far too seriously, and others understood moderation.

The place was steadily busy. Jan dropped off our order with a quick hello to both of us and a gentle tap on the shoulder as she walked on to chat with the table behind us.

I was fine with Teddy being my birth father, but I couldn't give him any type of title besides the guy who knocked up my birth mom and took off for years afterward. That was just an awkward way of introducing someone. Sometimes, I forgot Teddy had grown up and had a history in this town. Running away like he had twenty years ago doesn't erase that.

We made small talk about the weather before our food arrived.

After my first bite, I moved on to better topics. "What brings you to River Bend so early?"

"I've been going back and forth between my brother's place, my mother's, my sister's, and home, and I have been staying with a friend nearby. A central location between all of them. I think I put more miles on my car these past few weeks than I did all year."

"Sister?" I asked. I had a lot to learn about

him and his family, but that was a stunner.

"I thought you knew. Still hard for me to grasp all this. Wasn't it all explained?" he said.

"I haven't met anyone. I've seen your boys' pictures, and I may have seen your wife when my family attended your church services, but really didn't take notice of her. At the time, I didn't know my connection to you."

"Melanie is not handling all this much better than me, but I would have thought by now you knew."

I was confused. How would I know what was going on in his personal life? He was talking in circles, but I was standing outside a square box. Like he was an apple, and I, an orange, should understand what he was saying.

He was still talking. "I have been all over the place these weeks with my brother, the letter, my wife, and my mother, so I landed here."

It was already warm outside, and air-conditioning was blasting out at seven a.m. in the café. I was simultaneously sweating and shaking. The only thing I was learning was that I had a lot to learn about this man. He was talking about a sister, some letter, and saying was he living here.

"Letter?" I asked, not wanting to pry, but I was genuinely curious why he was bringing it up.

"You should have or will be receiving a letter from a lawyer. Apparently, my father had some land when he died, and he had instructions on how it should be divided up. It will explain it better than I could or want to."

He seemed bitter and almost childlike. Like he'd gotten a bad report card and it was not his fault. He picked up two more sugar packets and added them to his coffee.

My head was bouncing between all the words he was saying, and my wheel landed on "Landed here? Staying in town?"

"Yes, with a friend from high school." He looked down when he spoke.

"I sometimes forget that you were raised here. You must still know a few people. EG is always surprised when she sees people she grew up with. Despite her living here, I don't think she understands the draw for most people to stay. She seems to consider herself a part-time resident of River Bend since she spends so much time at her loft in Chicago."

"Is that where she is now?" He took another bite of his sandwich and grabbed a napkin, avoiding looking at me again.

"No, not this time. Sherrie and I are making ourselves comfortable in the house. It must be nice to be able to crash at someone's house and not be living in your car, driving back and forth. Were you able to walk here this morning?" I asked.

He nodded before drinking more coffee and

seemed to be calculating his words or letting the caffeine offset the alcohol from last night. "I'm staying three blocks over with . . . Tommy."

I put my sandwich down, sat back, and unconsciously, my left hand touched my right arm and held it on my lap.

Two months ago, Tommy's wife, Jean, had attempted to run me over, thinking I was EG. Luckily for me, I had only broken my arm before she'd taken off.

That same weekend, she confessed to killing Teddy's father twenty years ago but had let Teddy believe he had done it. Tommy and Teddy dumped the body in the river and, along with it, buried their secret for decades.

I learned that the body pulled out of the river was Teddy's father, my grandfather, and that EG and Teddy were my birth parents.

That same weekend, after a long night, Jean fired a gun into EG's house, missing everyone the first time. The second time she fired the gun, the bullet grazed Sherrie's arm.

That same weekend, Jean went into a mental health facility.

That same weekend, we discovered Tommy, the sheriff, had been covering up Jean's illness and snooping inside EG's house.

That same weekend, EG and her friend, Abigail, discovered Tommy's blackmail scheme to win the election for sheriff.

That same weekend, Tommy resigned from his job and had stayed out of the public eye since then.

That same weekend shifted everything in my life.

"Listen, I know what you must be thinking," Teddy said.

"No, don't. You don't know what I'm thinking." Our casual morning coffee conversations had just shifted past pleasantries about the weather, funny work stories, and that I supposedly have an aunt out there.

"You're right. I don't know what you're thinking. Tommy is a friend. An old friend. He helped me during a tough time twenty years ago, and he's here for me again. Someone who is misunderstood by most in the town."

I had a hard time connecting the dots: friendships, marriage loyalty, secrets, predator, victim, family. A drop of sweat ran down my back and clung to my shirt, and I tried to pull the pieces together. What piece was I? What dot was Teddy? Did it matter if I couldn't connect all the dots?

"Are you ok, Claudia?" Teddy asked. "You seem lost in thought."

"I just thought this place was probably not the best option for breakfast. If I had to guess, I have a handprint of powdered sugar on my shoulder from Jan. I should probably go home and change before work."

"I get it." He looked down and reached for his coffee.

I finished my egg sandwich in two bites while making a big deal of looking at the time. "I'm sorry to cut this short, but I want to put on a fresh shirt before I head in." He started to get up, and I kept talking. "Stay put. Just because I have to rush out doesn't mean you need to. Finish your coffee and relax." I made a semibelievable attempt of fumbling with my keys, wallet, phone, and coffee. I didn't want to position myself for any type of embrace. Why start now.

"We can try this again when our schedules are better," I said.

"That would be great. Next time, you could bring EG or Sherrie if you like?"

"Sure. Gotta go. Don't want to be late."

I went straight to Debby and got in. Just before I pulled out of the parking spot, I stopped and watched Teddy through the large window of the café. He had stood up to grab a newspaper someone had left behind, took his coffee, and moved to one of the sofas. He was clearly in no hurry to go anywhere this morning.

I drove straight to Chambray. I really didn't care if I had powdered sugar on my blouse. We could have almost made it a drinking game in town. Every time someone saw another person with powdered sugar on their clothes, they'd do a shot. Half this town would have been loaded by noon.

I sat in the car with the windows down, listening to the birds and watching a senior couple walk around the grounds. They were holding hands in their seventies. It was one of the most romantic things to witness at eight a.m. on a Wednesday morning.

I couldn't get it out of my head. Why would Teddy be staying with Tommy? Why should it bother me?

CHAPTER THIRTY-SIX

I was put at the main desk in the Administration building. Answering calls, sorting mail, and organizing the community newsletter were the official job duties. The unofficial but highly coveted role was being the pivotal keeper of all the residents' secrets and gossip.

There was a restaurant and bar for the residents, and it was open to the community. The bar did not open until eleven, but the lounge area was the morning hot spot. It started with the men reading the morning newspapers around 6 a.m. After their morning walk, around 8 a.m., couples wandered in, and then by nine thirty ladies filled the place, exchanging all sorts of information, of which very little was recipes or knitting techniques.

Today was no different than any other. The

phones were quiet, but the talk was everywhere.

Kay and I had developed nicknames for most of the morning regulars. She would be delighted to know our two favorites, Always-Wears-Pink and Needs-A-Breath-Mint, asked about her. I had learned this was her usual Wednesday morning post when SnapPea brought in an orange raisin muffin for Kay, but I was the not so lucky recipient. It should not have been considered a muffin but rather used at the gym for a weight. I could not imagine what could weigh so much and still be able to be baked.

My morning flew by, and while I was eating lunch, I learned that Kay had switched her schedule to come in at two today. Apparently, Ryan had made such an impression on her Monday she had already been maneuvering her schedule around before she'd met up with them at the bar yesterday. I didn't have to ask how her night had gone. It must have been better than how Sherrie and Brady had concluded their night.

I had just a few minutes to catch Cheryl and pump her for information. I was in luck because her trainee, Denise, was gone, but I wasn't sure how much time I had until she returned. Just before I stepped into Cheryl's area, Kay grabbed my elbow and pulled me back. We huddled in the hallway, whispering.

She talked about Ryan nonstop for several

minutes. I wanted to hear the details, but this was not the time. I saw my window of opportunity had closed when Denise came back from her break. I had to come up with a new plan and decided to ask Kay for help.

"I want to hear more about you and Ryan." I blushed because I knew she thought I wanted bedroom details. I had to make it interesting to keep her focus away from Ryan for a minute. "But I need your help. I can't go into details, but someone has been following me around. Someone called here asking questions."

"Holy shit!" Kay said rather loudly.

"Keep it down. I just need you to talk to Cheryl and find out as much as you can about that call."

She switched from giddy, starry-eyed, and gushing about Ryan to wildly entertained at the prospect of detective work. "You can't let on to Cheryl that anything is amiss. I cannot have her talking any more than she normally does."

"Just when I thought my day couldn't get any better, you give me this nugget. I am on it, girl." She smacked my ass when she walked away like a football player headed onto the field.

I was nervous about sharing what was going on but had no reason to be ashamed or embarrassed. I hadn't done anything wrong, or at least I didn't think I had. I was starting to think more help was not a bad thing.

CHAPTER THIRTY-SEVEN

The interview was the best part of the day. Gloria, the hotel manager, and I hit it off instantly again. The initial job title and responsibilities were not as good as expected, but held the promise of much more to come.

My official job would be a front desk agent, checking guests in and out of the hotel. A medium hourly paying position with the hope of overtime. She promised me plenty of opportunities to cross-train in all areas of the hotel. She had the philosophy that cross-training makes for better employees. Her honesty really earned my respect when she said they were short-staffed and employees tended to work in other departments than what they had been hired for, and she wanted everyone to be prepared to help where needed.

Before letting me think she ran a chaotic place with high staff turnover, she explained she turned out more employees for promotion and transfers to other hotels in the company than most of the other hotels in the region. If all went smoothly, I would have the chance to be promoted to supervisor or manager in six months and, in a year, move on to a bigger hotel in the city of my choice if I wanted to leave of River Bend.

That promise alone was what made me excited about the job. The six-month and twelve-month dates may have been a fluid estimated time frame in Gloria's mind, but I now had goals and a calendar to follow.

I was eager to get back to the house. I wanted to get on the company's website and look at my options. I wanted to make a conscious decision about my future and not just let it happen to me.

Assuming all went well with the drug test, I would start my training a week from Monday.

I parked on the street, went to the porch door, but the hook was on. Sherrie refused to get up and unhook it, so I had to go around to the back door. I found Sherrie lying on the sofa with a paper plate full of pizza balancing on her stomach and a notebook in the air, her pen scurrying down the page, and the television on the local news. The weather had held up nicely, and she had the downstairs windows open but the doors locked.

She made up for it by having a salad made for me, and it was topped off with three slices of pizza.

"There's beer in the fridge," Sherrie said loudly from the living room.

I grabbed my food and a beer and went to the dining room table, watching her write. "What are you doing there?"

"Just making a list of everything I need for school. Everything I need to buy and do before classes start. I am also trying to figure out how many shifts I can handle with my workload. How much do you think it snows here?"

"What?" I shoved the pizza in my mouth, savoring the cheesy goodness.

"I'm trying to maximize my time. Do I take another course or add a shift? I have to account for my time—eating, sleeping, studying, working, dating, grocery shopping, and shoveling? Do you know my father has me take a picture each time I cut the grass, and he monitors the rainfall here. He was so delighted that EG is letting me stay rent-free and helped expedite my admissions. He is doing everything in his power to make sure I don't blow it. If he has been that uptight about the grass, can you imagine him when the weather turns?"

"I love your dad. Robert is the best," I said with a mouth full of salad.

"I know." She put down the paper and pen

and turned her focus to the pizza. "What's up with you? Anything new with your shadow, dark vengeance, hawker the stalker?"

"Nice names. Let me know when you land on one. I got more than you can probably handle. You might want a fresh beer for what I got for you."

"I'm good. I just opened this one."

Ignoring her, I walked to the fridge and got a beer for her, then sat in the love seat.

"Lay it on me." She was sitting upright, double fisting the beers.

"Starting backwards. I got the job at the hotel. Starting a week from Monday. When I was leaving work, I saw Kay. I didn't have time to get into details, but apparently, she and Ryan are happy coupling."

"Whatever." With an eye roll, Sherrie said, "She can have a summer fling. I should have known something was off with his friend the shithead when Jenna turned him down."

"I told Kay that someone might be tracking me. I put her in charge of talking to Cheryl to find out more information. I figured it couldn't hurt if more people knew. Safer in a larger number of people helping me, correct?"

"By people, you mean Kay, not Cheryl and definitely not my folks. I am not risking them yanking me from here. For shit's sake, I'm scheduling shoveling times."

"I'm not talking about your parents—just Kay. But you know that means Jenna. Well, that did mean Jenna, but with Ryan in the picture, who knows?"

"Can you imagine him and Brady going all commando on someone?" She let out a laugh.

"Remember they are ex-military and they got the know-how and the guts," I said.

"But remember Khaki Number One manhandling Brady? I don't think he's coming to rescue either one of us. Now that I know Khaki One and Two aren't freaks, I wish I had gotten a better look at them. I think Number Two was kinda cute. Maybe my opportunity for a summer fling is still an option."

Our conversation lulled as we watched the news anchors banter back and forth about the best fried foods at the county fair.

"I have a beer and a half left. You want to tell me what has me holding these two?"

"This morning, I had breakfast with Teddy. I'm not sure if I smelled last night's booze or a morning kick start." I put down my pizza and picked up my beer. "He said a few things that struck me as kinda odd. Before I forget, he invited you and EG the next time we meet for coffee."

She flinched but remained silent.

"He said he had been traveling a lot these last few weeks. Weeks, not days. If something so intense happens, you don't confuse weeks and a weekend. The cashier at Peaches asked if he wanted his regular order like he has been there a lot. Seems he has been in town for a while."

"What about his job? Is he still preaching?"

"I don't know. I would think he has to be at the college in Vermont fairly soon."

"You didn't ask?"

I shook my head.

"I want to say something, but don't take it as a slight to you," Sherrie said.

I nodded. "Ok."

"What if Teddy's visits are not about you but EG?"

I was raising my beer bottle and stopped midway. "How do you mean?"

"Don't get me wrong, I'm sure he wants to get to know his daughter, but c'mon, why include EG and me in your gatherings? I am sure the guy has the gift of conversation. He is a preacher by trade. He does not need us to help fill the awkward pauses. If I had to guess, that invite was less about me and EG and more about EG. Remember when he showed up here drunk, and he made no attempts to hide the fact he was looking for EG?"

Now I took two sips of beer. "You're right. They do have a history together. They liked each other in high school and then got together one evening while in college. I am literally living proof of that. But that was over twenty years ago."

"Maybe you never get over your first love or first crush no matter how many years it has been. I still remember Kurt Davidson from fifth grade. He was in eighth grade, and I thought he was the man for me. I still get giddy when I think about him, and I don't think we talked more than two or three times. I have not seen him since he moved away when high school started. That was only a minor schoolgirl crush from ten years ago. You still get funny talking about your high school crush, and you never even kissed him."

"Maybe you're right. Do you think Teddy is the one stalking the house? He knows we're not EG."

"I don't think he is the nut bag out there."

"Did you put the mail somewhere? He said something about a letter. I guess his father had some property when he died."

"Inheritance?"

"Wouldn't it go to Teddy's mom?" I said.

"Depends if there is a will. With the mail, I was doing the same plan as normal. I put everything on the island, but with EG gone, I put her stuff in her room on her dresser."

"Ok, I'll look in a minute in case something got tossed in her pile. Hang on, I got one more tidbit for you. Drink up. Get ready. You won't believe where he has been staying."

Sherrie just looked at me and followed my advice the second time I said, "Drink." I waited a second before continuing. "Ready? He is staying with Tommy."

Cool and stealthy Sherrie let that hit her like a ton of bricks. She didn't move, but her face looked like a cold bucket of water just slapped her twice.

"He has been in town for an undetermined amount of time and has been at Tommy's."

"When you say 'Tommy' "—she used air quotes as if that was not his real name—"you mean the husband of the nut job that shot me."

"She didn't shoot you, per se; you were more or less in the way when the gun in her hand fired, and the bullet had grazed your arm."

"Tommy, the former sheriff?"

"We don't need to go over his complete resume. I did all the same calculations, and yes, the very same 'Tommy.' " This time, I used air quotes around his name.

We sat in silence for a minute before the conversation took an unexpected turn.

Sherrie said, "I'm going for a bike ride."

"Now?"

No response. She took her plate and beers into the kitchen, then went upstairs to change. When she returned, I was in the same spot, not knowing what to do, holding my beer in my left hand and my right thumb spinning the ring.

She opened the door to the porch and pulled her bike from the corner. She struggled, turning it around, and then fiddled with the simple hook on the screen door. The same hook she would not open for me earlier.

It was a simple maneuver she had done numerous times, but she seemed caught in a hamster wheel of haplessness. She had not turned the wheel and was jammed in the corner, unable to get a solid hold on the lock's elementary eye hook.

She finally put the bike down, stepped over it, and walked out. "I'm going for a run."

"Sherrie?" I said.

She stopped on the bottom step but did not turn around. "Lock up behind me."

"Ok," I said, so softly I wasn't sure she had heard me. My heart was pounding.

"I just need to clear my head." Almost to the sidewalk, she turned to face the house. "Claud, you and I are good. Just need to clear my head."

CHAPTER THIRTY-EIGHT

I slouched deeper into the fold of the love seat's cushions until I could no longer sip my beer. I sank so low my knees extended out into the middle of the room and my chin was resting on my chest. I needed to stretch and finally rousted myself out of the cushions.

I went upstairs and took a shower, my second of the day, wanting to clear my head and shake off this day. I put on my satin pajama top and shorts and went down to the porch to mindlessly flip through magazines.

I heard a car slowed down, and my heart started beating faster, then eased up when I saw it was Jorge. He turned into his driveway twenty feet from EG's house, and the car's headlights lit me up like a Christmas tree.

I was surprised when the passenger door opened. I didn't recognize the woman. She appeared to be the same age as Jorge, midthirties, and was casually but smartly dressed in a wrap skirt and light summer blouse.

"Hi, Claudia," Jorge yelled.

"Hey, Jorge."

He walked around the front of the car and waited for the lady to join him.

"Why don't you come out here? I can introduce the two of you," he said.

It wasn't even seven p.m., and I was in pj's, no makeup, with slicked-back, wet hair. I was in no form to meet anyone. This lady was beautiful, well put together, and he expected me to waddle out there and present myself.

"Come on, why so shy?" When I still did not have a good answer or begin to move, Jorge got a worried look on his face. "Everything ok? Any updates?"

"I'm fine." A shitload of updates, but this was not the time to clue him in.

"Claudia, this is Addie. Addie, this is Claudia. One of the ladies I was telling you about earlier. Usually, not a shy one. Come on out. Let's make sure you're ok."

Dang, he was not letting it go. He seemed to like this date because he would not have made such an effort with a dud.

"It's just . . ."

"Hi, Claudia, nice to meet you," Addie said.

"Yes, nice to meet you as well. I'm sorry I'm . . ."

From the porch, I could see she had brown hair and kind eyes. She spoke again. "No need to apologize. I understand." She was twenty-plus feet away but leaned in towards the porch. "I love those pj's. I have the same ones in lavender. Did you splurge on the slippers?"

I couldn't help but smile. "Nah, I was too cheap. Maybe I will put them on my Christmas list."

"They are worth it. Nice to meet you. We will let you enjoy your evening." She turned to Jorge and said, "Let's let Claudia enjoy her relaxing evening. You've got kitchen renovation updates to show me."

We all waved, and Jorge put his arm around her, looking at me when they stepped towards his house. I gave him a thumbs-up, and his smile got bigger.

Sherrie returned twenty minutes later and sat on the arm of the oversized chair on the porch, swinging her legs up on the seat.

I didn't mean the surprise in my voice when I said, "You don't look very winded." I tried to recover by saying, "You're in good shape."

"After pounding two beers, I figured

running might not be my best idea, but I needed to clear my head, so I just walked."

"I get that. Believe me, I get it. I know whoever is coming after me has an impact on you. And I definitely know how bizarre this whole Teddy thing is."

"I'm trying to figure out how freaked-out we need to be about this?"

"Freaked. I am not freaked-out as in scared. I am freaked-out in this bizarro world that is becoming our lives," I said.

"Really, let's think about this. Jean is locked up, but we don't know for how long. We are assuming Tommy and Jean are still married, but we really don't know anything about that. Teddy is staying with Tommy. He is not living at home or staying closer to his brother. I just find that odd. Is that the right word, odd?

"I'm still stuck on bizarre."

"Let's go with bizarre." Sherrie kept going. "What do we know about Tommy? He is a disgraced former sheriff who was caught cheating his way into office."

"What I find interesting is their friendship. What you said earlier about holding onto a silly grade school crush from ten years ago—think about what they went through twenty-four years ago. They had a real bond. If they weren't close friends before that night, what happened pretty much made them brothers. Teddy stumbled upon his father's body and thought he had been the one to kill him. Tommy stepped up that night. Teddy was in a panic and wanted to hide the body because he really thought he and EG had unknowingly killed his father two hours earlier. We now know Jean did, but that is neither here nor there right now. Teddy didn't own up to his mistake; he hid his mistake and then ran away like a coward. Did he do it to protect EG or himself? Tommy was the hero that night. Yeah, he helped hide a corpse, but he did it for his friend. Right or wrong, that is a friend we could all use."

Deadpan, straight-faced, without moving a muscle, Sherrie simply said, "I'd hide a body for you."

"Right back at you." I laughed, but became slightly worried, so I cautiously asked, "No dead bodies out there for you?"

"Not yet." She unlaced her tennis shoes as if I had asked her about the weather.

"So let me get this straight. On a balance scale of good guys versus bad guys, Tommy is looking better than your father, Teddy."

"I guess so. I really don't like referring to him as my father. My dad is my dad. Matthew is the man, the father, the dad. Always has been and always will be. Even before this week and Teddy showing up all drunk, he is just a guy in my life.

Maybe like a teacher. Someone who influenced part of my life's direction but is not considered family or friend.

"That 'Blood is thicker than water' philosophy people say is bullshit. You mean more to me than I think Teddy ever will. Friend is a more powerful word than family. A person chooses a friend and each day continues to make that choice. When people say, 'She was like a sister to me,' it's not as powerful as saying she was a friend. I love my brother because of who he is as a person and how he treats me and others. The word brother identifies a connection but does not guarantee a good relationship.

"Family you are bound to whether you like them or not, but friendship is earned, it's a gift. Saying Teddy is my father gives him a title. That usually comes with implied special meaning, but I am not buying into that theory anymore. Even a mentor or coach can have a deeper impact with creating relationships with meaning even more than a family gathering each holiday."

Sherrie had stopped moving and was just looking at me. I thought she might have heard or seen something I had not, but then she said, "That was beautiful. How you said that."

She pulled off her shoes, slid down the arm of the chair, and sat up, putting her feet on the table. "Did you see the text Mia sent? I can't believe it."

"My phone is inside. What did she say?"

"That ain't cool. We have talked about always having a phone within arm's reach. Don't get sloppy on me."

I gave her a mock salute.

"She heard from that guy, Parker, who lived next to us in the townhouse, that the bar where Jackson's band played in Chicago got raided. Last Saturday, he was helping Jackson carry in equipment because the drummer and bassist would be late. One or two guys were drinking at the bar; otherwise, the place was empty since it was so early. They had carried the last piece of equipment in and went to the bar. Suddenly, from the front door and back doors come in some SWAT dudes."

"SWAT team?" I repeated.

"SWAT, FBI, or ATF. I don't know. This is all coming from Mia, who got it from Parker. They were wearing blue windbreakers, and someone flashed a badge. One guy yanked the three of them off the barstools and tossed them out the front door, then told them to get out and stay the fuck away. It all happened so fast, they have no idea what happened to Jackson. Parker did say Michael, the bartender, looked freaked but not surprised. The bar has not been open since it happened on Saturday."

"You got all that from a text?"

"That is your first question! Sometimes you can be exhausting," Sherrie said.

I shrugged, and Sherrie kept talking.

"All Mia said on the text was SWAT team and no one heard from him since. Call for details. So I called. That is what one does when you get a message like that. It was a needed diversion on the walk just now. So what are you going to do now?"

"What do you mean?"

"You have to call Jackson and find out what happened."

"I have no desire to call Jackson. I don't care that much about him to find out if there is more to the story."

"Of course, there is more to the story. I'll tell Mia to keep working on it."

"One drama at a time for me, and right now, I will take on the one who chased us down."

"Fair point. Oh, you won't believe who I ran into on my walk."

"That was a short but productive walk."

"Yes, very productive. I ran into Officer Patrick."

"Now that is interesting. You swing a date with him?"

"Still working on it. It better happen soon. I can't handle a slow and sweet country guy. I want a take-charge country man. He did say there were no other sightings of the car that chased us or any other odd reports. They have been driving past the house but have not seen anything. He also said he stopped by yesterday to check on us."

"Us or you?"

That put a smile on her face.

"That reminds me we have to get the doorbell camera installed," I said.

"Looks like Jorge is home. I'll go over and get the name of the electrician he knows."

"Tomorrow. He has a date there now."

"That's cool. At least somebody on this street is getting lucky. I don't think lady Jolston, across the street, has given up the booty to old man Jolston since Reagan was in office. Do you see the way he attacks those bushes when he's out there trimming? That guy has some pent-up issues."

"I have nothing to contribute to any of that," I said.

"Let's change the bulbs. We can easily do this one." She pointed to the ceiling and stood up.

"And we can do the back door light. It creeps me out, not having a light in the back. I have been parking in front because you can't see anything back there. I spent five minutes the other day trying to get my key in the door. I nearly dropped my phone while I was juggling the keys, phone, purse, and food."

"Now? I'm in my pj's. I want one easy night. How about tomorrow?"

"What about the mail?" Sherrie asked.

"I forgot to look. I can't believe that I—"

"Don't overthink everything. Just get up and check the mail. There is no need to ponder why, just keep moving forward and don't read into every action or forgotten action. Just take care of it now."

"Ooh," I drawled out, feeling scolded but rightfully so.

I went to the mailbox secured to the siding underneath the large screen windows. I found a stack of catalogs and coupons, which I tossed to Sherrie on the porch, and went to EG's room to look at the mail Sherrie had stacked up on her dresser.

There were several letters addressed to EG, and I threw them back down. One fell to the floor, and I picked it up. On top of the pile, the next letter was addressed to me. Kinda. It was also addressed to EG. Kinda.

It was her address and the name was Claudia Graham. My first name and her last name. The postmark was from over a week ago. Either Sherrie or I could have tossed it in the pile if we read the last name, and seeing it was from a lawyer's office, we just would have assumed anything beyond a Pottery Barn catalog belonged to EG. She was so delighted about her weekend in Minneapolis and then the cruise, she wouldn't be bothered with anything official looking.

I thought this must have been the letter

Teddy was talking about. I was smad, that is sad and mad. That man did not even know my name. He had assumed I had EG's last name. He knew my parents, Matthew and Katie Lyn Middleton, raised me as their own from the second I was born. I guess for Teddy, I will forever connect him to that night he'd spent with EG. He seemed to be frozen in that time period.

I would do anything not to be like him.

I took the letter back to the porch. Sherrie was texting or pretending to text to give me time to read through it.

"You want to hear it?" I asked her after a few minutes.

"Don't be dumb or dramatic. Come on, give me the highlights."

"From what I can understand, George, Teddy's father, bought some land, but I am not sure when. He made arrangements for someone by the name of Leann Smithford to remain on the property until her death. Then upon her death, the land is to be divided amongst his grandchildren. All this legal crap is confusing. There is more mumbo jumbo, but I have to reread it."

"So, you're a land baron now?"

"Yeah, right. I can't imagine there is much value to it. From what I understand, the guy could barely keep a job. There could even be back taxes. Not sure what my portion would even be considering there are several of us out there."

"How do you find out more?" Sherrie asked.

"There is a meeting set up for the end of August. But I guess I could call the law firm and try to get some explanation of what this all means beforehand."

I should have been excited about the prospect of owning something, but at that moment, it felt like something else I had to do, like a chore, like taking out the trash.

I laughed a little when I pictured myself driving up to the big fancy lawyer office in Debby. I pictured The Beverly Hillbillies, the '70s television sitcom. Some poor folks discovered oil in their fields, struck it rich, and moseyed into Beverly Hills in their old jalopy, looking completely out of place and not caring they did.

I knew the office was closed for the day, but I left my name and phone number with the answering service and why I was calling. I didn't expect to learn anything new and thought I would probably be told it would be explained at the meeting, but I had to try.

Later, I tossed the letter on my dresser and easily decided not to waste too much energy guessing what it meant for me.

Who could have guessed that letter was one of the pieces I needed to solve the mess I was in? Looking back now, getting a letter from a lawyer is a pretty good clue—too bad that seeing the obvious is not my forte.

CHAPTER THIRTY-NINE

We had an easy night of channel surfing in the living room. I was delighted to be bored. I did not even flinch when we heard a car drive slowly past the house. It was nice to go to bed out of boredom and not exhaustion. My mind still sometimes circled back to who I could have upset that would want to come after me.

I woke up at seven after eight hours of sleep but not fully rested. I showered and did my hair and makeup before heading downstairs.

It was a perfect-weather day. Sunny with the occasional cloud and a manageable humidity level.

I put on my cute workout clothes, designed for working out but never expected to be worked out in. A heather-gray three-quarter-length wide-sleeved shirt with a large oval opening in the back, which exposed my deep-purple sports bra that matched my black and purple spandex knee-high yoga pants. I owned several pairs of yoga pants but had never taken one yoga class.

I expected Sherrie to be out bike riding or midway through painting the exterior of the house. That woman was always on the go. Some days, it was kinda annoying. Other days, I totally envied her.

I found her at the kitchen island eating cereal in her pj's. Always the same look for the four years I have known her. Some old T-shirt and cutoff sweatpants. Her bare feet swung back and forth around the stool, and she was using her energy this morning, fiercely writing more items on her back-to-school to-do list. She was listening to the same country music mix that was playing at the bar the other night. Pete's musical taste was seeping into her playlist. I wondered if she knew where that influence was coming from.

I grabbed some cereal and joined her at the island while I waited for my coffee to brew.

"Anything else besides light bulbs we need from the hardware store?" Sherrie asked without looking up.

"Check downstairs in the garage. I can't imagine EG not having any bulbs. When do you have to be at the bar?"

"Two. I have an appointment with the

financial counselor on campus at one. I have to review my plan for the next two years. I want the smallest loan possible, but I don't want to be eating ramen noodles every day either. Since you broke up with Aaron, I suppose our bread and pie connection is gone. I have to factor in the additional expense."

"Last night, you were calculating random snow-shoveling times, and now, you are adding baked goods to your list of expenses. Do you realize that my parents are about to be in the baked goods business? They are close to signing a lease for the industrial kitchen with Aaron's aunt and his mom. By late fall, we will be swimming in bread and pie."

"How close is Aaron to joining that group?" Sherrie asked when she stood up and poured herself more coffee, her back to me.

"You are never shy. Go ahead and ask the real question."

"How are you with seeing Aaron working with your parents?"

"That's not the question you want to ask," I said.

Sherrie came back to the island and sat down. "How are you getting along with your breakup?"

"Not great. I keep going back to why I broke up with him."

"And that was because . . ."

"That is what I have been sputtering around about. I was in such a lull about where everything was going for me. Two months ago, I graduated college with good grades, a boyfriend, a shitty job waiting for me in Chicago and an easy summer driving EG to chemo. Nearly two months later, I had a job, but because of community service hours, I was only getting paid fifty percent of the time I was there and with no clear career opportunity for me. I waited less than twenty–four hours to get together with Aaron after breaking up with Jackson. I was living rent-free and freeloading off EG, and all the while, I watched you—"

"Watched me? You're blaming me?"

"I am not blaming you. You're inspiring. I saw that when you came to visit two months ago. You enrolled for your master's program, got a job, sublet your old apartment, and left only to get your stuff here. All that after getting grazed in the arm with a bullet from Tommy's wife."

"Is that what you see? How about the way I see it? I quit a minimum-paying job that had nothing to do with my degree to start taking classes again before formally being accepted into the master's program. That's right, EG didn't get me into the program but gave me the idea to take classes and set myself up properly to get accepted. That was her idea. I couldn't come up with that good of a plan. I needed her just to talk to the registration office to get me signed up for a few measly classes. From my perspective, I am freeloading off my friend's aunt. That same friend who got her boyfriend to give me a job so I could afford ramen noodles."

"Oh."

"I tripped and stumbled through my whole summer. I am teetering between my own fear of not officially getting into the master's program and the real fear of having to tell my parents. You see what you want to see and not my reality."

"Oh. Fair point," I mumbled.

"You—"

"Stop. I was trying to say you are inspirational, or in the spirit of what you were saying—I was looking for inspiration, and I pulled it from your actions so take it as a compliment."

Sherrie rolled her eyes. "You have yet to answer the question . . . how are you getting along without Aaron?"

"Not good. I keep wanting to call him, but I am so mad at him for the whole Jo-Lee thing. I figured he would start dating sooner or later, but she was spending the night there less than twenty-four hours after we broke up. Then I remind myself about breaking up with Jackson and making out with Aaron the next day."

"Sleeping together and making out are two different things."

"Yes, but it was not too much longer," I said.

"So, to answer the question . . ."

"How can I forgive myself for the quick leap but can't get past what Aaron did?"

Sherrie picked up a piece of cereal and chucked it at my head.

I raised my hand to shield my eyes, and it bounced off and landed in my coffee. "What was that for?"

"Do I have to spell it out for you?" Sherrie sounded exhausted.

"Maybe. I haven't been able to connect the dots."

She stood up and opened the kitchen window above the sink to let fresh air in. The sunlight streamed in, causing the temperature to rise like an oven slowly preheating.

She leaned against the sink, crossed her arms over her chest, and looked right at me. "You have feelings for Aaron. More than the fact that he is a good guy. You seriously like the man; otherwise, you would not care about Jo-Lee. Last night, I told you Jackson was at a bar that got raided and no one has heard from him since, but you could not care less. If I had to guess, you broke up with Aaron because that was one thing you could control. You have been lollygagging and putzing through the summer. I bet if you took control Friday morning and took off your cast then, you would not have broken up with Aaron.

"Stop puttering and be your own inspiration! Remember how good it felt when you took control of the right stuff, like your cast, blocking Jackson, getting the new job. Your creepy secret admirer/shadowmonger, did not stop you from doing any of that stuff. It's ok to take a moment or a few weeks in a summer to figure out what you want to do. Our college degree is not the golden ticket to life. Four years of college and a degree just gives you something awesome for your resume, a hangover, and a college friend turned roommate turned friend for life. Taking control does not mean starting completely over."

"You have been sitting on all this insight and not sharing it with me. That's kinda rude." I snickered. "Keep working on those names for the person that is hawking us."

"Whatever. I sometimes have a hard time reasoning out the fact you or we have a stalker, and it is easier for me to deal with it if I called it something other than stalking." She smiled. "I'm gonna get dressed and look for light bulbs."

She went upstairs, and I grabbed a glass, adding some ice. When I saw the orange juice in the fridge, I started to cry. I grabbed the bottle and sat down hugging it. I let every emotion sweep through me. All the words Sherrie had said cascaded over me.

Only I got to decide what I wanted, and I wanted my guy back. I was delighted that I let myself feel that. It's ok to make a mistake. The problem was, it did not just involve me. I was playing with someone else's emotions, and that was not fair to Aaron.

I switched from pity to anger when I realized I couldn't tell Aaron I had been wrong. I was mad there was no option for him to take me back. What right did I have to interfere with his emotions now that he was with somebody else?

Do I have to live without ever telling him I want him back? What kind of person invades another relationship for her own benefit? Am I that kind of person?

CHAPTER FORTY

I pulled myself together. I would not waste the day wallowing in my feelings now that I had a decent understanding of everything.

I went to the garage and pulled the small ladder out to the porch. Of course the hook was still latched on the inside of the screen door. I left the ladder there and went back through the house to unlock the front door and the porch door. I heard Sherrie downstairs forging for bulbs, and she emerged victoriously.

We started with very little luck. The only bulbs were one hundred watts. The single bulb lit the porch and front yard, and every bug in a three-mile radius would be climbing the window screens to get in. We thought it would get too hot for the shade and opted to get new ones for the porch and use the bright bulb in the backyard.

Not using our heads, we decided to move the ladder from the porch through the house instead of going around outside. We made it through the living room, past the dining table, and made two turns in the kitchen without a problem. We were at the back door, so close to our destination, concentrating so hard on not nicking the walls that when we made the turn to head outside, we took out the bare bulb lighting the basement stairs.

After sweeping up, we moved outside and really lost our luck. I was up on the ladder, and the light fixture fell into my hands because the rusted nail could no longer support the weight after I jiggled it while getting out the old broken bulb. Sherrie supported the ladder, and I took a step down, holding the light fixture. I forgot that it was still connected to the wiring. The small tug I gave it separated the fixture from the wall. I pushed the wires back into the hole because I didn't want them to get wet if it rained.

We were both delighted that I hadn't dropped the light fixture or cut my hand on the broken bulb.

I stepped off the ladder while Sherrie stood facing the sun. I put the light fixture in the garage before I joined her. We soaked in sunlight before the high heat of the day crept up.

"I guess our electrician will have more than one job when he gets here," Sherrie said.

"I think I have a lot to tell EG when she gets back."

"You think? I hope you hear the sarcasm," she said.

"Just that I am possibly being stalked, and we are ripping apart her home bit by bit. A hole in the stairwell and missing light fixtures. Do you think she'll get a kick out of it or kick us out?" I asked, knowing full well EG would not be bothered by anything except the stalking.

"Hey, we patched the hole. You can't even see it. We could get this fixed even before she comes back," Sherrie said.

"Don't sweat it. She is not going to kick us out or report you to your father."

"I know, I know. I just like not destroying things or telling lies."

"Lies? What lies are being told?"

She looked over at me. "I need to talk to Aaron."

"Really? You?"

"I never did the background check and phone reference calls on Jo-Lee and the other chick he interviewed as he asked me to do. I forgot about it. I had Pete make a few calls and tell me what he learned. When Aaron asked about them, I fumbled my way through it. After she was hired, I made the call to her former employer. The response was odd."

"How so?" I asked.

"The person gave a great reference but kept referring to her Jo, not Jo-Lee, and was very surprised about the call because she had worked there for almost ten years but abruptly quit without notice. I was going to say something, but then Jo-Lee started and was pretty good at the job. Quiet but hardworking. I was going to say something again, but he is dating her. I didn't want to make it look spiteful after your breakup."

I chuckled. "Good luck with that one. You need to tell him. Honesty is a big point for Aaron. If he finds out about the lie and it possibly jeopardizes the bar or license, I am not sure how he'll handle it. He will appreciate the truth sooner than later."

"I know! That's why I still did the reference call after she was hired. Thank god she is a good worker. Do we have this place cleaned up enough? I have some time before my appointment on campus. Let's go for a bike ride."

"We can't handle a ladder without damaging the house, and you want me on a bike that depends on me braking with my weak hand?"

"How about walking along the river before lunch?"

"If you can handle putting away the ladder

and locking the garage door, I will lock the house up."

Five minutes later, we were walking down the street toward the river path. The sun and trees were casting shadows on the sidewalks, and three girls had made a hopscotch game with chalk on a driveway. Sherrie bounced in for two skips across the numbers before we moved on.

"You know what I have been thinking about?" I said.

"You've got a crazy stalker, you want your old boyfriend back, some militia manhandled your ex-ex-boyfriend, we are slowing tearing apart EG's house, Teddy is a drunk living with either a criminal or a hell of a friend, your new job, or that you have two different socks on?"

"Wow, you can sum up my life in under seventy words. That is a little unnerving. It was nothing that well composed and self-referencing. I was just curious why the river path has never been extended farther north."

"Wetland preservation. A committee is continuously monitoring the land, and they hope in the next three years to have a plan in place. Most likely build some type of boardwalk bridge structure that meets up with the path on the northern side of River Bend."

I stopped walking and just looked at her. "I was kidding. But where did all that come from?"

"When I'm bored at work, I listen to the regulars talk. The days following a town council meeting is the best for town news. When I'm cleaning behind the bar, I listen. Wait until I tell you what they're planning for the city dump."

"Thanks but no thanks. I will read about it in the paper," I said.

We walked from the boat launch parking area to the path. The river was on our right, and we watched a barge float down the Mississippi River.

"What I was thinking about before and can't seem to stop focusing on is who did I piss off. I am not that interesting," I said.

"Maybe we have it all wrong. Maybe it's not about you. Not directly. You are only seeing one side of things. Like you admiring me for thinking I have it all together while I'm thinking I am barely hanging on, leeching off EG, and squeaking my way into a master's program. Two sides to every story. Maybe it's not somebody who's mad or vengeful; maybe they want something you have."

"I really don't have anything of value, and why run us off the road? I could see breaking into the house, but why the car chase and casing my car?"

"What about Aaron's ex-girlfriends—jealousy?"

"No. He would have said something the other night when we were all at the house if it was even the slightest possibility. Plus, there hasn't been anyone remotely serious for about a year."

"This will be harder to figure out, but does someone want to get to EG through you?"

"I'd say that is great insight if you had any answers to those questions. Now, it's more for me to think about."

"I know this has been bothering you. That's not necessarily a bad thing. You should keep searching for the answer because it's about your safety."

"How can you tell?"

"You are usually humming some song from the eighties. These past few days, the radio dial in your head has been turned off."

CHAPTER FORTY-ONE

We walked back in silence. If I had to guess, Sherrie was repeating her to-do list in her head. I was thinking about everything she had said.

She quickly left the house to start checking items off her list. That inspired me to make my own list like some type of vision board. I'd had a professor in college who preferred circle diagrams to the traditional outline. His theory was not everything was neat or orderly and could not be lined up in order of importance. Some things related to more than one item. Starting with the central idea in the middle, we would then create other circles or bubbles shooting off it.

Sometimes, the central goal might shift to a smaller side bubble, but that was ok as long as we kept coloring in the bubbles as we accomplished things.

I tore a sheet from Sherrie's notebook and got to work at the dining room table, turning on my instrumental music playlist on my phone. I had about five hours' worth of the classics from Bach, Mozart, and others. It was my go-to study music. My college roommates initially made fun of me, but slowly, they each created their own playlists featuring old dead guys that couldn't be rocked out to.

I stumbled initially but told myself I was not outlining a chapter from a sociology book from college. I punched myself in the arm and permitted myself to self-indulge and wrote me in the middle of the paper. In the first bubble from the center, I wrote in career. The rest came easy—savings account, down payment for a home, car, vacation, time with mom and dad. My brother, Connor, got his own bubble. I wanted more time with him before he disappeared into college life. I was writing so fast I barely hesitated when I created the last two bubbles . . .the first one was stalker, and on the other side of the paper, I drew a little stick figure of me. I couldn't write the word yet, just a remedial drawing of a stick figure running.

This assignment was not all about goals and fun. This was a get-off-my-ass-and-do-something list. I could not ignore that fact that someone was still out there. I needed a serious game plan.

I kinda surprised myself with the last one. I'd thought it would be cool and had always been curious about it but also too scared and intimidated to try it. Aaron had talked about it but had never done it either. The truth was I'd always thought it was something I might try later on in life, like those fantasies about traveling the world or starting a charity, but why wait? I suddenly felt very inspired to step outside of my comfort zone. Only this time, it wasn't stepping—I was gonna run a damn marathon.

I read all my bubbles again, knowing I'd missed one, a big one. I didn't want to label it love. I hoped to have someone to love and someone who loved me, but I didn't want it to be something to check off or, in this case, a bubble to color in. I would keep looking, dating, and putting myself out there. Getting a man did not equal success. Just being me and putting myself out there is all I wanted. I drew a heart, and inside it, I wrote me.

I was positively impressed with myself, and I laughed again. All I had done was write some stuff down on a sheet of notebook paper, but it felt empowering to see it in writing.

I made myself a sandwich and almost dropped the pickles because my hand strength was not 100 percent yet. I smiled at the thought of EG and Aaron making sure I could open everything. My arm was looking more on the normal side but had a ways to go yet.

I cleaned up my lunch mess, putting music on and dancing my way around the kitchen. I took out the garbage and cleaned the sink disposal. There was a strange smell hanging in the air, and I could not pinpoint it.

I looked at my diagram bubbles again and made additional circles. From the career bubble, I wrote supervisor/manager and transfer. Savings account had two bubbles listing budget planning and find a financial consultant. I had an action plan for almost everything.

I got a text from Gloria that my drug test came back clean, and I was set to start in ten days. I'd had no fear of failing the drug test. Anyone graduating college and looking for a career should have known to curb any recreational habits before the interview season began.

I spent ten minutes wiping down the island—it should have taken thirty seconds.

What if Aaron knew how I felt? Is he serious with Jo-Lee? Is he with her to bug me? I tapped a nail on the island. Nah, he's not that kind of guy. I had initiated the breakup. I have been the one to stay away. I was the one who walked away from him in the hardware store. Who am I to judge about Jo-Lee when I was kissing him a day after I broke up with Jackson?

I needed to see him. I needed to see his face.

I wanted to see how he would react to me. Cordial, of course, that is him as a person. Was he going to be distant? Was he going to be friendly like I was just another bar patron? Would there be any sign of hope? I just needed to know if I had hope.

I will put myself out there, and let him know I am open to something.

I was not going to insert myself into his relationship with Jo-Lee, but I wanted to see him. I needed to see him. But why? Did I miss him or just having someone? Then I remembered what Sherrie had said about Jackson: I heard half a story about him being at a bar that got raided, and I had no interest in the rest of the story. Did I break up with him because that was one part of my life I could control?

Damn.

I wanted Aaron. I wanted to listen to him. I wanted to be in the back of the pickup truck at 2:00 a.m. when the bar closed and go to the river and watch the barges head south. I wanted to be standing in his kitchen after eating pie and for him to kiss the nape of my neck and for us to stay like that until we couldn't stand it any longer and then dash to his bedroom.

I ran upstairs for my keys. I was on the porch when I stopped, remembering to lock up. I left the kitchen window above the sink open a crack because of the undetermined smell. I closed the back door and hesitated because the scent was more substantial.

It smelled like metal grinding or maybe plastic burning. I figured it was either Jorge working on something in his garage or the neighbors behind him burning the dead tree they had taken down earlier in the week. But I couldn't tell because they had tall wooden fences, and I couldn't see into the yards.

Could it be a dead animal under the house? Maybe it had been an animal that had moved the doormat or rammed into the door, making Sherrie think we had left through the back door when she'd returned last week. But there was no way an animal ran us off the road.

There was only so much I could handle telling EG when she returned.

CHAPTER FORTY-TWO

I really did not want to drive. All the extra driving I was doing was costing me gas money. The early afternoon weather was beautiful, the sun unobstructed by clouds.

No one is going to come after me as I walk to town.

I got mad at myself for not getting any closer to figuring out who had chased us down.

Shaking it off, I texted Jorge for the name and number of the guy who could look at the wiring on the porch.

He said his brother-in-law, AJ, would come over Saturday morning. He also asked if any other strange things had happened. I assured him I was ok.

He really must like this woman he's seeing

because, normally, he follows up with me daily, asking if everything's ok.

That was another thing to update EG on. At least that was fun gossip.

Walking gave me a few minutes to figure out what I was going to say. Should I just go with the "Hey, can we talk for a minute?" approach? But then I would have to speak.

I could walk in like a regular customer and sit at the bar and chitchat.

What the hell am I going to chitchat about with a guy I have seen naked and hope to see naked again?

I could ask for Sherrie when I get there. She wouldn't get there for another thirty minutes, so I would have to chitchat about crap while "waiting." I was not carrying anything that I could have pretended to drop off for her.

I walked back to the river and the same parking lot/boat launch area Sherrie and I had walked through earlier. I found a park bench and sat on the backrest, my feet on the seat. I took off my top and let the sun wash over me. My sports bra would give me a weird tan line, but I didn't expect to be out there long. I texted Kay, asking if she had a minute to talk. I got an immediate response of

NEED 5

INTELLIGENCE GALORE.

Waiting five minutes to hear everything Kay found out washed away the relief I felt from the sun rays.

Taking control and going to see Aaron felt good.

Control. I was back to having Chuck and Sherrie in my head: take control, take control, take control, press to get the ball back. I shook my head. Oh god, something has to change. I can't have those two stuck in my head.

I watched some kids skip rocks, a granddad teaching his grandson how to fish, and a group of high school girls work on their tans. The river in that area was three-quarters of a mile wide, and there was a lock and dam about a mile north.

Two guys were fishing off a boat not too far from there. One appeared to be having some luck catching, and the other was having luck retrieving beer from the cooler.

A rare cloud floated overhead, and I could see the two guys fishing a little more clearly now that the sun was not making me squint. I surprised myself by recognizing them sooner but was not surprised it was Tommy catching the fish and Teddy catching the beer.

Kay called and barely let me say hello before she launched into her day. "You would not believe this place today. A pipe broke here in the admin building, flooding the bathroom and part of the hallway. Cheryl was forced from her desk and took up a seat with me behind the reception desk. She went for a late lunch now, so I don't have much time to chat in case she returns. I have to tell you, it has made my day go by really fast. Normally, her talking would have driven me insane, but thanks to your project, I used this as a chance to break her. Wait, hold on a sec—" She put down her phone and chatted with Singing Cynthia and Sangria Sara before she ushered them along. "Sorry about that."

"I heard. It sounds like happy hour started early. So what did you learn?" I asked.

"A lady called last week as if you had applied for a job and she was doing a background check. To be honest, I may have put the call through to Mrs. Baron's office. I couldn't understand her. It was like she was mumbling or eating. I just assumed it was about your community service hours, and it was busy at the desk."

"Don't worry about it. Could you get from Cheryl what the lady was focused on?"

"It took me forty-five minutes to keep her on track. Despite her complaining about not being able to work at her desk, I think she was savoring the fact she could talk to me and everyone that walked by. She was milking all this attention every second, so it was hard to keep her focused without her clamming up. I guess Mrs. Baron was headed past Cheryl's desk during the call and took notice of what it was about. Cheryl transferred the call to Mrs. Baron and heard her give dates of employment and job title. She knew she had probably screwed up by talking too much. She has gotten into trouble for this before." Kay and I both laughed, and she continued. "I didn't get much else except somehow EG's name got into the conversation. I also learned Cheryl thinks EG should write more romance. You know the sweet-enough-to-make-you-puke Hallmark Christmas movie romance."

"You mean like you and Ryan," I said and waited.

She didn't say anything.

Crap. Did I hit a touchy subject with her?

"Hey, did you say something? I had to drop my phone. Stuart was walking through the lobby doors, but he turned around to chat with the residents. I gotta go. He's coming back. We'll chat later. I'm meeting Ryan after work. I'll text you and you can join us." She didn't wait for me to respond. The line went dead.

Me and EG. Me and EG? Me and EG. What did that mean?

My attention went back to Teddy and Tommy on the fishing boat. Teddy stood up on the back seat of the boat and looked around, seemingly to steady himself. His back was towards me as he faced west. I was curious what he was looking at.

Tommy was in the front section of the boat, casting towards the east. I realized he wasn't looking at something but was relieving himself. Sometimes guys had it so easy.

Me and EG. Me and EG? Me and EG? I got lost in my thoughts again, causing me to lose track of time and my surroundings. Everything I should not be doing. At least Sherrie would be at the bar by now.

CHAPTER FORTY-THREE

I left the bench and walked over to the wooded area near the boat launch, standing in the shade for a couple of minutes before heading to the bar. I had crossed over from soaking up the sun to sweating through my sports bra.

I looked around. Six days ago, I had sat here waiting to break up with Aaron. Now, I was waiting to get him back. Besides of being aware that I was screwing with his emotions, this felt different. I felt alone but at peace with my attempt to have him hold me again.

The last time, I'd thought someone had been watching me, and I didn't think I'd been wrong. That memory prompted me to head towards the bar, at least to the town square where more people would be walking around. I walked through the boat launch parking lot, where only about a dozen empty boat trailers were hooked up to trucks and SUVs. I saw Sheriff Thomas's—oops, former Sheriff Thomas's truck. I walked between two trucks and spied in the bed of his truck. There were several flattened beer cases, a fishing pole, and a cooler.

I didn't know why, but I stepped on the bumper and reached in, opening the cooler. I wanted to see if they were ready to party all afternoon. Oh, hell, the surprise was on me. That cooler held the fish they'd caught. And it appeared they hadn't properly cleaned it the last time they used it. I shut it fast, stepped down, and away from the truck.

I didn't know what had caused me to snoop. I got mad at myself. I have someone invading my life and chasing me down. What gives me the right to go into someone else's stuff, even if it is just a cooler? It was too easy to cross that line of curiosity to breaching personal space.

I continued towards the bar, and more so than during the walk to the river, I was highly aware of people on the street and what cars were driving past. I tried to memorize license plates but got jumbled up after two cars.

Reaching to open the door to the bar, I was nervous. I could have been setting myself up for failure, but if my goal was just to see him, what could really happen? I had to confront myself with all the possible emotions before I headed in so I could be more prepared. Maybe this is all a waste of effort if he's not even here.

No need to worry about that, because Aaron was the first thing I saw when I walked in. His arms were raised, and fists clenched like a champion boxer after a fight. He yelled, "Take that man!"

"Easy peasy. Stand back," Pete said. "This is not over yet." He fixated on a tower of small wooden blocks stacked precariously on the bar.

I took several steps inside. My heart skipped a beat or five when our eyes locked.

Aaron greeted me with a smile. Deep down, I knew that smile was for anyone walking into his bar, but it still made my stomach flip. His attention was drawn back to the game when Pete triumphantly placed his brick on top of the stack. Sherrie and Pete were concentrating on the game and were oblivious that I was there.

The place was slow, but had a few tables occupied. A group of six college students day drinking, several notebooks torn apart at their feet—probably celebrating the end of the summer term. Two women were enjoying pizza and, if I had to guess, diet sodas. Two townies took up seats on the short end of the bar away from the game, where I had sat a few days ago.

Three of the students started chanting Pete's name. The old guys didn't seem to care or to understand the game of Jenga and watched the golf tournament on TV.

One of the middle-aged ladies walked over to the college kids and said, "I got five bucks on Sherrie to win it."

"In a game of three players, there is not a winner, only a loser."

Another student nodded. "The last one to lay a brick on top is the winner."

The woman was apparently not up for a debate and wanted to have some fun. "Fine, five dollars, Aaron loses."

Only four of the students took up in the pool, each one picking the player who would lose the game. The other two didn't seem to be poor sports, but maybe just poor students.

Sherrie's move was swift and effective, with massive applause from the group of students. Aaron's turn was next. The second lady, who was still sitting, booed when everyone else clapped at Sherrie's success because she had put her money on Sherrie to lose. Pete went to the music controls and cranked up some death metal rock band, and everyone in the bar booed, and he caved and changed it back to softer rock music that could be heard on FM radio stations everywhere.

"I don't care what you do, Pete, you cannot ruin my concentration," Aaron proclaimed.

The game was nearly over for the lack of

reasonable possible remaining moves, but everyone had thought that on the last round as well. Aaron removed a block with a steady hand and was about to place it on top when one of the old men at the end of the bar slammed his fist and said, "Son, what does it take to get a fresh beer around here?"

The slender old man—probably a hundred twenty pounds soaking wet and unable to hold a pint of beer without his arm shaking when he drank—managed to smack the bar top enough for it to rattle the wood the entire length of the bar.

The tower of wood blocks shimmied. Everyone held their breath, and Aaron stood anxiously determining if he could safely rest his block on top. He went to make his move, and the tower collapsed, making him the loser.

The bar erupted in loud cheers. The women and college kids exchanged their money, and the old man laughed. Evidently, he knew the game and had planned his move perfectly.

Aaron shouted from the backside of the bar, "Earl, I should ban you from this place."

"Fine by me, but who would you have left in here?"

The old men chuckled and went back to watching the game.

Sherrie skipped over and hugged Earl. "Earl, I would have had it. There was no way Aaron could have made that move, but thank you for the assist."

She spun around and finally saw me. "When did you get here?"

"Just in time for the big win."

"What's up? Why are you here?" she asked.

I paused before I spoke. The two ladies had paid their tab and left. Two new guys came in, and Sherrie told them to have a seat wherever they liked.

"So?" she said.

"I just wanted to see him. I don't know, but I think I need to say something."

"Here? Now?"

"What have I got to lose?"

"Don't know if this is the place and time, but I am not you. I have to take their orders." She gestured toward the two guys who had come in. "Aaron went back to the office. At least there, you have some privacy."

She left to talk to the two guys, and I slowly took twenty-seven steps, counting because I was too nervous to do anything else.

The office was smaller than normal with two empty kegs and a life-size cardboard surfer holding a margarita advertising tequila. The surfer's face seemed to be all crumbled up, and someone had put a pink-and-aqua flannel shirt on him.

"Hey," I said, leaning against the doorway.

Aaron sat in the desk chair, looking at his

laptop.

He looked up. "Hi."

I couldn't read his expression. "I was wondering if we could talk for a second."

He closed his laptop and pushed his chair back but got stopped by the kegs. He slipped out of the chair, pushed it in, and stood behind it. "I'm glad you stopped in. I wanted to talk to you too."

My heart skipped again, and my stomach did a double flip. I willed myself to stay grounded.

"What's up with cardboard hang-ten dude?" I asked.

"That was a not-so-funny prank. The liquor delivery guys dropped this off with the order yesterday. Sherrie dressed him up and put him up by the water skis on the wall, but I thought it looked stupid, so I told them to move it when they closed up. This morning, when I unlocked the door, this was positioned in the doorway waiting for me and I kinda punched it. It was a reflex. I thought somebody was robbing me. I was going to save it and try and scare someone else."

"Great story. Let me guess—you're going after Chuck."

"That could be a good guess." He smiled.

Ahhhh, he smiled. My knees were weak.

"You wanted to see me?" he said.

"You go first. You said you had something to tell me." I couldn't spit out the words. I was too nervous, but maybe I wanted him to give me some encouragement to say it was ok to want him back.

"I don't know how to say this." He rubbed his chin, pondering.

This is it. I was right. He still wants me back. One hand was pinched around my keys, and the other was making my phone case sweaty. I was ready for him to pull me into his cramped office.

Wait, what did he say?

"Stop. Start over," I said.

He looked uncomfortable, shifting from foot to foot but his gaze never dropped from my face, so I knew he was not lying or making this up.

"This morning we had our BOMB meeting."

BOMB was the abbreviation for Business Owners Meeting Bimonthly, an informal group of business owners on or near the town square that got together twice a month to talk about things going on in the community. It was not a political group and had no real agenda other than keeping everyone updated on things in town and determining if they need to take action on something. I called it a bunch of people gossiping for an hour. Aaron had always said that was pretty accurate, but they always learned stuff, and if someone didn't show, they were likely to gossip about them.

He continued. "Today, the meeting was held here before we opened. I didn't hear the whole conversation, but Jim from Draw Tavern and Henry were talking about how much Teddy has been in lately, and he seems to have closed the bar a few nights. It didn't seem like he's caused any problems but has been quite the regular lately. Sorry."

"No need to apologize. You're just passing out information. I am really not that surprised to hear it."

"Your turn. You said you had something to say?" He tried to step back, but the empty kegs were in the way. He looked down when he talked, his face flushed.

Between me, in the doorway, surfer guy, and the two kegs behind him, he looked trapped.

"Why the empty kegs in the office? Especially an office of this size."

"Let's be honest. This is not an office but a broom closet. This was funny idea number two today. Pete was trying to tell me something about my beer selections. I'm not sure how empty kegs prove his point, but he wants something different on tap." He put his hands in his pockets. "I'm sure you didn't come here to talk about my office."

"You're right about that. Could we maybe go for a walk?"

He took a half step forward, and his foot hit the chair leg. I wanted to grab his hand, but he looked over my shoulder and yelled, "Pete, get these damn kegs out of here."

Pete was behind me in seconds, and I felt like sliced meat between two slices of bread. He seemed to have forgotten I was back here until he came sliding up.

"Hey, we got—"

"I was just yelling for you to get these kegs out. I got the message. I will get different beer when I want."

"Ok. Just trying to have some fun here. We got . . . we got game," Pete said, fumbling for words and his voice trailing off when he saw me.

I didn't know what that meant. I looked back down the length of the bar. One more table had filled up since I'd walked back here. It was a group of pretty college girls.

Aaron reached out and touched my elbow. He looked directly at me. "I think you should head home. We will catch up later."

I looked at the table, and I looked back at him. "Don't worry about it."

I turned and walked back. Sherrie stood behind the bar, smiling at me like a kid in a candy store. I shook my head to signal nothing had happened. Nothing happened.

We got game, whatever. Let the boys pick up college kids. I guessed I didn't matter anymore to him. Maybe Jo-Lee returned to her boyfriend, Adam, and Aaron wants to really win the breakup game.

Sherrie dropped the pitcher of beer at the table of hotties and caught up with me at the door. "Where are you running off to so fast?"

"Home to pout and rethink my bubble action."

"Bubble action—what?"

"It's nothing," I said. Her good mood was beginning to get under my skin.

"Officer Holton Patrick was just in here."

"You like saying his whole name."

Sherrie giggled. "He was only here for a minute before he got a call on his radio. He had to run, but I had a feeling he was going to ask me out. He made up some lame story about doing walking patrol around the square, but I think he was looking for an excuse to come see me."

"You got all that in the minute I was in back with Aaron."

She was shaking her head when Aaron walked up to us.

"Why don't you call it a short shift, Sherrie? We're not busy. You can go home with Claudia."

"I appreciate it, but it's Pete's turn to go early. I could use the hours, and whatever little tips are to be made tonight will add up to something."

"Sorry, but I made the call. You go and Pete is staying. Whatever you two worked out before can be saved for another time."

Flashing lights of a cop car through the window got everyone's attention. The car had stopped in front of the bar, double-parked, and Officer Patrick hopped out. He ran into the bar and stood in the doorway because the three of us were blocking the entrance area. "Sherrie, Claudia, I'm glad you're both still here. The call I just got was about a house fire." He had everybody's attention and quickly grasped that he had left out the important part of the story. "The address is eight-oh-three West Thirteenth Avenue."

Sherrie and I looked at each other and whispered, "Hells bells. EG's house!"

I pushed Officer Patrick out of the doorway and ran. Sherrie was a step behind me. One block later, the squad car drove past. We turned the corner onto our street. Fire trucks were lined up by the house.

While we ran the rest of the way, I couldn't help thinking a few hours ago my concern was that I would have to tell EG there was a dead animal under the house.

CHAPTER FORTY-FOUR

Two fire trucks and two squad cars were parked in front of the house. We stopped on the edge of the property near Jorge's driveway to get our bearings. The hose was hooked up to the hydrant in the front yard of the house on the other side of EG's, running down her driveway between the houses. Debby was parked at the edge of the driveway, and they were maneuvering around it. I couldn't see any flames, but smoke rose from the backyard.

I couldn't stand there any longer so I ran, following the hose. One firefighter yelled for us to get back to the sidewalk. Sherrie and I ignored him and went down the driveway and stood in front of the garage. The backside of the house above the doorway was beyond charred. I still didn't see flames, just a lot of smoke filling the sky.

Two retired couples, Frank and Mary and George and Alice, came out of their houses to get a good view. Three young teens rode up on their bikes so close to the hose the firefighter had to tell them to move back. Across the street, Mrs. Jolston had shut all the windows and drapes before coming outside with blankets. She covered up her plants like people do when the weather drops below freezing. Before she scurried into her house, she refused to look in Fred and George's direction after witnessing Alice carrying four beers out to the group. Maybe I wouldn't have to tell EG about this after all because Mrs. Jolston would take care of it before EG even gets out of the car.

"Claudia, you again," Officer Patrick said. "You're beginning to make me believe in my job security with all the action you provide the force."

I gave half a smile. He was only trying to lighten the mood and maybe comfort me, but it was just a reminder of everything that had happened. Had someone taken this too far?

Sherrie stood with her arms crossed, shaking her head. "Seriously, who did you piss off?"

My body was rigid, but inside, I was melting. My cheek started twitching. I was trying my best to hold my shit together.

Officer Patrick must have recognized my emotion of nearly breaking down when he called the fire captain over and introduced us as the house's occupants.

"This is only a preliminary report, but it looks like it is an electrical fire," the captain said.

"Not arson?" Sherrie asked.

"Can't rule if it was intentionally set. We just know it started in the exterior wall and did not spread beyond a few feet from what we can tell. The guys upstairs pulled apart the drywall beyond the fire damage to ensure the fire was contained to the one area. The power to the house has been terminated, and the gas has been shut off. It's best to find someplace to stay for a while. The investigation guys will be here for a bit longer, but the trucks will be gone shortly."

My feet felt like lead. The only thing moving were my lips. I heard everything he was saying as if it were in slow motion.

The captain continued. "You're lucky that he called it in so fast. The fire was contained mostly to the outside wall with the stairwell on the other side. A few minutes later, it could have reached the bedroom and those boxes of old papers, and this whole place would have gone. The silly garden hose did its job until we got here."

"I smelled something earlier. Could that have been . . ."

"Possibly, burning plastic or smell of fish, dead fish. As I said, preliminary findings suggest electrical."

"When can we go in?" I asked.

"Not for a while, but as I said, you are lucky he was here." The captain pointed toward the rear of the backyard and then walked back into the house.

I still was unable to move, and the shock of seeing Jackson standing back there rattled my brain. I could not process it until Sherrie confirmed it when she screamed his name. He stood there next to the fence like he was trying to blend into the background. His lips moved, but I couldn't hear him. Rage was building up. He stood there with his hands in his pockets, a baseball hat pulled down over his eyes. He shifted slightly. I had never seen him look so nervous.

"Jackson?" I screamed.

He didn't move. I don't know how I got to him. I don't know if I ran, walked, or flew the fifty yards to him. He was not moving.

I poked him in the chest. "You. You did this? What is the matter with you?"

He put up his hands to defend himself and stepped sideways towards Jorge's garage. I followed him. He walked backwards along the garage towards the house while I kept yelling at him until he'd had enough.

"Stop! I didn't do it. I tried stopping it. You heard the guy. Somebody tell her I'm right." He didn't look for the fireman or even Officer Patrick, who was watching this all play out. He was talking to the fence. He couldn't face anyone. Coward.

"What is going on? Why are you here? Don't say backpack!"

"I need the backpack," he said, still looking at the fence.

"I told you I don't have it. I never did."

"What was that all about dropping it in the river? Did you take it to the river?" "No! Get it through your head. I never had the backpack. Sherrie and I were just messing with you. We figured if you are too dumb not to understand that I don't have the backpack, you would be just smart enough to realize we were screwing with you." I poked him in the chest again, the anger coming out with every jab. "Sooner or later, the lazy side of you would emerge, and you'd assume we wouldn't dump it in the river."

"What? I need you to tell me where the backpack is."

"Are you seriously listening to music in your earbuds? This house is burning down, and you got tunes jamming through that head of yours. Stop shouting, take out your earbuds, and listen to me."

His face twitched, and sweat dropped from underneath the baseball hat. He hesitated before removing one earbud.

I continued my rally. "What is so important about this backpack I don't have? I have never seen you so crazy about something besides your guitars. Do you have music sheets in there?"

"Listen, I just need to get it back. When you moved here two months ago and I came to visit, I might have left it then. I'm not sure the last time I saw it. I cleaned out my apartment and it's not there. I don't know if I left it in your apartment back on campus or if it was in my car."

"So you came here, broke in to search the house, got pissed it wasn't here, and set fire to the house."

"I . . . I . . . I tried putting it out. Ask them." He looked at the fence. "Please, just help me."

"What does this damn backpack look like?" Sherrie demanded.

I nearly jumped, having forgotten she was there. I had pretty much forgotten about everyone watching this exchange, including Officer Patrick. I had thoroughly sweated through my sports bra, and the billowy shirt clung to my body with all the sweat and anger pouring out of me.

"What does it look like?" she asked again.

Jackson looked at me as if he was asking permission to speak to Sherrie.

"Answer her!" I roared.

"It's black with blue-and-green stripes with duct tape on the side."

Sherrie stepped forward. "You moron! That is not a backpack! That's a duffel bag. Do you know the difference? All you had to do was say duffel bag with duct tape, and you could have had your answer months ago. Fucking moron!"

She had everybody's attention. One fireman was leaning out Sherrie's bedroom window, and Officer Patrick had gone to the sidewalk to push back the kids on the bikes and maintain crowd control.

I turned to Sherrie, and almost in a whisper, I asked, "You have it?"

"No! We tossed it."

"Tossed it? Where? When?" Jackson was shaking and almost crying. "I need it. Where is it?"

"What's in it?" I asked.

Jackson just stood there. He was close to breaking down and couldn't answer.

Sherrie answered for him. "Just some dirty, sweating gym clothes. Maybe a month ago, when Mia and I were packing up the apartment, we found it behind the couch. She opened it, and the smell was so retched she zipped it up and tossed it in the donation pick up pile."

"What pile? What donation pile? Did you drive it somewhere?" Jackson asked, practically begging.

"Back off!" Sherrie yelled.

He was hitting a nerve with her now.

"Don't you pay attention to anything on campus besides yourself? Seriously, what did you see in this guy?" She looked at me.

I had no answer for her. I was surprised he was taking all her shit. I thought he would have walked out at this point.

She shook her head. "At the end of each school year, the dorms and apartment complexes coordinate with different charities. They set up big metal containers so students moving out can donate stuff instead of it all going to the dump."

"What about the stuff in the backpack . . .?" Jackson's voice trailed off, and we could barely hear him.

"Duffel bag," she said, and someone laughed. "We didn't take anything out. The smell was so bad. Mia unzipped it, and a few seconds later, she closed it. If I remember right, she took that and the kitchen floor mats straight to the donation bin. I laughed when she said she put it in the donation bin instead of the garbage. What is the big deal?"

Jackson looked beaten down, then more scared than ever. He was frozen in place but again turned towards the fence. "Help me." He paused and put his hand to his ear. "What color was the container? Did it have a logo from the charity?"

Sherrie snickered. "I think the one nearest our building where Mia would have gone was a rusty-brown color. It had a penis and a chicken spray-painted on it. I think. I had to pass a few of them on the way to campus, but I definitely remember the penis and chicken."

"So, you don't know where it is now?" Jackson said softly. His shoulders slumped.

Branches snapped behind the garage, and I turned.

Someone was charging Jackson. He screamed, "You are going to pay you son of a bitch!"

CHAPTER FORTY-FIVE

If the fire had me in shock, what happened next put me into a different universe. Within seconds, a guy had pummeled Jackson to the ground and got one punch in before Jackson rolled over.

In a gargled voice, Jackson tried shouting, but I could only understand "Help . . . protect—"

Another noise came from behind me. A guy flew over the fence—in one motion, his hand was on the top of the fence, and his legs swept over horizontally like a gymnast on the pommel horse, and his dismount was solid but swift as he took three strides, reaching Jackson and the other guy in less than two seconds.

The firefighter, who had been leaning out the second-story window, was now between the back door and the three scuffling on the ground.

His feet were solidly planted and arms stretched out with a gun pointed at Jackson and the other guy.

I stepped closer to Sherrie. We locked our arms and took two slow steps backward, whispering, "Hells bells."

The fence jumper flattened the guy that had come after Jackson. His knee was on his back, and his hand was on his head. Jackson remained on the ground until Officer Patrick came back and helped him up. His nose was bleeding, and he was crying.

The guy on the ground continued to yell obscenities at Jackson.

"Where were you guys? You promised I would be fine." Jackson reached for his nose. "This is all your fault."

I didn't know who Jackson was talking to, but he was no longer talking to the fence.

"What is going on here?" I said, not sure if anyone but Sherrie heard me. It felt like this was the world's shittiest mystery, and somehow, I was a character in it. I stepped forward, but Sherrie pulled me back.

She elbowed me and whispered, "It's him and . . . and."

She stopped talking, and we silently pieced the puzzle together.

All the other firemen had disappeared. I could not see anyone on the sidewalk. Only the six of us remained in this soap opera.

The fence jumper was Khaki Guy Number One from the bar. He cuffed the guy on the ground and pulled him up.

Sherrie and I looked at each other, eyes wide. It was Brady. He stood there cuffed and yelling.

The fireman slipped out of the oversized yellow firefighter jacket and stepped out of the pants. Underneath came Khaki Number Two. Still in khakis and this time in a black T-shirt and a badge hanging around his neck. Khaki Guy Number One was wearing a blue windbreaker, and below that was his badge and shoulder holster.

Brady, still cuffed, still yelling at Jackson, was calling him an idiot among other names. Khaki Number Two told him to shut his mouth before he was arrested for stupidity. Brady opened his mouth to challenge him, but quickly changed his mind.

Khaki Number One stepped towards Sherrie and me. "I'm Special Agent in Charge Fitzhugh, and that's Agent Moekel, FBI. We want to search the house. Do we have your permission?"

"Search?" I asked.

"How about a warrant?" Sherrie said.

"It will be here shortly, but we'd rather expedite this and be out of your way."

"I am not the owner."

"We know. As a legal occupant, you can

consent."

Everybody was looking at me.

"Give me a minute." I pulled Sherrie back and whispered, "I don't know what's going on, but I think I'm going to allow them in, but is there anything you wouldn't want them to find?"

She hesitated. I could see her mind wheeling around. "All good on my part, but I don't think we have a choice."

We walked back to the group.

"Kha . . . sorry, Agent . . . Fitzhugh. Agent Fitzhugh, you may search the house, but I will tell you there is a registered gun in the first-floor bedroom in a locked box in the closet."

"Really?" Sherrie said from behind me.

Agent Fitzhugh made a call. Thirty seconds later, several men and one dog stepped out of a van parked across the street, and we heard some commotion on the sidewalk. EG's house on the left and Jorge's house on the right gave us a limited view of the show unfolding in front.

The onlookers on the sidewalk had returned, and Officer Patrick went to push back the crowd, trying to get a hold of the situation. We heard him telling another officer to allow someone through. We looked around to see who he was talking about and saw Jorge walking down his driveway. He cut through the grass and walked into the backyard toward us.

"Took you long enough to get here," Sherrie said.

"Why are you yelling at him?" I asked.

"Because I don't know what else to do. I texted him like a million years ago when we were watching them put out the fire."

He looked at Jackson and the others before coming up to us and putting his hands on our shoulders. "Are you ok?"

We nodded but said nothing.

"What's happening here?" he asked.

"You would not believe it if we told you. Actually, we aren't quite sure ourselves."

"Jackson, what is going on?" I took four giant steps and was in his face. "Speak now, or would you rather have me hear it from them?"

"I will tell—" Brady said, but Khaki Number Two—I mean Agent Moekel held up his hand and said, "You don't get to talk. You almost blew the whole thing."

Blood trickled down Jackson's lip, and his nose and eyes were puffy. I was sure those eyes would slowly develop a nice black-and-blue coloring.

"Start talking. Take out your headphones. They are standing in front of you, so stop talking to the fence and start telling me what's going on." I was losing my patience, and I turned towards the agents.

Jackson spoke like a scolded toddler. "Remember that bar my band played at a few times in Chicago?" He waited and realized no one needed to answer. "Back in May, after a gig, we were packing up, and I grabbed the bartender Michael's backpa—Michael's duffel bag by mistake. I thought it was no big deal. It turns out—"

Even with his arms still cuffed behind, Brady lunged for Jackson, kicking at him, but he got pulled back by Agent Moekel before he made impact.

"You are going to let him get away with it!" Brady shouted. "How could you do this to her? Somebody has to give her peace." He broke down crying, hanging his head and turning away from us.

Agent Moekel stepped back, giving him space.

Agent Fitzhugh had had enough of the slow talk. "Michael Ariens and his business partner, Quinn, are currently in federal custody being held under three federal charges including drug possession, intent to sell, and first-degree manslaughter with other federal and state charges pending."

"She did not deserve to die. She was not supposed to be there. He is going to get away with it," Brady said through gritted teeth, waving his arms in anger. "Let me out of these cuffs. I did nothing wrong."

"Not until you calm down," Agent Moekel said.

"We believe nineteen-year-old Alicia Stretton, sister to Brady Stretton, was with her boyfriend, Kurt Lidger, when he tried to make a deal with Michael and Quinn. Things went from bad to worse, and Ms. Stretton was shot and found dead three days later. We're here in search of that gun and other items."

"The . . . duffel . . . bag," I said, putting the pieces together.

"Yes, ma'am," said Agent Fitzhugh.

"That's why you are searching the house, the fire, and all this commotion because I . . . because she made me send some lame text because dipshit didn't know the difference between a damn backpack and duffel bag!"

I didn't wait for anyone to say anything and started after Jackson, jabbing him in the chest, trying to pound out answers. He was holding his nose and using his other arm to defend himself from me. He flinched to his right, and I saw past him.

The police had opened the road back up, and a truck slowly drove past. The face I'd wanted to see all day looked back through the window. He was coming here for me, I thought, but then he smiled with relief when our eyes met. He looked away and kept driving.

Jackson had put his arm out in defense, but it must have looked like some type of embrace to Aaron. He had it all wrong.

He thinks I wanted to tell him about Jackson but he could not be more wrong.

I felt like I had been punched in the gut. I had no energy left to fight Jackson.

I looked at Brady. "I am so sorry for the loss of your sister. I can't imagine what you're going through."

He didn't say anything.

"I don't understand what he is doing here," Sherrie pointed to Brady.

"I was at the bar when it got raided. I went to confront Ariens. He didn't know who I was. I decided to order a beer and get a feel for the fool. The next thing I know, the doors are busted down and Ariens is gone. Before those of us seated at the bar got tossed out, I heard about the band that was setting up. When they were detained, I knew there was some connection. I tracked down Jackson and forced him to tell me what he knew. I guess later, these guys finally made a deal with him to come up here thinking the back—the duffel bag was here."

I turned to the agents. "You guys were at BAR the other day."

"We just got to town, were waiting for our

assignment details, and needed some place to eat. The fact that you were all there was a coincidence," Agent Moekel said.

"Sherrie, listen," Brady said. "All that crap I said at the bar was a lie. Well, not all of it—I do like you. I just freaked out when Claudia mentioned Jackson, and then I realized who the two of you are. I didn't want you to think I was using you. Flirting just so you would get me the evidence. I thought it would be better for you to hate me than to think I was being nice and using you. I had to do something for my baby sister. Her killer needs to pay. I didn't know these guys were going to be here. I wanted the evidence found. I couldn't leave it up to him."

"I don't want to hear any of that. It was wrong, all wrong, and I am not sure I believe anything you have to say. I am sorry about your sister, but don't give me any more lines. What you said is never acceptable in any situation," Sherrie said.

"What about Chuck, Ryan, and Clint? Do they know?" I asked.

"No! It was just luck that I knew Chuck and Clint here in town. That was a great excuse to get Ryan to come with me. I told him we could fish and golf for a few days before he left for his job. I thought he might be of use if I needed backup, but then he got all tangled up with what's-her-face."

"Kay. Her name is Kay," I said, crossing my arms.

This guy was exhausting, and I understood he must be in pain, but that did not excuse his behavior.

I turned to the agents and asked, "Did you know who he was when you dragged him out?"

"Just thought he was a twit who was about to get his ass kicked by a girl," Agent Moekel said.

Sherrie stepped forward. "Is that embarrassing for you? Having a woman kick your ass?"

"Now is not the time," I said.

Jorge joined the conversation. "So let me get this straight. Right now the FBI is searching the house for a duffel bag that is several hours away." He chuckled.

"What's so funny?" I asked.

Jorge stole my line. "Now is not the time," he said to me and continued to speak to the group. "What about the fire?"

Agent Fitzhugh said, "According to the captain, that was an electrical fire. Something sparked in the wall. Jackson being here waiting for you probably saved the house from further damage."

"I had to come to the house because you blocked my phone. I smelled something and came back here and saw the flames. I grabbed the hose and called 9-1-1." He looked proud of himself.

Agent Moekel said, "Yeah, that's how he stepped up."

Jackson's look of pride withered away.

With the voice of a whiny adolescent kid, Moekel said, "Fire, fire, there's a fire!"

"Agent Moekel! Now is not the time," Agent Fitzhugh hissed, but his lip twitched in a motion that could have been considered a slight smile.

"Did you know he was in the bushes? How long have you been there? At the O'Brien's."

"They had no clue I was there," Brady barked.

"Really? Who do you think was chucking acorns at you? When I realized you weren't going to budge, we let you sit. We I'D you after the incident at the bar and hoped we scared you out of town. You should not have risked Jackson's mission to get the girls to tell him where the backpack was." No one corrected Agent Fitzhugh.

"We had someone posted at the O'Brien's for a few days for Jackson to come on board with our plan."

"What? Where are they? Why there? Why not come to us directly?" I asked.

"The O'Briens are fine," Agent Fitzhugh said.

"Fine? What crap is that?" Sherrie said.

Fitzhugh stood with his hands on his hips. "Look, we don't have to—"

I was done. There came a breaking point in every high-pressure situation that would send someone over the edge, and Mr. Blue–Windbreaker-and-Badge-Wearing, No–Emotion-Having Classified Government Agent had just pushed me off that cliff. "Right, you don't have to tell us squat. You stand there with no evidence to be found in that house, your key witness has a broken nose, and I am not sure that guy should be in handcuffs. You know, that guy over there who you let invade your stakeout." My voice got louder and louder as I spoke.

Nobody volunteered to hold me back.

"At least have some guts and make up a story to tell me as I am sure you gave the O'Briens some BS story."

Agent Fitzhugh did not budge or crack a smile. "Yes, ma'am. We told them we were with the gas company and needed to repair the line feeding through the backyard. They decided it was best to head to the cabin."

It appeared they were playing good cop, funny cop.

Agent Moekel added, "They didn't buy our gas company story. We showed them our badges, and they offered up the house and yard without question as to who we were watching. On the way out, Mr. O'Brien told us beer was in the fridge in the garage and the good cookies were above the microwave."

"He is a retired detective from Milwaukee. He could spot you guys a mile away," Jorge said.

"We didn't know how connected you were to Jackson and if he was protecting you or if you truly did not know about the bag. We couldn't risk exposing us with the search of one house when you had time to move it anywhere."

Agent Khaki Number Three came down the driveway and approached Agent Fitzhugh. It was meant to be a one-on-one exchange, but nobody was moving, not even Agent Fitzhugh. "All clear but . . ." He dropped his voice lower, so we couldn't hear the rest of what Khaki Number Three said.

Agent Fitzhugh looked at him pointedly. "How much?"

Khaki Number Three gave an inaudible answer.

Fitzhugh nodded. "That's fine. Leave it."

Jorge laughed at that. I couldn't imagine what was so funny.

Fitzhugh said for all the men to clear out of the house and let the fire captain resume his investigation.

Of all people, Jackson spoke next. "Can I use the restroom?"

"The captain has to clear the house before anyone can go in, and I'm not sure you will be able to return at all today," Fitzhugh said.

Jorge gestured towards his house. "He can use—"

I fiercely interrupted, "No! He does not get to go inside anywhere. Go take a leak behind the garage. Seriously, go now. I can't stand to look at you anymore."

He looked at the agents, who didn't budge. He seemed to have to pee so badly that he didn't care. He trotted over to the other side of the garage.

I turned to Jorge. "I didn't mean to snap at you. You're very kind. He is worried about peeing, and I am worried about telling EG about her house. However, could you get him some ice and a rag to wipe up his nose?"

Jorge left with a nod, and Sherrie and I just looked at each other in disbelief and moved under the oak tree for shade. The two agents conferred, and Brady just stood there, still cuffed. Jackson returned from the backside of the garage, and Officer Patrick moved to help Jorge, who was returning with ice for Jackson and bottled waters for everyone else. I'd forgotten Officer Patrick was even there.

Officer Patrick brought Sherrie and me our waters and stayed with us. I stepped away a couple of feet, letting them have a semiprivate moment while I listened to the whole conversation.

"Are you ok?" Officer Patrick asked Sherrie. "The two of you have seen some crazy stuff."

Sherrie smiled, twisting her toe in the dirt. She seemed nervous. "You know, just the typical week in River Bend."

"Now that this is all clear, how about I come over one day when I'm not in uniform and maybe ask you out?"

"You don't need to wait," Sherrie said.

"Yes, I don't mix the two. I feel out-of-bounds while there's someone in handcuffs, but I wanted you to understand my position."

"I appreciate that. Well, you know where I work and live, so I'll leave it up to you."

He walked over to the agents and spoke in a hushed voice that we couldn't hear. Sherrie came over and shrugged her shoulders with a small smile.

I whispered, "I thought you would be happier."

"I don't know about that line 'I don't mix the two', but I will ask you some time. That is kinda weasel-like. Do it or don't do it."

"How about you date him before you break up with him," I said.

"I'll go on a date if he ever asks, but all this gets me thinking about dating a cop. Is this a good thing?" She seemed to be asking herself.

We stood there for what felt like forever but was probably ten minutes, listening to the fireman going through the house.

Agent Fitzhugh took a call, grunting a few times before he finished and put the phone away. He looked at Agent Moekel. "All good, we're done here." He turned to Sherrie and me. "Sorry for the disturbance." And then something from a previous sensitivity course must have kicked in. "Sorry about the house, best of luck."

He turned his back to us like he just disconnected a call and took a step to leave.

"Wait a minute. Is that all we get?" I said.

Nobody moved. We were not in the mood for a cliff-hanger.

Agent Fitzhugh looked a bit peeved. "The team on the ground near your old apartment located the duffel bag."

Brady, who had been standing there, handcuffed, rather patiently, stepped towards Agent Fitzhugh, but Agent Moekel blocked him.

Fitzhugh continued. "The charity had not gone through all the metal containers they'd picked up, and from your description, they were able to locate it quickly. They found the bag with the weapon, drugs, and other items."

Agent Fitzhugh looked at Brady. "We got the son of a bitch. Your sister's murderer will get what he has coming to him."

Brady broke down crying. Agent Moekel uncuffed him and led him to the back fence, where he kneeled down and cried.

Agent Fitzhugh turned to Jackson. "You held up your end of the bargain, and Ariens corroborated your story that you mistakenly took the bag, undoubtedly not knowing what was in it." He addressed us again. "Michael didn't know Quinn had hidden the bag behind the stage in the bar until a few weeks later when he went to retrieve it and found a very similar looking bag instead. Quinn and Michael invited your band back to play to figure out what happened to their bag. That night our agents showed up and put this all into play. You will probably have to testify if Quinn and Michael don't take a plea agreement."

Jackson went from pale to ghostly sick.

Agent Fitzhugh looked to Sherrie. "The same goes for you and your roommate. I will need a written statement providing a timeline of the possession of the bag and the names of others who may have had access to the apartment."

"How did it end up in our apartment?" I asked Jackson.

"After our gig at the bar, I showed up at your place at, like, two in the morning. I grabbed what I thought was my backpa—duffel bag—from the van when the guys dropped me off. You let me in, and I tossed the bag towards the futon but missed, and it must have slid underneath. You were still mad about me missing lunch with your parents after your graduation ceremony. You didn't understand I had to set up and play a gig that night, so you wouldn't let me stay over. I got mad and left, forgot I even brought the bag inside."

I closed my eyes and lowered my head. "Leave. Just leave." I had no energy left for this guy.

"C'mon, it's not my fault. You heard them. I didn't know what was in the bag!"

"Not your fault. Such a moron. Leave!"

"Ease up. Let's get something to eat, and I'm sure at some point this could be a funny story." Jackson thought that was funny until he saw Brady's face.

Agent Moekel put his hand gently on Brady's shoulder.

"Sorry, man. I mean about your sister. That's not funny," Jackson mumbled.

"Leave now," I said calmly.

"I have no car," Jackson said.

"Get out!" I screamed. "The next time I see you better be in the courtroom, and thank god for you that there will be witnesses and guards around. So help me if I see you or get one text message from you, I will crush you."

"Are you threatening me?" he said.

Agent Moekel shook his head. "I heard no

threat."

I looked at Agent Fitzhugh. "You got him here. You get him out of here, and by here, I mean River Bend."

"Yes, ma'am."

Officer Patrick stepped up and asked Jackson, "Sir, would you like to press any charges against that man for assault?"

He touched his nose, not looking at anyone. "No," he said and walked towards the front of the house.

Agent Moekel said to Brady, "You are also clear to go, but I must advise you to stay away from this house, these women, that man out front, and the investigation. Any further action taken that affects this case in any way, you will be charged with interfering with a federal investigation. You could have done more harm than good. The people responsible for your sister's death will be held accountable. Do you understand me?"

Brady nodded and looked at Sherrie and me. She started to speak but stopped and remained stoic.

"Officer, will you walk Mr. Stretton away from here? Make sure he gets in his car. Also, let the other one know someone will come by in five minutes to pick him up, but best to stay in the front yard for now." Agent Fitzhugh turned to us. "Ladies, sorry for the disturbance. We appreciate your help."

"What about Mia, our roommate?" Sherrie asked.

"Someone has already made contact. We ask you to not discuss this with anyone until it is all over. There is an agent up front to take your statements."

Agent Fitzhugh walked towards the garage and down EG's driveway.

Agent Moekel walked closer. "We appreciate your honesty. Sorry about the house. Please tell EG her books are great."

"You read her books?" I didn't know why that surprised me.

"Not until I got to town. I think Mr. O'Brien consults for her. He had a manuscript lying out with notes written on it. After I read it, I picked up a book he had of hers. Good Book, but if she ever has questions on a federal case, she can give me a call."

He pulled out a business card and held it up until I took it, and he walked away.

"I guess they get bored when staking out a house. The house, this house," I said to Sherrie. Something occurred to me. "Wait," I yelled. "Obviously, you have been watching us. I got a question for you. Have you noticed anyone else watching us or anything strange?"

"Good thought," Sherrie whispered.

"Don't worry, ladies. Quinn and Ariens are not getting out. They have no reason to look for you."

"That's not what I meant, but good to know. Anything strange going on here?"

"You having problems?" Agent Moekel asked.

Despite having a federal agent at my disposal, I felt too anxious to speak up for myself. Although I was the victim, I was scared to look like a fool for saying something. I'd had all the roar and control drained out of me this afternoon. If something were wrong, he would have to tell me.

"No problems, just taking advantage of what you may have seen," I said.

"Besides Miller and his car that keeps passing by. He has a clean record. We ran a check on 'em."

"Miller?" I asked.

"We give everyone code names. By chance, we had first seen him coming out of Spirits and Things, and we ran everyone's plates that came near the house. Seems like a busy family."

"I get it. I know who you mean. Thank you, I know you were probably not supposed to share that." I gave a weak smile.

He walked towards the driveway softly singing "Ebony and Ivory" by Stevie Wonder.

Sherrie whispered, "I don't get it? Miller?"

"Miller beer. Teddy was probably walking out of the liquor store with a case of beer."

"Hey, wait. I got a question for you," Sherrie yelled.

Agent Moekel looked like we were overworking him until I casually waved his business card like a mini paper fan in front of my face. I was definitely giving off the vibe that said if you want credit in a book by a famous author, you better play nice with us.

"There is more in that duffel bag than your partner let on before," she said.

He used his pinky finger to pick something out of his tooth. "I don't know what you're talking about. All details are classified." And he walked away still softly singing.

In the months that were to come, Sherrie and I closely followed the case online and with the help of EG's friends on the Chicago PD. We were never called to testify because Quinn and Ariens took a deal before it got to court. We would later learn that when Alicia Stretton's body had been found, she was missing her two pinky fingers. Sadly, Quinn had done this with two previous victims.

I asked Sherrie what had made her ask the question in the backyard that day, and she said the more she'd thought about it and the smell coming from the duffel bag, it had to be something much worse than sweaty gym clothes and a half-eaten sandwich.

Much worse. Just like our evening was about to be—much worse.

CHAPTER FORTY-SIX

Sherrie had gone into Jorge's house with Khaki Pants Agent Number Four and wrote up her statement, and then we switched places. I finished my statement and stayed in the kitchen at the makeshift island made of a sheet of plywood, two sawhorses, and three mismatched chairs with my head in my hands, thinking about the last few hours.

The only image I vividly saw was Aaron's face when he'd driven past and witnessed Jackson reaching out to me. There was no smoke, no fire, and no federal agents. There was only his smile in the office at BAR, and then my mind jumped right to that look of disdain as he drove past.

A few minutes later, Sherrie, Jorge, and the fire captain walked in. Sherrie took a seat next to me, and Jorge grabbed a bottle of water for the captain and stood by the sink behind me. I extended my hand to the captain, offering him the third seat, but he declined.

He was wearing dark-blue pants and a navy polo shirt that hugged his belly, every beer he'd guzzled, and every nacho he'd eaten in his fifty-something years of life. I don't think he could pass the physical to get into the academy now, but he held command of the three of us.

"I understand that's EG's house."

I nodded. "She's on a cruise and will be back in a few days. I can try to call the cruise company and get a message to her."

"That's up to you. You're lucky someone was there when the fire broke out."

I rolled my eyes. I did not want to have to thank Jackson for anything right now.

The captain continued. "The fire started in the wall above the back door. The wiring in the house is original and is probably older than I am. Look at the shape I'm in. At least I got layers to protect me." He put his hand on his belly like Santa, laughing at his own joke before continuing. "It is not that uncommon for houses built in that time period to have walls stuffed with newspapers and other flammable material for insulation."

I was sitting upright like a child on the first day of school listening to the teacher, and suddenly, my stomach dropped. The feeling someone might have gotten in class when they thought they knew the answers, but then the teacher asked about the one chapter they didn't read. And they would pray she didn't call on them. I slowly raised my hand but kept my elbow at my side because I was nervous about my question and his answer.

"Would me accidentally pulling on the light fixture above the back door cause the wires to spark?"

"This is not a confessional." He smiled, waiting for someone to laugh this time, and Jorge volunteered a chuckle. "That very well could be. Although it was only a matter of time. Any fierce wind or heavy ice sitting on the light sconce could have pulled it out. Upon inspecting the house, I'm surprised it didn't happen on the porch. That wiring and the wood framework is a giant tinderbox. EG gives you any problems, let me know and I will explain to her it was only a matter of time."

"I appreciate that, but if you know EG, she will end up consoling me."

"You got that right. I do have some bad news for the two of you now."

"That wasn't it?" Sherrie asked.

"I can't let you back in the house. Well, at least upstairs for sure and in the basement, you can go in with one of my men for a minute to grab what you need. The water damage was confined to the house's rear wall, the back quarter of the bedroom on the south side of the house, and the stairwell leading up to the second has been compromised, so no going up or below it to the basement. While most of the house has very little damage to the structure, the smoke has infiltrated most everything. Power and gas have been cut off. You will need to find someplace to stay for a while."

"They can stay here," Jorge offered.

"I will leave that up to you. But you need to secure the back of the house. Officially, I can't recommend anyone, but if you ask my guys at the house, they know a couple of cleaning services that can help. They will be there for about another twenty or thirty minutes if you want to get in."

"Thank you for all the information," I squeaked out.

"Have EG contact my department if she needs the report for insurance. Don't beat yourself up. It was only a matter of time."

I silently nodded, and Jorge stepped forward, shook the captain's hand, and started to walk him out.

As they were leaving the kitchen, the captain turned back and said, "Usually, my department is the headline story, but we got upstaged by the feds. I hoped that all worked out for you."

That was a punch to the gut. Jorge walked the captain to the front door, Sherrie stood up and paced behind me. I put my head in my hands again.

Jorge came back to the kitchen. "Are you girls ok?"

I sat back up, put my hands in my lap, and my shoulders drooped like I'd just played ninety minutes of basketball. "I guess we're ok. Sherrie? What do you think?"

She grabbed the kitchen chair, sat down, and put her feet up on the plywood table. "I say we're ok."

"I was serious about what I said about you staying here. I will go someplace else."

"You don't have to do that. We can stay with Kay and Jenna," I said.

"No way! EG would do the same for me and my family. You know that," he said.

Sherrie and I nodded in agreement.

"And she would absolutely kick my butt and yours if you are not somewhere I can make sure you guys are fed and have a decent place to stay."

I held up my hands, accepting the truth of his words. "You're right."

"Why don't you guys go see what you can salvage from the house before they won't let you in. Phil, from the hardware store, is on the way with some tarps and plywood so we can secure the opening in the rear wall. He is also bringing a wet-vac, but I don't know if it's needed. Don't worry about that stuff. Phil and I will take care of it. Just get what you need."

I jumped up and gave him a hug. Everybody needed a Jorge in their life. Sherrie gave him a high five when she walked past. We walked around to the front door, and all the commotion was cleared away except one fire truck. The hose was cleaned up, and all the spectators were gone. Mrs. Jolston still had her shrubs covered and shades down.

"We need a game plan. We have to get upstairs. For Christ sake, I can't wear this flannel shirt for the next week."

I noticed for the first time that she still had her black apron tied around her waist.

"You're right. Do we sweet talk them, maybe storm the stairs? Can they stop us both?"

"Do we really want to charge a stairwell that has been compromised?" Sherrie said.

"Good point. Let's just wing it. I am too mentally drained to come up with strategies."

We could not use the stairs or convince them otherwise. We compromised that we could enter Sherrie's bedroom window using one of their ladders. Only one of us was allowed up. I grabbed some empty trash bags and literally pushed Sherrie aside so I could climb the ladder.

The water damage was in the back half of

Sherrie's room, but it only affected the boxes of old research materials. I pushed them apart so the mold would not build up, but the fireman stopped me. He was only giving me five minutes.

I filled up two bags' worth of Sherrie's clothes, and the fireman tossed them out the window. I went to my bedroom and did the same. I went back through both of our rooms and collected our laptops and phone chargers. The fireman went to the window as if he was going to toss the bag out, and I freaked. He apparently thought this was funny and said he would carry it down. I went to the bathroom to get our toiletries. The fireman yelled at me to hurry up.

I had no idea what Sherrie needed for her hair. She would have rolled her eyes if she'd been there. The bag was getting really heavy, but I risked it pulling apart and I grabbed everything of hers I could. It is the least I could do for her. I did one last look at the rooms—I hadn't noticed that everything was slightly out of place from when the agents had searched the house.

I climbed down the ladder. Jorge had already taken the garbage bags to his house. Sherrie gathered up some of EG's stuff and grabbed the perishable food. When I returned from carrying the electronics bag to Jorge's, Phil was in the backyard with another guy boarding up the giant hole in the house. Fire damage had been contained pretty fast, but the firemen had torn away some of the siding to make sure there were no other hot spots.

I couldn't believe I was standing there thinking I was lucky Jackson had been there to call the fire department. The image of him standing there with the little garden hose trying to undo the kinks so the water could flow, then the firemen showing up with their big hose made me laugh.

Sherrie and Jorge came around the corner. "What's so funny? Because nothing looks funny to me," Sherrie said.

"I either need to laugh or cry. Laughing seems like less energy. I was thinking of Jackson trying to get the hose and running around like a maniac. Speaking of which, what was making you laugh before?" I asked Jorge.

Sherrie turned to him. "Yeah, what was all that about?"

Jorge smiled, holding out on us. Finally, it seemed he decided he should tell us. "Hell, EG will probably tell you. Remember, after the search, the agent came out to talk to Agent Fitzhugh, and Fitzhugh asked 'How much?' They must have found EG's stash."

"Stash? She's got weed!" Sherrie said rather loudly.

Jorge nodded. "It makes her feel better after chemo treatments."

"I could use a hit about now," Sherrie said.

"I can't believe you let the FBI in to search. It's not a lot, but more than someone should have in this state."

"Not so loud." I pointed over my shoulder to Phil and the guy helping him.

That got another chuckle out of Jorge. He stepped forward and grabbed a hammer to help board up the house. He turned back to us and nodded towards Phil. "Who do you think gave it to her?"

CHAPTER FORTY-SEVEN

The fireman left but not before informing us that we could not enter the house for any reason and doing so could result in a fine or worse. Phil told us EG could pay for the materials anytime, and to call if he could do anything for us. Sherrie started to speak, but I elbowed her so fast that she understood this was not the time to score some weed. We just said thank you and goodbye.

We went back to Jorge's. A voice called us into the kitchen. Addie was in there, and on the plywood table were three square tin containers full of hot food.

"I was at the grocery store when Jorge texted me what was going on. I wanted to help, and the only thing I could think of was food. I got some fried chicken, mac and cheese, and steak fries. I figured comfort food at a time like this would be good for the soul. I also got a jumbo Greek salad in case the calories are too much.

I picked up a piece of chicken and sat down before I said hello and thank you. After my first bite, I introduced Sherrie and Addie.

Sherrie took a chair, and Addie sat on the counter.

"Girls, I didn't know if you were beer or wine or—"

"Beer us," Sherrie and I said in unison.

Jorge pulled three beers out of the fridge. After handing us our beer, he gave Addie a kiss on the cheek and stood next to her.

"Thank you. Thank you both," I said.

With a mouthful of food, wiping the grease off her chin, Sherrie echoed, "Yes, thank you."

"Let's get a few things straight here. Enough with the thank you. As I said before, you both would do this for me, and EG would kick my butt if I didn't help. One key is over there, and I will grab a second key later. The house is yours for as long as you need it. I will be here in the evenings working in the garage and finishing this kitchen. The downstairs bathroom is working just fine, but the floor tiles are back-ordered," Jorge said.

Addie said, "I threw a load of towels in the washer so you will have clean towels, free of sawdust. I grabbed extra paper plates at the store.

From the stories EG was telling me, this kitchen may take years to finish, and the real china may be a decade away from seeing the light of day. I bought laundry detergent if you want to start washing your clothes."

"You know EG?" I asked.

"Oh, she introduced me to Jorge! I have known her for a few years. I have a loft in the same building as she does in Chicago, and she told me about the open visiting professor position at Jameson College."

I watched soon-to-be graduate student Sherrie straighten up in her chair. She reached for a napkin to wipe her face.

"I'm teaching several botany classes this summer and will be here for the fall and spring classes."

"Welcome to River Bend," I said with a mouth full of fried chicken. I hadn't known I was hungry until I'd seen the chicken and hadn't stopped eating since I'd sat down.

"If you don't mind me asking, what happened to your arm?" Addie asked.

"I broke it back in May and just got the cast off. I was hoping the zombie look was going to make a comeback."

"Jorge, go to the garage and get the gloves I brought over the other day."

He rolled his eyes but did as he was told.

Addie hopped off the counter, dug through a milk crate full of spices, and pulled out coconut oil.

"I helped him stain the kitchen cabinets, and I was not about to ruin my manicure, so I brought these big yellow gloves over here. If you can eat one-handed, give me that arm."

The coconut oil had the consistency of butter sitting in baby oil. She gently coated my arm and then slipped on the big yellow glove. "Do this every other day for a few days, and it will be looking as good as new. Just be careful when you take off the glove; your hand will be oily and a little sweaty."

"That's awesome. Thank you."

After we'd eaten, Addie and Jorge left but not before he pulled me aside and asked if I was really ok and if I'd had any more problems with people following me.

I assured him Sherrie and I were fine. He was embarrassed by either the big hug I gave him or the two thumbs-up I gave him when I said that Addie was a good catch and he shouldn't let this one get away.

CHAPTER FORTY-EIGHT

Ten minutes later, I was standing in Jorge's backyard when Sherrie joined me. "What are you doing out here? I was calling your name for five minutes. I couldn't figure out the washing machine. By the way, the laundry room is upstairs next to the master bedroom. That was half my problem. I was trying to open a jammed door in the basement, thinking the washing machine was in there."

"Sometimes you leave me speechless," I said.

She rolled her eyes. "Whatever. Seriously, what are you doing out here?"

"I was putting the dinner containers in the trash cans, and I couldn't help but look at EG's house. I can't believe I started a fire."

"You? It was me who needed the ladder."

"But I'm the one who broke the bulb and yanked the fixture from the house."

Sherrie looked at me pointedly. "Only because I wanted to paint."

"We could do this all night—playing who is more to blame," I said.

"The captain said it was only a matter of time."

"I know, but what a way to come back from a cruise. EG has a summer of chemo treatments and then gets to take a free cruise and smack. The two lovely girls she let stay in her house have to tell her that her house is currently uninhabitable."

"Obviously, I don't know EG as well as you, but something tells me she'll be cool about it. But I am freaked that I have to tell my father. I just have to find a place to live first and fast. Really fast. We can't stay at Jorge's forever."

"We are lucky there was no major water damage. I don't think they even turned on the big hose. I guess Jackson did save the house. I think the firemen spent their time pulling off the siding instead of using the water. Phil boarded up the house pretty fast. Why are you laughing?"

"You look funny standing here with the yellow glove on."

"My hand is sweating. I've got to take it off now."

We went back into the house and looked

around. Jorge's bedroom was clean but sparse with only a king-size bed and a dresser. One of the spare bedrooms had two twin beds for his niece and nephew with blankets straight from the Cartoon Network. The third bedroom was being used for storage during the renovations. The master bath was extraordinary with a steam shower, soaking tub, and amazing tile work. It was spotless. It seemed he had sealed off the master suite and spare bedroom from all the sawdust.

Sherrie carried our clothes upstairs to the laundry room, and I threw myself on the couch. Before he left, Jorge had removed the sheets on the furniture. I couldn't help thinking that he was taking forever to remodel his place, but the work was impeccable, the work of a master craftsman.

I pulled off the yellow glove and rubbed the coconut oil in. I probably should have left the glove on longer, but my arm felt too confined. I felt trapped. I was staying in someone else's home. Everything was spinning out of control and falling down around me.

My mind went back to my bubble diagram. I didn't know what had happened to it. Is it still sitting in EG's kitchen? Is it on the floor, kicked under a chair with a fireman's boot print on it? I pictured it in my head and imagined me making a giant squiggly line around all the bubbles like a frame and, on the bottom, me as a stick figure holding up the frame. I wanted now more than ever to color in or, better yet, pop a bubble.

Sherrie walked down the stairs with her hands in her apron and pulled out her phone. "Have you checked your phone? Kay has been texting us."

"Ah, shit," I said. "Everybody in town heard about the fire, I'm sure."

"No doubt about that, but she's asking what happened to Brady."

"I forgot about Brady being here with Ryan. What are we going to say? We're not supposed to talk about what happened."

"She will not settle for a nonanswer."

"Let's go tell her what we can, and then I'm going to finish what I started this afternoon." My legs were bouncing, and my left hand was as oily as my right arm. I was restless.

"Really? You still ready for it? I'm surprised Aaron didn't show up when the firemen were there."

"He did. You must have missed it. I saw him drive by when I was talking to Jackson. I think he misunderstood what was going on."

"Ohhh, that's not good. Sorry for stating the obvious. I have to go back to the bar and turn in these checks." She pulled out register receipts and some cash from her apron.

"Tell Kay we will meet her in the square.

You can close out your checks, and then I will finish what I tried to do this afternoon. It all may fail but I have to try."

I watched her text as I pulled out my phone. There were so many missed texts and calls. I owed Kay a favor because I had a message from Mrs. Baron stating she heard there was a fire, and I could have tomorrow off. It could have only been Kay working her magic at Chambray to take care of me.

It was strange to not be able to call my parents or EG. There was going to be a new rule put in place that all three of them couldn't be out of phone reach at the same time. It felt especially lonely not having Aaron to talk to. Thank god Sherrie was there for that roller coaster, or I might have lost my mind.

"You take the spare bedroom upstairs. I'll sleep on the couch," I said.

"Are you sure? There are two beds up there."

"I don't know if I'll be able to sleep, and I don't want to keep you up if I am tossing and turning. There is no way I could sleep in Jorge's bed. It's just too weird."

"I totally agree. I can sleep in strange places, but we know him. It is oddly intimate taking his bed. I thought you would think I was being kooky if I said something. Although with the air-conditioning on in this house, we both may sleep like babies tonight."

I tried locking the house, but the key kept slipping in my hand because the coconut oil had left a slightly greasy residue, so Sherrie had to do it. Before we started walking, we stood out front. The sun was getting low, but the sky was still light. We stood in Jorge's front yard, looking at EG's house.

Sherrie was still singing "Ebony and Ivory," explaining that she couldn't get it out of her head. From the front, there was no sign of fire damage. Damn, I was not going to let myself say or even think how lucky I was that Jackson had put out the fire.

We walked to the square with Sherrie singing the whole time. We found Kay and Jenna on the park bench we had sat on about a week ago, only this time, they had no beer.

"What the hell happened! Are you guys ok?" Kay asked.

"It is hard taking anything you say seriously with that hickey on your neck," Sherrie said, and Kay just smiled.

Jenna stood up and let me have a seat on the bench. "Are you ok? What about the house?"

"The house is fine. Somewhat. We tried fixing the light above the back door the other day, and the old wiring in the walls sparked. It was a slow-burning fire. Jackson was there when the flames broke through the siding, and he put it out and called the fire department."

"Your old boyfriend, Jackson? Back with him, are you? What was Brady doing there? Did you dump his ass? Why was he such a mess and screaming at Ryan that they had to leave immediately?" Kay asked, getting to the point of her concern. She was all fun and games until it interfered with her sex life.

Sherrie rose up on her toes, then lowered her heels. She was curling her anger inside her. "I was never with Brady. I threw him out of BAR. He came looking for Jackson and was told to leave."

"That is crap. How does Brady even know Jackson?" Kay said.

Sherrie and I exchanged looks. We were not as prepared for this as we should have been. I owed Kay a lot. She had done things for me all summer and had expected nothing in return.

I told them about what had happened to Brady's sister and the duffel bag brouhaha.

Kay said, "Ryan told me Brady invited him here for some fishing, but we didn't hear from him for a few days. I was getting ready to drive Ryan back to Chicago today. I changed my schedule and was going to make a weekend of it. Then, all of a sudden, Ryan got a text from Brady saying they were leaving now. He pulled up in front of my place, looking all beat down and twitchy. Not saying much except that he just wanted to get out of here. Ryan thought he looked too upset to be left alone. So they are currently driving back to Chicago." She looked shrunken in that black linen tank top dress and her black canvas sneakers. So small and heartbroken—a far cry from two days ago.

Jenna looked at me. "I was at work when somebody said there was a fire at EG's house. I don't know what spreads faster in this town—fire or gossip. How bad was it?"

"You got that right," I said. "You know better than anyone in this town, since you work at the courthouse, about things that get said and not said."

Jenna was a smart girl. She knew there was more to the story, but I hoped she understood we would not say anything more. Kay was sulking about losing her newfound boyfriend so suddenly, she didn't notice the gaps in our story. I kept the attention on the fire and away from Brady and the FBI.

"Not as bad as it could have been. Damage to the back siding and the staircase."

Keeping the conversation away from the things we couldn't talk about, I said to Sherrie, "Why don't you take care of your bar checks, and then we can move on."

The door to BAR opened, and two guys walked out. One yelled hi to Sherrie, and they walked over. She introduced them as Vince and Jim, two regulars at the bar.

"Good luck working tonight. Aaron just kicked out some women for making too much noise. We didn't want to stick around to see what got into him. We will see you next week," Vince said as they walked away.

Sherrie said goodbye and looked at me with no expression. "I wonder what could be bothering my boss."

"Go do your thing in there," I said.

Sherrie left, and Kay got a call from Ryan. She got up and walked to the gazebo to talk in private.

Jenna sat next to me on the bench. "I don't expect you to say anything. I understood your little coded message. I know you can only say so much, but I have to ask you something because, when I was at work, I overheard something in the cafeteria. I couldn't see around the corner, but a cop had his communication radio on and Central Dispatch said there were D'Blues around. It's some type of code meaning federal agents are in town. So just tell me this, do you need help? Is it creepy Judge Lobal? Do you need a lawyer?"

I didn't know Jenna very well. We had gone out for drinks several times this summer, and she had processed my paperwork for my community service hours. Beyond that, I really didn't have that much history with her. Despite that, all I wanted to do was hug her and say thank you. She was a woman that had your back.

"Thank you—just witnesses, not defendants. One day, we will tell all. Right now, I need to take care of other stuff."

"Are you sure?"

I just nodded. We sat there for a few more minutes before Sherrie returned.

"I was thinking of walking over to Peach's and looking at the bulletin board to see if someone has a place to rent," she said.

"Good idea. I'll text you when I'm done," I said.

Jenna and Sherrie walked to the gazebo and tapped Kay on the shoulder. They told her they were headed to Peach's. Kay followed behind, still on her phone.

I got a text from Teddy. He'd heard about the fire and wanted to know if everything was ok. I didn't have the energy for him and just responded, We are fine.

I waited on the bench to collect myself before I went to see Aaron. I was sad, but he was mad. Would he even talk to me?

Sherrie texted Good luck.

I looked down the street. They stopped at her car. She had driven to work, and we had run home when we'd heard about the fire. She finally ditched the pink-and-aqua sleeveless flannel for a T-shirt in the back seat. She waved at me and I waved her on, trying to convince her—and me—that I was good.

CHAPTER FORTY-NINE

Even if Aaron didn't want me back, I wanted him to know Jackson had not been invited back into my life. I might have jumped forward with him, but I don't fall back.

Inside, three tables were occupied and no one was at the bar.

Pete was bartending. "You just missed Sherrie," he said.

I shook my head. "I'm looking for Aaron."

He pointed me to the office.

I walked towards the closet/office, and he stepped into the office doorway. He stopped when he saw me. I froze in place. I looked down, realizing I was standing in a pile of napkins. When I say pile, I mean several hundred napkins. I didn't have time to understand what that was about.

When I looked up, he stood there with no expression. No acceptance or distaste showing on his face. More tangible emotion came from the cardboard surfer margarita man.

"You have a minute?" I asked.

No response.

The only movement came from me fiddling with the nail I'd broken opening the door to the bar. My weakened hand had slipped, and now, the crack in the nail was so deep into the flesh that it stung when I touched it.

But I was there to save my relationship, and I didn't know how deep I'd cracked it.

"How's the house? Sherrie said it was not so bad. EG will be relieved."

House! Sherrie! EG! What is he talking about? Can't he see I am cracking?

"I just wanted to tell you things are not what—"

"Hey, boss, we got game again," Pete said from over my shoulder.

Aaron didn't move.

"Yo, game on," Pete said.

"I got what you said. Cash out the tables. Tell them we're closing early."

I looked back into the bar area. The only change was that two guys had walked in and taken a seat at one of the tall tables near the front door. They had been there before, the last time Pete had said "We got game." Slow business was expected at this hour. I didn't understand why he was closing.

"Let me take care of business," Aaron said.

"If you're closing up, I can wait."

"No, let me take care of business." His arm reached towards me.

My heart skipped. Was he coming to hold my hand, maybe lean in and whisper "All good, we're good," and carry me away?

He didn't do any of those things. He took my elbow and tried nudging me towards the back hallway to the rear exit.

"Let me take care of business, Claudia Jo."

I didn't move. I looked back and saw Pete drop a check off at a table. He looked back to Aaron. This time, Aaron's hand pushed my elbow, forcing me to step farther down into the hallway. He was escorting me out of the bar and his life.

He left me near the exit down the hallway. I pressed my body against the cold metal bar of the door and paused before I slammed myself into it.

Aaron looked back. "Bye, Claudia Jo."

I threw myself outside and stood between the brick building and his truck, sorting through my feelings. I didn't know what I felt most: sad, mad, lost, lonely, confused. Claudia Jo. No one uses my middle name. I hadn't even known Aaron knew my middle name. What was that all about?

I walked to the end of the alley. I couldn't be with people now. If I joined Sherrie, Kay, and Jenna at a bar, I wouldn't leave. I just wanted to figure this out.

As I rounded the corner onto the sidewalk, Jo-Lee smacked right into me, and I stumbled backward. She grabbed my arm as I started to tumble down, but she caught me. I regained my balance.

A few people were high on my list of who I did not care to see right then. She wasn't number one, but she was clearly in the top with Aaron, Teddy, and Jackson.

"I am so glad to see you. He told me you guys talked about it. I've been wanting to find a way to talk to you. This is so weird. I had no idea when I started working at BAR how this all pieced together. I was going to see you the other day, but I didn't know if you knew everything so I thought you should hear it from him first. I've got to run and take care of some other business now." She winced when she said the last line but kept going. "I'll call you sometime."

Although I had regained my footing from our run-in, everything out of her mouth had kept me off-balance. She left me standing there, went into the alley, and opened the door to BAR.

What the hell was that.

CHAPTER FIFTY

I walked towards EG's house, feeling like a moron. I could not have cared less if somebody was chasing me.

My phone beeped, and for a second, I hoped it was Aaron, even though deep down, I knew it would not be.

The message from Sherrie read To be or not to be. I sent her a picture of a stick figure walking with its head down. Just because I was sad didn't mean I couldn't be funny. She texted back House, and I gave her a thumbs-up.

The sun had set, and it was moving past dusk. I watched some kid walking his dog and talking on the phone. I waved at Mr. Williams, who was watering his wife's pots hanging on the patio. I looked at everything, so I didn't have to think about anything.

Two blocks from the house, Sherrie drove past and parked in front of Jorge's, waiting for me. "I ditched Kay and Jenna. If you want to be alone, I could try and find out if Officer Patrick is on duty."

"When are you going to start calling him by his first name?" I asked.

"When he asks me out, I'll skip the formality. I thought his slow approach was annoying, but then I thought about how he didn't get scared off or care when Brady was talking about flirting with me. Now that is a man."

"Good for you."

"Are you going to make me ask what happened, or can you just spill the beans?"

We stood between EG's house and Jorge's. We knew we could not go into EG's house. However, we needed our safe corner of the world where we felt safe and most at home, so we went to EG's porch. I sat on the couch, and Sherrie took the big comfy chair like it was the most natural thing in the world. There were no lights or a fan to turn on, but we felt content. This porch was our home.

"I was just in Peach's, freezing. I think the little time I spent here in EG's house has conditioned me not to like cool indoor air," Sherrie said.

"Nice play on words. Been working on that one long?"

"Just came to me. So are you going to tell me what happened?"

I was lying on the couch looking up at the light bulb we had successfully changed earlier but couldn't turn on now. "You know, I was just thinking we're lucky the fire started with the light above the back door. I think if we torched the porch, EG would be pissed. Not much rattles her, but losing this porch would probably do it."

I managed to get a laugh from Sherrie, and she said, "That will be your T-shirt slogan 'Don't Torch the Porch.' The T in torch will be a ladder."

"She wants to be my friend," I said.

"Who?"

"Jo-Lee."

Sherrie sat up. "Well, well, well. No wonder you're talking about torching stuff."

"He tossed me out the back door before I could say anything. I ran into Jo-Lee in the alley, and she was headed to BAR. She was rattling on and on about how she was happy that he told me. She wanted to talk to me before, but she didn't know if she should wait. I don't get it. Did she expect us to be friends?"

"Weird." That was one of Sherrie's rare one-word replies.

"Understatement of the year."

"When I left you on the bench, I'd set you up for success; how did you blow it?"

"What are you talking about? I'm lost on how you set me up for success."

Sherrie was leaning forward with her elbows on her knees like a basketball coach talking to her players. My eyes had easily adjusted to the dark since we had no lights but the glow of our phones. I could see how serious she was.

"Just before I walked in, I guess Aaron threw out two guys. I don't know the story, but we ran into Vince and Jim again, and they said they had never seen Aaron act that way towards any customer. They didn't hear what happened but got a bad vibe, so they left. Aaron was in a foul mood when I went in. Pete cashed me out and asked if we were ok and how was the house. I got so mad—mad for you and mad that Aaron didn't give a shit his employee's house was on fire. Aaron told me to have a good night and to stay off the damn square again. What's up with that? I'm tired of his directing where I should or should not be. Then it dawned on me that I probably remind him of you. So I said, 'She is not with him.' He walked towards his office. I yelled it and still no response. Then I figured what gets Aaron's attention more than a woman yelling is a mess in his bar."

I sat up. "You threw the napkins at him!"

"I kinda flung them at him. Pete had them stacked up on a tray, so I took the tray and did the best I could. Paper napkins don't have much substance, so distance and high impact were not a success, but it got his attention. Aaron finally turned to me, and I shouted again, 'They are not together. She did not invite him here. He is gone.' I may have added 'dumbass' under my breath. He didn't say anything, but I think he was happy because he didn't yell at me about the mess and walked into his office."

CHAPTER FIFTY-ONE

"You called him dumbass, and he called me Claudia Jo."

"Claudia Jo. The only time someone's middle name is used is if they are in trouble or being baptized."

"There was no baptism going on in the bar."

Sherrie jumped up. "That's it. Trouble!"

"Holy crap! You're right. Sit down. I don't need you pacing," I boomed.

"Stay off the square—"

"They were telling us to stay away. Something is going on," I said.

"Do I see you smiling?"

"Maybe. Maybe Aaron doesn't hate me but was trying to protect us."

"Us?"

"You are living in this house with me. Remember when he wouldn't let you close the bar? You tried sending Pete home, but he overrode that decision. He told me a story about Teddy being the new town drunk. What do you think could be going on?"

Sherrie didn't respond. Several cars had driven down the street, but this time, the car slowed and parked in front of the house.

Sherrie whispered, "Can you see who it is?"

I shook my head. "Everybody we know understands we're not staying here."

"Lookie-loos?" she asked.

"At this hour? In the dark?"

Sherrie slid down the chair, grabbed my arm, and pulled me down. She wiped her hand on her shorts. My arm still had a residue from the coconut oil.

We crawled to the far corner and crouched between the chair she was on and the other big chair on the sidewall. Two car doors slammed shut, and we heard muffled voices. Sherrie said something I couldn't understand. She went to grab her phone, but I put my hand over it to cover the light.

The voices got louder. We listened without moving.

"No damage on the front. Let's walk around. I'm sure they're not staying here for the night," a man said.

Sherrie was shaking. I was kinda relieved to see something actually make her nervous. I had begun to think she wasn't human the way she powered through the car chase, her confrontation with Brady, and the house fire.

They walked down the driveway on the other side of the house. We stayed low. I shifted from crouching to sitting on my butt with my knees to my chest, wedged between the couch and the end table. Sherrie looked like she was in a track meet and was about to run the forty-yard dash with her low squat.

The men walked between EG's and Jorge's houses. We remained still, very still, and kept listening.

". . . Check next door?" that same man said.

"Don't want to bother him. They are probably someplace safe. Let's go," another man said.

"Do you know where the other one is?" Man One said.

I couldn't hear Man Two's answer, but I knew the voices. Sherrie saw my face when I made the connection. She made a thumbs-up and then a thumbs-down, asking if they were friend or foe. I pointed my thumb sideways and let it dip a little. They were not a threat, but they were also not a friend.

I was praying they would not come onto the porch. There is no reason for them to—the house was dark, clearly showing no signs anyone was there, but then again, we were there.

The car doors opened and shut. We relaxed a little, and when the car started and drove away, Sherrie rolled onto her back in front of the chair. I slowly stood up, stepped over her, and got back on the couch.

"That must have been his wife's old car," I said.

"Who?"

"The boat trailer is hooked up to his truck." I didn't mean to give Sherrie only parts of the answer, but I was putting it together in my head. "That was Teddy and Tommy."

"Ohhhh. The odd couple—"

"I am not in the mood for funny."

"No intention of being funny, but I have to give them a nickname so I can contain them in a place in my head without associating them with the weird family dynamics you got going on—one is a disgraced civil servant and married to a person who shot me; the other is the new town booze head. I could probably go on."

"Understood. I may have to borrow that line of thinking. What did they mean someplace safe?"

"They figured we couldn't be staying here," Sherrie said.

"The way it was said was like we're still in danger. They could see the fire was not so bad."

We went quiet again. After a few minutes, Sherrie started softly singing "Ebony and Ivory" again and only stopped to ask me what I was sitting on.

"The couch. I don't know how else to explain it," I said.

"Living with you can be exhausting, and I am not talking about all that bullshit from earlier. You are sitting on something that's making noise. Paper or something."

I stood up and didn't see anything, but it was dark. I sat down and heard the crumpling noise. Sliding my hand between the cushions, I pulled out an envelope.

Sherrie paused her singing. "What is that?"

"The envelope from the letter I got from that lawyer in Madison," I said.

"Oh my god," Sherrie said unusually loudly and then nothing.

"You know you can be exhausting too. Want to share what you just discovered?"

"What was that name again? The woman Teddy's father allowed to live on the land."

"I think it was Leann Smithford. I can go look."

"Ever since you said it the first time, the last name stuck with me, and I just figured out why," she said, leaving me hanging.

"Seriously, stop pausing for effect. It's getting annoying."

"It may or may not mean anything, but Jo-Lee's last name is Smithford. I couldn't remember why it sounded so familiar, but it just came to me."

I never knew the meaning of the word gobsmacked until now. I was leaning back on the couch, my feet flat on the ground, legs spread wide, and I raised my arms to the heavens before dropping them like weights on the cushions next to me. I was like an athlete coming off the field after an exhausting run.

"Do you think we're related? Is that what Teddy meant! In the café when he said something about having a sister and it will be explained in the letter. This is the letter. That's what Jo-Lee meant about wanting to talk to me when we bumped into each other. She was talking about Teddy, not Aaron. She said something to the effect of wanting to come see me. Maybe it was her that was driving past the house."

"But would she run you off the road?"

"Good point. Maybe it's like you said earlier. It's not what I did to someone. I didn't piss off someone, but I am a threat to someone and have what they want." I held up the empty envelope.

Sherrie sat there, soaking it all in, still humming that damn song. My mind raced through the last few days. I spun my ring so fast it almost flew off because of all the coconut oil.

Everything clicked. "He is not dating her; he's protecting her! Does someone want my inheritance?"

I jumped up and dug into my yoga pants side pocket and pulled out the business card for Agent Moekel.

"That's the answer!" That damn song. He has our answers.

"What are you doing? Who are you calling?" Sherrie stood, giddy. "Tell me, tell me!"

I held up my finger, telling her to be quiet. The call went to voicemail. I left a message. "Agent Moekel, this is Ivory calling. At least I'm assuming I'm Ivory. It would be pretty weird if I was Ebony. I'm hoping you can help me. You said that was one busy family. Can you tell me who in the family? This is my cell phone, and you know where I live. Whatever you can do, I would appreciate it. Thanks, bye."

CHAPTER FIFTY-TWO

"I'm Ebony?" Sherrie said.

"You think I am?" We sat down, laughing.

"How did you figure it out?"

"I looked in the mirror."

"Still trying to have a sense of humor?" Sherrie snarked.

"I was thinking about when Moekel called Teddy 'Miller,' and I wondered if we were given code names. With your never-ending singing, it kinda hit me."

"Sorry about that. I know what a person's singing can do to another person."

"Don't apologize. If we go down that route, we'll be here with me apologizing to you for everything you've gone through with me."

"Do you think Moekel was trying to tell you

more?" Sherrie asked.

"Maybe. He talked about a family being busy, not my family per se," I said,

still slowly piecing things together.

"It's him. He is coming for me and he is going after her. That's what he was trying to tell me." My head swirled as I saw the puzzle pieces coming together. "No! She wants the inheritance."

CHAPTER FIFTY-THREE

"Who? What are you saying? Who is *he*? Who is *she*?" Sherrie said.

I was already on my feet at the screen door when Sherrie grabbed my arm.

"Wait, what are you doing?" she said.

"I'm going to BAR!" I stopped and looked at her. I could barely breathe. I started talking and running down the porch steps.

"What are you talking about? Put it together for me." Sherrie was trailing behind me. I stopped when my phone beeped with a text from an unknown number.

High traffic vehicle report for non street residents.

Only two vehicles were reported, and both had Minnesota license plates registered to one person: Theodore Siusiac.

Theodore Siusiac—Teddy.

I replied Thanks, but I got an automated reply of Message was undeliverable. I had a feeling I was not getting any more information from Agent Moekel or his office.

I started running again, and we were at the end of the block before Sherrie grabbed my arm again and held me in place. "Tell me what is going on."

"It is Teddy. I'm a threat to him. His life, his wife, his job. A pastor with a bastard child who took away his inheritance."

"Whoa, girl. That is a big spin on what's going on. How can you be sure?"

"The two cars that have been driving past the house are both registered to Teddy. He said he found out he has a sister who would take another piece of the inheritance and I would take another piece."

"Maybe she's working solo, and he is trying to stop her?"

"Why are you defending him?"

"I am not defending him but trying to sort this out logically. I'm on your side."

"I know. I know. Thank you for always

being with me. I think Jo-Lee may be in danger. Earlier, Aaron told me Teddy has been in town drinking enough to get himself inserted into the local gossip scene. Maybe he went to BAR last Friday and freaked out Jo-Lee. Just tonight, he asked if we were someplace safe, or did he mean out of reach? The other 'one' he referred to wasn't EG but Jo-Lee. I have got to see what she knows."

"Do you think that's wise?" Sherrie asked.

Ignoring the question, I was too anxious to debate this anymore, and we continued moving down the sidewalk. Nobody was out at this hour, but a few houses still had the TVs on and a dog was barking. I was aware of every step I took, every acorn that dropped, and every squirrel who found them.

"Ok, then. I guess you think it is wise," Sherrie said to no one in particular.

We were run-walking to BAR.

I turned to her. "I have to talk to Jo-Lee."

We were about a block away and could see the outside lights to the bar were off. We looked through the window. Some people were still inside, but we couldn't make out who they were. I tried pulling the door open, but it was locked. I decided to try the back door.

We got to the alley, a patrol car passed by.

Sherrie waved. "Do you want to do this alone? I'm cool either way."

"She might be willing to talk if it's just me. I don't want to barge in there and for her to think we are accusing her of keeping secrets."

"I'll talk to Officer Patrick and see if he has seen Teddy or Tommy tonight while patrolling. Text me anything if you need moral support."

I pulled my phone from the side pocket in my pants. "I only have about three percent of battery life, although that's about two percent more than I have left in my body today. I will keep it handy if I need you."

"We said we were going to keep our phones charged."

"I'll remember that next time I'm talking to the feds while I look at a burning house."

She gave me a hug and went to play street detective, and I walked down the alley.

Someone went in the back door. I'd thought I'd been ready, but a whole new drama was unfolding.

I pulled the door open, and the alley light above the door illuminated me like a display window. When the door shut behind me, I realized most of the lights were off inside the bar. Only the shadow of the man that walked in before me was visible.

I started walking down the narrow hallway. There were no other sounds but footsteps, and my shoes were making a funny sound. I looked down and saw I'd made some footprints, but didn't know why. I must have tracked something in. But that didn't make sense because they started in front of the walk-in beer cooler.

The man in front of me turned around and didn't say anything.

"Hello," I yelled.

Still, the bar was silent, and the only light came from the office desk lamp's dim bulb, neon beer signs, and outside streetlamps flooding through the front windows.

I stopped in front of the restrooms. "Who are you?" I asked.

"I'm looking for a friend of mine. I was told she was here," he said.

Neither one of us moved, and no one else seemed to be there. I didn't understand why the place would be empty but the back door open.

My eyes adjusted to dim lights. The man was thirtyish, wearing jeans, a T-shirt, and work boots. He had curly hair hanging down his neck under a baseball cap and probably three days' worth of beard stubble.

"I think they closed early, so you might want to check another bar," I said.

"I can see that, but she works here."

"Who?" I asked.

"It's none of your business."

"Just thought I could help. I know everyone

that works here." The hair on the back of my neck tingled.

He didn't take his eyes off me.

"Who are you looking for?" I asked again.

"I don't think you can help. We should probably go." He came towards me, blocking my view into the bar.

"It's ok, you go ahead." I didn't want him coming close to me when he passed.

My gut told me to run. I stepped to my right to avoid him, about to turn and run, when I saw past him. A pair of tennis shoes and jeans lay on the floor at the end of the bar. My mind spliced together what I was seeing.

Someone was on the ground. On the floor, my footprints were painted in blood.

I lurched forward, but he had grabbed my arm.

I pulled from his grip and ran the eight steps to the end of the bar.

Pete.

He wasn't moving, but I didn't see blood. I knelt down next to him, touching his face. He was warm.

His arm moved to my hand, and he moaned something I couldn't understand.

"I didn't want you to see him. Something happened here. We should leave," the man said, standing over Pete and me.

"Who are you?" I said.

"I'm looking for Jo-Lee."

"Why?" I asked.

No answer.

The hum of the coolers and the neon lights' soft whirring were the only noises in the bar.

"Why?" I asked again.

"I am a friend of hers. I went to her place, but she wasn't there, so I came here and found this." He gestured towards Pete.

I rolled off my knees and onto my butt so I could see the man better. I gently held Pete's hand.

I couldn't understand what was happening.

"I am afraid Jo-Lee could be in danger. Do you know where I could find her?"

"You said she was not at her place. Then I might know," I said.

"Gimme the address. I have got to get her."

"I don't know the address, only how to get there. You from around here? If so, I can tell you."

"No, Lee and I go way back. I just drove up here looking for her."

"I think she could be in danger too."

I looked around at the bar. A few tables were pushed back and chairs turned on their sides. Teddy must have been losing his shit. I had never seen anger as one of his traits, and now all this was unfolding.

"Tell me again how you know Jo-Lee and

why she's in trouble," I asked.

"You tell me. Look at him," he said, pointing to Pete. "I need to get to her. Where is she?" His voice was teetering between coldness and eerie. "Let's go."

"Let me call the police. I can't leave him until I know someone is coming for him." I pulled out my phone only to watch it shut off.

"We can call in my truck. We're wasting time."

"Who are you? Tell me your name."

In a calm voice, he said, "I think you should come with me. We don't know if whoever did this will return."

He sounded logical. I thought about what I knew about Teddy and I was breaking inside. I was no longer s'mad—I was f'ing mad.

"We'll call the police in the truck. Take me to Jo-Lee."

I moved to stand up, and Pete squeezed my hand. I hated to leave him, but I had to protect Jo-Lee.

The man shifted a couple of steps towards the office into the light, and I had a clear vision of him.

He turned his back to me. In his back pocket, an envelope was sticking out. The return address and logo of the law firm were clearly visible, just like the envelope I'd held in my hand thirty minutes ago.

I took two significant steps towards him. Someone had crossed out the address and appeared to have written a forwarding address.

The envelope was barely inside the pocket, but I couldn't grab it without getting too close or him noticing.

"Who are you?" I said.

He turned around. "What?"

"I am not taking you anywhere."

"My name is Adam. I'm a friend of Jo-Lee's, and I am beginning to think you're not a friend of hers if you are not willing to help me."

"If you are a friend of hers, then be a friend and call the police right now."

"My phone is in my truck. You are wasting time," Adam said.

"When was the last time you saw her? If you are such a good friend of hers, why haven't I seen you in here before?"

"What are you talking about? I'm a friend from back home. Now you are beginning to upset me. Come with me, missy."

Missy? Who calls someone missy? He was starting to cop an attitude and talk down to me. He is not a friend in need of help.

"I think you should come with me now." His voice was even, his lips barely moving and fists clenched.

I stepped back but tripped on Pete's legs and fell back into the bar. The man reached for my arm to steady me. He let go once I was stable but didn't move far away.

"We need to go. I can't let someone get to my Jo-Lee before I do. She has not mentioned me, has she?"

"I don't know you."

"I told you. I'm Adam. My Jo-Lee, sorry, I should say Jo-Lee is very private. I'm not surprised she hasn't spoken about me."

I was so confused. Trust your gut. Mom always says trust your gut.

Pete groaned. He tried to raise his arm, then dropped it. I had to figure out how to help him. His arms did not look broken, and his legs seemed fine. Three buttons of his flannel shirt were missing, but that could have happened anytime.

If Teddy had done this to Pete, I couldn't imagine what he would do to Jo-Lee. I needed to help her. I took a step towards the hallway. The man was ahead of me but kept turning back.

He had his arm out, whether to guide me or make sure I was within an arm's reach, I wasn't sure.

He walked slowly, making sure I didn't change my mind. "Tell me what's going on. Why do you think she's in danger?" I asked.

He stopped walking. His calmness was

unnerving. "She has a bad man after her. I came up here to protect her."

"Who?" I asked.

He hesitated, but with an even voice, he said, "Her father. He has been gettin' after her for some time, and she finally got out from under him. I've been watching him when I'm not at work. Keeping an eye on him, making sure she is safe up here. Just using my weekends to protect her. If I'm not here keeping an eye on her, I'm watching the old man's house."

He stepped past the cooler. I could see something I hadn't seen before: more blood droplets on the floor. He saw me looking and stepped back in front of the cooler door.

He reached for my arm, but I pulled back. "C'mon. Let's get to my truck, and we call 9-1-1 for your friend." His voice had changed. He was getting angry.

The back door opened. Another man I had never seen before stepped into the doorway, holding open the door.

He was clearly older than us, between fifty and sixty maybe. He wore jeans, a short-sleeve button-down shirt, and tennis shoes. Cigarette smoke wafted all the way down the hall.

He looked at me and then to Adam. All I could see was the rage in his eyes. His face turned crimson, his eyes narrowed and focused.

"Where is she, you son of a bitch? Is she here?" the new man said, standing in the doorway like a bull ready to charge.

"Who are you?" I screamed.

"I'm Victor. Jo-Lee's father—stepfather. I am here to take her home. Is she here?"

My knees were shaking, but my feet felt like they were in cement.

"Is she here?" he yelled again.

"Nnnno," I spit out.

How would I get help for Pete and the person I thought is bleeding in the cooler? I took a back step, thinking I could make a run for the front door.

"Where are you going?" Adam demanded.

"I was going to leave you two be, but I think you should both leave." I tried to sound assertive, but instead, it came out like a whining teenager.

"I am not leaving without my daughter," Victor said.

Adam stepped closer to me, tried grabbing my arm again, but I would not let him.

He whispered, "We will walk out together. Stay close to me."

Victor said, "I don't know who you are or how you know that man, but stay away from him. This is your chance to go. Do yourself a favor and leave."

I took two steps towards the bar. Pete was

moving his arms again and now his head. The men yelled at each other. I bent down and helped Pete sit up, putting his back to the wall and his legs out of the hallway. He was still mumbling.

"Who did this?" I asked him.

He mumbled again.

"Was this Teddy?" I asked.

He gargled no and pointed to the two men who had come out of the hallway. They were still yelling and shoving. I was unable to follow who was saying what. A freight train of information was plowing through my head.

I crawled to the center of the bar. Near the register, Aaron had installed an emergency alert. He would get a signal.

Please let him get the alert. Please don't be bleeding in the cooler, I prayed.

I hit the button. A second later, a phone beeped. Aaron's phone was sitting next to the register.

Damn it. Where is he?

My hands and body were trembling. I went back to Pete, checking his head for injury and felt a bump on the back.

I didn't know if I should leave him and run for the back door or stay. I couldn't imagine leaving him, but I needed to get help. I hoped the emergency button activated some alert not only to Aaron but to a security company or, better yet, the police. I wasn't doing much for Pete, Aaron, the bar, or me.

"They will be here—"

"I will get her—"

"You will pay—"

"How could you?"

Between the grunts, pushing, punches, the tables scraping across the floor, and the refrigeration motors, I didn't know who was saying what.

The shoveling escalated, and then I saw a gun. Both men wrestled for control of it. I tried pulling Pete behind the bar, but he was too heavy. The men pushed and shoved each other, their arms twisting in the air.

This was not going to end peacefully. Rage flashed in the eyes of both men.

One of the men yelled for me to run. I couldn't leave Pete.

The men tumbled into a table. Adam was on top of Victor, their arms still twisting and fighting for control of the gun. Despite being older, Victor seemed to have more strength and pushed Adam off him. They flew into the bar. The sudden jolt of the hard stop startled them. The gun slipped from one of their hands and fell at their feet only inches from me. They tumbled back and tripped over some chairs, which separated them.

Instinct made me jump for the gun. I threw

my body over Pete's legs and grabbed it. Standing, I faced the men but kept the gun down.

Common sense should have made me run, instead I stood firm, knees shaking, but the rest of me was solid.

Finally, the yelling stopped. They had looked like shadows dancing, but now, they were like idle bulldozers standing, separated by the fallen table. A neon light flickered an orange glow across their faces. Each man tried to catch his breath. Victor was rubbing his left shoulder.

Adam said, "Give me the gun and let's get to her."

"No," I said in a soft voice.

They did not move.

"Run," Victor said.

"Don't listen to him. Take me to her. We can make a call for your friend," Adam said.

"Don't go anywhere with him," Victor pleaded.

Adam took a step towards me, shaking his head. "You can't listen to him. I told you, he's a bad man. Look at what he did here."

Who was right? Who was wrong?

"I am a dad, and I know that your dad, god willing you got a good one, will want you safe. Go and get help." Victor's voice was soft yet emphatic.

Adam jumped forward. "You can't listen to him. She came here to get away from him."

I raised the gun. My arms were shaking, but I had control. Some control. I had to hold it with both hands because my right was still slippery from all the coconut oil.

"He has the story twisted. Take care of yourself." Victor took two steps closer to me, inserting himself between Adam and me.

Bounce, bounce, bounce. My thoughts were all over the place.

I heard something behind me and chanced turning around. Down the hallway, the back door was still closed. When I turned again, each man had taken a step closer to me.

Again, I heard a noise. It was coming from the walk-in cooler. The door was being pushed open. Someone was trying to get out. I spun around to the men when they moved closer again.

Adam tried coming forward, but Victor blocked him. I looked down. Adam was standing on the envelope from the lawyer's office.

The noise came from behind me again. Cold air rushed out when the cooler door opened. To my horror, Aaron collapsed, and the heavy metal cooler door was trapping him in the doorway.

The men grunted. I turned to see them charging me. Desperation was written on their faces.

It was swift.

Trust your gut.

I knew evil when I saw it.

I had to protect her.

I had to protect me.

I fired once.

My arms were jolted by the recoil. Everything happened in slow motion. All sound was drowned out by the gunshot.

Both men collapsed. One rolled away out from under the other.

I stepped back, hitting the office door. Someone touched my shoulder.

I screamed and threw myself against the opposite wall, keeping the gun raised. I didn't know how many bullets were left, but I was still ready. The gun shifted in my hand from nerves and coconut oil.

My finger shook on the trigger, a microsecond away from firing. My mind focused as the figure fell to the floor. I kicked them in the face. A button snapped off the person's flannel shirt and rolled to my feet. The cardboard margarita man glared up at me.

I mumbled, "Hells," and in my head, Sherrie said, "Bells."

I ran a hand through my hair and crawled over to Aaron. I used my legs to push open the cooler door. He grabbed my hand.

Back in the bar, Victor took off his shirt and used it to apply pressure to the gunshot wound in

Adam's chest. "You bastard should live so you can die in prison. I want no mercy for you."

Seconds or minutes later—time was a vague concept at this point—the back door flew open.

Men in blue bounded down the hallway. Someone pulled me away from Aaron, and I slid up the wall. Someone picked up the gun at my feet.

I didn't know how long I stood there. Time had frozen. More men in blue came in, and—I think it was minutes later—one stretcher carrying Adam went past. An EMT yelled to the officer near me, "Aaron has lost some blood, but the guy on the stretcher is the priority."

They put Aaron on another stretcher and took him out.

I walked straight to the bathroom and threw up in the sink.

An officer in the bathroom doorway waited for me. He held up his arm so I couldn't leave. Pete walked down the hallway and out the door assisted by a policeman and an EMT.

I heard Sherrie screaming in the alley and another female voice, which I could only guess was Jo-Lee.

I tried walking towards the rear exit but was not allowed to leave. The officer directed me to a table and stood next to me.

I will probably be taken into custody.

Officer Patrick came over. "You again."
I didn't laugh this time.

CHAPTER FIFTY-FOUR

I was escorted out of the bar and helped into the squad car. The car ride was a blur of trees and streetlights. Someone opened the back of the squad car. I stepped out. The cool night air felt good on my skin, but the light coming from the police station windows was blinding.

Inside, a tall sizable desk stood in front of a large room with bright lights. They took my phone and keys, the only personal items I had on me.

They took me to a small carpeted room with a small table pushed against the wall, three chairs, and two cameras in the upper corners of opposing walls. I sat there by myself for a long time.

Eventually, two officers came in and took my statement. I recounted everything I could remember and told them it was probably all caught on security video. I was never read my rights and had probably been there for two or three hours. Time was in a tunnel, and I was stuck in the middle.

The officers left, and a woman about fifty years old, wearing gray slacks and a black button-down oxford came into the room.

I was drained of energy, and she brought no emotion or sign of humanity with her. I gave my account of what happened again, wanting her gone. She did not interrupt and asked a few questions when I was done. I mentioned the security cameras again. She said she'd reviewed the tapes but needed to hear my statement. She allowed me to use the restroom without being escorted but told me to return to the room promptly after.

One of the first detectives who had interviewed me came back. "Do you want to call someone?"

I nodded, but another officer said there was a Mr. Lawrence here to see me.

"Mr.? Mr. Lawrence?"

"Yes, ma'am. Follow me." The officer walked me to the open reception area.

Seated on the bench were Sherrie and her parents. They stood when they saw me.

I walked past several desks, and the officer pushed open the half door that marked the reception area.

Before I had finished stepping into the room, Sherrie's mom, Evie Lawrence, grabbed my arm and pulled me into a hug so strong that we looked like one and a half people instead of two adults. I wasn't sure how long I kept that warm blanket of love around me before we released. The moment my arms started to slacken, Mr. Lawrence put his hands on my shoulders. It was the second blanket of love.

Sherrie pulled me out of her dad's embrace and gave me a hug. She whispered, "I figured I was going to have to call them sooner or later and thought this might be the time."

"We got here as soon as we could. Made good time, eighty minutes. Been here thirty, hoping to see you," Robert said.

"Are you here by yourself?" Evie asked.

I nodded. "I'm not sure if they brought anyone else here."

"Hon, I am talking about a lawyer."

"I don't have a lawyer."

Evie turned to the officer on the other side of the half door. "I want to speak to the detective in charge."

A few minutes later, one of the detectives who had taken my statement came over and introduced herself to Evie. "I'm Detective Angie Decorah."

"I'm attorney Evie Lawrence. Can you tell

me—"

"Just a moment. You can all follow me back."

Evie put her hand on my shoulder, and the four of us, plus another officer, followed the detective to a small conference room. A long oval table that probably sat twenty sat in the center of the room. Bright fluorescent lights beamed over the center of the table.

Evie directed me to the head of the table near the door. Sherrie took the seat to my left, Robert was next to her, and Evie stood behind me.

Detective Decorah adjusted the lights to a comfortable non-eye-piercing level and sent the other officer for coffee.

Evie held up a finger. "Could I get hot water with lemon, if possible please?"

Detective Decorah wore jeans, a light-blue polo, and tennis shoes. Heavy eye makeup and long blonde hair pulled into a tight, twisted braided bun contrasted the casual-looking outfit. If I had to guess, she had been somewhere fun when she'd gotten the call and changed out of her dancing clothes before coming to the station.

She took a seat, leaving a few empty chairs between us, shuffling papers until the officer returned with coffee. A tray with a thermos, several mugs, and sugar were brought in, and the officer left relatively fast. If I'd had to guess, it was to avoid being asked to do any more gofer work.

Evie handed me a mug of hot water with lemon and whispered, "This will be better for you."

I wrapped my fingers around the warm mug and held it close to my chest. Robert and Sherrie took some coffee and settled in their chairs. Evie kept her hands resting lightly on my shoulders. I felt like a bear cub, and mama bear was ready to strike.

Detective Decorah took control. "First of all, let me start by saying Ms. Middleton here is not under arrest, and that is why you are both allowed to be here." She directed her comments to Sherrie and Robert. As she continued to speak, her eyes floated between Evie and me. "We have reviewed the security video footage, and it matches everything Ms. Middleton and the witnesses stated. The shooting was self-defense."

Sherrie gasped, and Robert twitched but otherwise remain motionless. It dawned on me that the three of them knew nothing of what had happened inside the bar.

"We are just waiting on the final word from the district attorney. She was the woman you spoke with after you gave your statement the first time. No charges are pending."

"What about Aaron?" I asked. My hands were still locked around the mug, and my feet were glued to the floor.

"I am unable to comment about anyone's medical condition."

"Come on, seriously!" Sherrie's voice was loud. Neither her dad nor mom stopped her. "Gossip in this town is more abundant than the corn in the fields. Let me go use the restroom, and I will find out." She turned in the chair.

I started shaking.

Finally, she said, "Mr. Rhoimly just got out of surgery, and full recovery is expected."

I dropped my head and closed my eyes, letting the tears run down my cheeks. Relief flooded out of me.

Sherrie pulled the mug from me and handed me some tissues.

I raised my head. "What about Pete?"

"I am really not—" the detective started.

Evie turned toward the detective. "We are not here for the fun of it. Can you please just tell us what you can so we can leave?"

"Mr. Morris has a bump on the head but will be fine."

"What about . . . the other one?"

"Who was there?" Sherrie asked.

I didn't move to answer her.

Detective Decorah looked at Evie, pausing before she spoke. I thought the detective must be a mother. She waited for Evie to sit.

Evie took the chair on my right and placed

her hand on my leg.

Detective Decorah spoke in a calm voice as if she was reading a how-to manual. "Mr. Adam Darnel died two hours ago on the operating table. A single gunshot wound punctured his lung."

I lurched forward in my seat, putting my head on my knees. My stomach heaved, but nothing came out. I eventually sat up.

Footsteps sounded in the hallway, and Detective Decorah excused herself.

"Whenever you're ready, you have got to explain everything," Sherrie said softly.

I nodded. I looked at Evie and Robert and teared up. "Thank you for coming."

"Of course, darling," Evie said. "I don't know what went on, but I am happy there are no charges. I do real estate law, and the only courtroom I ever see is on reruns of Law & Order."

"Thank god I did not know that, or I really may have thrown up. But thanks again for coming."

Robert sat forward a little. "When Sherrie called, we knew it was trouble; otherwise, we would have only gotten the highlights when she comes home next month to raid the pantry shelves."

"Can you tell us what happened?" Sherrie asked.

I started telling the story from when I

walked into the bar. Then I backed up and told them about someone following me and how I thought it was Teddy. Evie and Robert exchanged looks, but they did not interrupt. I explained about seeing Pete and the blood on the floor, my confrontation with Adam, and finally Victor walking in.

Sherrie spoke only when I was done talking. "Why Adam? I am confused—you said Jo-Lee's dad had been coming after her."

"It all came together for me. I don't know what piece fell into the puzzle first. Adam had said Jo-Lee's dad had been abusing her, and he had been watching him. Somehow, I remembered what you and Aaron were discussing last Friday in the living room. Her father is a long-haul truck driver on the weekends. Adam couldn't have been watching her dad when he was out on the road instead of at home. He was lying. Everything he was telling me was a lie.

"Victor kept telling me to run and take care of myself. It wasn't about him; he was worried for me. Adam must have been here last Friday night, and that's what freaked Jo-Lee out. That's why she took off running when I saw her in the alley."

"Stay off the square," Sherrie mumbled.

"Aaron and Chuck were trying to keep us away from the chaos," I said.

Sherrie raised an eyebrow and smirked.

"Who would have figured they are good guys trying to be better guys? Why did you break up with him again?" She knocked her knee into mine, and we smiled at each other.

"I saw the envelope from the lawyer's office in Adam's pocket. He came back to River Bend because he had gotten her address. Her dad had written the forwarding address on the envelope, and Adam must have snagged it from the outgoing mailbox.

"When the gun dropped, I picked it up. Adam's rage and passion was nearly palpable. He was not going to stop until he got Jo-Lee. Before Victor showed up, I was thinking about taking him to Aaron's place where Jo-Lee was." Tears streamed down my face. "But when Adam came forward, there was such fury in his eyes I knew he would not stop."

"Fight or flight. Instinct. You did the right thing, and don't let anyone tell you otherwise," Robert said gently.

Detective Decorah returned and took her seat. She placed her arms on the empty table, clasping her hands together. "Let me update you. As I said, Adam Darnel died on the operating table. He came to town with a friend, a Mr. Mitchel Gorman. He does not appear to be directly involved in the incident at the bar. Mr. Gorman came forward several hours ago and gave us a statement. He confirmed that Mr. Darnel came to River Bend to find Ms. Smithford. The men separated when Mr. Darnel became obsessed with finding Ms. Smithford this evening. Mr. Gorman has left town and is no threat. As far as Mr. Adam Darnel is concerned, there was a warrant out for his arrest for domestic abuse and murder. Most recently, he was involved in a DUI. The passenger of the car he hit was killed, and the driver was seriously wounded. The man had a rap sheet longer than my arm. He is no longer going to be a burden to anyone.

"I tell you this so you understand what the man was like. It does not lessen what you did, but it may bring you a little bit of peace. We offer counseling services for those involved in traumatic events. Here is the card with the phone number. You may call at any time. Someone will answer twenty-four hours a day."

I was shivering and sweating, hearing every word she was saying. Everything was being tattooed into my memory.

"I have to ask—did he have a family?" I said.

"It's only natural to have questions. I don't have those answers. Even if I did, those answers might never help you settle up what's inside. As I said, no charges are being filed. You are free to go. Thank you for your cooperation." Detective Decorah stood.

Robert stood also and extended his hand to her. "Thank you."

"One more thing. We will put out an official statement within the next twelve to twenty-four hours; until then, we don't comment on an ongoing investigation. However, you and I both know how small this town is, and once the story gets out, you can expect local and possibly statewide news coverage. Speak or don't speak to reporters. That is your option. I just wish to tell you sometimes less is more. Beware of the lurkers and the quiet press personnel. Especially those that pretend to be your friend, those are the ones who will tear you down the most. If you have trouble with anyone, please give me a call. I would love to deal with them myself," the detective said as the rest of us pushed back our chairs and stood.

I shook Detective Decorah's hand. She showed no reaction when she touched my cold, oily, and scaling hand. She was a professional who had seen a lot even in this small town.

She was almost out the door when she turned back. "Please really consider calling the counseling center. Maybe not tomorrow or the day after, but soon."

Moments after she left, another officer came in. "Ms. Middleton?"

"Yes," I said, raising my hand a little.

"There has been a Mr. Steiger trying to

contact you."

I shook my head. "I don't know anyone by that name."

"Victor Steiger. He was brought here in the other squad car."

"Jo-Lee's stepfather," I said, addressing the group.

"Actually, there's another lady and gentleman as well. All three are asking to see you."

"Jo-Lee and Teddy. Are they out front?" I asked.

"They're in a conference room down the hall. They could have left hours ago, but I think they were waiting to see you."

"Can you tell them I am ok please? I'm in good hands and will contact them tomorrow."

"Come to the front and get your personals. I'll walk you out the back door." The officer turned her attention to Robert. "Sir, if you would exit from the front, you can pull your car around to the side. I will walk everyone to that exit if you're more comfortable with that."

Before anyone moved, I said, "Wait, is there anyone else out front or in the parking lot?"

"Last check it was all clear."

"If you could just keep them in the conference room until we leave, we should be ok going out the front."

She instructed us to wait until she was

confident the conference room door was closed. After getting my personal items, we left and did not turn back. I wanted no chance of seeing Teddy. He was not the one who had come after me, but he still had a lot of explaining to do, and now was not the time.

CHAPTER FIFTY-FIVE

When we got in the car, I asked to go to the hospital, but Evie insisted I go home to change and shower. While I was aware of the wetness and dirt on me, it never occurred to me that some of it was blood from Aaron's bullet wound.

Sherrie sat in the back seat with me and helped her father navigate the way to Jorge's house. It was nearly two a.m. The streets were empty. I was surprised that Sherrie didn't navigate him past the bar, and suddenly realized I didn't know what happened to her.

"So I told you about my . . . my . . . a-a, I guess let's call it my incident. What happened to you?" I asked.

"I got bored and sat on a park bench, waiting for you to text me, but I guess you were preoccupied." Sherrie smiled as she spoke.

"Whatever." That was all I could come up with in the moment.

"I left you in the alley. Sorry about that. I should have gone in with you."

"Don't you start with that. Who knows what could have happened, better or worse, we will never know," I said.

She shook her head, but I was not sure she believed it. "I went to the square. A squad car was parked on the other side. I went to see if Officer Patrick was in it. Halfway past the gazebo, I saw Teddy and Tommy walking around. To be honest, I froze in place for a minute. I didn't know if I should run to the squad car or if I should speak to them."

"I felt the same thing. Trust your gut," I said.

She nodded in agreement. "I knew you thought Teddy was behind everything, but I couldn't put it together as you had. I had my doubts about Teddy, but the more I thought about it, I couldn't see him driving us into a cornfield. Teddy and Tommy saw me, so I went to talk to them. They were worried about how we were doing. Asking if we had a place to stay and said it would be best if we left the area and you and I remained together. I tried pushing them for answers. Teddy said something about Jo-Lee was being trouble or in trouble. I couldn't understand his thinking and what he was saying.

"Then Officer Patrick and Officer Baumann were walking towards their squad car, and then they took off running. Seconds later, we heard the sirens from another car and the ambulance. We ran to the alley but were not allowed back. Two stretchers and Pete were loaded into the ambulances. I was close to making a run for the ambulance, and then you walked and got in the back of the cop car. I tried Aaron's phone and got no answer. Then I called these two." Sherrie gestured to the front seat. "I figured it was time. I don't know if I was more relieved that you weren't on the way to the hospital or more proud you were being arrested for something."

The rest of the ride was quiet and thankfully short. We arrived at Jorge's and took a hot and fast shower. The thought of standing still was nerve-wracking. I had been in the police station by myself for what seemed like days, but I was sure it was hours.

I went downstairs and found Robert in the upright chair with a glass of whiskey on a table next to him, nodding off to sleep. Sherrie and her mom were in the kitchen.

Evie sent Sherrie out of the kitchen for something and slid over a plate with some cheese, crackers, and sliced apples, insisting I put something in my stomach.

She smiled with a nod when I took a few crackers. "There you go. Have you called your parents yet?"

"Not yet," I said. "They will be in port sometime Friday."

Evie held up a finger. "Well . . . it technically is Friday. Friday afternoon in Europe, actually, a respectable time of day to call them."

"It would be crazy to ruin their vacation. Nothing can be done about the situation, and they won't be able to get here any sooner. Same goes for EG."

"You're mistaking this as a conversation instead of understanding it as a directive."

Sherrie came back with my hairbrush. After Evie brushed my wet hair, she pulled it back into a cool twisted braid.

I looked at Sherrie, and she said, "This is what my mother and my aunts do. She can't cradle you in her arms, so she does your hair. In your family, your mother cooks and cleans. EG orders takeout and rubs your feet to show love."

While Evie had done my hair, I negotiated to call EG at a more reasonable hour in Florida.

I went to the bedroom to call my parents. The call went to voice mail. I said I was fine, but some things had happened that I needed to tell them but not to worry. I also texted my brother, not caring if I woke him up, but got no reply.

Back downstairs, Robert was up with his keys in his hands. They seemed to understand I was going to the hospital regardless of the time and with or without them, and decided it would be best for Robert to come with me. Sherrie was not staying back either. She had our purses and a phone charger for me. Evie stayed at Jorge's house, sitting in the chair Robert had just vacated, and took ownership of the remaining whiskey.

On the way to the hospital, I sent a message to Jorge telling him things were fine and that Robert and Evie were at the house. He responded relatively fast, considering it was the middle of the night. I tried to keep it brief and assure him all at the same time. I promised full disclosure at a more reasonable time.

We got to the hospital. Unsure of where to go, we got a little turned around. Finally, someone else who was waiting pointed us in the right direction. I turned into the waiting area, and before I knew it, I was being hugged by Lesley, Aaron's mom, and then by Jan, his aunt. Chuck sat in the corner, enjoying me getting smothered by the ladies. He got up when he saw Sherrie and introduced himself and the rest of the family to Robert.

Lesley and Jan were so happy that I was ok and were not surprised to see me. They led me back to the line of chairs and sat on either side of me.

Aaron's dad, Jack, was in the room with him.

Jan and Lesley told me Aaron was shot in the left shoulder below the collarbone and would be fine. The surgery had gone better than expected because the bullet had missed the lungs. The nurses had highly suggested they go home and get some sleep since only one person was allowed in his room, but they refused to leave.

I realized Aaron might not have told them we had broken up. He'd barely told them we were dating. Not because he was hiding it, but as I was told years ago from some guy friends, that's a guy thing. Barely telling their family about their dating life was a guy thing. As long as you met the family, you were in good standing. I had always kept that nugget of information tucked away for times like this.

Chuck filled me, Sherrie, and Robert in on what had happened before I arrived at the bar. He had seen everything on video before turning it over to the police. I was sure he'd made a copy for himself.

Chuck was missing some pieces of information because he only had the video and no audio. He had gotten the alert I'd triggered and pulled up the camera feed when Aaron didn't answer his phone. Chuck went through the video several times and figured out Adam had come in earlier when Aaron had told me to leave. It appeared Aaron had asked Adam to leave, or at least they exchanged words. We figured he went to Jo-Lee's apartment since he had her address but came back and got into it with Pete and Aaron.

Adam had walked in the back door, snuck up on Pete, grabbed him, and threw his head into the wall. Aaron pulled Adam off of Pete, and they got into it. At some point, Adam pulled out his gun but only managed to get him in the shoulder. His mom and aunt winced as Chucked recalled this part of the story. Aaron got himself into the cooler and must have jammed the handle somehow because Adam tried to open it. He left the bar then and came back right before I got there.

"He must have seen Sherrie and me walking and turned around to make it look like he was just getting there."

I started telling my part of the story, but Sherrie interrupted. "How is Pete?"

Chuck answered. "Serious headache. It will last a long time, but he should be fine. The nurses told me that if we call his family, he will sue and come after anyone who calls them as soon as he can stand without getting dizzy. Two of his roommates showed up after they heard something happened at the bar."

"Is he still here, or did they take him home?" Sherrie asked.

For some reason, Chuck found that funny.

"The doctor would not discharge him into the care of his roommates. That's one of them over there." He pointed to the corner.

A guy was sitting in a chair with his arms crossed, head back, and mouth open. A gentle snore came from him. "The other one was slightly less drunk and is probably sleeping in the room with him."

Sherrie stood up and looked at me. "Do you mind?"

"Of course not. Go," I said.

Chuck pointed down the hall. "Second door on the right."

Sherrie went into the room. A minute later, a twentysomething woman came out, walking a not-so-straight line and sat next to the sleeping guy.

Jack had come out of Aaron's room, sat next to his wife, saying it was her turn to visit Aaron.

I introduced Robert and assured him I was fine.

Chuck started chuckling again.

His aunt leaned over and looked at him. "What is so darn funny?"

I could appreciate that he kept finding things amusing tonight even if I didn't have the strength to laugh.

"Ask Claudia about the other one that came after her," Chuck said.

Everyone turned and looked at me.

I shook my head and rolled my shoulders. "I have no idea what you are talking about."

"I have to commend you on your calm under pressure and doing what had to be done, but kicking Margarita Man in the face was a bit much." Chuck pulled out his phone with the five-second video cued up. He had even put it on a loop. He had been waiting for the right moment.

Everyone, including me, got a laugh out of me kicking a cardboard surfer wearing a flannel shirt.

After the laughing stopped, I told Robert to head back to Jorge's house and get some sleep. He didn't put up much of an argument, knowing Aaron's family would be there all night. He said goodbye to Sherrie, and Chuck walked him to the car under the pretense of giving him directions. Robert was probably telling Chuck he better keep an eye on Sherrie and me.

I decided I'd better send EG a text to call me before she called anyone else in town. Between the house fire and all this tonight, I was sure some of the gossipy ladies would be reaching out to her. I could just imagine her phone being flooded with messages when she got back to port and had a phone signal.

I took some time coming up with the right words and left it at WE ARE FINE. CALL ME FIRST. Some stuff happened you should know about.

I sent the text, and almost immediately my phone rang.

CHAPTER FIFTY-SIX

EG had seen my text and called immediately. "Just got your text. I'm already awake because the cruise ship docked yesterday and I'm taking an early flight back. It's barely dawn here in Florida. I'm in a cab on the way to the airport. Is everything ok? Has something happened?"

"There are so many details, but this is the time for highlights." I gave her the short version, but left out my role in all the activity. "That is a big story, but the other story, you should probably sit down for."

"Claudia, I'm in a cab." She chuckled.

"Oh, yes, ok. Well . . ." I said and proceeded to tell her about knocking out the light above the back door, Jackson, the damn duffel bag, the feds, and the fire.

She just asked a few questions as if I had told her about this year's corn crop. There was no anger, only concern for us. Once I said Jorge and Phil had taken care of the house, she was back to worrying about Sherrie and me.

"We're unable to be in the house because of the stairs.

Not surprisingly, she wasn't upset. "We'll figure it out when I get back. Oh, also, your parents' ship was delayed getting into port because of bad weather off the southern coast of Spain."

"Did you speak to them?"

"No, but I made friends with the cruise ship's captain, and he was able to track their boat."

"You will have to tell me about your cruise ship romance." I laughed. "Anyway, Jorge is taking care of us at his house, so we're fine."

For the time being, I left out Robert and Evie being there because that would send signals that the incident at the bar was bigger than I had let on. I wanted her to enjoy her happy memories of the cruise as much as she could before returning to River Bend and the nightmare of tonight.

CHAPTER FIFTY-SEVEN

I must have fallen asleep around four a.m. in the waiting room for a few hours. I woke up and found my head on Lesley's shoulder. Chuck had switched places with Lesley in Aaron's room, and Jack had gotten everyone coffee from the cafeteria.

I was awakened to the smell of breakfast. Lena, Jorge's sister, worked as a nurse in the emergency room. She had been getting off duty last night when Aaron was brought in. This morning, she'd sent Jorge in with an assortment of tortillas filled with eggs and sausage.

I gave him a mini version of what had happened to Aaron and stopped the story when I got to what happened at the bar. "Robert and Evie are at your house, and EG will be back this afternoon."

He nodded. "I'm going to talk to Lesley and Jack. Glad you're ok."

Jan appeared from the elevator with several bags full of fresh baked goods. She stopped at the nurse's station and dropped off two bags before coming into the waiting room. Jorge made a point to grab a scone before leaving.

Chuck came out of Aaron's room. "If you want, you can go in, but don't expect much." He must have seen the look of panic on my face. "Only because he is still groggy from the meds. He may not remember the conversation, but you have a few minutes before he falls asleep again."

I left them in the waiting room and felt like I was tiptoeing down the hall. I pressed lightly on the door, preparing myself for the worst. Sunlight framed the window shades giving a soft glow to the other side of the room. A monitor hummed. My eyes followed the blankets from the foot of the bed up to Aaron's chest. He was looking at the ceiling and turned when he heard the door creak behind me.

He smiled and tears instantly started down my face. He raised his hand to me, and before I knew it, I had my hands wrapped around his, not worrying about the tubes taped to the back of it.

He spoke first. "Let me get this straight." His speech was slow but steady.

I was nervous because I had so much to say

to him. None of it mattered though. I just wanted him to keep holding my hand and not send me away.

He cleared his throat. "I understand you took out Margarita Man."

We laughed, and he winced in pain.

A nurse had come in behind me and said, "If you guys don't let me in on the joke, you're gonna have to leave," she said with a smirk.

"I am not leaving," I said, my eyes not leaving his.

Aaron squeezed my hand a little tighter.

The nurse had shifted my body so she could get close, but he didn't let go.

She had some powdered sugar on her uniform, but I didn't say anything. She gave us about twenty more seconds before she kicked me out of the room.

In the waiting room, I found Sherrie and Pete's roommates, Cameron and Jesse, munching on breakfast sandwiches and scones. They were talking to Jack, Lesley, and Jan. At eight a.m., Evie came to the hospital to check on us, carrying a box with ten fresh hot coffees from the corner deli on Broadway.

"Everything my daughter tells me about this town and your family, I knew you would be well taken care of when it comes to baked goods," she said.

Introductions were made, and the mood was much lighter than it had been in hours.

Chuck tossed Sherrie a key. "There will be a second key on the kitchen table. On Monday, my place is yours. I will be in Texas for several weeks for work. I'll text you the address. It's small, but it will get Jorge his house back to him. There's not much for food, but the kitchen has the equipment you need to cook."

"Good Wi-Fi?" Sherrie asked.

Ignoring her, Chuck continued. "Unfortunately, the garage is full, but two cars can fit on the driveway. I will leave the Wi-Fi passcode next to the key. Please text if you have any problems. Mrs. Traeger on the right will be nosy, but all the others keep to themselves. It's not far from the bar."

"I will make sure it's clean," Lesley said.

Chuck rolled his eyes.

"I have to do something. If I sit here every minute, I will go nuts, and Aaron will throw me out, so let me be productive," she said.

The doctor came out to update us. "Aaron is recovering nicely, but we're not going to release him until Sunday or Monday at the latest. Sleep is what he needs now. He'll be taking short walks around the nurses station starting this afternoon."

Pete was being discharged within the hour. He would have a headache for a while, but everything long-term was expected to be fine. Chuck said he would drive Pete and his roommates back to their apartment and then check on the bar.

He also had asked Jacob, the other bartender at BAR, to care for Rita and help him watch the bar. Jacob and Pete were not family, but they would have done anything for Aaron and Aaron for them. Again, three people with a strong bond, and they weren't family.

At eight thirty, I didn't want to go, but my head felt like a fifty-pound weight. The morning sun was piercing my temples, and any faster movement was blurry to me.

We said our goodbyes, and Evie drove Sherrie and me back to Jorge's. I went up to the guest bedroom and fell asleep thinking about Aaron smiling at me and holding my hand.

I woke up around noon to a loud bang and assumed it was someone downstairs.

My phone had several messages. I texted Teddy back, agreeing to meet him at the square in a few hours. I also texted Kay and Jenna, telling them I was ok and we would connect later. My brother had left a message saying he and some friends were still in Canada fishing. The signal was horrible, and he would be back to the land of Wi-Fi probably Monday. He didn't understand my message that I was fine, and if he had forgotten something like my birthday, he apologized.

Brothers.

I went down to the living room, walked past Sherrie dozing on the sofa, and found Evie and Robert in the kitchen with Jorge talking about the remodeling.

"What was that loud noise?" I asked.

Evie looked at Robert and Jorge and then back to me. "Hon, we didn't hear anything."

"It was probably something out front," Jorge said, exchanging a look with Robert.

"Come and sit and have something to eat. I'll make sandwiches," Evie said.

"Jorge, we will be out of the house Monday. Chuck will be gone and offered up his house," I said.

"Whatever time you need is fine by me, but if I don't get out of my sister's house soon, I will gain ten pounds," he said.

"I thought you might be staying with Addie."

"No," Jorge said.

"A man of a few words. Things must be ok," I said.

He smiled. "Sure."

"I guess I'm not getting anything else out of you."

"Addie did give me something to give to you and Sherrie," Jorge said.

From the living room, Sherrie shouted, "I

heard that. What do we get?" She got up and shuffled her way into the kitchen.

Evie pulled out all the sandwich stuff and placed it on the counter. We started making lunch, and Jorge retrieved a bag from his car. Inside were two pairs of slippers that matched my satin pj's. Sherrie squealed in delight.

"She is a keeper Jorge," I said and turned to Robert and Evie. "EG will be here this afternoon. I really appreciate that you came here in the middle of the night."

"We will stay another day or so to make sure you two are ok and see what we can do for EG."

"I'm sure she will appreciate that, but she will not want to keep you—"

Robert held up a finger. "Listen to me, young lady. I will do anything to make sure that daughter of mine and her friend are safe and secure. And, most importantly, that my daughter is set up here in River Bend, so she does not end up back at home. I have already started to gut her room and turn it into an office for Evie."

"Dad!" Sherrie cried.

I gave a nod. "Understood."

CHAPTER FIFTY-EIGHT

Shortly before two p.m., Sherrie and I left Jorge's house. Evie was not happy that I wasn't taking it easy, but she let it go when I told her I was meeting Teddy and would have Sherrie with me. I felt slightly bothered by all the hovering. I knew it was out of concern so I got over it, but it felt like another thing I would have to manage.

We stopped at Peach's, and Sherrie got us some coffee. I waited outside, leaning against the brick building, letting the sun wash over me.

I was snapped out of my meditative state by another loud bang. Again, I couldn't pin down the noise.

When Sherrie finally emerged, I was reading a text from Lesley telling me Aaron was doing better than expected. I asked if I could come back, and she suggested maybe around dinner.

We walked to the square. Someone called Sherrie's name, and she waved.

"The one on the left is Monday. I don't know his name, but he shows up every Monday. The other one is Marco. He comes in more often."

Tommy drove past with Teddy in the driver's seat. Seeing the two friends together made me think about titles given to people. Their friendship was as strong as ever. They weren't brothers but friends. I hoped Sherrie and I would still be close twenty years from now. Maybe I shouldn't associate Tommy with his sick wife and what she had done to me and Sherrie. Teddy hopped out of Tommy's truck, which had the boat trailing behind it.

I ran up before Tommy could take off. I knocked on the back window to keep him from driving away and turned to Teddy. "If Tommy wants to join us, that's fine by me and I would like it."

"Are you sure?" Teddy asked.

"Go park, and we'll meet at a picnic table in the square," I said and then saw him hesitate. "How about we meet you at a table near the boat launch?"

I nodded in agreement, and he jumped back in and waved when they took off.

"What was that?" Sherrie asked, her tone telling me she was not pleased.

We walked past the square to the river.

"We are all gonna sit and talk it out," I said.

"I was only walking you here, so my father wouldn't insist on being your chaperone."

"I want everything out in the open. If we are going to live in this town, we need to understand each other and I won't have to repeat everything."

"Ok, but if at any point you want time with just Teddy, let me know and I will hang back," Sherrie said.

We walked the few remaining blocks in silence. Tommy had parked the truck and trailer in the same spot as a few days ago. They were standing near a table with their backs to us, watching the Mississippi run past them. I couldn't help but wonder if they wanted to hop on the boat and go with the current until they were only forgotten memories of this town.

They turned around as we walked up. I sat on the bench, Sherrie next to me, and they sat down on the other side with Teddy positioned between Sherrie and me and Tommy on the edge of the bench.

"How is Aaron?" Teddy asked.

"Fine. He was hit in the shoulder, but it missed the lungs. He will be going home tomorrow or Monday."

"Pete?"

"He's already out, and besides a giant

headache, he's fine."

"And you?" Teddy asked.

"I'm fine. Please tell me everything," I said.

"Me? You seem to have been in the middle of everything last night," Teddy said.

I didn't know what I'd expected, but denial or cowardice were not at the top of my list. Whatever I'd felt in fear last night paled in comparison to the anger building inside me now.

"I am giving you one more shot, or I walk away for good."

He looked at me without expression as if he was reading a menu board above a deli counter. Sherrie's head swiveled so fast I thought she snapped a muscle. Tommy was as still as a bronze statue.

"I don't have time for this. Actually, I have the time, but what I don't have any more is patience." I started to stand up.

"Claudia, you have to know this is not easy . . ." Teddy said.

I turned, slid my legs over the bench, and stood up. No one else moved.

The sun was hitting my eyes, but I could see him clearly.

I threw my hands on the table, leaned in, and through gritted teeth, I said, "Bullshit. Easy? You want easy? How about being chased down. How about someone walking through where you live.

Calling your job and digging for personal information about you. Following you in a grocery store. Invading my space and hers." I gestured to Sherrie. "You think it's hard now. Stop protecting her, and man up before I get a restraining order on your wife."

"Wife?" Sherrie said softly.

I nodded and crossed my arms. Sherrie swung one leg over the bench and waited before she stood up.

Tommy stopped her. "She's right. Tell her everything. About Melanie and all of it."

Teddy nodded and motioned for me to sit. It was a childish power play, but I refused.

CHAPTER FIFTY-NINE

Teddy sat on the other side of the table. I gave him a minute to collect himself. Tommy stood up and stayed at the head of the table, his arms crossed. He seemed, like Sherrie and me, to be waiting for the puzzle pieces to finally fall into place.

Teddy was looking at no one but spoke to each of us. "It took me some time to figure it all out. I didn't know what Melanie had been up to. Let me back up the story.

"For years, I had dreams—actually—nightmares about that night I and Tommy put my father into the river. Until this summer, I thought EG and I had killed him. I was forever grateful that EG never lived with thinking she helped kill a man. Now, knowing that we didn't do it and that it was Jean is a huge relief. I hope you will never know what it's like to live with that on your hands."

Sherrie looked at me. I was paralyzed. I was not going to share what I had done last night. He must have heard, but it was not time for me to connect the dots for him.

Teddy continued. "I would have these literal nightmares and wake up screaming. Sometimes, I would say the words dad or EG. I always told Melanie I didn't understand the dreams or what they meant. I told her from the beginning that my father walked out on my mother, brother, and me. I had told her everything except the night we put him in the river.

"EG meant so much to me. Being with her that night was so special. I know it sounds crazy after all these years, but I thought that night EG was the one for me. What was the best night of my life was also the worst night of my life. I connected with EG but lost her a few hours later."

I was still frozen in place and getting more upset. "Don't play on your emotions for EG you carried all these years. I want to know about now."

Teddy wouldn't look at anyone. He kept speaking as if he hadn't heard me. "I found solace in the church and eventually married Melanie. For a while, the night terrors stopped.

"When the fisherman discovered my father's remains, everything came flooding back. The years of abuse and neglect he'd subjected me and especially my mother to. The raw emotion of it all. I only told Melanie my father's body had been found. I left everything else out."

Teddy looked at me for the first time. His flat tone did not change, and as he spoke the words that connected a story, he lacked empathy for himself and me. "I did not tell her about you or EG or how I was involved in hiding his corpse.

"About six weeks ago, I abruptly gave my notice to the church and accepted the teaching job in New England without consulting Melanie. I think some part of me didn't want her to come with me. I did not deserve to have this family. All of it was too much for her, the job, my refusing to talk to her, less time I spent with the kids—I was becoming a recluse. She was nearly pushing me out the door, and I was relieved."

"You showing up at the house looking for EG. Chasing down old memories." I didn't know if I'd said that out loud. Nobody acknowledged the words. I realized he had been always trapped between his past and current lives.

Teddy continued. "About a month ago, my brother and I got a letter from a lawyer's office after we filed for the death certificate for my father. We did it for mother. To give her final peace of mind.

"The letter stated our father had owned land in southern Wisconsin. The land was to go in a trust for his grandkids. I spoke to someone at the law firm. My father had said to make sure his kids didn't get a dime from the land because we were worthless and maybe his grandkids would be less of a disappointment.

"How is that for a punch in the gut? Two decades later and from the grave, my father is still a bastard.

"The woman at the law firm explained that Leann Smithford had been allowed to live on the land until her death. Then the land is to be sold for the benefit of the grandkids for my brother, Christian, and me. My father had affairs with Leann and other women throughout his marriage to my mother. Leann remained important to my father, and four years before his death, twenty-seven years ago, they had a daughter together.

"George Joseph Siusiac and Leann Smithford named her—"

"Jo-Lee," Sherrie and I said together.

I sat down on the bench and said, "Continue."

"George couldn't or wouldn't even give his daughter his first or last name. Only a portion of his middle name. I guess that is better than living with his family name stuck to you.

"Leann died a few months ago. She had always told her daughter that her father was from River Bend, but not much else about him. Apparently, he treated Leann only slightly better than my mother. Jo-Lee got messed up with Adam and tried breaking things off with him. Her stepfather, Victor, for the last sixteen years, told her it might be best to get out of town for a while. It might help get rid of Adam once and for all. Adam was not one for letting things go easily. Jo-Lee thought this would be her chance to escape from him and learn more about her birth father, so that's why she came to River Bend.

"She did not want anyone here knowing who she was and anyone from her past knowing where she went. It was a coincidence that she stumbled into Aaron's bar and met the two of you.

"While all this was going on with Jo-Lee, Melanie and I were having trouble. When the letter came from the lawyer, she got it in her head to take the money from the sale of the land and buy a home for her and the kids. But I didn't know the value of the land, and it would have to be divided three ways. At first, she understood it to mean between my kids, my brother's kid, and Leann's if she'd had children. Melanie had my bags packed. I was hardly taking care of my church responsibilities, spending most days holed up in our home office. I was planning on going to the meeting at the lawyer's office at the end of the month by myself."

I leaned forward. "Because you still haven't told her about me."

Again, he didn't look at me but just shook

his head. "She must have seen some of the paperwork from the lawyer lying on the desk. She had your name and the address here. She learned the address belonged to EG, and she spiraled out of control. She thought I had an affair."

I didn't bother to correct him on my last name. He'd told the law office I was Claudia Graham. EG Graham had given birth to me, but Katie-Lyn and Matthew Middleton had made me family.

Teddy continued. "At first, I didn't understand when she threw me out of the house. She said I am just like my father. I stayed with my mother, then Melanie showed up there, upset and saying I was destroying our family. I couldn't put my mother through any more pain. That is when Tommy offered me a place to stay."

I had forgotten he was standing there. He didn't acknowledge what Teddy had said in any way.

"Melanie was obsessed with her marriage, her life as a minister's wife being destroyed, not realizing her actions were against everything she was fighting for. She was caught between protecting her way of life and punishing me for failing in the eyes of God."

I couldn't believe the judgment coming from Teddy. I wondered if he ever had given a sermon on empathy.

Tommy looked uncomfortable hearing his friend speak. I saw pity in his eyes. Tommy, whose wife was receiving treatment for mental health issues and who had lost his job as sheriff, understood empathy and was there for his friend, even though Teddy did not understand it.

Teddy kept talking. "I'm not surprised at all the things you said. I caught her trying to sneak into Tommy's house, and once, I saw her walking around town, dressed funny with a hood and sunglasses on. I thought she was watching me. I never dreamed she would come after you."

Tommy nodded. "When we heard about the car chase, we got really worried."

"How did you hear?" I asked.

Tommy understood my concern. "We weren't being nosy. I still have a few friends on the local blue squad. Having been county sheriff, one of them asked if there was a problem with street racing in other towns or if there was a history of it somewhere else. It was all informal stuff. I miss the job, and they like an outside professional opinion. I can also tell you the best roads to maintain the speed limit if you want to avoid a ticket."

Sherrie and I each gave him half a smile.

"All I'm saying, I don't want you to think I was invading your space," Tommy said.

"We appreciate that," I said and turned back to Teddy. "Go on."

"These last few days, I learned who Jo-Lee was and what she was doing in town and how she was hiding from Adam. We didn't know if Adam had your address and would think Jo-Lee was there. Jo-Lee, nor her stepfather, read the last letter from the lawyer. I did not know if all those receiving a portion of the trust were identified in the letter."

"What about Melanie?" I asked.

"She and the kids are with her parents. We were due to move out of the house provided by the church at the end of the month. Before the last two weeks or so, we have been trying to figure out if they will come with me, or maybe we wait until the second term begins in January. We have things to work out."

"That's nice." I hoped he understood my sarcasm. "What is she going to do about me? EG? EG's house? I will tell you this once since you don't seem to have understood what I was asking. If I see her near either me, Sherrie, EG, the house, or even this town, I am going straight to the police. If she wants to be out of jail and there for your kids, she better listen the first time you talk to her. She does not get a second chance. She used up her nine lives when she came into EG's house, tracked me in a grocery store, called where I worked, and chased us down. I don't know what her intentions were with that car chase, and I don't want to know. She could have seriously hurt us. If that doesn't do it for you, I have an FBI report of each time she drove past the house this week. Either you can stop her, or the police will."

"I hear you," Teddy said and stood up. He seemed to need more than two feet of space between us. "I can't imagine what it has been like for you."

I couldn't imagine he had ever thought about what it had been like for me.

He turned towards the river, seeming to lose himself in the moving current.

I felt the sun beating through my cotton shirt. Sherrie had been sitting silently next to me. I got up and took our empty coffee cups to the trash can to give everyone a moment to themselves. I had not even heard a few more cars pull into the parking lot.

Teddy walked a little closer to the river. He seemed lost in his own thoughts. A Frisbee flew close to him, and he didn't flinch or shift when the kid picked it up.

Tommy sat down and looked at us. "I have wanted to talk to both of you. This may not be the right time, but I don't know if there will be another opportunity."

Sherrie and I sat there silently, open to listening to him.

"I never got to apologize to you. Both of you.

What Jean did was not right. Worse was me enabling her to carry on as if she was ok. I didn't know how bad she was, but that does not excuse me from any responsibility. Jean is getting help, and I am working on things too."

Sherrie displayed some grace. "Thank you, I hope you mean all that."

"I do. After what you two have been through, you are not only surviving but thriving. You continue to fight for yourselves, and at your age and this stage in life, it's something I admire. You don't have to accept that from me, but I wanted to say it."

"That was nice to hear," I said.

We all turned and looked at Teddy.

Tommy said, "One of the things I learned was we are not responsible for other people's actions but must account for our actions around that person. Teddy is still learning that. I am not saying that so you go easy on him, but he has not dealt with stuff in twenty years and he has created this snowball effect and doesn't know how to step out of it yet."

We nodded in agreement.

Sherrie seemed to accept everything Tommy had revealed, and broke the anxious tension. "This isn't a funny situation, but I have to say, you guys sure can pick 'em." This made the three of us laugh, and Sherrie continued. "I appreciate everything you said. I admire how you stood by your wife."

"Thanks. Before, that was my choice, an easy choice. I loved Jean. Still do. Through her illness, I always have, but I wasn't certain about our future. Now, one way or another, she will be a part of my life."

Sherrie and I looked at each other. He seemed to be telling us something.

He must have seen the look on our faces. "Jean is five months pregnant. She went off her medication about a year ago. There was little hope of us conceiving, but she was desperate to try anything."

"Wow, congratulations," I said.

"We are just trying to figure out the best course of action for Jean. She is currently in an amazing hospital and treatment center. The doctors think it is best for her there and that she may not be able to handle the responsibility of motherhood. So I will be raising our daughter on my own. I can only hope she has the tenacity of you ladies."

CHAPTER SIXTY

Teddy rejoined the group. I had said what I had wanted to say and was beginning to feel as if I were the parent scolding a child. I waited for him to say something.

The future of our relationship from this point forward was unclear. I couldn't see anything to gain from having him in my life. It would not be a loss if he was not in it anymore, and for that, I was grateful but also unwilling to completely shut him out.

"How much longer are you in town?" I asked.

"I'm not sure. I have three weeks until I start teaching. I need to straighten things out with Melanie. I would like to have some time with Jo-Lee before I go. Speaking of which, she and Victor would like to see you as soon as you are ready."

"Can you tell them I will meet them at Peach's in thirty?"

He pulled out his phone. I walked towards the river, and Teddy followed me, several feet behind.

This time he spoke first. "I am sorry for everything. Showing up at the house in that condition, Melanie, everything."

I nodded to tell him I'd heard what he was saying. I couldn't tell him it was all right or agree to accept his apology. It wasn't that he was not sincere about apologizing for the chaos; it was that he was missing the fact he was the trigger point for most of it. I felt like the adult in our relationship and decided to give him some advice. "I have no right to tell you how to live or what you should do, but you do have some things to figure out. While you are figuring out your family life, maybe you should also think about how much you have been drinking."

"What? I don't think you are in a position to—"

I turned to face him. "Just my opinion. I have seen and heard things and have been around enough people to know when they are blowing off steam or when they are hiding. It may not be rehab-needed drinking, but don't hide behind it."

I walked past him, then stopped. "I do wish

you all the best. Stay in touch. Sorry to end on this note, but if I see Melanie around here, it will not go well."

CHAPTER SIXTY-ONE

I left Teddy standing on the riverbank. Sherrie and Tommy gave each other a hug and said goodbye. I waved to Tommy and wished him luck with fatherhood.

As we walked to Peach's, I called Lesley for an update on Aaron. She said he was doing fine but a little winded because he had just done two laps around the nurses station. I told her I would be there in an hour or so.

Sherrie broke the silence between us. "Thank you for that. I was not sure I wanted to see Tommy, but listening to him actually helped me."

"I wish I had to the peace you do. I surprised myself by speaking to Teddy like that. Thankfully, he was slow to respond because I'm not sure I could have handled any pushback. I am kinda sad—not about what I said, but the fact that I had to say it."

Sherrie nodded. "I get that. Are you ready for those two?" Sherrie pointed.

Outside BAR, Jo-Lee and Victor were looking through the front windows.

"Not really, but I just want to get it over with so I can see Aaron."

They saw us and suggested we go to Bumbles instead. As we walked the few blocks, Victor talked nonstop. He was not loud, but I felt like everybody was watching us. The smell of cigarette smoke wafted off him despite no cigarette in his hand.

We sat down, and I watched the two of them. It was enduring watching daughter and stepdad worry about each other, even if it was just about the right table. She wanted him to have enough light to read the menu, and he was concerned if the air-conditioning was too much for her. Victor had a nervous energy, his leg bouncing the whole time. Jo-Lee was quiet and seemed self-conscious about each movement.

Rose came over from behind the bar and insisted I get up so she could hug me and then placed her hands on Sherrie's shoulders. "Chuck was here a few minutes ago getting sandwiches. He and Jacob are cleaning and giving us some of their inventory."

"Inventory?" Sherrie asked.

"He wasn't sure when the bar is going to open again. So I'm taking some of their product. Hush now, we ain't supposed to be doing that, moving kegs between our places. The city would yank my liquor license, but I am helping them regardless. Those Rhoimly boys are good folk. Sherrie, hon, if you want to pick up some hours here, just let me know. I think you could teach some of these kids I got working here a few things."

"Absolutely," Sherrie replied.

We ordered, and Jo-Lee apologized for not telling Aaron the truth up-front, but he had figured out she had been hiding something. She'd told him everything about Adam and that she was hiding from him. One of Adam's friends had been in the bar a few weeks earlier, had recognized her, and must have told Adam she was in River Bend. That was why he'd shown up on Friday. At that point, he didn't know where she was living, but only that she was working at BAR. Even though she had a restraining order out on him, it wouldn't stop him. She didn't go into the details about him or his past. Victor looked uncomfortable the entire time she spoke about Adam.

She'd had her birth father's name and knew that he was from River Bend. After her mother, Leann, died earlier this year, Victor had gotten a letter from the lawyer about the land and the trusts set up for the grandkids. She had no idea when she took the job and eventually met me that we were related. It wasn't until she met with Teddy and Christian a few weeks ago that they laid it all out.

I nearly choked on my burger when she said a few weeks. Teddy wanted to tell me himself, she explained. Sherrie stopped eating and watched me.

I excused myself to throw some cold water on my face in the bathroom. Standing at the sink, I thought back to the night Teddy had shown up drunk at EG's house. Even in his drunken state, all he'd cared about was seeing EG. It wasn't even on his drunk mind to tell me Jo-Lee was my aunt. He was waiting for me to get the letter from the lawyer's office.

I knew Teddy was not to blame for Adam coming to town. But if I had known why Aaron was hiding Jo-Lee, things would have turned out differently.

There were many maybes in the timeline, but if I had known someone was after Jo-Lee and it was not Teddy, maybe things would have changed. Maybe the cops would have caught Adam at Jo-Lee's apartment, maybe Pete and Aaron would have had the back door locked. Maybe Aaron would not be in the hospital. Maybe Sherrie would not have hesitated to talk to Teddy and Tommy, and they would have been at the bar with me. Maybe Adam would not have come back. Maybe I would not have shown up at the bar when Adam was there. Maybe . . . I would not have needed to pick up the gun.

I bent over the sink and heaved, but my lunch stayed down. I was sweating, my hands gripping the sink.

I heard the loud noise again and looked around the bathroom, but no one else was in there. I pulled myself together.

On my way back to the table, three people looked at me. One of them said, "She's the one." I heard the words and understood what they meant, but I wouldn't or couldn't acknowledge to them. That would have been too much for me. I needed to finish here and get back to Aaron.

Victor looked at me with concern. "How are you doing, Claudia?"

I looked at everyone at the table. "I promise you, I'm fine." I didn't want to share my feelings about Teddy. Jo-Lee had just discovered she had brothers. I didn't need to be feeding her my sour feelings about Teddy.

Victor dipped his head. "Despite all the craziness, there is some good in this for you." He smiled at me.

I could not imagine what he was talking about.

"The inheritance. Leann never talked much about George, or if she did, it was not very nice. Besides Jo-Lee coming into the world, the only other decent thing George did was buy the house and land and pay it off before he disappeared," Victor said.

Jo-Lee continued to explain. "We don't know the details and probably won't until we all meet with the lawyer at the end of the month. I don't think I receive anything. The figures are an estimate, but when divided amongst George's grandkids, your portion will be approximately, after taxes, about thirty thousand dollars."

Victor got a chuckle out of that. "Isn't that crazy? Georgie boy hit the real estate market right. Leann never wanted to leave the area, even after all the development. Good thing because the land just kept growing in value."

Sherrie leaned in. "If you don't mind me asking, what about future grandkids?"

Jo-Lee shrugged. "I not sure how it's worded in the legal documents, but the proceeds from the sale go only to Teddy's and his brother's kids born between certain dates. George made it like some type of inheritance game. Only the players, Teddy and Christian, didn't know they were pawns in their father's game. He thought I would be able to marry a man with money, and then my kids would be taken care of. When I called the firm, one of the old lawyers told me it would be all explained at the meeting. He gave me a few additional details like I just explained. He was a funny old bugger and seemed to have been waiting decades to execute this will. The lawyer called George a 'twisted son of a gun with the devil's eye for responsibility.' "

Sherrie spoke again. "Sorry to hear that."

"That's ok. I don't need or want anything from that man," Jo-Lee said.

"So, what's our sharpshooter gonna do with your share of the cash?" Victor asked.

"Me? I don't know. What's gonna happen with you, having to leave the house? I don't know about me." I looked around the restaurant, and the neon beer lights seem to blur into one giant sign that wrapped around the room. I focused on the empty chair behind Victor to center myself.

Victor chuckled. "That's right. What's the hero gonna do with the money? It's like winning the lottery. Some people invest wisely, and others blow all the money in a few years and end up poorer than before they won. I see you as a smart one. Me, I am headed to Florida. Me and Leann bought a house years ago, and I'll make the move permanent. Gonna become a fisherman and give up life on the road as a trucker. Hope this one joins me at some point, but she is smart and could go anywhere." He pointed to Jo-Lee with delight. "I hope you buy something nifty for yourself."

I hadn't touched my food since returning to the table. The smell was suddenly too much. Sherrie handed me her water. Everyone seemed to be waiting for me to answer.

"I don't know for sure. I would like to share some of it with you. I think you should get some," I said to Jo-Lee.

She shook her head. "That's very kind, but as I said, I don't want anything from that man. You keep it. I appreciate the gesture."

"I understand. I will probably give a portion of it to a women's charity for domestic abuse."

Jo-Lee raised her hand to her mouth, and her eyes welled up.

"From what I have been told, George was not the greatest man out there, and for what you and others have been through, I want to do something good."

Jo-Lee reached out and gave me a hug from our seats.

"The other thing that popped into my mind was maybe a trip to a special island with some special ladies." I turned and punched Sherrie in the arm. "Wanna go?"

"You two relaxing on a beach sounds great," Jo-Lee said.

"No, I was thinking of somewhere else, maybe take our mothers with us. I'm thinking of Guernsey Island, in the English Channel. I read about it, and it always intrigued me."

Sherrie let out a soft yip, her hands doing a quick light clap, and her legs bounced under the table.

"Well, you deserve it after what you did. You will be a hero forever to me," Victor said.

"Please don't say hero," I said, suddenly getting the shakes and sweating again.

My phone rang. I was relieved to see it was my mom. "I'm sorry I have to take this."

I didn't wait for them to say anything; I answered the phone, giving them a half a wave goodbye. I went to the back of the restaurant and out to the alley for some privacy. I bumped into Chuck coming back in. I stood between the dumpster and the brick wall so no one would see me, not wanting anyone pointing at me, saying, "She is the one."

When I heard my mom's voice, I melted. She put my dad on speakerphone, and I told them everything. I went day by day, from someone following us, Jackson, Teddy, taking my cast off, the house fire, the letter from the lawyer, inheritance, going to the bar, and Aaron being shot.

My parents listened without interrupting. I pictured them standing next to each other, Dad listening over my mom's shoulder while he rubbed her back. Mom would be putting her hair behind her ears. Eventually, they would be holding hands.

I stopped to catch my breath. Choking on my words, I said, "I killed him. It was me. He is no more. Me . . . me . . . I killed him."

I was on the ground, sobbing. I wasn't really coherent, but later, I remembered someone taking my phone and talking to my parents. Someone picked me up and carried me. I kinda remembered the car ride. It wasn't until we turned down the dirt road to Aaron's house that I was able to break back into the present.

Chuck stopped the truck, hopped out, and opened the door for me, helping me out. He guided me by the elbow into the kitchen. He had me sit at the table, then got me a glass of water and a box of tissues.

"I'll be back. Go ahead and use the bathroom."

I did as I was told, then threw some cold water on my face, never looking in the mirror.

I returned to the kitchen to find Chuck standing there with an old backpack sitting on the table. He had me sit down, and he sat across from me.

"Listen, I don't have all the right words or the all professional tools to help. I do suggest you get someone professional to talk you through this, but for now, I want you to listen and do what I ask," he said.

I shook my head and listened.

"What I do have is experience in this: you have to become comfortable with the fact you killed someone."

I flinched and looked down at the table. My hands were between my legs, and every muscle in my body tightened.

Chuck continued. "Being comfortable is not saying you are a murderer, but you have killed. There is a difference. Being comfortable is making it so you can deal with it. After I returned from my first deployment, I was at a party. As a joke, someone asked if I'd killed anyone. Let's just say that evening did not end well for all that were there. Words get tossed around too much, and people don't know the impact they can have on someone. There will be other triggers. For some people, it could be a sound, a smell, a song, a bell ringing, or the feel of metal against your hand. All, real or imagined, can trigger the moment for you. You need to be ready to deal with it. What you have going for you is that you're allowing yourself to feel. The man you shot was a dirtbag, but you recognize him as a person and that is good.

"You cannot go down the rabbit hole of what-ifs. That will not get you anywhere. You can't imagine what would have become of him. Would he have become a good person? You don't know, and that's ok. He could have been a good person, but you were in a position and you had to react. You trusted your gut and did the right thing. Do you understand that?"

I nodded.

"Fight or flight. You chose to fight. And, goddammit, that is special. Not everyone has that. Sometimes running can be the best option. For you, at that moment, it was to stay and fight. Be proud of your actions but understand they come with consequences such as accepting that you took a life. It's ok to mourn the loss of life, but please don't regret your actions, especially actions you cannot undo.

"I want you to do something for me now. I want you to stand up and carry this bag. Walk around the lake—yes, the whole lake—and while you walk, I want you to take the small rocks from the bag and toss them in the lake. You with me so far?"

I nodded again.

Chuck pressed on. "Each time you throw a rock, I want you to say one line. Go through the list and repeat.

"I killed someone.

"It's ok.

"I am ok.

"I live today.

"I live tomorrow."

"Throw a rock, say a line. Now with me, let's say it together."

Chuck knelt beside me, put his hands on my knees, and shifted my body so I was facing him.

Together we said, "I killed someone. It's ok.

I am ok. I live today. I live tomorrow."

Chuck had me repeat it by myself and helped me stand up. He put the backpack on me, so the bag was in front. It was heavy, and he had me support the bottom with my hands as if I was carrying a chubby toddler.

The weight of the bag seemed to snap me out of a fog. I'd felt like I was watching someone play me in a movie, but the cold, heavy canvas sack woke me up. "Can I do this later? I want to see Aaron."

Chuck's eye twitched. "No, you have to do this now. I will tell him you were asking to see him. Follow me."

We walked out of the house and down the path to where Sherrie and I had stood on Saturday. Chuck repeated the instructions to walk all the way around the lake. "When you get done, there will be a blanket to sit on until you're ready to leave."

"When will I know I'm ready or done?" I asked.

"You'll just know. Or a rainstorm will hit, and the lightning and thunder will chase you back." He smiled, but I didn't say anything. "It's ok to laugh—that's part of why we're here. Get you back to smiling and living. Real living, not just going through the motions. Don't worry, Sherrie and everyone know where you are. Robert will be here when I leave. You will be ok. Just remember, this is one exercise to get you started, but talk to someone. A professional. This is not a cure, just one tool to help you."

Chuck reached in the bag, put some pebbles in my hand, and turned me towards the lake.

I walked.

I threw a rock. "I killed someone."

I threw a rock. "It's ok."

I threw a rock. "I am ok."

I threw a rock. "I live today."

I threw a rock. "I live tomorrow."

CHAPTER SIXTY-TWO

I walked and walked. I don't know how long it took me. I didn't know what time of day it was. I didn't hear anything but my footsteps for a while, and then the noises faded in and out. I kept walking and repeating.

The bag was getting lighter. I slowed my pace. I heard birds singing, and I kept walking.

I didn't know if it was one hour or three, but I eventually made it around the lake. Some blankets and two other bags sat on a log nearby. I spread out one blanket on the grassy area and brought both bags over. One had a sandwich and water and the other had more rocks.

I drank the water, then picked up some rocks and threw them in the water. This time, I didn't repeat anything. My mind wandered to all the people in my life. Eventually, each rock I threw, I said their name and smiled. All my family, friends, college pals, Kay, Jenna, even Mrs. Baron, and Cheryl got a smile. I went back to repeating what Chuck had taught me.

I heard a noise behind me, but I didn't look, figuring it was Chuck or Robert. That gave me another smile. I went back to throwing pebbles. The sun was setting, but I didn't want to leave. I made a pillow of the second blanket but realized one of Aaron's sweatshirts was caught up in the blankets.

Despite the humid sticky air, I put on his sweatshirt. Pulling it in around me, I could smell him. I fell asleep almost immediately to the sound of crickets and dreamed of all things good.

I woke up once to a loud bang, angry something had interrupted my dream of all my favorite people sitting around a large table eating as if it was Thanksgiving. The table was impossibly large, but everyone I loved was there. I remembered what Chuck had said—anything can trigger a memory—real or imagined. I'd heard gunfire in my dream, and it had interrupted everything good. I was going to have to learn to cope with this.

I fell asleep again and woke to sunlight. I ate the sandwich that was in the bag, watching the light reflecting off the water. Someone had brought a thermos of hot coffee to the blanket while I was sleeping.

The air was muggy with the rising sun, but I had a chill around me. The coffee warmed me from the inside.

I sat there a little while longer and finally decided I was ready. I'd have to deal with this, but I had my family and friends for support. Those that didn't understand the burden I had to carry were not my problem. I could learn to ignore them or educate them and, most importantly, not let them get to me—I had my own thoughts to deal with.

I stood up and stretched, actually feeling good. I emptied the last of the pebbles into the lake and packed up the blankets. Walking up the path, I was disappointed to see there were no cars. I hoped my phone was in the house. I needed to call Sherrie so she could drive me to the hospital.

As I got closer, I saw someone sitting on a folding chair on the lawn, wrapped in a blanket. The person had a view of the path I was on and was too short to be Chuck and too small and pale to be Robert.

I couldn't believe my eyes.

At the edge of the wooded path, my eyes focused.

I dropped everything and ran. Halfway to the chair, Rita plowed into me. As I bent down to scratch her chin and get some kisses, I watched him struggle slightly to stand up. When I was nearly to

Aaron, he held out his hand to stop me from coming too close so he wouldn't lose his balance. His arm was in a sling, and he looked a little drowsy.

He took my arm and slowly pulled me close. We kissed gently. I took a half step back and looked at him, not believing my eyes. He seemed a little shaky. I had him sit and knelt next to him, holding his right hand in mine and petting Rita with my left hand.

"What are you doing here? This is amazing. I was coming to see you. How long have you been here?" I said, panting.

"Probably an hour. Chuck came in this morning before he left to give me the update. Last night when you didn't return, I got a little nervous."

I looked down, unable to look at him. Tears welled up in my eyes. I had broken up with him and hadn't been there when he was in the hospital.

"I'm sorry, I wanted to be there, but I kinda had a meltdown."

"I know. It's ok. That's why I'm here." Aaron squeezed my hand.

Through my tears, I said, "If you tell me he has my Bumbles back alley episode on video, I am going to be mad."

"Nah, at least I don't think so." He wiped away a tear from my cheek as he spoke.

"Why didn't you tell me what was going on with Jo-Lee?" I asked.

"To be honest, I didn't know everything. I only knew she was running from Adam, not about her connection to you or Teddy until a few days ago. You broke up with me. There is being friends with your ex, and then there is a matter of how much crazy shit do you tell your ex. By the time she told me about Teddy, Adam showed up looking for her. I was still mad at Sherrie for lying about doing the reference checks, and I was taking it out on both of you."

"She knows she's in trouble with you," I said.

"She was at the hospital last night, telling me what happened at Bumbles and apologizing. She would not stop. It got so bad, her nonstop talking, I buzzed for a nurse to come so she would stop," Aaron said.

We both laughed. He winced a little in pain.

"The other reason I didn't say anything, to be honest, you and her can kind of be wild cards. I mean, look at what happened when you didn't know what was going on. Could you imagine what kind of trouble you and Sherrie would have gotten into if you'd known Adam was after her? He kept showing up, and I had to keep the two of you out of the bar and away from the square. I don't have enough insurance on the bar to cover what you and

Sherrie could have done." He laughed again.

I didn't laugh. "I was so excited when I realized you were protecting and hiding her here and not dating," I said.

"I had to set it up that way so you would stay away if Adam showed up. I would rather have you mad than physically hurt."

"How did you know I was at the lake last Saturday and came out when Sherrie and I were in the woods?"

"Molly called offering more brownies, making chitchat, and said she saw a car come down the drive. I didn't know who it was and went to investigate."

"Molly? Phil's sister?"

"Yeah, Molly Douglas. You met her husband, Wally. They have the land next door. I am surprised you haven't met, but then again, she keeps a pretty low profile around town."

"Oh." I didn't have much else to say at that point.

"I can't tell you how nice it is to have this over with. Jo-Lee is nice and very grateful and so is her stepfather, but I was stressed. I spent my nights at the loft. Once she realized Adam found her in River Bend, she reached out to an old friend and got a new job a in Milwaukee. She was going to leave at the end of the month."

"I had lunch with them yesterday. They

were both very grateful for everything you did," I said.

"They also stopped by the hospital yesterday before they left. Jo-Lee was headed back home with Victor. I told her she could have her job if she wanted when I reopen since she has no reason to flee if that's ok with you?"

"With me?" I asked.

"I want to make sure you're comfortable having her around." He hesitated and then squeezed my hand. "I want you around too."

"Really?" I looked at him.

"Yes, but we have to talk some things out. You can't shut me out. I am not saying you have to tell me everything, but you can't shut me out."

"I get that. I was trying to figure out some stuff and got all up in my head about moving forward meant starting over on everything. I never meant to hurt you. It wasn't about us. It was about me fumbling and fixing the wrong puzzle," I said.

"In some ways, dealing with Jo-Lee and her issues were a good distraction. I was not ok with seeing you around the bar as just a friend. The whole 'Let's be friends' thing was more painful than helpful. I was trying to be cool about it."

"So, does this mean we are—"

He kissed me before I could finish the sentence.

We didn't stay like that for long. I was

cramping from crouching in front of him, and he was a little winded. I helped him up, and we walked towards the house.

"How are you out of the hospital so early?"

"When Chuck came by to tell me what was going on with you this morning and that he left you by the lake, I had to come. The nurse and I had a few words of disagreement. I said I was leaving regardless of whatever they said was best for me. I was to be discharged later today, so I forced the issue and had the staff expediting my departure. I may have to go back and apologize for some of my words," he said.

"That's sweet of you, but I am sure as nurses, they've heard a lot worse from other patients." We stepped slowly up the steps, and I said, "I have decided I want to do something. I kinda want to do it on my own. I know it's been your thing that you do and have encouraged me to try it and maybe I have been listening. While figuring out my future, one of the things I wrote down that I wanted to do was run a marathon."

Aaron stopped walking and looked at me. "Really, that is awesome. I've thought about it but haven't got past eight miles. I admire you. My legs are fine, but this shoulder will have me sidelined for a while, but I heard what you said about wanting it to be your thing."

"I figured if I am going to plan my future

instead of doing it one step at a time, I'll do it one mile at a time. I hope you will be there to cheer me on." Mentally, I pictured myself coloring in my last bubble on my vision board.

He leaned over, kissing me on the cheek, and whispered, "I will always be there, wherever you need or want me."

We walked in, with Rita trailing behind us. Inside, sitting at the table were his mom and aunt. They had sent Jack to take Robert home and to Peach's to pick up some breakfast for the group. They took Aaron from me and led him to the couch, doting on him as if he were a child. It was neat to watch.

In the kitchen, I called EG. She was happy to hear from me and had gotten to town late afternoon yesterday. EG said my parents were on a plane and would be here tomorrow. I promised to come see her in a few hours. I called Sherrie and gave her an update. She and her mom were waiting for Robert before going to breakfast, and then she was going to give them a tour of River Bend and the campus. I suggested a great place for donuts on the other side of the river.

Jan came into the kitchen and took the plate of brownies. We walked back into the living room together. I sat next to Aaron. Rita was at his feet. I teased Jan, saying it was kinda early for dessert.

"Darling, this ain't dessert; this is therapy,"

she said.

"That sounds like a good plan. Maybe I will have one," I said.

"I don't think that's the best option for you," Aaron said.

"What do you mean?" I asked.

Jan laughed. I looked at her, bemused.

"Those aren't Jan's brownies. They're not from Peach's. Can't you tell? There's no powdered sugar. Those are from Molly. I had them here for Jo-Lee, hoping to calm her nerves."

Slowly, it came together—the brownies Aaron had in his truck and would not share. Molly, Phil's sister. EG's pot.

Lesley was about to take her first bite of a brownie.

"Those are pot brownies!" I said.

"Aaron!" his mother said. "How could you let me?"

"I would have stopped you, but apparently, Jan knows what they are," Aaron said.

"Damn right," she said.

CHUCK'S STORY

I should have stayed with Claudia at the lake, but I couldn't be there when she was so vulnerable. I had to take Robert to the house and knew he would check on her. He was a vet and understood what she was dealing with now. I could not be the one to stay with her.

Once she accepted what had happened, she would be fine and would continue to be a fighter. I didn't have to be in Texas for another week, despite what I'd told my family. When I'd gone to the hospital the night Aaron was shot, the emergency room nurse asked me who Claudia was. Aaron had kept asking about Claudia while he was all loopy from the medication. He hadn't asked about Pete or what had happened to that bastard who'd caused all this mess. She'd captured his heart.

I was going to have to let my feelings for her go. I'd almost lost my brother years ago because of a woman. I promised never to let that happen again. Ever since Claudia and I had the best phone date ever, I couldn't get her out of my head. I had hoped things with her and Aaron would burn out, and then I could make my move.

I was wrong to think I would have a chance with her. I can't be there to watch them heal together. I would be like a hawk in a tree waiting to strike.

Too bad Sherrie didn't pick up Aaron's phone months ago, and we could have talked for an hour instead. It would have made things a lot less complicated.

I'd said goodbye to the family this morning when they were wheeling Aaron out of the hospital. I couldn't help but wonder if Aaron knows why I'm driving ninety miles an hour to get out of the state.

BOOK CLUB DISCUSSION QUESTIONS

The book demonstrates Claudia's fight-or-flight instincts, but what about Sherrie? Sherrie stayed closed to Claudia and became protective. Sherrie did not leave or coward away. Who would you drive into a cornfield to protect?

Claudia's relationship with Aaron was easy, and she confused that with being stationary. Balancing career aspirations and a relationship is never easy. Can Claudia move out of River Bend and keep dating Aaron? Can they have a future?

Chuck put aside his feelings for Claudia to preserve his relationship with Aaron. Can a friendship or sibling relationship survive when someone has feelings for someone else's significant other?

Claudia was a victim of stalking and refused to speak up to EG. Was she protecting EG, or did she feel ashamed as a victim?

After the fire and all the chaos of the day, Claudia and Sherrie return to Jorge's house, but instead of going into his house, they retreated to EG's porch and sat in the dark. Do you have a happy place?

Can Claudia salvage her relationship with Teddy? Claudia already has amazing father but is there a place for Teddy in her life?

Claudia went through a traumatic event in the bar when she killed Adam. She finally broke down in the alley, and Chuck gave her one coping technique. But, if Claudia continues to suppress her feelings, will it hinder her future relationships and mental well-being?

Is there a small town you love? What makes it charming-location, architecture, ice-cream stand, restaurant, or an annual festival?

Join a book club.
Start a club or find one at a local library.
Reading is amazing- talking about what you read with a group is even better.

ACKNOWLEDGMENTS

If you are family or friend, you may find your name or some variation of your name in the book. Large and small characters, heroes or villains, endearing or annoying, just know there is no correlation between you and the character. I needed a name, and I chose from what I know and what means something to me. Just know the name was used out of love and familiarity.

Thank you to my sister, Heidi, for inspiring me to read that Mary Higgins Clark book many, many, many years ago. It started my love of reading and eventually led me to writing.

Thank you to my editor, Starr Waddell. The story and mistakes are mine, but Starr helped smooth out the rough edges.

Thank you to my beta readers for the feedback—Alexis, Molly, and Mel.

A special shout-out to Molly Stretton. I don't have enough words of appreciation to express my gratitude for all the rolls you cover-beta reader, social media coordinator, PR rep and for always answering the weird and mundane questions and for all the encouragement.

Mel, would you please join the world of writing? Most of all, thank you to my husband, Brian, and son, Alex, for their love and support.

ABOUT THE AUTHOR

After graduating from the University of Wisconsin-Stout, TJ embarked on a career in the hospitality industry, which led to multiple moves across the country. An avid marathon runner, TJ turned to writing after her knee eventually gave out. The author lives in Kansas with her husband Brian, son Alex, and dog, Reba. When not writing, TJ can be found hiking our national parks or traveling with her book club.

GO

Printed in the USA
CPSIA information can be obtained
at www.ICGtesting.com
LVHW091213260424
778284LV00007B/2